Hunted

Anew Book Two

Josie Litton

About this Book

*A*melia undoes me in ways that I can't fathom. With her, I can feel the coils of pain and memory that entwine so deeply inside me beginning to loosen. Far in the back of my mind, I can't help wondering what will happen if they unravel completely. Will she know how to gather them up and reweave them into something new and better? I sure as hell don't."

Amelia and Ian's story continues in Book Two of this erotic retelling of "Sleeping Beauty" set in the near future. Torn apart by the revelation of Ian's tormented past, the lovers are caught in a web of deadly danger they can only survive by confronting together.

As the collective madness of Carnival descends on the glittering world city of Manhattan, Ian's fight to redeem himself takes him into the depths of the nightmare that has haunted him for so long. At the center of it is Amelia, at once a pawn in a monstrous game of evil and the only hope of ultimately defeating it.

In a world ruled by sensual excess, the passion of these lovers holds the power to transform despair into hope and betrayal into justice. But a fateful decision will change the course of their lives forever.

Praise for the ANEW Trilogy by Josie Litton

"Most beautiful, erotic twist of Sleeping Beauty! Can't wait 'til the next book!!"--Chrissy Dyer, Goodreads Reviewer

"...a new twist on futuristic romance! And let me tell you, it's totally worth it!!!...Cannot wait for the next installment. FIVE STARS FOR THIS AUTHOR!!!"--Summer's Book Blog

"5 Explosive stars...nothing less than spectacular...sensual, explosive and revealing."--Dawn Marie Carpintero, Goodreads Reviewer

"I loved every minute reading this book...What an amazing start to this series, thank you Josie Litton."--Kerry Callway, Goodreads Reviewer

"...a completely unique and creative story that had me captivated from the start."--Melissa Cheslog, Goodreads Reviewer

"I love Josie Litton's creativeness. She will capture you and keep you conquered in everything she writes."--Twin Sisters Rockin' Book Reviews

"As an avid lover of romance novels of all genres, I am always so happy when I discover a new type of plot line or a book that has a superb story to support all of the steamy bits that make me blush. That's definitely what you'll get in this book."--Loredana, Goodreads Reviewer

"...a completely unique and creative story that had me captivated from the start."--Melissa, A Risque Affair Book Blog

Hunted

Contents

About this Book..3

Prologue...7

Chapter One..11

Chapter Two..23

Chapter Three..31

Chapter Four 37

Chapter Five..47

Chapter Six..57

Chapter Seven..63

Chapter Eight...73

Chapter Nine..81

Chapter Ten...89

Chapter Eleven...95

Chapter Twelve...103

Chapter Thirteen...111

Chapter Fourteen..119

Chapter Fifteen...129

Chapter Sixteen 141

Chapter Seventeen 147

Chapter Eighteen...155

Chapter Nineteen..165

Chapter Twenty 173

Chapter Twenty-one..181

Chapter Twenty-two..189

Chapter Twenty-three..199

Chapter Twenty-four..207

Chapter Twenty-five 213

Chapter Twenty-six..221

Chapter Twenty-seven 229

Chapter Twenty-eight...237

Prologue

Amelia

*T*he small gold plaque bears a single line of cursive script, "The Cabinet of Secret Delights".

A shiver of anticipation runs through me. I know this place. I recognize it. I'm back at the estate where Ian and I first met. But it isn't real. It's a dream.

I don't care. Awake, I am forlorn and alone. Only in dreams do I come alive.

At my touch, a hidden door beside the plaque swings open. The room I step into is a study in beauty and opulence. Its intimate size is magnified by the gilded mirrors hanging in ornately carved gold frames beneath a soaring dome. The floor is covered by a finely woven carpet in shades of hunter green, ivory, and ox blood red. The same colors are picked up by the ceiling mural that depicts the god Zeus in pursuit of various nubile females. Successful pursuit, it appears, as he is shown plunging his impressive endowment into a succession of startled beauties.

But it isn't the god who commands my attention.

In the middle of the room stands a gilded cage, six feet in diameter and at least half again as tall, constructed of roped wrought iron curled into scrollwork. I stare at it as my heartbeat accelerates. Everything about the room arouses and alarms me--the padded benches fitted with discreet restraints, the armoire filled with exotic toys, the aura of carnality that hangs thick in air lightly scented by leather and sandalwood. But nothing affects me more than the cage. Aside from its obvious purpose, I have no idea why it is here.

But perhaps I'm about the find out.

In the world beyond dreams, the one we call real, I've only been in this room once before and then I was alone. Now I'm not.

A man steps from the shadows. Black jeans hug the long length of his legs and his narrow hips. Under a snug black T-shirt, I see the movement of muscles across his broad shoulders and chest. His arms hang loosely at his sides, the fingers of each hand curling inward as though he carries weapons that are invisible to me. His hair is dark brown, thick and slightly long. The sun has burnished his skin. He has strong, symmetrical features, the facial bones angular and chiseled.

He hasn't shaved in a day...two? I wonder suddenly how the stubble along his square jaw would feel against my fingertips. Is it coarse? Raspy? Silken? The thought shocks me with its presumption of intimacy.

When no more than an arm's length separates us, he stops. This close, he appears even larger, more formidable but also young, still in his twenties. At last, I can see his eyes. Set under arching brows, they are a rich golden amber shading to brown, framed by thick lashes. In them burn the barely banked fires of heart-stopping hunger.

Distantly, I am aware that this is how Ian appeared the first time we met. Such a short time ago. An eon. The pain of missing him fills me with every breath I draw, threatening to blot out everything else. I push it aside resolutely. The dream is fragile. I can't risk any thought that might shatter it.

He holds out his hand. Without hesitation, I step toward him. At that moment, what I want most is to hear his voice. When it comes, the deep, slightly husky timbre sends a shiver through me. I watch in unwilling fascination as his full, surprisingly sensuous mouth--the only hint of softness I can see in him--shapes a single word: "Amelia."

My name on his lips is at once an acknowledgement and a command. I obey without hesitation and place my hand in his. At the first touch of his skin against mine, pleasure sings through my veins. I am overwhelmed by a sense of relief. This is where I belong. Where I want to be.

As I move, I feel the thin sheath that skims my body from shoulders to ankles. Beneath the diaphanous fabric, I glimpse blushing alabaster skin. Ian's eyes darken. His gaze lingers on my breasts, the indentation of my navel, the small gap between my thighs that reveals my bare cleft.

I feel the wetness gathering in me, the excitement, the all but unbearable need. I want so badly to touch him and be touched in turn. He knows my body better than I do but even more, he reaches beyond mere flesh and bone to the center of my being, soothing my fears, freeing my hopes, fulfilling my dreams. In his arms, I have found the one place where I am complete.

Without him...

A wave of anguish curls through me. I flinch and instinctively step closer to him, seeking the comfort only he can provide. But between one beat of my heart and the next his hand slips from mine. He takes a step back and smiles with gently chiding regret.

No! My desperate effort to deny his rejection falters against my knowledge of his implacable will. And with that, the edges of my dream begin to fray.

Instead of Ian's embrace, the wrought iron bars of the cage close around me. As I struggle to shake them loose, the mirrors that line the walls of this sensual retreat suddenly begin to crack. Through the jagged wounds, skeletal fingers of dank mist rush into the room. They spread quickly, encircling Ian. Far from trying to elude them, he stretches out his arms as they weave around him, swiftly cloaking him in darkness.

I cry out, pleading with him to resist but it's too late. He is vanishing before my eyes. My sobs, my pleas, my curses have no effect. They fall away, mere gasps on empty air, until at last nothing except the memory of him remains. I am left alone, anguished and bereft, trapped in the gilded cage.

The coldness of the metal seeps into my skin. I begin to shiver uncontrollably. Curled in on myself, I lie sobbing until the dampness of my tears on linen pillow cases scented with lavender draws me back into a reality from which no dream can grant release.

Josie Litton

Chapter One

Amelia

Manhattan Island
May, 2059

"Amelia--?"

I look up, meeting my grandmother's concerned gaze across the oval breakfast table spread with white linen and set with old family china and silver.

"Your breakfast is getting cold," Adele prods gently. Although we have known each other only since I arrived in Manhattan a month ago, I don't doubt that my grandmother's concern for me is genuine. I'm grateful for it, even though I'm sometimes at a loss as to how to respond.

On this occasion, I force a smile and poke my fork into the perfectly made omelet scented with fragrant herbs. Adele waits as I take a bite, chew, and swallow.

"Are you excited about tonight?" she asks.

I'm dreading the Crystal Ball, the gala event that precedes the start of Carnival. The hours that will be spent smiling, making idle conversation, and pretending that I am delighted to be among the cream of society hold no appeal. All I really want is to creep away and hide but I am not about to inflict that unpleasant truth on a kind woman who wants only what is best for me.

"Of course," I say. "It's the most anticipated event of the season, isn't it?"

As short a time as I've been here, I've learned that everything involving this glittering enclave of the elite is 'the most'--exciting, important, exclusive, desirable, whatever. The city, so beautiful in many respects, is a testament to excess and self-regard. While everything is 'the most', nothing is ever regarded as 'too much'.

"I suppose that's true," my grandmother says with a smile. "Certainly, everyone who matters will be there."

I glance at her in time to catch the hint of challenge on her lovely, ageless face dominated by eyes the same aquamarine shade as my own and framed by elegantly coiffed silver hair. It's on the tip of my tongue to ask if she thinks that Ian will be at the ball but I stop myself. I've already learned that to speak his name, even as a whisper in the tormented night, only makes my longing for him all the more unbearable.

Realistically, I know that I don't need to be concerned about encountering Ian tonight. His power and position allow him to shrug off attending such events without consequence. My situation is far more tentative. Despite the lengths that he and others have gone to protect me, I can't risk drawing the wrong kind of attention. As a member of the McClellan family newly arrived in the city, I am naturally a focus of curiosity and interest. But that is nothing compared to what would happen if people suspected for a moment who--and what--I really am.

The soft ticking of the ormolu and marble clock on the mantle draws me from such cheerless thoughts. I set my napkin aside with a flicker of relief and rise.

"I should be going. Sergei doesn't tolerate tardiness." The ballet master is as demanding as he is gifted. I'm fortunate to be taking classes with him.

Adele frowns but she doesn't object. "Of course, dear. Just be sure that you're back by three o'clock. The dressers are arriving then."

I smother a sigh and nod. On my way toward the front entrance of the manor, I make a brief detour. At the far end of the living room, a life-sized portrait of a beautiful young woman hangs looking out over the gardens. Susannah McClellan, Adele's other and very beloved grand-daughter, Edward's older sister, dead now for more than a year.

In the painting, she is wearing a white, pleated gown of Grecian design that leaves one shoulder bare and skims her perfect figure. Her head tilts slightly to one side, as though she is lost in thought. She looks delicately beautiful with an air of waiting for something that she accepts will never happen.

Her hair, like mine, is chestnut but straight, perhaps not naturally since my own is a tumble of curls. Her eyes are the same shade of aquamarine. An accident in Susannah's youth that required reconstructive surgery left her cheekbones a little lower than mine, her jaw a bit rounder. But that is only the beginning of the differences between us. On my best day, I could never manage her air of serene acceptance. My nature is far more inclined to impetuousness and defiance.

The contrast in our personalities inevitably makes me think of Ian. Susannah was the woman he chose to be with and whose loss he has truly mourned. Whereas I... He never asked for me to be a part of his life. I was thrust on him without his prior knowledge or approval. Merely by existing, I've forced him to confront the nightmare that he thought he had long since escaped.

The pain of that is agonizing yet I can't bring myself to blame Susannah for any of it. Everything I have, all that I am, I owe to her. If she hadn't acted with such courage and grace at the end of her life-- I push aside thoughts of the macabre fate that would have been mine and reach up, touching two fingers to the side of the frame. It's a small gesture but one that I find myself making every time the complexities and challenges of this world threaten to overwhelm me. Fittingly enough given the connection between us, she has become my talisman.

Moving on, I take a quick glance in the gilded mirror that hangs on one wall of the mahogany-paneled entry hall. My appearance tells me little more than it did a month ago when I saw myself for the first time. Still, I no longer feel as though I am looking at a stranger. Little by little, I am coming to know myself.

My hair is brushed as smooth as possible given its inherent wildness and coiled into a bun at the nape of my neck. I've lost weight in the last few days with the result that my eyes look even larger than usual in the pale oval of my face. At least the raw silk pants and fitted black velvet jacket that I'm wearing over my practice clothes are elegant enough to pass unremarked on the city's streets where appearances count for everything.

Outside, I stand for a few moments just beyond the entrance to the mansion and tilt my head up to the sun. The warm spring air carries the scents of flowers and newly mown grass from the park on the far side of the avenue. Beyond the stand of Lombardy pines that screen the residence, cars skim by soundlessly. I can hear the call of gulls who come inland from the harbor along the rivers that surround the island city, looking for whatever spoils they can find.

They aren't alone. A faint rumbling under my feet reminds me of the network of conduits that take workers back-and-forth between their micro-apartments and their places of employment. Deliveries arrive the same way and waste materials leave. Nothing is allowed to mar the city's pristine surface.

Farther down in the abandoned tunnels of the old subway system and the derelict sub-basements of buildings long since demolished is an even less welcoming world, home to the scavengers who flock to the city out of desperation, smuggled in by human traffickers and abandoned at the first hint of trouble from the heavily armed Municipal Protection Services.

Yet the beautiful, tree-lined streets that I walk along on the way to Sergei's studio exude a sense of harmony and serenity. Not coincidentally, those are the twin virtues emblazoned on the banners fluttering gaily from flag poles, street lights, and passing cars. Combined with the other decorations going up for Carnival, it's all very festive.

I can almost forget that beneath the veneer of culture and beauty lurks a far more hedonistic reality. Almost nothing is off-limits or even particularly difficult to obtain. Clubs abound where the most beautiful and skilled sex workers--men and women alike--serve every taste. The most popular among them become celebrities, paid huge amounts to endorse products. Recreational drugs are everywhere. The brilliant and darkly handsome Jorge Cruces, head of the world's largest pharmaceutical company, is one of the most respected men in the city. His success in keeping his products out of the hands of those too young to use them legally assures that he is left free to sell them to everyone else. Yet as ruthless as Cruces is said to be, there are still rumors of illicit substances coming from hidden labs, drugs that promise to overcome every inhibition and release the darkest, most powerful desires.

It's all still so new to me. My impulse is to drink in every sight and sound but I try to control that. I've learned from harsh experience that the sensory overload that results leaves me confused and exhausted.

Although thoughts of Ian are never far from my mind, my mood lightens as I walk. It's a relief to lose myself in the anonymity of the passing crowd, however briefly. I've paused to wait for a light to change when I feel a prickling between my shoulder blades. The familiar sense of being watched descends on me. I experience it regularly yet I can never discover what is causing it. We are all watched virtually all the time both outside and in public buildings but this is different. This feels personal.

Glancing around, I see only residents, who are far too involved with themselves to take any notice of me, and workers. Many of the former are dressed in the fashion of the moment--glaring neon colors, lush fabrics, plumes, and spangles displayed in styles intended to shock, amuse, or titillate. Any reaction is acceptable so long as attention is paid. The fashion faddists affect a pose of aloofness while keeping a sharp eye out for admiring glances. In contrast, the workers are dressed in utilitarian liveries that designate which household or corporation they serve. They keep their faces blank and their gazes averted as they scurry along.

I tell myself that I'm merely jumpy but the sensation of being watched continues until I step inside the elegant building on the other side of the park where Sergei has his studio. As I do so, I hear the soft thud of feet on the floor above accompanied by the sharper rap of the staff that the ballet master uses to beat out time and, when necessary, correct an errant dancer.

I slip into the communal dressing room, take off my outer garments and tuck them away in a locker. I've just finished tying on my toe shoes when a gaggle of young dancers enter. They are from the corps de ballet of Sergei's company and are preparing for a special performance to be given the first night of Carnival. Flushed and sweating in their leotards after what has no doubt been a strenuous work out, they eye me covertly. I can't really blame them. As Sergei's only private pupil, I'm bound to attract their curiosity.

My previous attempts at friendliness having failed, I smile at no one in particular and leave the dressing room. Sergei is waiting in the sun-filled studio. The young, intense Russian dance master is almost too good looking with a long, sinewy body packed with muscle, dark golden hair tied at the back of his neck in a small ponytail, and harshly beautiful features. He is brilliant, mercurial, and volatile. None of that troubles me but he is also far too perceptive.

Narrowing his gaze, he says, "Still brooding, I see. If I were staging 'Anna Karenina', I would cast you in the lead."

Ignoring the reference to Tolstoy's tragic heroine who plunged into a doomed affair that drove her to suicide, I say, "How fortunate then that you've settled on 'Medea' instead."

He's planning a bloody extravaganza--stage blood, I hope--to showcase the fury of history's most legendary scorned woman. The Russian dance master has a rare ability to hold an audience spellbound while compelling it to witness the consequences of abused powers and broken promises. It's a favorite theme in his work, one I fully support despite the fact that Sergei himself admits that it's only a matter of time before he's made to pay for his candor.

He tilts his head to one side and studies me. "You should be over him by now, whoever he is. If you were properly focused, you would be dancing professionally but instead--" He waves a hand in frustration.

The assertion startles me. I've only known Sergei for a few weeks, hardly much time for him to assess my ability. Yet he seems certain.

Positioning myself at the barre, I say, "Thank you but I doubt that's true."

He frowns. "Why not?"

What can I say? That however physically adept I may be, I lack the emotional experience that is as vital to dance as are music and movement?

Sergei would rightly want to know how any twenty-two year old could have lived as little as I have. I can hardly explain to him that when I woke a few weeks ago in the garden of Ian's estate two hundred miles north of the city, I had no idea who I was and only the most scant memories of the time that had gone before, memories I would prefer not to have at all.

Putting that aside, I say, "Don't you think I'm too pampered and privileged to be capable of the discipline that would require?"

He narrows his gaze. "Are you? That had not occurred to me. But if you think so... " His staff raps against the bare wooden floor. "Let's see what you're really capable of."

∞ ∞ ∞

An hour later, my muscles straining and my body damp with sweat, I whirl through the final steps of a grand adage from Tchaikovsky's 'Sleeping Beauty'. My stamina has surprised me but perhaps it shouldn't. The rigor of dance provides my only relief from thoughts of Ian.

"Good," Sergei says over the last notes of the music. He looks vindicated. "I knew the first time I saw you dance that you had great potential. Miraculously, whoever trained you in the past didn't muck it up. Your technique is excellent, your interpretation natural, unfeigned. All you need to do is focus, Amelia."

Since I can hardly tell him that my ability is only a reflection of the knowledge and skills Susannah gave to me, I remain silent.

Gracefully, he extends his long, muscular arms en bas as though to embrace the studio and all that lies beyond. "Focus and the world can be yours."

I want to believe him, not because I aspire to dance professionally, I don't. But I do need to find a purpose, something that will give meaning and structure to my life. I've tried to tell myself that there is some benefit in being forced to part from Ian. I am thrown back on my own resources, compelled to become more independent and self-sufficient. Surely, all that can only make me stronger. Yet the pain of being without him remains anguishing.

I reach for a towel and drape it over the back of my neck. Holding onto the ends, I say, "It isn't that simple--"

He makes a dismissive sound. As much as Sergei embodies the sublime complexity of dance, he sees human relationships in far starker terms. For him, a man and a woman give each other what they need or they go their separate ways.

But what happens when the only way to give what is needed is to part? Does longing cease? Does yearning ever die? How much does the heart have to shrivel before it no longer aches?

With a start, I realize why I don't want to give up what I feel for Ian. Not because I enjoy torturing myself, far from it. But the pain that has taken up permanent residence inside me is a constant reminder that I am alive. And where there is life, there is hope, however forlorn it may seem at the moment. If I am nothing else, I am the living proof of that.

"Yet again your mind wanders," Sergei says in exasperation. "Where does it go, Amelia?" Shrewdly, he adds, "Or should I ask, who does it go to? Who is this man who has cast a spell of enchantment over you?"

I can't help but smile at such a whimsical thought. The first time I saw Ian, moments after I awoke, he seemed so commanding that I fancied he was a prince. I was not entirely wrong though he is a dark one to be sure, hardened by adversity and haunted by his past. I can't forget that he is the man who left me, collapsed on the floor of his penthouse, stunned in equal measure by his coldly calculated possession and the shattering revelation that accompanied it.

Despite my pleas, that ruthless, implacable man is putting his own life at risk hunting down the fanatics who endanger mine. As much as I want to be strong, to take care of myself, I can't deny how bereft I would be without Ian's protectiveness. Surely, I can do no less for him no matter what the cost to me?

Sergei frowns. "You are tired. We will stop."

I am about to insist that I can continue when I realize that I should not. I have done this before--pushed myself too hard too fast--and suffered the consequences. Given how anxious I am to make up for all the time I lost adrift in the prison of sleep, a certain degree of impatience is understandable. But if I am to survive the loss of Ian, I need to pace myself.

"I'll do better next time," I promise.

"Or you will think of him again. Go back to him or forget him, Amelia. There is nothing in between."

Only the chasm and myself hanging suspended above it. I turn away toward the dressing room.

When I emerge half-an-hour later, having showered and changed, another rehearsal is underway. Sergei truly is indefatigable. But he breaks off as I head toward the exit and joins me. Holding the door open, he says, "Are you being picked up?"

The question surprises me. I assume that I leave Sergei's mind the moment I leave the dance studio. That he would give any thought to my life beyond there is unexpected.

"It's a beautiful day. I prefer to walk."

He frowns. "You should be careful."

I look at him closely. His gaze reveals little but I have come to know him well enough to realize that he is genuinely concerned. "Why?"

"You didn't notice that there are more police than usual on the streets?"

I was too busy thinking about Ian to do so but I'm not about to admit that. "I've been here such a short time, I don't really know what is usual."

"Then take my word for it. There are rumors..." He stops, as though suddenly remembering himself. "It's the Russian in me. We are bred to suspicion. All the same, in this place caution is always called for."

One of the municipal drones that are constantly on patrol passes overhead, at a level with the upper floors of nearby buildings. It hovers for a moment and moves on. I watch it go as a cloud drifts across the sun, chilling me.

"What kind of rumors?" I can't help wondering if they have anything to do with Ian. The power he commands and his refusal to use it in blind support of the elite has made him enemies among those who hold high office in the city and beyond. But in the final analysis they aren't much more than puppets. The real danger lies with those behind the scenes, pulling the strings.

"Most are the usual fear mongering," Sergei says. "But there are others--" He cocks his head toward the floor and what lies beneath. "Claims of unrest below," he murmurs, " alarming our illustrious citizenry and prompting calls for a crackdown."

I tense at the thought. Life is hard enough for the scavengers without subjecting them to even greater deprivation. Too vividly I recall seeing a young man beaten for no greater offense than having the misfortune to be caught above on the street.

"Surely it won't go that far," I say even as I know that I may very well be wrong.

Sergei shrugs. "Just be careful, all right? Stay alert. Don't let your mind wander."

"Yes, maître," I say with a smile, employing his title with only a hint of teasing. I have enormous respect for Sergei even if we don't see eye-to-eye on the nature of human relationships.

He's still standing at the door watching me as I go down the steps and outside. While I've been inside, the wind has picked up but the day remains invitingly bright. I decide to walk back through the park. On the way to it, I can't help noticing that Sergei was right, there are more police around. Never mind that they're referred to as the "protection services" and wear blue uniforms rather than black or camo. Their faces are concealed behind helmeted visors and they grasp deadly weapons positioned across their chests, always at the ready.

I'm relieved to step inside the park, an oasis in the center of the city that is the exclusive preserve of residents. Only a handful of workers-- nannies, landscapers, and the like--are permitted here. The almost eight hundred acres encompass lawns, ponds, riding paths, and playing fields including the polo club where Ian and I had a passionate encounter that I recall all too vividly.

Despite my assurances to Sergei, I can't help thinking about Ian. He's foremost in my thoughts as I cross the stone Bow Bridge that arches over a picturesque pond. To the south, the magnificent skyline of the city rises but I see only the silver and black spear that is Pinnacle House, the headquarters of Ian's defense tech company. Is he there now? Does he think of me?

Suddenly feeling shaky, I stop for a moment and lean against the sun-warmed stone of the bridge. A turtle slides off a nearby rock into the water. Ducks glide by. In the distance, children are laughing.

The sound pierces me, evoking thoughts of the childhood I never had even as I am swept by longing I cannot bear to acknowledge, involving as it does a future with a man I long to love with all my heart and the children we cherish together.

I squeeze my eyes shut for a moment. When I open them again, the world glistens behind a sheen of tears.

How absurd! I have far better things to think about. The Crystal Ball, what I'll be wearing, all the fascinating people I'll be meeting with their inane chatter and calculated smiles. The men I will dance with because it's expected and fend off because I have no interest in any of them. The relief I will feel when I can finally leave and crawl back into my empty bed.

My gaze turns once again in the direction of Pinnacle House. I'm entertaining the thought that I am doomed to long for Ian forever when a flutter of movement nearby catches my eye. A metal grate concealed by bushes rises with a soft creak, followed quickly by two small heads. Children. Dirty, ragged, and definitely not laughing.

As I stand, frozen in place, they scamper out, run to a nearby trash bin, and begin searching through it. They move quickly, pulling out a half-empty bag of popcorn, a partially eaten hotdog, and, to their apparent glee, a box that rattles with a few stray candies. One of them is a boy of perhaps seven and the other a girl several years younger. They look enough alike to be brother and sister, although it's hard to be sure given the layers of grime.

While still searching the trash, they begin stuffing food into their mouths, swallowing without hardly pausing to chew. They're gulping it down as though they know it can disappear at any moment.

I'm wondering what I can do, how I can help them when they suddenly become aware of my presence.

At once, the boy steps in front of the little girl. Clearly intent on protecting her, he glares at me and raises his small fists.

I stare at the children. They are so thin! And so frightened. Under the grime, their skin is pale, as though too rarely exposed to the sun. Yet despite all that, they are defiant, not yet ground down by their cruel circumstances. The thought that they see me as any kind of threat is horrifying.

I do the only thing I can think of and press a finger to my lips in what I hope they will recognize as both a warning and a promise to keep silent.

For a long moment, the children gaze at me in wary disbelief. Only when I remain unmoving, not calling for help or sounding an alarm, do they finally act. Grasping the little girl's arm, the little boy runs for the safety of the tunnel they emerged from. As they disappear back into the darkness, the metal grate clangs shut behind them. No sign remains of their presence except the abandoned bounty from the trash bin.

My legs are shaking. I have to lean against the side of the bridge. Waves of shock and disgust surge through me. I've been in the city for a month. I've seen enough to know what is going on. But nothing, not even the beating that I witnessed, has hit me like this. Children! There are children down there, which means there are probably also babies. I cannot bear to think of that but I can't turn away from it either.

I know what it's like to be trapped and helpless. To be subjected to cruelty made all the worse for being coldly impersonal. To be denied even the most basic humanity. But in my case at least I was assumed to have some value, even if it was only to be gutted and harvested so that another could live.

Odd how things worked out. The woman I was supposed to save is dead and I am here, Susannah's version of the ultimate make-over, struggling to adapt to this strange new world.

The tinted glass of the chamber gives the liquid within it a blue-green hue. I am floating in a sea as ancient in its composition as the vastly larger one where life itself began. Long, undulating ribbons run from my body to points around the walls of the chamber. Nourishment passes through then, oxygen is provided, waste is removed, muscles are stimulated--painfully. Time passes, endless, empty, tormenting time.

Bile rises in the back of my throat at the memory and the others like it that I'm not supposed to have yet cannot escape. I wrench my inner gaze from the nightmare that still lives in me and stare at the remnants of discarded food that the children abandoned. In this perfect world where nothing matters more than appearance that evidence of their presence is likely to attract attention. Rather than risk anyone discovering the grate and sealing it--or worse tossing a grenade down it--I pick the trash up and put it back in the bin before I move on.

Chapter Two

Ian

There's blood on my hands. I thought I'd been more careful than that but hell, it's not as though it's the first time. It wouldn't have happened if the idiot head of the Human Preservation Front hadn't surfaced from his drug-enhanced stay in a sensory deprivation tank, mistaken me for some monster from his twisted id, and made a move on me. Last one he'll be managing for a while.

Apparently, you don't need much in the way of brains to run a terrorist organization responsible for killing well over a hundred people and blowing up billions of dollars' worth of scientific research. All in the name of preserving humanity, of course.

Asshole's lucky I didn't wring his neck, I'm in that foul a mood although I shouldn't be. Everything's gone well. Hunt down the HPF crazies who declared an all-out war on replicas. Check. Stress them with a combination of drugs and deprivation until they tell me everything I want to know. Check. Clean up whatever's left. Check.

Staying busy and productive has kept me from thinking about Amelia as much as I would otherwise. As it is, she doesn't go through my mind more than a thousand or so times a day. Each and every memory of her is a punch to my gut. In the ten days since we were last together, the pain of missing her has become as constant as breathing. Weirdly, I'm glad of it. In a strange way, it makes me feel as though we are still connected. Pathetic, I know, but it's all I've got.

I come out of the bathroom still drying my hands to find Edward stretched out on the couch in my private office on the penthouse floor of Pinnacle House. He's my age, twenty-eight, and has the same aquamarine eyes and chestnut hair as Amelia. Otherwise there isn't much resemblance between them. Not surprising since she's exquisitely beautiful and he's just a guy.

The real surprise is how little Amelia resembles Edward's older sister and my former lover, Susannah McClellan, the woman for whom she was supposed to be nothing more than a source of replacement parts. The moral and ethical issues of human cloning are tough enough but the replica technology that allows the digitized pattern of one individual's brain to be imprinted on another has introduced a whole new level of controversy. So far we're not handling it well.

Except for Susannah who made a selfless decision in her last days before the disease that had overshadowed her life finally took her. Not only did she choose to forego any further chance to extend that life, she sought out the most cutting-edge replica technology so that she could give Amelia only knowledge and abilities rather than her entire neural imprint. By doing so, she made her unique among replicas--free to be her own self, form her own memories, and live her own life.

The truth is that I can't imagine what it's been like for Amelia, awakening into the world as she did. I'd say that she suffers from amnesia except a person has to be allowed to live before she can have anything to forget. However much she knows, and that appears to be a great deal, she has no context of memory or experience. Everything--every sight, sound, taste, every touch is entirely new to her.

If I were any kind of decent guy, I would have backed the hell off and given her time to find her own way. Instead--

I close my eyes for a moment against the image of Amelia that first night on the balcony in the rain and later under me in the golden bed. In the aftermath, I couldn't evade the sickening possibility that I had taken advantage of a vulnerable young woman who had no ability to deny me. To my infinite relief, the truth turned out to be otherwise. Amelia possesses free will in abundance. She is in every sense her own person, able to make her own choices. I'm the one who can't resist her. Or at least I couldn't until I realized what a danger I am to her. Now I'll deny myself what I want more than anything else in this world before I'll compromise her safety for an instant.

Yet despite all that, she still has no existence in the eyes of the law except as property.

My property, to be precise, according to the terms of Susannah's will. That's something I try very hard not to think about.

My cock stirs at the reminder. He and I used to get along great but these days we're definitely on the outs.

"There's some useful stuff here," Edward says, indicating the intel we've squeezed from the HPF fuckers. "Enough to get me started at least."

Amelia's brother may look like he was born for the boardroom and the polo field but he's shown yet again in the last few days that he doesn't mind getting his hands dirty. At least not where protecting his sister is involved.

I toss the towel aside, glad that he has no idea what's going through my head--and other parts. "Good. I want to know who the money is. Find him or her and I'll be able to finish this once and for all."

That's my real goal. As much as I have sympathy for people who feel threatened by the sweeping changes that technology is bringing to all our lives, I have zero tolerance for the fanatics who want to kill anyone they decide isn't sufficiently human. Until the source of the money that made the HPF's activities possible is found and crushed, the whole sorry mess could start up again. Amelia would never be safe.

Not for the first time, I wonder how Susannah's parents managed to love one child enough to take such desperate measures to save her while being willing to deny her clone--essentially her identical twin only younger and even more vulnerable--the most basic human rights. Maybe I'll just never understand how we decide who's one of 'us', worthy of being valued and respected, and who isn't.

Edward levers himself off the couch and stretches. His hair is a mess, he needs to shave, and there are shadows under his eyes. I don't look any better. We've been at it hard for a week, ever since my team and I brought the HPF leaders back to Pinnacle House. I'm not going to dwell on what was involved in capturing them except that all my people came home safe.

"You going tonight?" Edward asks.

"Going where?"

"The Crystal Ball. It's tonight."

I'd forgotten about that, not surprising given that I'd have a hard time choosing between an ocular probe straight through the eye into the cerebral cortex and an evening spent in the company of the city's 'elite'.

"I've got a headache," I say, smirking.

"Lucky bastard. So are your mother and sister going?"

The question sounds casual but the mere fact that he's asking gets my attention. Marianne--my twenty-two-year-old, beautiful, and very sheltered sister--seems to have a thing for Edward. So far I haven't seen any sign that he returns her interest but I've been distracted.

Eyeing him, I say, "Yeah, they're going. What about you?"

He nods. "I'm escorting Amelia and our grandmother."

On the one hand, I'm relieved to hear that. Adele is a feisty grand dame who I happen to really like. But it's good that Edward isn't letting Amelia go into the shark tank without him. On the other hand, now that I know where she will be this evening, I have to fight the temptation to drop by just to catch a glimpse of her. Our paths are bound to cross again in public at some point. What's the harm if I just make that happen sooner rather than later?

There wouldn't be any if I could trust myself where she's concerned. The problem is that I can't. I want her too damn much. She's a fire in my blood that refuses to be extinguished.

"My father's son." The words I hurtled at her the last time we were together haunt me, not in the least because they are true. Marcus Slade was a monster who got his kicks hurting women in the very exclusive BDSM club that he founded and to which he lured select members of the city's elite. He initiated me into his practices when I was fifteen. A year later, I broke free but the damage was done.

I've spent every day of my life since then fighting his legacy only to have Amelia come along and shatter all my hard-won control. Through absolutely no fault of her own, she's awakened the demons inside me. I'll tear out what passes for my heart before I let them hurt her.

"You okay?" Edward asks. He looks concerned. We've known each other since we met at school more than a dozen years ago. He's gone on to become a pillar of the community, head of his family's financial empire. While I'm...hell, if I know.

"I'm good," I say.

He nods but he doesn't look convinced. Indicating the intel, he says, "Let's go over this again."

We do, looking into every nook and cranny that might provide a lead. I'm impressed by Edward's breadth and depth of knowledge. He's a totally honorable guy who I'd trust with my life--and maybe even with my sister--but he still understands the shadow world of money manipulation better than almost anyone. I'm as above board as I can be given my line of work but I sure as hell wouldn't want him coming after me.

"So you think the source of HPF's funds has been deliberately hidden?" I ask when we're done.

"No question," Edward replies. His confidence is unshakable. "Only thing I'm not sure of is how many layers I'll have to dig through to get to it. But don't worry, we will find out who's behind this."

"Good to know. I'll have a team on standby."

He glances at me but he doesn't say anything. We both know that when he comes up with irrefutable proof of who was funding the HPF, he'll be signing that man or woman's death warrant. In a world where wealth can corrupt any court, the only justice is personal.

Edward leaves a short time later. When he's gone, I wander out onto the terrace that wraps around the entire floor. The building is tall enough that on many days I'd be looking down on a cloud bank but today the weather is clear.

I stand, hands driven into the pockets of my jeans, and stare out over the wide swath of the park that splits the upper east and west sides of Manhattan. I'm so high up that the people down below are no more than tiny specks but I can make out the curve of the pond tucked into the southeast corner of the park. Not far from it are some of the city's most exclusive residences including the McClellans'. I wonder if Amelia is there now, getting ready for the ball.

I could find out. All it would take is a quick call to the security that I've had on her ever since she arrived in the city. Although the HPF effectively no longer exists, I'm not about to ease up on her protection. Not until I know who was behind the threat in the first place. And why.

I'm still contemplating the question of who was really responsible for the recent destruction of the Institute where the customized replica technology that made Amelia possible was developed when the link in my pocket chimes. I step through the nearest door before answering, into the art gallery that divides my apartment from the reception and meeting rooms on the other half of the penthouse floor.

I'm standing in front of a holographic image of men on patrol in a narrow street, taking fire from adjacent buildings yet continuing to advance. This side of the gallery is devoted to images of war. The real thing, no chest-beating triumphalism, just the horror of it coupled with the courage and decency to uphold values that, however fragile they may be, are still the best hope for humanity.

I worry about that more these days, wondering where my own country is going and whether I'll find myself fighting on home ground eventually. I'll move heaven and earth to prevent that. This thing with the HPF could give me an edge but I'm a long way from figuring out what that might be.

My gaze drifts down the length of the gallery to the side that could be said to represent the nature of eroticism that can be as powerful and dangerous in their own way as war itself. The statues of the bound ballerina that were on display as a favor to a friend are gone. I couldn't bear to have them around after my last encounter with Amelia.

I can still see her pleading with me to believe that I could only hurt her by letting her go. She went on thinking that up to the moment when I coldly and deliberately fucked her all but senseless even as I revealed the truth about how much she really had to fear from me.

In the end, crouched on the floor staring at me with those huge eyes that are windows into her soul, she accepted that we really don't belong together.

I haven't been back in the gallery since. If I'd been thinking straight, I wouldn't be there now. The way I'm feeling, it'll be a cold day in hell before I set foot in it again.

The link chimes once more.

Answering it, I snap, "What?"

"Thought you might be grabbing a little shut-eye," Brad Hollis says, arching a brow at my curt response. He was my commander in the Special Forces, recruiting me shortly after I enlisted in the military in defiance of my father's plans for me. Hollis saved my sanity and quite possibly my life. I owe him more than I'll ever be able to repay.

"I'm good," I say more calmly. "What about you?" He was with me on the raids to round up the HPF leadership and he fully shared the burden of the interrogations that have just concluded.

"I was thinking of treating myself to a nice warm bubble bath but I've been diverted," Hollis drawls.

My mouth twitches at the image of the straw-haired, buzz-cut Kentuckian with ice blue eyes and a penchant for boar hunting lolling around in a bubble bath, at least without appropriate feminine company.

"What's going on?" I ask.

"Not sure but Gab's concerned so I thought we'd better give you a heads-up."

Gab is Gabriella Innocente Darque, the six feet plus French-Haitian cyber-engineering whiz kid who runs information security for Slade Enterprises. If she's worried, I am, too.

"Go on." I say.

Ten minutes later, I get off the link and stare into the distance, thinking about what I've just learned. Rumors, that's all there is, nothing more. Gab made that clear when she joined the conversation.

"It's just a vibe I'm getting," she said. "But I can't shake it. For a couple of days now we've been hearing about more unrest below. That's why there are so many police on the streets. The problem is I'm not picking up anything like that myself. As far as I can tell, the scavs are as beaten down as ever. Plus there's the gala tonight at the Crystal Palace. If the situation is as tense as the city leaders want us to believe, why aren't they increasing security there?"

I can think of a couple of reasons why not. The Crystal Palace is in the park, an exclusionary zone for almost all workers and a place where a trespassing scavenger would be lucky to get out alive. But in addition, surrounding the place with heavily armed police would put a damper on the night's festivities and make people question the competency of the city's leaders.

I consider calling Edward, telling him what I've learned, and suggesting that he enjoy a quiet evening at home with his grandmother and Amelia but the whole thing may be a false alarm. Not that I think Gab's wrong, I don't. Something's up but the chances of it having anything to do with the Crystal Ball seem remote. All the same, I'm not about to take risks with Amelia's safety.

In the back of my mind, I know I'm grabbing a convenient rationalization for what I really want to do anyway but I don't care. Heading for the shower, I can't contain a wry smile.

Gab may be a weird pick for Fairy Godmother but thanks to her I'm going to the ball after all.

Chapter Three

Amelia

Set on the edge of the park beside a reflecting pool filled with hundreds of floating lanterns, the Crystal Palace looks as though it belongs in a fairy tale. Sparkling panes of glass supported by an almost invisible titanium lattice reflect the glow from the building's vast interior. Entering, the guests become shadows back lit by the radiance. I can't help thinking that they look as though they have ascended into a world even more rarified and beautiful than the one that surrounds me.

To the west beyond the park the sun is setting in a blaze of glory that turns the building's dome into a prism casting rainbows across every surface. Music wafts from speakers in the nearby trees--Mozart's "Eine Kleine Nachtmusik". The air is filled with the scents of rare perfumes and the laughter of beautifully dressed men and women.

Gravel crunches under the thin soles of my ridiculously high heels as I walk beside Adele and Edward from where the limo dropped us off. The smile I've pinned on is making my face ache. I can't stop thinking about the children I saw. They've even managed to push Ian from my thoughts, if only for the moment.

My hand is tucked into the crook of Edward's arm. He places his own over mine and squeezes gently. "You look lovely, Amelia."

I know his intent is to help me relax and I'm grateful for that. But the truth is that I could be as ugly as sin and I would still be drawing admiring glances because I'm wearing the McClellan diamonds. Edward brought them to me in my room as I finished dressing. As my maid stood off to one side, trying not to gape, he opened one black velvet box after another and laid them out before me.

"Susannah rarely wore these," he said. "She thought they were a bit ostentatious but they are a family tradition and I think you might find them...useful."

I understood what he was telling me. By wearing the pieces, I will be distinguishing myself further from Susannah. People would be even less likely to suspect the connection between us.

As much as I understand that, my first glimpse of the diamonds that now collar my throat, dangle from my earlobes, encircle both my wrists, and nestle in my hair stunned me. The smallest is at least a carat, the largest many, many times that. Beautifully cut, set in white gold, they glitter with the fire of the inner earth.

Among the larger stones, Edward tells me, are fabled gems smuggled out in the garments of aristocrats fleeing revolutions, pilfered from the treasure palaces of rajahs, and discovered amid the ruins of ancient Amazonian temples. Any one of them is worth a king's ransom. Taken together, they are a declaration of my family's power and my own identity as a McClellan.

Approaching the Crystal Palace, I am vividly aware of the avid stares directed at me, the quick tilting together of heads, and the groundswell of whispers. The thought occurs to me that more than any guest, the McClellan diamonds are the real belle of the ball. For the first time that evening, my smile is genuine.

The three of us give no sign of noticing the attention we're drawing. My brother has been pre-occupied since we left the residence but my grandmother is livelier. She leans close to me and says, "Chin up, my dear. It's all in a night's work."

A few weeks ago, the notion that attending a ball could be called 'work' would have baffled me. But now I understand that it is in settings like this that the true business of the city--and the world--is done. Business of all sorts, as it turns out.

Adele has let slip that inquiries have been made regarding the young, previously unknown, and apparently very eligible McClellan who has suddenly appeared in Society. Discreetly, young men--and young women on the chance that such is my inclination--are being put forward by ambitious relatives or on their own behalf. It's the way of such things, my grandmother assures me. Money is drawn to money. Love, or at least affection, can follow or not as the case may be. What matters is that there be no disruption to the established social order. It's all very pragmatic, she says, even as she dismisses the thought that I should consider any such marriage for myself.

I wonder what the ambitious parents and their progeny would think if they had any idea of the truth beneath the identity that Ian arranged for me. Would they recoil in horror or would they be too blinded by the glare of the McClellan diamonds to care?

Not that it matters. The only man I can bear to think of in such intimate terms is--

Here.

My head turns in response to an attraction that my body acknowledges even before my conscious mind is aware of it. I glance around quickly, certain that I must be wrong. The Crystal Ball is exactly the sort of event that Ian stays away from.

At first, I see nothing apart from the mass of people. But then the crowd shifts enough to give me a clear view across the ballroom. I catch a glimpse of a head towering inches above smaller men, dark brown hair shot through with shards of gold, the sweep of broad, muscled shoulders tapering into a powerful back and--

My reaction is visceral. In an instant, the tempo of my heart increases. I am swept by a wave of heat that makes me belatedly aware of how cold I have felt throughout these long, empty days and nights. Shamelessly, I drink in the sight of him even as my thoughts tumble over each other.

Does his presence mean that the threat from the HPF is over? If that's the case, I'm immensely relieved that he's no longer putting himself in danger for my sake. But why would he choose to attend the Crystal Ball? Does he have a fondness for dancing that I don't know about? Nervous laughter bubbles up in me at that thought. I press my lips together tightly.

Unlike many of the men, he is conservatively dressed in formal eveningwear, the black waistcoat and trousers contrasting with the ivory slash of his shirt, dove gray tie and matching waistcoat. The veneer of elegance suits him yet it is also at odds with the aura of barely contained power that he exudes. I cannot bring myself to look away from him.

"Is everything all right, dear?" my grandmother asks. Her beautiful face creases with concern. She follows the direction of my gaze and immediately brightens. "Oh, good, Helene and Marianne are here. Let's go say 'hello'." She grasps my hand, intent on drawing me along.

"No!" I pull back sharply, fighting to control myself. At her startled look, I say more softly, "That is, you go. I'll join you...later." Much later as in never. My single greatest goal for the evening has just become to avoid contact with Ian for his own sake. There is nothing I yearn for more except to be with him, held by him, my breath filled with his, his mouth claiming me and his--

"You look flushed," Edward says, glancing down at me. "Is something wrong?"

"It's the heat," I blurt even though the temperature inside the Crystal Palace is perfect. It would never be allowed to be anything else. "I'm just going to--" I gesture vaguely toward where I think the ladies' room may be.

"Of course," he says. "I'll hold off the hordes of your would-be dance partners as long as I can but hurry back."

With a nod that in no way expresses my true intentions, I flee. I can't get away quickly enough even though there is really nowhere for me to go. I could hike across the park to the house but as secure as the park supposedly is, I'm not about to do that while weighted down with enough diamonds to buy a small country. Not to mention all the concern I'd cause Edward and Adele if I suddenly disappeared.

I just need a few minutes to myself. Ian may only be putting in a token appearance with the intention of leaving shortly. But even if he plans on remaining all the way through to the grand finale fireworks, the Crystal Palace is huge and it's filled with hundreds of people. There's no reason for our paths to cross.

A sudden thought occurs to me. What if he isn't here alone? What if he's with a companion? That debutante people were whispering he might be interested in, or the divorcee, the one who's rumored to be into light bondage? The bolt of jealousy ignited by the thought of Ian with another woman makes me reel. The lights are suddenly too bright, the sounds too piercing. Colors swirl behind my eyes. My vision begins to blur around the edges as dizziness threatens.

Forgetting the ladies' room, I push my way against the crowd toward the main doors. The sharp edge of panic is building inside me. I taste metal and realize that I've bitten my lower lip hard enough to draw blood.

The physical pain is of no consequence but the emotional... That's entirely different. I blink back tears as it occurs to me that not long ago I was afraid that I had no will of my own. As it turns out, I needn't have worried. I'm perfectly capable of getting furiously angry at Ian, disobeying him without a single qualm, saying 'no' to him, arguing with him, and even sending him away. What I can't do is stop longing for him. Logic, I'm realizing, has little part to play in human relationships. The heart wants what it wants, devoid of reason or sense.

Outside, I quickly move away from the guests who are still arriving. I'm not paying much attention to where I'm going until I realize that I'm standing beside the reflecting pool. By the time I notice, it's too late. The dizziness returns with a vengeance, hurtling me into another agonizing memory.

The white-coated technicians are priming their machines. Soon the pain will begin. I open my mouth to scream but my throat is paralyzed. Panic strikes and I struggle to breathe only to realize that I can't. I have never taken a breath, never eaten, hardly moved of my own volition. My body is maintained. My mind is left to fend for itself. As for my heart...

Where do the people go when they aren't on the other side of the glass walls? Where am I when I am not awake to see them?

Time passes, moments merging one into another. Suddenly, in a flicker, there are more beings on the other side of the glass, many more, working intently. So many, so busy that I try to brace myself for the agony that is to come. It does but not in any way I could expect.

Motion--I am moving!

Different walls surround me, a room I have never seen before but I hardly notice.

The level of liquid in my chamber is suddenly dropping. Terror fills me. How can I exist without the medium that has sustained me all this time?

I begin to thrash and am restrained. A tube is forced down my throat. Air fills my lungs for the first time.

Light unfiltered by fluid strikes my eyes. Sounds assail me...the murmur of voices, the beep of machinery...

I am strapped down on a hard surface. Something that I can't see is attached to my head. Pain and fear are so much my normal companions that I hardly notice them anymore. But suddenly there is more...much more...something faint, elusive, growing...

Someone.

Awareness explodes within me. For the first time, I have words and with them a flood of concepts and ideas that they illuminate. From all that, my mind forms a single, transforming thought:

I.

I exist. I am.

I blink and Ian is coming toward me out of the shadows. His stride is steady, his eyes intent. The world is falling away before me. I reach out frantically, feeling the brush of his fingers, the touch of his breath in the moment before hope slips from my grasp and I plummet into drowning darkness.

Chapter Four

Ian

*A*melia!"

I lunge forward as she's about to fall into the reflecting pool. All the breath goes out of me. What the hell? Edward told me she was all right, back to classes with the damn Russian and the usual social round. I wasn't going to follow her when I saw her leaving the ball but she looked upset and I couldn't stop myself--

Several of my men are converging out of the shadows. I order them off with a jerk of my head and carry her to a stone bench far enough away from the entrance that the guests who are still arriving won't see us.

Her face is pale against my shoulder, the delicate fringe of her lashes casting shadows across her cheeks. I can barely feel the faint rise and fall of her breath. She was always slender but now she's too damn light. I mutter a curse and sit down, holding her on my lap.

"Amelia, sweetheart, wake up." I can hear the fear in my voice. What if there's really something wrong? She's been going flat out ever since she awoke, thanks in no small measure to me. Could sensory overload have done this to her? What if she doesn't wake up? Everyone who knew squat about the customization protocols used when she was imprinted got vaporized when the Institute was destroyed by the HPF. Where will I find someone to help her? I should have known better. Should have taken better care of her. She was entrusted to me and all I've done is--

Her lashes flutter. She stirs in my arms. Relief hits me so hard that I gasp, sucking in air. It's a good thing I'm already sitting down.

She makes a soft sound and opens her eyes. For a moment, they're filled with confusion but then she focuses on me. At once, she stiffens.

"Ian--"

Yeah, Ian. The guy who fucked you with cold calculation while he told you about the demons that urge him to forget that you're a thinking, feeling human being and use you like the possession that the law says you are.

That guy.

I still have nightmares about the Club, something I didn't tell her. Lately, they've gotten a hell of a lot worse because she's in them.

"It's all right," I say quickly. "I'll let you go in a second. I just want to make sure that you're okay."

Her hand grips the lapel of my evening jacket. "Don't," she murmurs.

Don't what? Hold her? Talk to her? What?

"Don't let go."

Oh, shit. It's hard enough to hold on to my resolve where she's concerned without her giving me any excuse not to.

"Just for a minute," Amelia murmurs. "That's all. I just need to--" A shudder runs through her.

I can't help myself. My arms tighten around her. I touch my lips to her forehead as I inhale the unique, arousing scent of pure Amelia. She feels so fragile in my arms but I don't doubt her strength and courage any more than I do her passionate, honest, and giving nature. She's generous to a fault. She certainly has been with me and apparently still is given that she isn't pushing me away, screaming bloody murder, and demanding that I never come near her again. After ten days without her, it's all I can do not to carry her farther into the park, find a secluded spot and--

"Need to what, sweetheart?"

She doesn't answer, only presses closer to me. I'm savoring the feel of her, not even trying any more to figure out what's going on, when she gives a soft sigh.

I know that I have to put a stop to this. There's no question about that. Life can be murky as hell but where she's concerned right and wrong are so clear that the blinding clarity feels like an ice pick straight through my skull.

Let her go.

Simple, no brainer. Besides, I already did that when I told her the truth about myself and walked away from her.

There's no going back from that. Is there?

I look down and see my hand wrapped around her wrist. How the hell did it get there?

Her bones feel so delicate under my fingers. At least I'm not squeezing, just holding lightly. I've got that much control left, although I can't say how much longer even that will last.

The light of the floating lanterns, falling across her face, reveals a small injury to her lower lip.

"You're hurt." My voice is unintentionally harsh. I wince at the sound of it. The last thing I want to do is frighten her. The mere thought of doing so is like a knife twisting in me.

The tip of her tongue touches her lip for just an instant. A flare of heat moves through me.

"It's nothing," she says softly. Her eyes still won't meet mine. She's so damn lovely but far too pale. I can see the faint blue tracing of a blood vessel along the side of her forehead. She looks as though she's become almost translucent. The thought that she's fading away scares the shit out of me.

I take a breath and shift her a little on my lap, enough so that hopefully she won't be aware of the erection that's straining against my trousers. My cock has absolutely no sense of timing or anything else apart from the need to be deep inside her, thrusting hard, driving us both to--

I clear my throat and ask, "What happened? Why did you faint?"

She hesitates and I can tell that she's debating what to tell me. Finally, she says, "I just got a little dizzy, that's all."

She's withholding something. I don't have a clue what it is but I'm certain all the same. I can't blame her for not trusting me but I also can't stop myself from resenting the fact that she doesn't.

"If you weren't feeling well," I say, "you'd tell someone, right? Edward or Adele, someone. You wouldn't keep that to yourself."

The question seems to surprise her. "Yes, of course I would but I'm fine."

That's obviously not true but I don't want to argue about it so I change direction. "You shouldn't have come out here alone."

The irony of the situation doesn't escape me. I sent her away because I'm a danger to her but I don't trust anyone else to keep her safe, not even my own men. No wonder I'm tied up in knots, unable to sleep even when I get the chance, and so on edge that Hollis and Gab are tip-toeing around me.

"I needed some fresh air," she says.

I nod, pretending to understand. "It's a crush in there."

She's silent for a moment before she finally lifts her eyes to mine. Her gaze is unfathomable, her voice a thread of sound that makes me want to draw her even closer. "I didn't think you would be here."

What does that mean? That my presence makes her uncomfortable or... It hits me then, what I'm feeling from her. She's deeply, profoundly sad, as though her world has turned as dark and bleak as my own.

My chest feels as though it's about to crack. The need to comfort her is so overpowering that I know I'm on the verge of forgetting everything else and giving into it. Rather than let that happen, I stand abruptly, steadying her on her feet. I pull my hands away and take a quick step back but I can't help devouring her with my eyes.

Distantly, I notice that she's draped in diamonds. They encircle her throat and extend down over her delicate collarbones, clasp her wrists, adorn her ears, and nestle in her upswept hair. But their brilliance fades to insignificance beside the woman herself. Her gown is a deep, rich velvet, the color of aged claret. It's the perfect foil for alabaster skin suffused with a slight blush. Her chestnut hair has been mildly tamed and swept up to expose the delicate line of her throat. I stare at the pulse fluttering there and fight the urge to press my lips to it.

Hoarsely, I ask, "Amelia, what's wrong? And don't tell me again that you're fine because you obviously aren't."

She doesn't answer me directly but she does ask, "Why are you here?"

I run down a quick mental list of plausible reasons. Escorting my mother and sister is probably my best pick but I refuse to hide behind women.

"I need to know that you're safe." What the hell? Is telling her the truth becoming a habit?

She shoots me an anxious look. "The HPF--?"

"Gone," I say quickly. "You don't need to worry about them anymore."

"And the--"

She pauses delicately as I recall giving her the short version of what I intended to do to the HPF leaders once they were captured. Reduce them to babbling husks of men, was how I think I put it. Way to go, Slade, sensitive and reassuring as always.

"The information you wanted," she says. "Did you get it?"

"Edward and I have everything we need," I assure her, wanting to drop the subject. "We'll track the money, find out who was behind them. You don't need to worry about that either."

She nods and I think she's relieved that she's safe but then she opens her mouth and completely blows my world apart. "Thank God! I've been so worried about you."

About me? I'm the bad guy, sweetheart. The one other people lie awake at night worrying might be coming after them. Evil people, scumbags but still human in their own special ways.

"Going after the HPF was a horrible thing to have to do," she continues, oblivious to my thoughts. She's looking at me with those huge aquamarine eyes that are filled with an emotion I don't want to recognize because it looks dangerously like compassion. The shriveled thing in my chest that passes for a heart twists at the thought.

"I'm so sorry that you were dragged into all this," she says.

I've had nothing to drink. I don't touch drugs no matter how legal they are. So why am I hearing things?

And seeing them, too, because her eyes are glistening with tears, as though she's done something terrible that she can't ever forgive herself for. I'm so far out of my depth, so baffled that I can barely string a few words together.

"Uh...I think you've got it backwards. You're the one who didn't ask for any of this."

She looks at me as though I can't possibly be this obtuse. How little she knows! When it comes to Amelia, I've cornered the market on dumb and dumber.

Patiently, she says, "You're doing all this for my sake. That makes it my responsibility." She straightens her shoulders, tilts her chin up, and meets my gaze head on. Her voice is small but unwavering as she says, "I'm very well aware that Susannah sprang me on you with no warning. You never asked to be involved with me. And now I also know the harm I've caused you. What you've had to relive because of me. If there was some way that I could undo all that--"

She thinks this is her fault? She thinks I'd be better off never having known her? How is it possible for an intelligent, seemingly rational woman to get everything turned inside out like that?

No memories. No experience. No context. Knowledge but nothing to put it up against, no way to make sense of anything except gut instinct which, in this case at least, is dead wrong. That's how.

But she still has strength of character and raw courage that astound me. I've known a shit load of people in this world who won't take responsibility for anything. Who always have some excuse why they're never to blame no matter what harm they do or how much havoc they wreak.

Hell, I've put some of them in the ground.

And this woman--this beautiful, brave woman--stands right in front of me and apologizes because I'm the dark, deeply flawed bastard that I am?

Hell, no. No way she gets to do that.

"Listen to me," I say. "You have nothing to be sorry about. You're the innocent party in all of this. You have been from the very beginning." Completely innocent as I would have realized before that first night with her in the golden bed if I had been thinking straight. I should have taken it a hell of a lot slower with her or better yet kept my hands off her entirely. If I were remotely the man she thought I was, I would have. Instead, I'm--

"I may be inexperienced, Ian," she says softly. "But I'm not a child to be protected from unpleasant truths. Please don't treat me like one."

If the suddenly steely glint in her eyes is anything to go by, she means it.

"All right then," I say, regrouping rapidly. "Tell me the truth. How are you really?"

Reluctantly, she says, "I breathe. I eat after a fashion. I would sleep more but when I do, I dream. How are you?"

What's wrong with her dreams, unless she means that they're nightmares? I want to ask her about that but I'm scared that she'll say I'm in them. Instead, I say, "I bench pressed four eighty the other day. That's a record for me."

She nods, smiling like that's great. "So you're working out. That's good...healthy."

It beats pacing the floor at night, my body feeling like it's been twisted into knots with longing for her and my skin burning for her touch.

"I've been playing a little handball, too," I add. In between interrogation sessions and only with the rapidly shrinking pool of guys willing to get on a court with me while I'm in the mood that I am.

"How is Hodge?" she asks suddenly. Amelia and the combination steward, jack-of-all-trades and voice of my conscience who pulled me out of the hell my father had consigned me to took to each other right from the start. Hodgkin--Hodge--has been giving me the fish eye ever since I got back and not because he gave a shit about what I was doing to the HPF assholes. He thinks I'm nuts to have parted from Amelia, which makes no sense at all given that he should know better than anyone how bad I am for her.

"And Gab?" she adds. "How is she?"

Oh, yeah, Gab, who's happily hitched to her beloved Daphne and these days just gives me pitying looks.

"They're both good. Edward says you're back to dancing."

Polite chitchat isn't part of my usual repertoire but I'm willing to do it if it distracts her and makes her even a little less sad and anxious.

She nods. "Sergei is very good about making time for me. Especially considering how busy he is putting together a production of 'Medea' for Carnival."

The Russian, a mad woman who kills her kids, and the city-wide insanity that descends every year with Carnival. Perfect.

"He's a prince." I have no doubt that good old Sergei would like to be doing a hell of a lot more than just taking Amelia through her dance steps. In my perfect world, he wouldn't get within a mile of her. But no matter what the law says, Amelia is her own person, fully capable of making her own choices. I wouldn't have it any other way. At least the rational part of me wouldn't.

Unfortunately, it's not totally in control at the moment.

I take a step closer, knowing I shouldn't, unable to stop myself, and frankly bewildered by what's happening to me. I've never been in a situation like this before, not remotely close. Amelia undoes me in ways that I can't fathom. With her, I can feel the coils of pain and memory that entwine so deeply inside me beginning to loosen. Far in the back of my mind, I can't help wondering what will happen if they unravel completely. Will she know how to gather them up and reweave them into something new and better? I sure as hell don't.

Her breath catches but she doesn't move. As though I'm detached from it, I watch my hand rise, the fingers curled. My knuckles brush very gently along the arc of her cheek. I savor the touch of her skin, the small tremor that runs through her, the sense, however brief, of being connected to her.

Her eyes close for a moment. When they open again, I see the desperate longing that mirrors my own. "Ian--"

The sound of my name draws me back into the here-and-now. What the hell am I thinking? I came out here to keep an eye on her, protect her, not to remind myself of how much I want to be inside her, filling her with incandescent pleasure, savoring the exquisite sight of her as she comes.

My hand drops. I take a step back. Whatever small victory that may represent is drowned in the sudden sense of desolation that sweeps over me. I'm swamped by the bleak reality of what it really means to face life without her.

Neither of us moves. We just stand there, staring at each other until, without warning, I feel a familiar prickling between my shoulders. Instinctively, I turn, putting myself between Amelia and whatever danger I've suddenly sensed.

But there's nothing. Only the glittering Crystal Palace, the light and music pouring from it, and the softly bobbing lanterns casting their glow across the reflecting pool.

Or so I think until a shape moves in the shadows to the side of the entrance. For just an instant, I catch a glimpse of silver hair and tanned, patrician features. I don't need to see more.

My hand closes on her elbow. I feel her start of surprise but ignore it.

"You should go back inside now," I say, my tone making it clear that I won't tolerate any argument.

I want her where I can keep a close eye on her and I need to have a quiet word with Edward. He won't be any more pleased than I am to learn that Charles Davos, a man we both have the darkest suspicions about, shows no sign of having gotten over his unhealthy interest in Amelia. He's there, in the shadows, watching her. Watching us.

The grim certainty settles over me that one way or another this evening is not going to end well.

Chapter Five

Amelia

The young man I'm dancing with is going on about something to do with his family's investment firm. I nod with what I hope is an appropriate degree of interest. The truth is that I scarcely hear him. I can't focus on anything other than Ian.

The shock of being in his arms again, surrounded by his strength and protectiveness has blasted apart the façade of calm I've only barely managed to maintain since we parted ten days ago. I am standing, I am breathing, I must appear normal enough because no one is reacting to me oddly. But it all feels as though it is happening to a stranger. I am outside my own body, staring at myself, wondering who that woman is who manages to look so composed when everything inside me is in turmoil.

I can't be wrong that Ian was also affected by our encounter. The way he looked at me curls my toes in my satin heels. For a moment, I indulge in the wild thought of what it would be like to be with him again, our bodies touching, entwining--

"Of course, it was an enormous coup for us," my dance partner says. "I almost felt sorry for the poor bastards on the other side. They never saw it coming." He chuckles.

"Fascinating." I speak by rote, too pre-occupied staring over his shoulder to be more than barely aware of what I am saying.

Ian is standing off to one side of the ballroom, an aloof presence whose manner is guaranteed to discourage anyone tempted to engage him in conversation. Earlier, I saw him speaking with Edward but since then he's done nothing other than watch me. That should be unnerving or annoying but for the first time in ten days, I feel a stirring of hope.

I cherish it even as I know that it's misplaced. Nothing has changed. I'm no better for Ian than I was the moment I awoke. If not for me, he could have gone on with his life without having to confront the demons of his past. I can't bear what my existence has cost him.

Any more than I can bear being without him.

The dance ends. Another eligible young man appears to sweep me away. I wonder vaguely how many of them there are but nothing about them can really hold my attention. They are more or less interchangeable, some slightly taller or shorter, more or less graceful, chattier or not. One has particularly sweaty palms, another holds me too tightly, making me glad of the added protection of the corset I'm wearing. But apart from that I notice very little about them. I'm functioning on automatic--dancing, speaking, smiling without any thought except for Ian.

At last, blessed relief, the chime sounds for supper. There will be more dancing later, followed by the fireworks that conclude the evening but I have a brief respite. Edward appears to escort me to our family's table. To my surprise, Ian is already there with his mother and sister.

The thinned, stern line of his mouth takes me aback. He was so gentle outside but now he seems anything but. Is he displeased that we're seated together? Or has something else angered him?

My grandmother is chatting happily with Helene Slade. Although Ian's mother is several decades younger than Adele, the two are good friends. Meanwhile, lovely, blonde Marianne is looking a bit flushed. I notice Edward's gaze on her and wonder who exactly arranged for our two families to be seated together.

Ian holds out a chair for me next to Marianne. As I sit, the backs of his hands brush the bare skin of my shoulders. I close my eyes for a moment against a wave of yearning that robs me of breath. When I open them again, he has taken the other seat beside me.

"Enjoy the dancing?" he asks with an edge in his voice that throws me further off balance. It sounds strangely like... jealousy? Is it possible that the sight of me in the arms of other men is responsible for his mood? I flush at the thought. We were only dancing, for heaven's sake! Strictly proper ballroom dancing, and I was barely conscious of doing that because all I could think of was him.

Belatedly, I remember what his own sister told me about him. Ian is highly possessive, at least when it comes to anything--or anyone--he really cares about.

A giddy recklessness sweeps over me. Throwing self-preservation to the winds, I say, "I love to dance, so much so that I've overdone on occasion. But you know that already, don't you?"

His lean cheeks darken at the reminder of an episode that occurred shortly after I awoke, when we were both still at his estate north of the city. Reeling from his revelations about how we had come to be together and anxious to discover what abilities Susannah had given me, I attempted a grand jeté without being properly conditioned for it. The agonizing cramp that resulted all but crippled me. Fortunately, Ian was on hand to soothe my injuries in the most effective way possible.

"I know that you need someone to rein you in," he growls.

I glance around the table nervously, hoping no one heard his suggestive tone. I needn't have worried. Adele and Helene are still chatting happily. As for Marianne and Edward...

At first glance, she appears to be looking at him as she would any man she has known all her life and regards as a friend. But I catch a glimpse of more personal interest in her gaze that surprises me. In contrast, Edward's expression gives away nothing. I can't help wondering why he is being so guarded. Marianne is lovely, Ian would surely approve, and society in general would consider them an excellent match. What then stands between them? Or is it who? I know nothing of my brother's personal life but my instincts tell me that there is far more to him than he shows to the world.

When I look away from them, my gaze falls on Ian's hand, lying on the damask tablecloth. The knuckles are scraped. My throat tightens as I wonder how that happened. My thoughts leap to his confrontation with the HPF, the danger he placed himself in, the acts he has committed in order to protect me. I try to force my gaze away, anxious that I'll make a spectacle of myself. But instead, I find myself remembering how that hand feels on my body--stroking, teasing, taking, his long fingers sliding inside me, unerringly finding that spot where I am so exquisitely sensitive.

My breath quickens. I reach out for the crystal water goblet at my place setting and almost knock it over. My face flaming with a mixture of embarrassment and arousal, I catch it and manage to take a small sip before the waiters arrive with the first course.

The food is superb, as it always is at such events. To my surprise, my appetite has returned. I eat but I skip the various wines that are poured for each course. If I'm certain of one thing. seated as close as I am to Ian I need to keep a clear head.

That's easier said than done. No sign of his displeasure remains as he morphs into a charming and attentive dinner companion. He listens with apparent interest as my grandmother describes the goings-on at an artists' colony that she supports. The mix of partner swapping, petty sabotage, and grandiose rivalries sounds like it would make a good basis for one of the reality shows that dominate the video stream.

I watched one the other night when I couldn't sleep yet again, something about people competing for a shot at a personal assistant job. Some of the tasks they were given seemed deliberately demeaning-- cleaning a bathroom with a toothbrush and cotton swabs, carrying a tray of drinks over a swaying bridge that dumped the unlucky into a vat of mud, and so on. But the winner--chosen by a panel of prospective employers-- was thrilled to the point of tears.

"What's wrong?" Ian asks.

Belatedly, I realize that I'm frowning. With a quick shake of my head, I say, "I was just thinking. It's so hard for people to find work without a patron or mentor to smooth the way for them. Doesn't that mean that a lot of human potential is going to waste?"

He turns further in his chair and studies me. I only just manage to hold myself still and not look away from him. The thought goes through my mind that he's taking what I said seriously and weighing his response.

After several moments that seem to draw out forever, he sighs. "That's the central problem of our age. We're learning that it isn't enough to meet the basic needs of human beings--food, shelter, and so on. Without a sense of purpose and the self-worth that comes from it, people flounder. Some escape into gaming, drugs, cults, whatever. Others get caught up in outfits like the HPF."

At the mention of the terrorist organization, I stiffen. I want to know more about the people who would have destroyed me and everyone like me. But I feel guilty enough about what Ian had to do for my protection without asking him to revisit a subject he may want closed forever.

Even so, he did bring it up and this may be the only opportunity I will have to learn more. Tentatively, I ask, "They really believed that the ability to imprint one person's neural pattern on another is a threat to the survival of the human race?"

I do understand their fear to some extent. The replica technology could enable very wealthy people to achieve a kind of immortality by preserving their own neural patterns through generation after generation of replicas. They could achieve a suffocating stranglehold on society, preventing any change that didn't serve their own purposes. But there are billions of human beings. How can anyone possibly believe that a handful of replicas could drive them into extinction?

That's bad enough but Ian has a different and in some way even more terrifying perspective. "The replica technology has enormous potential for misuse," he says. "The ability to customize replicas only makes that worse. If it hadn't been destroyed when the Institute was blown up, that process could have been used to produce individuals denied the free will that makes us human and condemned to a form of slavery worse even than any that has ever existed before."

The thought horrifies me, both for the sake of the poor creatures who could suffer such a fate and because Ian himself is clearly repulsed by the very idea. For the first time, I have to confront the fact that he has a highly negative view of the technology that made me who I am. What does that say about how he views me? Of our time together and the intimacy that I thought we shared?

My throat tightens. I only just manage to say, "It almost sounds as though you're defending the HPF."

He dismisses that idea out of hand. "Then I'm not being clear. Nothing excuses terrorism but in order to combat it, we have to understand its roots. As crazed as the HPFers were, they tapped into a fear that's shared

Josie Litton

by many. Technology was supposed to empower people. Instead, it's made far too many of us obsolete. Species that don't earn their own way don't survive for very long."

I'm struck by his use of 'we' and 'us', as though he can empathize with people who will never achieve anything in their lives remotely like what he has done. I can't help wondering how many of the other attendees at the Crystal Ball could do the same. The sense of privilege and entitlement is overwhelming among the very select group of individuals who are the winners in this brave new world. The problem is that makes everyone else losers, something people are bound to resent, if not worse.

"When you put it like that," I say, "I have to wonder why there isn't more unrest."

"People who commit what the government classifies as crimes lose their benefits," Edward says quietly. I hadn't noticed that he was listening but now I realize that the others have tuned into Ian and my conversation. Our table is an island of seriousness in a sea of frivolity. "With no other way to survive," my brother adds, "they have to become scavengers."

"That's a fate that anyone would fear," Marianne says softly. "I imagine that most people just accept their lot rather than risk having that happen to them."

"And to their children," Adele adds. "People who lose their benefits also lose their children. Minors in those circumstances become wards of the state unless their parents go underground with them."

I think of the ragged, hungry children I saw earlier and a surge of anger fills me. Dimly I realize that this is the emotion that has been building in me ever since I arrived in the city. I've fought against it because more even than my yearning for Ian, it frightens me. By any measure, I can be considered naïve, having been awake such a short time, but I am coming to appreciate the advantage of seeing with new eyes, not jaded by experience. Eyes that increasingly view the world with painful clarity, cutting through the façade of beauty and luxury to a far uglier reality.

My companions may see a more complex situation than I am capable of appreciating but that doesn't change the essential truth that I refuse to deny any longer.

"This is wrong," I say, gesturing to our exquisite surroundings and beyond--the park, the city, the world of excess and indulgence that presses in on me with claustrophobic intensity. "Profoundly wrong. Something has to change. The status quo isn't just deeply unjust, it's also dangerous. However fearful people may be, when their survival hangs in the balance and even their children are threatened, I have to believe that they will act. The only uncertainty is when and how. That and how many will die in the process."

A glance goes around the table. I sense a silent understanding that eludes me. "Another time," Edward says softly. "Another place." He isn't reprimanding me, only reminding me that the setting calls for discretion. I flush, suddenly feeling very young but knowing that he is right.

The conversation moves on to less sensitive topics. I try to be attentive to it but my dark thoughts about the world in which I find myself entwine with my vivid awareness of Ian. I can't help wondering where he stands. He possesses enormous power but if it really came down to it, which side would he choose--the privileged elite to which he undeniably belongs or the masses of ordinary people for whom he seems to have at least some empathy?

I can't answer that question. The man who has taken me to the heights of ecstasy and the depths of despair is still very much a stranger to me. That thought leaves me subdued through the rest of supper. When the dancing resumes, my body feels unaccountably heavy. I go through the motions as I did before but they require far more effort. My face hurts with the strain of smiling. I'm feeling trapped when an all-too-familiar presence suddenly appears.

Charles Davos gives my current dance partner a chill smile and jerks his head slightly in a gesture of dismissal. The young man--who presumably comes from an affluent, powerful family--doesn't hesitate. He steps aside at once, in effect handing me over to Davos.

Before I can get over my own shock at his sudden appearance, I am in the arms of the silver-haired, seventyish patrician who is rumored to control the city council and a great deal more. Despite his age, he is tall and fit, the result no doubt of every longevity enhancement that money can buy.

My instinct is to wrench myself free and walk away. But if I do that, I'll draw unwanted attention. Stymied, I remain as I am.

"Forgive me," Davos says. He looks well aware of my predicament and amused by it. "I couldn't bear watching you stumbling about with yet another hapless swain. I really don't know what ails young men these days. They are sadly lacking in both style and substance."

He is holding me in a perfectly proper fashion, one hand resting lightly on my waist and the other clasping my own. His skin is cool and dry. He smells of citrus but underneath that is a musky, oily scent that makes me recoil. His yellow-green eyes have an almost reptilian cast. I am truly ill at ease around Charles Davos, not in the least because he had an unhealthy fascination with Susannah that he seems to be transferring to me.

Above all, I'm afraid he knows that I have something to hide. He may even have an inkling of what it is.

I glance over his shoulder, looking for Ian or Edward. Neither of them would approve of my dancing with Davos but they are both absent from the ballroom at that moment. Perhaps it's just as well that I handle this myself.

"What do you want?" I ask. The question is too blunt for our gracious surroundings but I'm past caring. I just want to be done with him.

Davos raises a brow. "You're very direct, my dear. I can accept that...for now. I want to do you a favor. If you're as smart as I think you are, you'll be grateful."

The thought of owing Charles Davos anything makes my skin crawl. "I neither need nor want any favors from you."

Unperturbed, he says, "You should be careful about your dealings with Ian Slade."

I stumble a step. Ian and I have attended many of the same social events but we've almost never been seen together in public except as part of a larger group. Davos can't possibly know what happened between us at the estate or later in the city--at the opera house, the polo club, the gallery at Pinnacle House. All those times and places that I absolutely must not think of right now.

"I'm friends with Helene and Marianne Slade," I say, proud that my voice is rock steady. "But I'm scarcely acquainted with Ian."

Davos smiles. "That's very good. If I didn't know better, I could almost believe you. Susannah was a remarkable young woman in so many ways but sadly that didn't prevent her from succumbing to Slade. I would hate to see you make the same mistake, especially under the circumstances."

Despite myself, I rise to the bait. "What do you mean?"

He shrugs. "Ian has always walked a very fine line where the law is concerned. I'm sorry to say that recently he's crossed it. He will have to be held accountable for his actions. No one can be allowed to operate as a power unto himself. That simply isn't good for society."

"Accountable to whom?" The moment I ask, I know I've made a mistake. I've tacitly acknowledged that there is something Ian could account for, at least if he was so inclined.

"And for what?" I add hastily. "What are you claiming that he's done?"

"Besides lead his private army against civilians who had not been charged with any crime, take them prisoner, and interrogate them himself using who-knows-what barbaric methods? Make no mistake, such actions will not be tolerated."

I struggle to conceal my shock. To the best of my knowledge, only a handful of people know about Ian's involvement in the destruction of the HPF. How does Davos?

He draws me a little closer. "I would hate to see you caught up in the official reaction to Slade's disregard for the rule of law. You have a chance for a wonderful life here but that won't be the case if you are linked to him."

The anger I experienced earlier returns in force. How dare the likes of Charles Davos claim that being associated with a man of Ian's courage and honor could harm anyone? He isn't fit to wipe the mud off Ian's boots.

I'm about to tell him so and the consequences be damned when my breath catches. Ian has returned to the ball room and seen us. He is crossing the dance floor on a missile-like trajectory. Anyone who doesn't get out of his way is in danger of being flattened. The rage on his face makes me quake even as I know full well that I'm not the target of it.

Josie Litton

Chapter Six

Ian

*G*et the fuck away from her."

I don't even try to keep my voice down. All I can think of is ripping Davos' hands off Amelia and hurtling him against the nearest wall. Dimly, I'm aware of the shocked looks of the couples around us. They've stopped dancing and are either standing frozen in place staring or--the smarter among them-- prudently backing away. All I really see is Amelia's white, strained face. She knows perfectly well that I'm revealing to anyone with eyes to see how involved we are. I just can't bring myself to care.

Being with Amelia, holding her, hearing her voice has me on a kind of high that I can't really understand and sure as hell can't control. Worse yet, I don't even regret it. For a guy whose kept such a strict rein on his emotions for years, I'm a mess. Anger, worry, arousal and a bizarre giddy happiness are at war in me.

By forcing my hand, Davos has done me a favor in a weird way, although he'd be enraged if he realized it. Thanks to him, I'm doing what I've wanted most even as I've moved heaven and earth to avoid admitting it. I'm claiming Amelia as my own and the world be damned. I'll deal with the consequences later.

The look that flits across Davos' face confirms that his stratagem in approaching Amelia has worked. Any doubts he had about the nature of her relationship with me have been answered once and for all. If he puts that together with the fate of the replica-hating HPF and draws the correct conclusions, we'll have a real problem. But at the moment, I can't give a shit. Let the whole world know how I feel about her. I'm not the only danger to Amelia, far from it. If I can hold the others at bay by making it clear that she's mine, then that's exactly what I'll do.

"Just as I suspected," Davos says with a sneer. "You haven't changed at all, Slade. You're still a savage."

Ordinarily, I'd never consider striking a seventy year-old man but Davos is in a league all his own. He has been ever since I encountered him at the club my father ran. Some of the men had to be drawn in slowly, perverted step by step. Not Davos. He took to it all like the proverbial duck to water, the sick bastard.

But he's gotten as much from me as he's going to get. I take Amelia's arm and draw her away. To my great relief, she doesn't resist. I wouldn't have blamed her if she did. Yet I can't forget how she felt in my arms a few hours ago, the fear that consumed me when I thought she might be ill and my relief that she isn't. Right alongside all that is the passion she unleashes in me, making a mockery of the self-control I've practiced for so long that I was arrogant enough to think it had become second nature. Now I know better.

I should find Edward and leave her with him. Walk away and don't look back. But every fiber of my being rejects even the thought of that. Without moving, I watch as Davos vacates the dance floor, oozing arrogance with every step.

The music pauses, then begins again, a slow, languorous melody with sultry undertones from a sax that coil through the air and settle deep down inside me. I can feel the warmth of her body so close to mine. My gaze drifts to the swell of her breasts, rising and falling with each breath she takes. From the first moment I saw her, I've desired Amelia with an intensity that I've never experienced with any other woman. Even at our most intimate moments, when I've been deep inside her, pouring my life into her, my need for her has never eased. But it has changed, becoming as much emotional as physical in a way that frankly scares the shit out of me.

I raise my eyes and meet her gaze, seeing in it a depth of longing that I don't deserve but can't resist.

Hell, with all the damage I've just done, what's a little more? "Dance with me," I say.

She doesn't hesitate but instead flows into my arms as though they're the one place where she belongs. The realization is humbling even as it troubles me deeply. This woman is a lot of things, all of them remarkable, but she definitely comes up short on self-preservation. I thought that she'd accepted once and for all that I'm bad for her but now I'm wondering if I'm wrong.

As relieved as I am that she's got a full measure of free will and then some, I'm not totally sold on how stubborn she can be. When she gets that steely look in her eyes--

"Davos knows that you're behind what happened to the HPF. He claims that you're going to be held to account for it."

All I want to do is sink myself into her and-- "What's that?" I ask belatedly.

She shoots me a chiding glare that, heaven help me, makes my cock twitch. But then so does everything about her.

"Davos. You. HPF. Government. Trouble."

"Oh, right, that. Don't worry about it."

"How can I not?" she demands. "You did it because of me and now--" Her voice trembles. She looks truly concerned. For me.

My throat tightens. With an effort, I say, "Amelia, Davos is bluffing. He doesn't know anything, at least not for certain. He's just trying to frighten you. The government is glad to have the HPF eliminated without getting their own hands dirty. They're not going to question who did it. Even if they were inclined to do so, they're not going to pick a fight with me."

I'm not bragging, although it could be taken that way. The men and the few women who run the government--really run it unlike the puppets who front for them--don't care about anything except their own well-being. Some of them shelter behind the notion that what's good for them is ultimately good for everyone. I can only laugh at their vanity and arrogance. Others, the ones I consider more dangerous, have an even more self-centered vision of how the country and the world should be. Anything done to make that vision real is fine with them. They're a classic case of the ends justifying the means. Tangling with me is a complication they don't want. On the contrary, I know full well that they still hope to co-opt me to their side.

Amelia tilts her head back and looks at me directly. "Why is that, Ian? What reason would the government have to fear you?"

I shrug, partly because I'm uncomfortable with the question but mainly because I don't really know the answer. Not yet. My gut says that the time is coming when I'll have to make a choice. But for the moment, I duck the issue, saying only, "The government is happy enough to use defense companies like mine when they want to avoid public accountability. If they're waking up to the fact that there's a downside to so much power being concentrated in private hands, that's their problem."

"But they could still come after you," she insists. "They're hardly without their own resources and they can be influenced, can't they? By someone like Davos, for instance. He isn't making any secret of how much he dislikes you."

I choose my next words carefully, wanting to make her understand but also wanting to put an end to the subject.

"The authorities won't come after me just because of Davos. It would take a whole lot more than that. I haven't sought a direct confrontation with them and they have every reason not to do so with me."

Without giving her a chance to respond, I draw her closer, inhaling her scent. The effect almost pushes me over the edge. If we weren't in the middle of a crowded dance floor--

Not trusting myself with that line of thought, I look around for any distraction and stumble across the most obvious one.

"Nice diamonds," I say.

She flushes a little and shrugs. "I don't think anyone has seen past them all night."

She's serious, which has me shaking my head if only inwardly. Amelia is the least vain woman I've ever known. In a very real sense and despite everything we've shared, she truly doesn't understand the effect she has on me.

Or on other men, yet another thought that I don't want to entertain just now.

We sway to the slow, sensual throb of the music. I forget about Davos, the HPF, all of it and just concentrate on the pleasure of holding her. I'm wondering why we didn't do this before, back at the estate or since. Too busy having mind-blowing sex, I guess. But there's something to be said for just being like this, surrounded by other people but still alone together in our own bubble.

It doesn't last, of course. Nothing that good ever does. Too soon, I catch sight of Edward. We left the floor at the same time so that I could update him on arrangements to deal with any possible threat that could arise this evening. Davos must have been watching and seized his opportunity to go after Amelia. I won't repeat that mistake. The bastard's never getting anywhere near her again.

Edward's talking with Marianne. No surprise there. Our mother is standing nearby, smiling. She's well aware of my sister's interest in my old pal and apparently approves. I'm not there yet but I'm getting closer.

"She cares for him, you know," Amelia says softly. Her gaze has followed my own but I'm looking at her now and I see the wistfulness in her eyes. It puzzles me. Why would the sight of her brother and my sister together spark such an expression of longing in her unless...

The answer hits me hard. Edward's a fundamentally decent guy with the patience to bring an innocent young woman along gently. Any "wooing" I ever did of Amelia happened in bed...or against a wall, on a floor, anywhere that happened to be convenient. I regret that now. She deserved better.

I've sent her away twice--once from the estate and the second time supposedly out of my life altogether. Yet here we are.

Third time's the charm? I almost laugh at the thought. Nothing about my life has been charmed and for sure nothing about Amelia's has been either. Riding off into the happily-ever-after may be fine for Edward and Marianne. If he makes a move on her that had damn well be what does happen. But it's not for us.

Us. I turn the word over in my mind. It hurts but I take the pain and hold on to the idea. That feels good enough that I let it linger as the music picks up again. Amelia and I dance on.

Chapter Seven

Amelia

I can't fathom Ian's mood. He seems genuinely unconcerned about any danger to himself whereas I'm still shaking from his confrontation with Davos. What can I say to convince him to take the threat to his own safety seriously?

Even if I could find the words, I doubt that anything that would come out of my mouth right now would make much sense. Being with Ian again, in his arms, the warmth of his body driving away the cold that has sunk into my bones since we parted makes me feel as though I am flying apart. I'm torn between joyful relief and the sharp pain of knowing that we will go our separate ways when the ball is over and the evening ends.

How can we do otherwise? When we are together, he fears that he will harm me and I know that I am harming him. I can't bear to be the cause of his suffering. Yet here we are...dancing. His right hand holds mine with gentle firmness while the other rests possessively on my waist. My palm has drifted a little from the broad sweep of his shoulder. I can feel the powerful muscles of his upper arm even through the fabric of his evening jacket. Too vividly I remember what he looks like in his natural state, his body perfectly formed and honed, the ultimate expression of masculine beauty.

I close my eyes, swept by longing so intense that it robs me of breath. When I open them again, Ian is staring down at me. His gaze is darkened by concern.

"Are you all right? What's wrong?"

It's on the tip of my tongue to assure him that I'm fine when I stop myself. Treacherous longing uncurls deep inside me. I have so little time with him...

"I'm still a little dizzy. I could use some fresh air."

My cheeks flame at the bold-faced lie. Apparently there's nothing I won't stoop to in order to be alone with Ian. Just for a few minutes. Where's the harm in that? Hundreds of people surround us. More than a few of their eyes are on us. With such diligent chaperones, we can't possibly get into any trouble. Can we?

"Let's step outside," Ian says. Holding my hand, he leads me from the dance floor. I go with him gladly, only hoping that I can control my unease near the reflecting pool. I'm fully aware that the problem I have with standing bodies of water is directly related to the torturous years of intermittent consciousness in the gestation chamber. But recognizing that and being able to control it are two very different things.

When I realize that Ian is leading me onto a stone terrace that extends from the opposite side of the Crystal Palace, out of sight of the pool, I all but sag with relief. We are on the western edge of the park, facing a broad swath of lawn studded with gnarled trees. Beyond it lies a low wall of gray stone covered in lichen. On the far side of the wall is an avenue lined with tall, stone-faced buildings, many dating from the previous century. They are home to some of the cities wealthiest and most powerful.

The air is cool and slightly moist. Before I can stop him, Ian takes off his jacket and lays it over my shoulders. I breathe in the scent of the fabric that still holds the heat of his body. The sensation of comfort and protectiveness is all but overwhelming but I don't dare yield to it.

Instead, I say, "You don't have to do that."

"Do what?" he asks, his voice low and deep, close to my ear.

My hands clutch the lapels, holding onto them as though I am holding onto him. I stare out at the twinkling lights that fill the trees. "You don't have to take care of me. We aren't together anymore."

I'm reminding myself more than him. The world in which I find myself is too full of danger. I can't afford to indulge in any fantasies about the two of us.

He stiffens beside me. With surprise? Displeasure? I can't be sure which. "Maybe I'm just being chivalrous."

I turn, forcing myself to face him. "You feel responsible for me but you shouldn't. We both know that you never asked for me to be in your life."

He frowns as though he isn't following me. "I didn't know to ask. I could never have imagined you. You were a gift, in every sense of the word. The most amazing, remarkable, and--" His mouth quirks slightly. "--challenging gift that I would never even have thought to dream of."

His words and the warmth with which he speaks them bring a sudden rush of tears to my eyes. I blink it back fiercely, struggling for control. No matter how much I want to believe his version of us, we can't deny what my existence has done to him.

"A gift?" I scoff. "One that's forced you to relive the past and confront demons you thought had been put to rest a long time ago. Who would ever ask for that?"

He shrugs. "No one, probably. But knowing you, being with you has made me realize that not dealing with the past doesn't resolve anything. Old sins just fester and become even more destructive."

"They aren't your sins." At the very thought, anger rises in me. "You were only fifteen years old. The guilt was your father's, not yours. He involved you in that terrible place."

Ian is silent for a moment, gazing at me intently. Slowly, he strokes the backs of his knuckles along my cheek. The pad of his thumb finds and tugs lightly at my lower lip. At his touch, my whole body ignites. I can barely suppress a moan.

His eyes darken. I have the sense that he is struggling inwardly, weighing how much and what to say. Even so, his next words surprise me.

"What about the pleasure, Amelia?" he asks softly. "Do you imagine that wasn't mine, as well?"

I stare at him, unsure what he is telling me. He was an adolescent, in the throes of puberty. Of course, having sex would be physically pleasurable but that doesn't mean--

A faint, sad smile flicks across his face. "There were aspects of it--the dominance, the possession, the control--that appealed to me." He turns serious, somber even, as though he wants to be sure that I understand the full import of what he is revealing. "They still do."

A tremor runs through me. My own nature isn't remotely submissive. On the contrary, it's a good thing that I'm inclined to defiance or I would never have survived. And yet, when I'm with Ian, something dark and primal deep within me stirs to life. I become a being of pure sensuality, craving his possession more even than light or air. Too easily I remember how it felt to be beneath him, controlled by him, his cock thrusting into me, driving us both to ecstatic release.

Ian is staring at my mouth. "Don't do that," he says.

"Do what?"

"Wet your lips."

I didn't realize I was doing so. I stop at once but it's too late. Heat flares in his eyes. Passion? Anger? I can't tell. Starkly, as though to discomfit me as much as I just have him, he says, "It reminds me of how good it feels to be in your mouth."

The muscles at my core clench. We're in the midst of an ultra-elegant event attended by hundreds of the city's elite. But suddenly all I can think of the wetness pooling between my thighs.

"We should go back inside." My voice lacks even a hint of conviction.

"We could do that," Ian agrees. He takes my elbow but instead of guiding me back into the Crystal Palace, we go in the opposite direction, down a short flight of stone steps and out across the lawn. My heels sink into the soft ground. Excitement flares in me as I wonder what he is contemplating.

He slows his pace to accommodate mine but doesn't halt until we are twenty yards or more from the terrace, looking back at the ball. Light, music, and laughter spill from the glittering pleasure dome. But it is surrounded by deepening shadows and appears to be floating on a sea of impenetrable darkness.

"I used to come here when I was a kid," Ian says quietly. "There was an old restaurant at this location. Tavern on the Green, I think it was called. It was torn down the winter I turned eight and the Crystal Palace was built in its place. I found the whole process fascinating."

My throat tightens as I think of the innocent child he was before his father drew him into his own twisted nightmare and tried to make him nothing more an extension of himself. A part of me is fiercely glad that Marcus Slade ultimately drove his high-powered sports car off the side of a cliff. The world is a better place by far without him.

We are standing beside an ancient, gnarled oak tree. Its branches spread out above us, filled with new leaves unfurling from spring buds. I breathe in the scents of the night and try to find solace in the simple act of being close to Ian. It works, to a degree.

Even so, I start when he lifts my hand and lays it, palm down, against the rough bark. Quietly, he says, "I carved my initials into this tree. Right about...there. Feel them?"

Gradually, my fingertips find and trace the shape of an 'I' followed by an 'S'. Two decades have passed since an eight year-old boy stood here. The evidence of his presence has become blurred but I can still detect it.

"Why did you do that?" I ask.

He hesitates, long enough for me to wonder if he's going to answer. Finally, he say, "That was the winter when I realized how bad things really were between my parents." His mouth tightens with old, remembered pain. "My mother had bruises. I knew how she was getting them but I couldn't do anything about it."

"Did you tell anyone?"

He shakes his head. "Even then I had a sense of how powerful my father was. I knew that no one would take her side against him. When I tried to talk to her, my mother insisted that everything was fine. I realize now that she was doing what she thought she had to do in order to protect her children."

"She loves you very much." I haven't spent a great deal of time with Helene Slade but I have gotten to know her well enough to be certain that she was and still is a devoted mother. One who did find the courage to leave her abusive husband once she was certain that Ian had escaped him.

He nods. "She's a wonderful woman but nothing could change the fact that I felt completely helpless. That scared the shit out of me and made me really angry. I started ditching school, roaming all over the city, looking for something, anything that could help. In a weird way, watching a building being torn down and something new going up in its place was a reminder that nothing's forever, things can be changed, made better."

As the significance of what this place means to him settles over me, I ask, "That's why you carved your initials here?"

He shrugs. "I guess. I think that I wanted to leave some evidence that even though I couldn't do anything to help my mother, I was still real. I existed."

My throat clenches. I know all too well the pain that comes from trying to affirm one's existence to an uncaring universe. But at the same time, I'm well aware that Ian is opening up to me in a way he has never done before. First admitting to desires he has fought to deny and then revealing how vulnerable he has felt.

I could weep for the child he was but it's to the man that I turn. My fingers, coming away from the tree, twine around his. I rest my other hand on his chest and lift myself on tiptoe. Softly, I touch my mouth to his, giving him time to draw back should he so choose.

When he doesn't, I'm emboldened. If there's any chance that he's right about it being better not to let the past fester... Like the spring leaves, hope unfurls in me, small and tentative but present all the same.

"I'm not afraid of you, Ian. You have never done anything to harm me, and I don't believe that you ever could."

The muscles in his throat ripple. I draw closer, pressing my body against his, needing desperately to give him everything--passion, yes, but also warmth, comfort, and above all, acceptance. Or perhaps what I truly need to share with him is love, that mysterious, elusive emotion that I'm not even sure I'm capable of experiencing.

"You have too much faith in me," he says. "You need to be free, Amelia. After all the years that were taken from you before you were allowed to awaken, I can't bear the thought of denying you the opportunity to live to the fullest."

Passion flares behind his eyes. His hand cups the back of my head. "But at the same time, I want to keep you only for myself, to possess you completely. I want to be in your every breath, your every thought. I really do want to own you in a way that has nothing to do with any paperwork."

His lips brush mine, once, again, savoring, parting, taking. His tongue thrusts deeply. The spiral of need and pleasure spins upward, wilder by every moment, out of control. My fingers dig into his broad shoulders, my body pliant under his hands.

The taste of him intoxicates me. I want more. My hunger for him is ravenous. He is light, air, hope, promise. He is everything.

I cling to him, my arms wrapped around his waist, my hands savoring the feel of hard, toned muscles just beneath his shirt. He backs me against the trunk of the tree, reaches out to grasp my wrists, and stretches my arms over my head. His big, hard body holds me in place.

"I've missed you," he murmurs. "More than you can know."

"Not true. I've longed for you every waking moment and at night..." A quickening of remembered pleasure stirs in me. Helplessly, I flush.

"Amelia?" His voice is at once stern and amused.

Reluctantly, I say, "I had dreams..."

"About me?"

"Hmmm, yes."

His humor deepens but so does the dark fire stirring in his eyes. "Were they arousing?"

"Yes..."

He quirks a brow. "Did you come?"

I look away, my face flaming. Given all that we've shared, I can't imagine why I'm embarrassed but I am all the same. "Sometimes! All right? Can we move on?"

His answer is to thrust against me, making me vividly aware of his erection brushing my hip. His voice is low and hard as he says, "You've been in my dreams. I've cursed every dawn that's taken me from you."

Oh, my! When did Ian develop such a romantic turn of phrase? I'm far more accustomed to the stark, crude words he whispers in my ear as he thrusts deep inside me. They never fail to send me soaring over the edge. But I'm no more immune to this new, tender passion.

My throat thickens with unshed tears. "What are we going to do?" I whisper. I don't mean just now. How are we ever going to reconcile the seeming impossibility of being together? And what if we can't?

I don't think that Ian deliberately chooses to misunderstand me but he isn't willing to be distracted by so problematic a future.

"This," he says and takes my mouth with his. His kiss is a wild, primal claiming that robs me of breath and sets my heart to pounding. He gives no quarter, nor do I want any. But with my arms still held above my head, I can't touch him. The frustration quickly becomes unbearable. I lift a leg, kicking it free of my long skirt, and arch it over his hip. He grunts and slips a hand under my knee, drawing me tight against him. The smooth fabric of his evening trousers can scarcely contain his erection. I arch my pelvis, rubbing my slit over the hard, growing bulge. The pressure through the thin scrap of my wet panties is exquisite. I am desperate to be closer to him, needing him to complete me, longing...

He breaks off the kiss and stares down at me, his gaze wild and raw. I feel as though he is stripping me bare. "I'd like to make you come right here, right now," he says. His hips thrust, once, again... "You're close, aren't you?"

I can't deny it. All the pent-up desire of the past ten days is rushing together into a hot, urgent core of sensual hunger whirling at the center of my being. I'm trembling on the edge, an incandescent nova on the very verge of exploding.

The shadows around the ancient tree protect us. We're alone in a world of our own making. My need for him is unbearable. But still something holds me back.

"That won't solve anything."

The words are wrenched from me. My own body rebels against them, clenching painfully. But the truth is inescapable. The passion we share has never been in doubt. It's the results of it that we both fear.

Ian hesitates and for a moment, I think he isn't going to relent. But then a ragged breath escapes him. He rests his forehead against mine.

"What do you think would?"

He's asking me? The one with almost no experience in the messy, bewildering, sometimes frightening but still exhilarating struggle called life?

"I don't know...just being together? Taking things moment to moment? Is that even possible? Do people ever manage that?"

I have no way of knowing but Ian seems to think that the idea has merit. He takes a step back, gently lowering me until I'm once again standing on my own two feet. Slowly, he releases my arms and draws them down as well. Holding my gaze, he says, "Let's try, all right? If nothing else, we can see where it leads us."

Moment to moment. Each one allowed to unfold without the rush and clamor of expectations. What a difference that would make after the weeks of living between the shadows of both past and future.

A bubble of excitement rises in me. Buoyed by hope, however fragile it may be, I nod.

Josie Litton

Chapter Eight

Ian

n hour later, I grin down at Amelia, relishing the excitement in her eyes. She's practically jumping up and down like a little kid.

"Do you think they'll be coordinated to music?" she asks as we join the crowd moving outside where the fireworks are about to begin.

"Absolutely they will be," I assure her.

Her smile is radiant. "Something by Mussorgsky, maybe, or Elgar. Dvorak, perhaps, or Mahler?"

She has a nearly encyclopedia knowledge of classical music, thanks to Susannah. But when she plays for herself, she prefers twentieth-century jazz. Just one more way that Amelia is her own person.

"Uh, yeah, any of those would be good." I'm looking ahead toward the double doors. The crowd is bunching together in front of them. There's some sort of hang up. Patience runs thin in a group where everyone is accustomed to going first. Already, the grumbling is starting.

From the corner of my eye, I spot Davos leaving through a small side door. He's maintained his distance from Amelia ever since I warned him off but I've kept an eye on him all the same. I don't trust the slimy bastard as far as I could throw him. Several other sleek men in evening clothes are with him but the vast majority of the guests remain right where Amelia and I are, unable to get out.

The combination of the stuck crowd and Davos slipping away has hit the tripwire that's always present in my mind. Normal people, suddenly alerted to the possibility of danger, experience an adrenalin rush that either freezes them in place or makes them flee. It's different for me. Time slows down and everything takes on a heightened clarity, every small detail standing out in stark relief. I become hyper-focused, which is a big part of why I'm good at the darker side of what I do.

I spot Edward, thankfully on the fringe of the crowd. His mother, Marianne, and my mother are with him. Over the heads of the people surrounding us, I shout, "Go!"

I don't know for certain what's about to hit us but the strategy of bunching a target set as closely together as possible is classic. Whatever it is, I'm sure of one thing--the situation is about to get butt ugly.

I have to hand it to Edward, he doesn't hesitate. Nor does Adele. She grabs my mother's arm as Edward takes hold of Marianne. He lifts her off her feet and moves fast, keeping the two other women beside him, toward the far edge of the room. Anything that hits will be aimed at the center, which makes the margins not a good place to be but the best that's available.

Amelia and I are a lot more hemmed in. She's looking at me with the first stirrings of alarm. I grab hold of her and clasp the back of her head, pushing it into my chest.

"Close your eyes," I order and quickly do the same with my own, at the same time ducking my head against her shoulder, shutting out as much light as possible.

The first flash grenade crashes through one of the glass panels a moment later and instantly detonates. Several more follow quickly. Searing white light blast my retinas. I'm temporarily blinded but that doesn't prevent me from hearing the screams that break out all around us. People are panicking. When the initial surge of shock starts to wear off in a few seconds, they'll try to run. The biggest and strongest may manage it; the rest will be trampled.

"Hold on!" I tell Amelia as a countdown starts in my head. Ten...nine...eight... We don't have much time before the stampede starts. I push through the people around us, heading instinctively in the direction I mapped out in the few seconds before the grenades hit.

Beyond the screams, I can hear weapons fire outside. The sound is grimly satisfying. Only a handful of my men were close in to the Crystal Palace. The rest were hidden among the nearby trees, all of them well concealed by some of the latest tech to come out of my own labs. The attackers, whoever they are, are getting a nasty surprise. Whatever they had planned, they've been stopped in their tracks, buying us at least some time.

Edward is waiting on the edge of the chaos. The women are wide-eyed and obviously afraid but they're holding it together. Adele and my mother are both tough old birds, and I mean that as the highest compliment. Marianne's a different story. Nothing in her life has prepared her for anything remotely like this yet she isn't so much as flinching. I'm damn proud of her.

"We can't stay here," Edward says as soon as he sees me. "One stray energy beam and..."

I know what he means. The glass walls of the Crystal Palace offer no protection. Without further delay, we head for the escape route that we agreed on earlier. I take point, leading the way. By sticking to the edge of the vast ballroom, we avoid the worst of the crush but the going is still difficult. Edward guards the rear, keeping the women between us. Neither of us wants to hurt any of the poor bastards who are just trying to get the hell out the same as us but we're not about to let them get in our way either.

Before we can advance very far, half-a-dozen men come through the side door that Davos used. They're dressed in black, helmeted but with their visors up to be sure they can be recognized. The weapons they carry are the latest design straight from my R&D division. Hollis is in the lead. He and I exchange a quick nod as my men take up position around us. They form a phalanx that clears our path through the crowd quickly.

When we reach the kitchens, they're empty, the workers having sensibly scrambled for safety at the first sign of trouble. A trapdoor in the floor stands open, leading to a flight of wooden steps. Hollis and two more of my men descend swiftly. After several tense moments, Hollis sticks his head up and signals that the tunnel is clear.

I hang back as Edward helps the women descend. When they've done so, he jumps down to join them, then glances back at me expectantly.

"I'll meet you on the other side," I say.

Edward looks at me for a long moment, then nods. I don't have to worry about him, he gets it. Not so the ladies, who all stare at me as though I'm nuts.

"You aren't--" My mother begins.

"Ian, really--" Adele adds.

"You can't!" Marianne exclaims.

Amelia doesn't say a word. She just brushes past Edward and starts back up the steps as though she can somehow stop me all by herself.

Edward sighs, snags an arm around her waist, and pulls her back down. She doesn't hesitate but responds with a swift kick to his shins. "Let me go!"

Hollis chuckles. With an apologetic shrug to Edward, I lower the trap door back into place just as Amelia lets loose with a string of curses that turns the air blue. Where she acquired that vocabulary I can't imagine but damn, does she know how to use it.

Still shaking my head over the crazy idea she has that she could somehow stop me, I strip off my tuxedo jacket and vest, loosen my tie, and accept the body armor that one of my men holds out. Once its snapped into place, I feel more like myself. Moments later, weapon in hand, I head out into the fight.

The night is pleasantly warm with a hint of rain to come. I can smell dark moist earth sharpened by the ozone of high-energy weapons. I'm moving at a swift trot through the shadows, my muscles feeling loose and limber. This is what I do, who I am. I make no apologies for it even if there have been times, especially lately, when I've caught myself wondering about a different kind of life. One that more than anything else involves Amelia.

I can't afford to be thinking about her now. With the discipline that I've depended on my whole adult life, I force myself to refocus. The bodies of attackers are scattered on the ground. I flip one over and take a close look.

The dead man is clean-shaven, well-nourished, wearing camo with no insignia.

A high-energy beam strikes the ground inches from where I'm crouching. I barely notice. If it had hit me, the next-gen body armor I'm wearing would have absorbed most of the blast, assuring no more than a minor injury. All the same, my men respond instantly. More bodies fall.

I catch a flicker of movement out of the corner of my eye. My own weapon goes up automatically. I fire. Another of the attackers hits the ground and lies there, unmoving.

A short time later it gets quiet, except for the sirens I can hear off in the distance. The Municipal Protection Services are on the job or they will be shortly. What's the old saying? When seconds count, the police are minutes away? They can't really help that, of course, but the truth of that statement has never been more clear to me.

Knowing that lives hang on every moment, I move with my men toward the main doors of the Crystal Palace. As I suspected, they've been deliberately jammed from the outside. I can see the people smashed up against them, well dressed men and women who a short time ago were enjoying yet another pleasant evening in their privileged lives with no thought to the possibility of danger. Most of them are still pounding desperately against the glass, trying to get out. But a few are on the floor, ashen and unmoving.

Since there's no way for the people closest to the doors to back up, my men can't blast them open. Instead, they just sheer both sides off at the hinges, then do the same to several of the glass panels closest to the ground, creating other openings for people to escape through. They stagger out, gasping, crying, falling to their knees. The more aware among them are looking around frantically, calling out trying to find whoever they came with. I see several tear-filled reunions. Behind the crowd, on the floor of the Crystal Palace, a dozen or so bodies remain.

Whatever attack plan the assailants had in place has crumbled under the defense mounted by my men. The enemy has either fled or been subdued. I conduct a quick in-field debrief. We'll review the engagement much more thoroughly later but for the moment it's enough to know that our own casualties are minor and are already being evacuated.

With no interest in hanging around to deal with the MPS, I give the order to move out. My men and I are withdrawing from the perimeter of the Crystal Palace, advancing deeper into the park, when the air suddenly quivers all around me. In the next moment, I'm on the ground.

Spitting out dirt, I turn my head in time to see the entire structure of the Crystal Palace lift off its foundations in the instant before it flies apart. Huge, razor sharp splinters of glass rain down in a broad arc across the park. Diving for cover, I offer up a silent prayer that Amelia and the others are well away from the hell that is suddenly falling from the sky.

Hunted

Chapter Nine

Amelia

e're a short distance beyond where we exited the tunnel, deep in the park, when without warning the night shatters. I stagger a few steps as the ground ripples under my feet. Instinctively, I look back over my shoulder just in time to witness a sight that my brain can't immediately grasp. The sky is filled with--diamonds? Huge, faceted, shimmering shards radiating white light are falling toward us.

Beside me, the blond man with the crew-cut who I think is called Hollis yells, "Down! Everyone down!"

Without waiting for me to act, he grabs me and throws me to the ground, his body arched over mine, shielding me.

I hear thuds in the distance, and screams but they hardly register. All I can think of is--

Oh, God, Ian!

He's back there in the midst of this horror. That harsh, inescapable truth is agonizing. I can't breathe or move or do anything except endure the fear for him that is turning my body to ice.

Images flash through my mind. Ian holding me in his arms as we danced. Smiling at my enthusiasm about the fireworks. Arousing in me the hope that we could both put aside our darkest fears and give us another chance.

And now... Too vividly, I see one of the monstrous shards impaling him, driving the life from him, his blood pouring out. Nausea overwhelms me. I'm on my hands and knees, Hollis hovering over me, as I come close to retching.

When I recover enough to realize that I'm not actually going to do so, I become aware of my grandmother to one side of me. Marianne is on the other, using the hem of her dress to pat beads of sweat from my face.

"It's all right," Adele says softly. "Ian's tough and well protected. He'll come through this."

I don't even question how she knows the source of my distress. And I'm far beyond embarrassment over what fear for him as done to me. When I finally stagger to my feet, Hollis steadies me. I can hear sirens coming from all directions. Helicopters are overhead, the fast chop of their blades cutting through the air.

Over the roar, I yell, "We have to go back!"

He looks surprised but that's quickly masked as he shakes his head. "Not happening. My job is to see that all of you get to safety. Can you walk?"

I can but I'm not about to. He has to be out of his mind if he thinks that I'll just go off and leave Ian --

"If you can't, one of us will carry you," Hollis says emphatically. He looks as though he knows exactly what I'm thinking and is prepared to take any steps that he must to deal with it.

I glance at Edward. Any hope I had that he would side with me is dashed the moment he says, "We keep going. Ian has enough to deal with right now without having to worry about you."

The fact that he assumes Ian is still alive and in control gives me some slight comfort but it does nothing to ease the fear clawing at me.

"He could be hurt," I say. "No matter what you think. We have to go back!"

Edward and Hollis exchange a glance. Not for the first time, I resent the way certain men have of communicating silently with each other, quite literally over my head. They can agree on whatever they want, it doesn't change a thing.

I dart a quick look to the side. If I run, I'm certain that they will follow. The problem is that they're likely to catch me before I get very far, especially given the ridiculously high heels that I'm wearing.

None of which means that I'm not going to try. I grip the sides of my gown and surreptitiously hitch up my skirt, taking a deep breath as I do so. Hollis and Edward are discussing the best route out of the park. When they are both looking away from me, I bolt.

I run full out, taking advantage of the strength and stamina that I've built up dancing. I'm heading in the direction of the red glow rising where the Crystal Palace stood such a short time ago. Almost immediately I have to veer around shards of glass that have pierced the ground. Each is taller than I am. I'm struck by the sudden, fanciful notion that they look like the teeth of a giant, mythical beast, a dragon perhaps, set out to form a terrifying obstacle course. Seeing them makes me realize how close they and others like then came to raining down on us. For anyone closer at the moment of the explosion--

I hear shouts and the thud of feet behind me and speed up. My heart is hammering, my breath becoming labored but I don't care. Nothing is going to keep me from Ian--

The large shape of a man looms up suddenly in front of me. For a frantic moment, I think that one of them--Hollis, my brother, one of the other men--has gotten out ahead of me. I try to dart around but the man is faster. Big hands lash out. I'm hauled against a broad chest, all the breath squeezed from me, as a voice says, "Amelia! Thank God!"

Ian!

Relief more profound than any I've ever known rips through me, bringing in its wake a sudden, strange languor. If he weren't holding me, I'd collapse.

I look up into his face, taut with worry, and something cracks wide open inside me. In the next instant, I'm sobbing uncontrollably.

"I thought...I was so afraid..." The words come out as little more than gasps but he seems to understand. A tender, somewhat surprised smile curves his mouth.

"Yeah, babe, me, too. If anything happened to you--" He breaks off as his eyes turn dark and grim. The back of his hand brushes my cheek with aching tenderness but a moment later, he frowns.

"Why were you running? What's wrong?"

Seriously? Did he really just ask that?

"I thought you might need help."

The gentle man of a moment ago vanishes in an instant. A jagged pulse springs to life in his clenched jaw. He stares at me with disbelief that wars with fury.

"You were going back? Putting yourself in danger deliberately? Don't you have any sense at all?"

My momentary weakness dissolves in a flash. I am so tired of him or anyone else thinking that I am somehow fragile or less than capable. The hard truth is that I would never have survived all the years that I did with my sanity intact if I didn't have a deep reservoir of strength. To be fair, I've never told him about the memories I'm not supposed to have but fairness is very low on the list of my priorities at the moment.

"You're one to talk! You did exactly that for my sake but I'm not supposed to do the same for you?"

He looks at me as though I'm some species of creature that he's never encountered before. His expression is a combination of stark bewilderment and pure male frustration that under other circumstances might be funny. Not now, though, not here in this verdant sanctuary that has suddenly been transformed into hell.

Finally, in stark exasperation, he says, "I'm trained, battle hardened, this is what I do. You're--"

I hold my breath, more afraid than I want to admit of what he will say next. You're a replica, good only for pleasure? I have a sudden image of a porcelain, tutu-clad figurine in an old music box twirling to a tune plucked out by tiny pins on a metallic cylinder. An automaton without a life or a will of her own.

His voice drops, softening a little even as his gaze remains scorching. "You're an amazing woman but you're not equipped yet to take care of yourself in this world." As though he expects me to argue, he adds, "Running straight into danger as you've just done proves that."

In the last few hours, I've had hope for a future I thought gone for good dangled in front of me, been caught up in a savage attack, and feared for the life of the man I can't exist without. Only to discover that he doesn't acknowledge me as a fully functioning adult capable of dealing with challenges, someone who might actually be of help to him. And with that, something inside me snaps.

"Do you have any idea how much strength it takes to--" Endure what I did all those years in the gestation chamber? Make sense of the world that I've been plunged into? Cope with the astonishing reality of what I am? All that reveals far more than I'm willing to under the present circumstances.

Instead, I retreat a little, taking refuge in what I fully recognize is a metaphor of sorts for everything I have faced. "How much strength it takes to dance? How much stamina? How much pain is involved in making it all look effortless? No, obviously you don't. I am not a toy for you to keep safe on a shelf until you decide that you want to play with me. I'm a woman, your equal in every way. Either you get that, or--"

I break off because the blazing heat in his eyes makes me forget how to breathe.

"Are you giving me an ultimatum, Amelia?"

From the very beginning, I have understood that this wounded prince who walked out of the darkness to claim me is a man to soothe and placate, above all to please. More often than not I know how to do that. But this time when I open my mouth to respond, what comes out sounds inexplicably like, "Yes, I am."

The night turns suddenly very quiet. I can hear my own breathing and the rapid beat of my heart. The air between us feels charged as though by an oncoming electrical storm. It prickles along my skin, entering through my pores, settling deep within me.

Ian takes a step forward, another. I remain where I am, refusing to back down, unable to look away. The moment stretches out, seemingly endlessly.

And then he is there, right in front of me, his big hands cupping my face with exquisite gentleness. He bends his head, slowly, giving me time to pull away. I see the desperate yearning in his eyes that mirrors my own.

Without thought, I close the small distance between us. My lips brush against his, savoring, tasting, parting. My tongue slips into his mouth and finds his. The passion that explodes between us is instant and overwhelming. It blocks out everything else, even the nearness of death. Or perhaps it is that shared knowledge of our own mortality that fuels it. Life is precious, every moment counts, and we have been apart far too long.

A low growl wells up in him. His hands, gentle moments before, close on me with roughness that far from being frightening, elates me. I want this man, all of him, the light he doesn't believe exists in him and the dark that I long to banish. As maddening as he can be, he is mine every bit as much as I am his. Whether he understands that or not.

Fury, hurt, fear, all of it collides with sheer unbridled lust. I suck hard on his tongue, drawing him even deeper into my mouth and claw at the armor over his chest and shoulders. I love that armor; it may very well have saved his life. And I hate it. I desperately want it off and the two of us skin-to-skin, as close as we can be until I take him inside--

A throat clears behind me. In the small part of my brain that's still functioning, it sounds like a thunder clap.

I whirl around to find Edward watching us. All I see of Hollis is his back as he withdraws quickly. The man is nothing if not discreet. Unlike my brother.

"Do we have time for this?" he asks, arching an eyebrow. "We should be moving on."

Strong hands set me aside even as one twines with my own, fingers interlacing, keeping me close.

"We should," Ian says with a nod. "We'll go to Pinnacle House. Nowhere in the city is safer."

He sounds completely impervious to what has just happened between us. A dart of resentment moves through me. Once, at the estate, he indulged me with the illusion of control. Now I realize that I want the real thing, not forever, not even mainly, but I want to see him come undone and know that I am the cause.

Before Edward can reply, my grandmother joins us. Adele's silver hair is a bit mussed but otherwise she looks perfectly calm, as though nothing out of the ordinary has happened. I can only admire--and envy--her composure.

"You should certainly do so," she says to Ian, not unkindly. "The rest of us need to return to our own residences."

"With all respect, ma'am," he begins, "that isn't a good idea."

"On the contrary, the last thing we want to do right now is draw attention to ourselves." She holds up a hand, forestalling any further argument. "We are the innocent, shocked survivors of a terrible atrocity, no different from all the others who were here tonight and are fortunate enough to still be alive. We were not escorted away just as the attack began, escaping through a tunnel in the company of your men who were present in force and for unexplained reasons."

It takes several seconds for her meaning to sink in. When it does, I gasp. "You aren't suggesting that anyone could believe Ian was involved in the attack?" That's insane yet I can't overlook the fact that the city creates its own reality, different in so many ways from the world that normal, ordinary people inhabit.

"If the presence of his men here tonight becomes known," Adele says gently, "some will certainly suggest that. The Council won't want to accuse him openly, of course, but they need to assign responsibility for this quickly. A long drawn out investigation would be intolerable to the city's residents and would bring demands for political change."

"You're right," Helene says. She has joined the rest of us without my noticing. "Nothing counts for more in this city than appearances. Going to Pinnacle House would broadcast to the world that at the very least we lack confidence in the Council's ability to maintain security. Any hint of such disloyalty will invite questions that we don't want to have asked, much less be pressed to answer."

Frowning, Ian turns to Edward. "Do you agree with this?"

Reluctantly, my brother says, "I'm not happy about it but the ladies are right. We were all seen together at the Crystal Palace this evening and we all got out of there alive. If we now all hole up in Pinnacle House, we're bound to draw attention that could get in the way of our finding out who was behind this."

Slowly, Ian nods. Like it or not, and it's obvious that he doesn't, he accepts what the others are saying. I can't help thinking that this is one of his great strengths, the ability to see beyond his own formidable intelligence and experience and grasp when someone else is right. Now if only he could extend that to me.

"All right," he says. "But the security ring that's in place will be tightened. It will be discreet but it will be there."

What security ring? Suddenly, I recall the frequent episodes of feeling as though I was being watched. Could Ian have been responsible? Exactly how close an eye has he kept on me since I arrived in the city?

Before I can ask, he says, "But Amelia is coming with me. That's not up for discussion. Apart from everything else that has happened here tonight, Davos has left no doubt that he has an unhealthy interest in her. I've managed to make that worse."

He looks directly at me as he speaks, as though he expects me to object. When I remain silent, a flicker of wary surprise darts behind his eyes. I fight a smile, secretly delighted that I can keep him off balance at least a little, especially since he does the same to me so effortlessly. That's all well and good as far as it goes but I can't overlook the much larger issue. I accepted that he and I should part because simply by being with me, he's forced to confront his worst demons. Now, because of his concerns for my safety, he will have to do exactly that.

My throat tightens at the thought but there is one consolation: He won't be alone. Whatever comes, this time I am determined that we will face it together.

Chapter Ten

Ian

The sight of Amelia standing in the great room of the penthouse on top of Pinnacle House sends a bolt of relief through me. For the first time since walking into the Crystal Palace hours ago, the muscles at the back of my neck start to unclench.

She's here. She's safe. Besides that, nothing else--including my raging hard-on--matters. All my concern about needing to stay away from her has crashed and burned against the reality of imminent death. If I had gotten her out of there a few moments later... If one of those shards of glass had hit her... I close my eyes against the pain that lances through me.

When I open them again, my gaze meets hers. I take a breath and force myself to speak as calmly and steadily as I can manage.

"I'll let Hodge know that you're here," I say. "He'll see to anything you need. I mean that, anything." Casting around for some way to convince her that I'm down with whatever it takes to make her happy, I say, "If you need to go to class with that Russian, Hodge will arrange it."

My plan is to stay as far away from her as possible for however long she's here. I'll sleep in the single men's barracks, eat in the mess, work out, do whatever I have to while steering well clear of Amelia. That shouldn't be a problem considering that Pinnacle House is the vertical equivalent of a small city with a population of more than twenty thousand men, women, and children. One way or another, I'm responsible for them

Josie Litton

in addition to another twenty thousand or so in other locations around the world.

For their sakes, as much as Amelia's and my own, all my attention needs to be focused on figuring out what happened tonight, that and getting to the bottom of who was financing the HPF. My gut says that there could be a link, either that or two separate efforts are underway to undermine the established order. Unraveling that won't leave any time to think about Amelia.

Which is why I'm lingering just a couple of minutes when I know I should be on my way out the door.

She looks pre-occupied. I'd worry more about that if I weren't so distracted by how the velvet gown she's wearing has slipped off one creamy shoulder, yet further exposing the swell of her glorious breasts. Or how it clings to her narrow waist before flaring slightly at the curve of her hips that I love to grasp as she rides me--

In desperation, I force myself to look away from her, out through the glass walls of the penthouse to the city and beyond. It's almost midnight but Manhattan is still lit up, lights blazing as though a party is going on that will never end. Less so the outer boroughs where the working stiffs live, resting up in their micro-apartments for whatever the coming day will bring. How will they react when they learn of the attack on the Crystal Palace? With a certain vindictive pleasure is my guess, although they'll be careful to mask it.

Beyond the rings of light is the harbor, a black hole in the night except for the statue of Lady Liberty illuminated by high-power searchlights intended to discourage anyone who might think of dropping by uninvited. Visits to her island have been banned for the vast majority of people for longer than I can remember and there's a rumor that she's falling into disrepair. Personally, I wouldn't be surprised to look out one day and discover that she's gone. At best, she's become an anachronism. At worst, she's a potential rallying point and a threat.

But she can't hold a candle to the woman reflected in the glass wall. Amelia is watching me. There's a slight furrow between her brows that I find myself wanting to kiss away.

"Would you like some help?" she asks, meeting my eyes in the glass.

90

I turn back to the room, to her. "With what?" Leaving? I can do that under my own power. And I will...any minute--

"With your--what is it called, body armor?" she says. "It looks uncomfortable."

I open my mouth to explain that I've worn armor like this for days and nights at a time in the field. A few hours is nothing. I'll take it off when I get down to the operations floor for the debrief.

But before I can say that, Amelia closes the distance between us. She's kicked off her high heels. The top of her head tucks neatly under my chin. Laying a slim hand on my chest, she says, "How does it come off?"

Walk away, go downstairs, do the debrief. Take a cold shower. Take a longer one. Jerk off. Do anything I have to do to--

"Like this," I say. My hand is over hers, guiding her. I have to be out of my fucking mind. My fingers slip under hers, pressing against the biometric sensors that release the armor. The front and back pieces that protect my torso separate and drop onto the floor. A million bucks worth of the most advanced survival equipment on the planet, forgotten.

Because Amelia isn't done yet. I'm also wearing armor on my legs where a hit can sever the femoral artery, making for a very bad day. Without breaking eye contact with me, she lowers herself slowly and gracefully to her knees.

Amelia and my cock have gotten along really well in the past. He doesn't give a shit about the demons that haunt me or my very genuine fears about how I could hurt her or much of anything else besides being deep inside her. By the time the rest of the armor hits the floor and gets kicked to the side, he's more than raring to go.

Worse, still on her knees, Amelia tosses me a look that walks the line between sweetly shy and ready to have me for her next meal. She reaches for the button of my waistband.

Whoa, not happening.

I grab hold of her and lift her back onto her feet. "You've been through a terrible experience. You're not thinking straight."

Her eyes narrow. I get the distinct impression that a calculation is going on in that complex, often bewildering brain of hers. After a moment, she turns her back, glances over her shoulder, and says, "You're right. I should really lie down. If you wouldn't mind returning the favor?"

How's that?

"The buttons," she prompts. "I can't undo them myself." When I stand there frozen, she adds, "Perhaps you'd rather call Hodge to help me?"

Cold day in hell. Pigs flying.

I stare at the long--extremely long--row of tiny pearl buttons that marches down her back from just below her bare shoulder blades to the curve of her ass. Each is secured with a velvet loop that matches her dress. When I touch a tentative finger to one of the buttons, it slides right off. On top of everything else, they're so polished that they're slippery.

We live in the era of high-tech everything when inhuman speed and efficiency overrule all other considerations. And this is the best way they can come up with to fasten a dress? What kind of sicko sadists work in the fashion industry?

"This isn't a good idea." I'm talking to myself. Amelia definitely isn't listening or if she is, it's not having any effect. She shrugs, freeing her other shoulder so that the dark claret-hued velvet slips all the more.

"I could just sleep in my dress," she says. "But I'm wearing a corset and it's a little tight."

The Universe has to be doubled over laughing. For ten days, I've struggled to do what's right and here's where it's gotten me. Maybe it's the epic hard-on or the incipient blue balls or something a whole lot deeper and darker but in the next moment, I'm watching my hands gripping both sides of the velvet that's warm with the heat of her body and--

Tiny pearls fly in all directions and skitter across the penthouse floor. The gown falls away, pooling around her feet. Amelia is left in nothing more than a black lace corset, matching thigh highs, and a tiny excuse for a thong.

That and the diamonds that encircle her wrists and throat, dangle from those delicate earlobes I love to suck and nestle in her hair. No goddess adorned by her worshippers ever looked more enthralling.

She turns again and stares at me. Her luscious lips have formed a surprised O that has me instantly thinking what I would like to be doing with her mouth. To it. In it. In her.

Fuck.

"Amelia--" I'm drowning in need for her, grasping at a last thin filament of reason, and she isn't helping. Every dark reason I have for staying away from her is ricocheting around in my mind. I can't escape them any more than I can avoid my overwhelming need for her. Those opposing forces threaten to tear me apart.

"Don't," she whispers as she steps gracefully out of the pool of clothing at her feet. Her hands reach up, her fingers lacing in my hair. On tip-toe, she presses closer. My breath fills with the intoxicating scent of her skin. "Don't think," she whispers. "Don't worry. We're alive, we're together. That's all that matters."

It isn't. I'm fairly confident she knows that as well as I do but I'm forgetting why I should care. All I can think of is the sight of her trying to come back up the steps out of the tunnel because she didn't want to leave me. Running to me in the park. Keeping her hand in mine.

After everything that's happened between us, she still trusts me.

Nothing matters beyond that except the raw hunger that's eating me from the inside out. I'm coming apart in some way that I've never experienced before--not in battle, not in my darkest moments, never.

Knowing that I shouldn't, terrified not to, I lift Amelia into my arms.

Josie Litton

Chapter Eleven

Amelia

*I*an carries me up the floating glass staircase that connects the two floors of the penthouse. My heart is pounding and I can't catch my breath. It's dawning on me that I've pushed him past his limits into territory that he never intended to revisit. Now I'm about to face the consequences.

Given the choice between remaining mired in the anguish of missing him or reaching for even a chance that we can be together, I feel no hesitation at all.

At least I don't until Ian sets me down in the master bedroom, paneled in glass and looking out over the rooftop Japanese garden. The setting should encourage a sense of peace and serenity but all I can feel is the raging fire of my need for him.

The mouth that has tormented me so exquisitely is tightly drawn as he says, "Tell me this isn't insane."

The words are far more of an order than a plea. That makes me smile. However concerned and vulnerable he is, he's strong willed as ever. I wouldn't change that for anything.

"You think this is funny?" he asks.

I rest my palms against his chest and look up, meeting his gaze. His pupils are dilated, leaving only a narrow ring of tawny gold around the outer rims. The planes and angles of his face are even more sharply defined than usual. I can't help but think of how beautiful he is, this passionate, wounded man who has struggled so valiantly to do what is right.

"This is what we both want," I say, seeking only to reassure him. "What we both need."

That horrible day in the gallery, I said a great deal more, about wanting him without condition or judgment, all of him, the light and the dark. In hindsight, I feel as though I babbled on and on although realistically I know that wasn't the case. Whatever I said, it didn't work. Words don't with Ian, something I should have realized before then. Actions count-- his, mine, ours together.

I take a step back, reach around to the hooks holding my corset closed, and undo them. The garment falls into my hands. I hold it for a moment, a shield of black lace and silk scarcely protecting me from his gaze.

Ian's eyes darken even further. A long tremor runs through me. I want him so desperately, want to hold him inside me, watch his pleasure build, know that I'm the cause of it, and finally see him come undone. Above all, I want him to know that we can both have this without either of us being hurt, him by his demons and me by whatever harm he imagines he could do.

I want to end even the thought of that for good, shatter it as thoroughly as the glistening panes of the Crystal Palace were blown apart tonight.

The corset slips to the floor. I stand before him. Despite the thong and thigh highs, I feel more exposed than I ever have before. The cool air of the bedroom contrasts sharply with the heat of my skin. My nipples are puckered and I'm all too aware of the wetness gathering in me.

When he still doesn't move, I force myself to walk over to the bed. Slowly, I sit down on the edge, lift my right leg, and begin rolling the stocking down along my thigh, over my knee and calf until finally I slip it off my foot. The length of ivory silk dangles from my fingertips for a moment before I let it fall. Lifting my other leg, I repeat the process until I'm left with nothing more than a rapidly dampening scrap of black lace between my legs.

Ian's scrutiny is making me acutely self-conscious. I lean back as nonchalantly as I can, resting on my elbows, and study him.

"Your turn."

The corners of his mouth quirk ever so slightly, giving me hope. Without taking his eyes from me, he unbuttons his shirt. When it falls open, revealing his broad chest defined by perfectly formed abs and the V of muscle pointing toward his groin, my throat goes dry. But not before I notice a scattering of small, faint bruises that I don't remember from before. They don't so much mar the perfection of his beauty as accentuate it.

All pretense of casualness dissolves. I straighten and reach out to him. "What did that?"

At the brush of my fingertips along his ribs, he stiffens. "It's nothing."

"No, really, what did that?"

Ian shrugs, clearly uncomfortable with the subject. "Weapons blasts, ninety-nine percent of which was absorbed by my armor. The rest is inconsequential."

But it wouldn't have been if he hadn't been wearing the armor. Any one of the small marks could have been a lethal blow. All the air goes out of my lungs but a moment later, it rushes back accompanied by a healthy dose of anger. He was in a battle in the middle of what is supposed to be one of the safest and most civilized places on earth. An actual battle!

"What the hell is going on?"

I don't realize that I've spoken out loud until Ian takes my chin between his long, hard fingers and lifts my gaze to his.

"I'll find out," he says solemnly, "and I'll deal with it. You don't have to worry."

I don't mistake the words for mere reassurance. They're a promise that he will keep at any cost. The thought of him going into danger yet again fills me with dread but Ian seems to feel none of it. To the contrary, he appears entirely focused on the moment.

He releases me and in the same motion holds out his arm. "If you wouldn't mind--"

I stare at the patch of tanned skin, lightly dusted with hair, visible where the sharp folds of linen meet and have a sudden, almost irresistible urge to press my lips to the veins hidden just beneath there, to feel the pulse of his life's blood.

"Amelia--" He says my name cautiously, as though he is unsure what is going on in my mind.

He may be but I'm not. I know exactly what I want.

Even so, my fingers shake as I unfasten first one, then the other cufflink. I hand the pair to him. He slips them into the pocket of his trousers and shucks off his shirt, tossing it onto the floor

I inhale deeply. Ian bare-chested should come with a warning label. No man has the right to look that good. Inevitably, my gaze lowers to the impressive bulge visible against the finely woven fabric of his trousers. A wave of heat moves through me. I want him, all of him, naked, ready, in my hands, my mouth, my body. Now.

But Ian has other ideas. The breath I've been holding without even realizing it leaves me in a rush as he slips his hands under my knees, unbalancing me just enough that I fall back onto the bed. Before I can react, he drops down in front of me.

Holding my legs apart, he says, "Your panties are wet."

I gasp at the smug pleasure in his voice but even more so at my reaction to it. If I thought that I was aroused before--

He lifts my legs over his shoulders and nuzzles the inside of my thighs. He must have shaved before leaving for the Crystal Ball. I miss the soft rasp of scruff where my skin is so sensitive but this is good, too.

I try to move downward, wanting nothing so much as to take his magnificent cock into my hands and guide him to me, but he stops me. Holding me still, he says, "I need this, this way. To be sure."

Sure of what, I wonder? Of me? He must know that I am his, freely and of my own choice. I've done everything I possibly can to assure him of that. Haven't I?

What more can I do or say or give to him? What part of me hasn't been his? A flush moves over me as I recall that there actually are some things we haven't done...yet. Is that what he wants? Me in every possible way? Nothing held back, nothing forbidden?

The thought is darkly exciting, if more than a little daunting. But I trust Ian and if he wants--

His fingers slip under the thong and part the folds of my slit, probing lightly, stroking me.

I gasp as my back arches. After ten long, agonizing nights of twisted sheets and dreams from which I wake in the grip of arousal so intense that it's painful, his merest touch there is almost enough to send me--

Almost but not quite. I tremble on the edge, wanting, needing...

He withdraws as a moan of frustration tears from me. I try to grasp his hair but his hands close on my wrists. He growls, "Be still."

Our eyes meet down the length of my body, mine so filled with need, his-- I'm far less sure of what he is feeling...or planning. Before I can wonder, he pulls the thong to one side and suddenly thrusts the tip of his thumb into me, making a mockery of his command. My hips come up off the bed, swiveling in a vain attempt to deepen his penetration. A dark flush spreads over his lean cheeks. Watching me intently, he murmurs, "So impatient."

I subside but reluctantly and am rewarded when his tongue follows the path of his finger, stroking from top to bottom before beginning to circle around my clit. Slow circles, fast circles, feather light one moment, pressing hard the next...round and round but never coming close enough.

"Ian, please!"

He lifts his head and meets my eyes up the length of my straining body. "Please what, sweetheart?"

"You know..."

His gaze is scorching hot. The air between us feels as though it is vibrating with our mutual need. "Tell me," he demands.

I hesitate, wondering if this is the time to remind him that I am not naturally submissive but before I can do so, the raging arousal of my body blocks out every other consideration.

"Please let me come," I whisper.

I feel his smile against my heated skin as he ducks his head again and catches my swollen clit between his teeth, nipping lightly before he sucks hard.

There is no sweet build-up, no languorous climb. The orgasm that hits without warning clenches every muscle in my body and bows my back. The effect is explosive. Intelligence, reason, sanity itself all dissolve into nothingness. I become a creature of pure carnality.

The cry that rips from me turns into a long, gasping sob. Dimly, I'm aware of Ian, resting back on his heels, watching me as I come. His eyes are heavy-lidded, his mouth slightly slack. I can see my own juices glistening on his lips.

As the last spasms finally subside, he eases the thong down my legs and tosses it aside. I reach for him, desperate to feel his weight on me, his cock thrusting into me, but he catches my wrists in one hand and presses me back down onto the bed. Before I realize what he intends, he slips two fingers into me and strokes unerringly against the spot where I am so acutely sensitive.

With the echoes of that first orgasm still resonating, I don't think that it's possible to come again so soon but Ian proves me wrong. The second hits even more ferociously. Blackness threatens at the edge of my vision as I cry out helplessly.

"Feel," he murmurs against the taut skin below my navel. "Just feel."

I don't have any choice. The days and nights without him have left me so primed that I'm helpless to deny him. His lips move against my skin, his voice sinking deep into me, dark, explicit, shredding whatever tiny kernel of resistance I have left.

"Your pussy is like hot, slick velvet," he murmurs. "I love seeing you like this--swollen, quivering, soaked with the pearly juice that's oozing out of you." The flat of his tongue laps at me. Pleasure pools low in my belly and radiates upward, arching along my spine.

"I can't--" My voice catches as all the breath goes out of me. Ian tongue-fucks me with ruthless intensity as he rolls my clit between his thumb and index finger.

I can't come again. I won't survive it but my body is no longer my own. His head is burrowed between my thighs, the powerful muscles of his back flexing under taut skin. I'm on the verge again, so near...

"That's it, baby," he murmurs, "come for me." He drives his fingers into me again, hitting the spot exactly, and I clench hard around him as lights explode behind my eyes. Before the waves of pleasure even begin to subside, Ian slides the thumb of his other hand along my pussy, coating it with my juices. Separating the cheeks of my ass, he probes gently and slips into me just the smallest distance. The shocking, forbidden sensation drives me up yet again. Coming on top of everything else, it's too much.

"Ian!"

I hear my own voice from a distance. My senses overwhelmed, my body shattered, I fall away into oblivion.

Josie Litton

Chapter Twelve

Ian

The man I see in the mirror over the bathroom sink looks better than he has any right to. Watching Amelia come again and again is a hell of a mood booster, and not just because she's the most sensual women I've ever known. I've taken a step toward believing that I can be with her and still stay in control. One step, that's all. I don't mistake it for anything more but it gives me hope. Never mind that my cock, still hard and aching, may never forgive me.

I finish splashing cold water on my face, towel dry, and head downstairs for the debrief. Everyone else is milling around shooting the breeze while they enjoy the high that comes with a job well done. I dump my armor on a chair and nod to Hollis to begin.

We start with what matters most. "Five injured," he reports. "All being seen to in Medical. We might have a couple of guys off duty for a few days but that's it."

I take a moment to give thanks and at the same time make a mental note that the Research and Development team deserves another bonus.

"Good, what about the other side?"

"We counted twelve dead before we withdrew. Plus there were another fourteen bodies of civilians in the Crystal Palace before it exploded."

"Everyone else got out?" If they did, it's thanks to my men.

"Looks like it. A few more were killed or injured by falling debris but most got away unharmed."

"All right then. Let's see what we've got."

Hollis activates the screen that takes up one wall of the conference room. Officially, my company controls several surveillance satellites that we use for mission-appropriate tasks. Unofficially, I have backdoors into many others, including one in geo-synchronous orbit over the city that gives us a detailed, time-lapse view of exactly what went down at the Crystal Palace in the minutes before it exploded.

"The assault force haloed in from stealth fliers," Hollis says as we watch the shapes of men falling from high altitude, their chutes low opening at the last possible moment to give minimal warning of their approach. "They took up position around the building and immediately jammed the main entrance as well as several side doors. Only one was left open. Our men waited to engage until the first flash grenade was launched. At that point, when there was no possible doubt that we were dealing with hostiles, we opened fire."

I nod. We all take a moment to acknowledge the shock that the attackers must have felt when what they would have expected to be a cakewalk turned into a fight to the death. One that more than a few of them lost.

The images continue to flow as I go around the room, listening as each of my lieutenants reports on his team's part in the engagement. The consensus is clear. The Crystal Palace was attacked by a professional force that nonetheless was unprepared to deal with serious opposition.

"They were good," one of my guys says, giving credit where it is due. "But I didn't get the sense that they'd worked together a lot. There wasn't much cohesion."

We all know what he means. Group cohesion turns individuals focused solely on their personal objectives into members of a team willing to sacrifice for a larger purpose. It's essential wherever the stakes are high and performance is critical, which is why we're never done drilling for it. That's paid off big time tonight but then it always does.

"They seemed to only be prepped for a quick in-and-out against a soft target," another lieutenant says.

Both observations agree with what I saw and they beg a key question. As the sat feed continues, I ask, "What about their objective? Do we have anything on that?"

Mercenaries like the man I saw commonly have no identifying marks, even their fingerprints have been removed. They don't exist in any DNA banks. Figuring out what they were after likely will be the only way to unlock the identity of whoever sent them.

Gab says, "The chatter we intercepted suggests that they intended to take control of the Crystal Palace and everyone in it."

"For what purpose?" I ask. "Hostages?" Most of the city's elite were in attendance, people wealthy and powerful enough to be valuable bargaining chips. But to what end?

"Could be," she allows. "But some of what we heard suggests that they were really after only a handful of individuals."

"Who?"

"Don't know," she says. "The targets were referred to by code names."

"If they were only after a few people, why blow the whole place up?"

"They were ordered to when it became obvious that the mission was failing," Gab says. "The order came in the open, not encrypted, which suggests that it was spur of the moment."

"As in someone was watching in real time, didn't like what they saw, and wanted to destroy any evidence of what had gone down?"

Gab nods but she adds, "Or whoever was running the op just lost it and went off the deep end. My thinking is tending in that direction, which could mean that we're dealing with someone who isn't entirely rational. But we need to do more analysis." She pauses for a moment, listening to the feed coming in through her head com.

Frowning, she says, "MPS officers are removing the bodies of the attackers and what's left of the dead civilians. They're not waiting for any forensics, nothing, just dumping the remains into security vans."

Sanitizing the scene is par for the course but it won't limit the panic that will already be setting in as news of what happened spreads through the city.

She listens again, then says, "Okay, this isn't good. They're bringing in dead scavs and arranging them around the ruins of the Crystal Palace."

We've all seen some really fucked up stuff but this is a new low in a city that bills itself as among the most cultured and refined places on earth.

"One guess who the city council is going to blame for the attack," Hollis says. He doesn't mask his disgust.

"At least publicly." I say. Behind the scenes, they'll be scrambling to find out who was really responsible. The short list of private companies with the resources to conduct such an operation starts with Slade Enterprises. I know without asking that the sat feeds have already been scrubbed of any evidence that it was my men who took out the attackers. All the same, between my take down of the HPF and what's happened tonight, I expect to hear from the council before long. I need to put together a strategy to deal with them.

"We're not going to figure this out right now," I say. "Everybody check in with your families and get some rack time. Until this is over, we stay on high alert. I don't want anyone below par. We'll reconvene in eight hours."

The nods and grateful looks that go around the room tell me that my consideration is appreciated. I don't ever question my men's level of commitment but I also never abuse it. They're the best in the world at what they do and they deserve to be treated as such.

The room empties except for Gab and Hollis. The three of us help ourselves to more coffee and settle around the conference table. The sat feed is still running. It's jumped to real time. Where the Crystal Palace stood a few hours ago there's nothing left but a smoking ruin surrounded by the grisly remains of poor bastards who could never have come close to pulling off such an attack but who are the fall guys anyway.

"The council just happened to have a bunch of dead scavs on ice to use like this?" Gab asks. Her skepticism couldn't be clearer or more deserved. The ugly reality is that the bodies are likely still warm, having been rounded up and killed expressly for that purpose. After all, who's going to miss a few dozen scavs except those who are equally powerless?

They'll have heard by now, the men, women, and children who scratch an existence from what their "betters" throw away. Some will flee off-island, others will burrow deeper into whatever sanctuaries they can find. They'll wait it out as they do whenever the city authorities see fit to blame them for some fuck up and declare a crackdown. But this is bigger than anything that's ever happened before. I'm skeptical that the city's residents will buy the idea that scavs could have pulled off such a coordinated and well-armed attack, let alone its explosive ending. Whoever made the call to blow up the Crystal Palace definitely didn't do the powers-that-be any favors. Their ability to maintain control is about to be pushed to its limits and just possibly beyond.

"The council must have seen this coming," Hollis says, voicing what I'm thinking. "Not the particulars, obviously, but they had a heads up that something was going to happen. That's why they put more cops on the streets."

"But not where they would actually have made a difference," I point out. "If we hadn't been at the Crystal Palace tonight, the outcome would have been very different." I turn to Gab and tell her what has emerged front and center in my mind. "Charles Davos and a half-dozen other men left right before the attack began, through the only door that wasn't jammed."

Her eyebrows arch. "You think they're responsible?"

"Possibly. If they are, they were smart to put in an appearance so no one would remember afterward that they weren't there and ask why." Grudgingly, I add, "But they could have been the targets and someone warned them just in time for them to get away. Whatever the case, you should be able to identify who left with Davos from the sat feed. Once you do, I want to know every association they share, every communication between them, anything that links them. If they've pissed in adjoining urinals recently, I want to know about it."

She grimaces but nods. "Nice image, boss. I'll see what I can find out."

I'm running down a mental checklist for anything I've forgotten when Hollis says, "This sure has been a night for surprises." He shoots me an amused look. "Top among them, Miss McClellan. It's not every day that I get outflanked by a ballerina."

"Fast was she?" Gab asks, deadpan.

"Oh, yeah, and hell bent on making sure that the boss here was okay." With a nod in my direction, he adds, "Probably just as well that you brought her back with you. Left to herself, she doesn't seem to have a whole lot of regard for her own safety."

Ignoring the fact that I agree wholeheartedly with that, I say, "She's a guest here." A loaded word weighted down with warnings about courtesy owed, respect due, and the wisdom of backing the hell off.

Gab and Hollis exchange a glance. She stands, grinning. "Sure thing. If that's all, I'm going to get on that urinal research."

"And I'm going to get some of that rack time you mentioned," Hollis says as he, too, rises. Innocently, he adds, "You should get a little shut eye yourself, boss. Looks like you could use it."

I knock back the dregs of my coffee and push away from the table. The talk about getting some rest reminds me of how Amelia looked when I left her in my bed. Fast asleep, her soft, plush lips slightly parted, her breathing soft and deep, the diamonds still gleaming against the pale perfection of her skin. A sleep of utter exhaustion and, I hope, satiation.

I straightened her and laid her head on the pillow, catching the scent of her perfume as I did so. My hands lingered until I forced myself to step back and pull the duvet over her. Even then, I could hardly bear to leave her.

And I can't wait to return. Just for a moment to be sure she's alright. Still determined to prove that I'm in control, I stop by the gym showers first. Standing under the pounding jets of hot water, I feel myself really relax for the first time in days. Having Amelia close at hand where I can keep her safe makes everything else more manageable.

Half-an-hour later, wearing gray sweatpants and a sleeveless T-shirt, I head upstairs. The apartment is hushed and dark. Beyond the walls of windows, I can see the city, suspended in the brief interval between when the late night clubs close and dawn breaks. The impression is deceptive. In some of the towers below me ambitious young men and women are in the middle of their work day. They rarely see the light, living as they do in sync with the Asian time zones and beyond. I wonder what nerves they're having to soothe as word of what happened spreads.

I step out onto the terrace. The wind that's almost always present at this altitude follows me as I walk around to the north side, facing the park. At this hour, it would normally be cloaked in darkness but to the west where the Crystal Palace used to stand banks of mobile lights blaze. I watch for a few minutes, envisioning the scene--officials, many of them survivors of the explosion, struggling to reassure the public, the media dutifully transmitting every word while the disaster voyeurs congregate, lapping up the excitement as though it's a drug.

Finally, I get around to admitting that I'm only out here because I'm postponing the moment when I'll have to leave Amelia--again. Once I know that she's all right, I'll have no excuse to linger and plenty of reason not to.

Might as well get it over with.

I take the floating stairs two at a time. The small, discreet lights embedded in the upper floor provide the only ambient illumination but it's enough to see by. I can hear the ripple of water in the garden's stone and bamboo fountain but another sound punctures the stillness--soft, desperate moans.

My first thought as I race into the bedroom is that Amelia was injured in the escape from the Crystal Palace and unforgivably I didn't realize it. What I see seems at first to confirm that. She's thrown the covers off and is curled on the bed, her knees drawn up to her chest, hugging herself as though she's trying to disappear. Tears course down her cheeks. My breath leaves me in a rush. Deep inside, in the darkest most primal part of myself, a scream of fury rises. A red mist moves in front of my eyes. Whoever has harmed her, I will take them apart piece by piece and crush them out of all existence.

But first...

I'm about to scoop her up and carry her down to Medical rather than wait for them to reach us when I suddenly realize that Amelia's eyes are closed and moving rapidly under the pale lids.

I force myself to breathe and take a closer, marginally calmer look. What I see fills me with anguish.

She isn't physically hurt after all but that's scant comfort. Instead, she's clearly in the grip of what must be a gut-wrenching nightmare.

Josie Litton

Chapter Thirteen

Amelia

An immense shard of glass slices into me, splitting me open. My blood and organs flow out, a writhing mass drifting all around me.

I would scream but I have no breath. Helplessly, I bang against the wall of the gestation tank, desperate to attract the attention of the white-coated technicians standing just beyond. Busy with their dials and monitors, they ignore me.

The shard shifts, digging deeper. The pain is unbearable. Horror fills me. I am dying without ever having lived. I will never fill the sun on my face, hear the laughter of children, know the love of my brother and grandmother.

I will never be with Ian.

My struggles redouble. I thrash frantically, desperate for an escape that I am terrified does not exist.

Iron bonds surround me. I am pressed against stone that feels oddly warm and pliant.

A voice--low, urgent, tender--whispers, "It's all right, sweetheart, you're safe. I won't let anything hurt you."

Slowly, the fear that grips me begins to ease. I take a breath, followed by another. The claustrophobic sense of being trapped once again in the gestation tank slips away. A hand--strong but gentle--strokes my back. Pleasure shimmers along its path.

I open my eyes.

And meet Ian's amber gaze, shadowed by what looks strangely like fear. I don't make the mistake of thinking that such a seemingly indomitable man isn't as prey to that emotion as anyone else but he's normally far better at concealing it. Not tonight though. Something has broken through his defenses, if only temporarily.

I'm far too distracted to ponder what that could be. We are stretched out on his bed together, my body nestled tightly against his. I can feel the soft fabric of his sweatpants and T-shirt against my bare skin. But I'm more distracted by the heat pouring off him and the strong, steady beat of his heart under my cheek.

"Are you all right?" he murmurs.

I don't know how to answer because I both am and am not. The nightmare is over but its effects linger, filling me with a desperate need to affirm that I truly am alive and free. I murmur something in response but all my attention is focused on the feel of him pressed along every inch of my body. The pleasure he gave me so recently still resonates but incredibly I want more. My nipples harden as inner muscles clench.

"Do you want to talk about it?" he asks when I don't respond.

Oh, god, no. To speak of such things is to make them real in a way I cannot bear. I would rather do anything than that.

"I could ask you the same." I'm not sure that I'm ready to hear the details of what happened to him with his father but I am certain that we need to address the shadow that still haunts him. "Do you want to talk about it?"

He doesn't pretend not to understand what I'm asking but he still shakes his head. "I can't. I probably should have years ago with a professional but I didn't and now...I just can't."

The anguish he tries to hide from me is heart wrenching. At that moment, I conceive an even deeper, more visceral loathing of his father and everyone else involved with his damnable "club" than I have yet experienced.

The coil of fear that has been wound so tightly inside me since the attack on the Crystal Palace began suddenly snaps. I know exactly what we both need. Squirming against him, I push myself upright and press my hands against his broad, sculpted shoulders, holding him down. His eyes widen slightly but he lets me.

My palms tingle as I skim them down his bare arms, savoring the sensation of muscles bulging beneath taut skin. I love this evidence of his strength, of the power he's so skilled at holding in check. But I also resent it. I want him to give himself to me completely, holding nothing back.

Slipping my hands under the bottom of his shirt, I pull it up as I explore the hard ridges of his abdominal muscles, lingering over his flat nipples. A low groan breaks from him.

In my urgency, I'm shameless. Without waiting for permission, I pull the shirt up over his head and drop it onto the floor. Sitting back on my haunches, uncaring that I am wearing only the McClellan diamonds and a smile, I luxuriate in the sight of him. His sweatpants are tied below his navel, exposing the hard V of muscle arching downward and the trail of dark, silky hair thickening to his groin. The soft fabric conforms to the swell of his erection, already impressive.

I can only marvel at my greed for him. Despite having been driven so recently to heights of orgasm by his oh-so-skilled mouth and fingers, I desperately want to feel him deep inside me, filling and stretching me, completing me as only he can.

The ache between my thighs grows more insistent. I pull the pins from my hair and toss them aside, letting the chestnut strands fall over his chest as I bend and swirl my tongue around his nipple. Is he anywhere near as sensitive there as I am?

Hmmm, maybe not as much but he's hardly immune. A long shudder runs through him. "Amelia..."

Whatever he's going to say--warn me, discourage me, whatever--I don't want to hear it. There's only one way I know to silence him. I lower my mouth to his, teasing his lips apart, and at the same time slip a hand into his sweatpants, brazenly stroking his length. My fingers can't meet around his girth. I'm amazed by my body's ability to contain him in the throes of passion.

The tip of my tongue traces the ridges of his teeth and slips deeper, stroking with the same rhythm as my hand. He groans. His hands fist in the sheets, the veins and tendons of his arms standing out in high relief.

In the thickening silence, I hear only the rush of my own blood, know only the touch and scent of him. Everything else--the room, the world, all the clamor of recent events--fades away. Driven by overwhelming need, I yank his sweatpants down further, freeing his cock, and keep yanking until I can pull them off and toss them aside. I know from experience that Ian's reflexes are lightning fast but he makes no move to stop me. His gaze is hooded, his breathing harsh. I can feel the heat pouring from him.

I am so tempted to mount him at once, take his magnificent cock deep inside me and ride him to sweet oblivion. But I want what I always have, a righting of the balance between us, a way to offset the seemingly overwhelming advantage he has by virtue of having lived so much more than I have. I possess little of memory or experience but I was gifted with knowledge, even if it is still largely theoretical. I'm determined to make the most of it.

Without taking my eyes from him, I treat myself to a long, slow lick up the shaft of his cock and swirl my tongue all around the crest. He tastes clean, a little salty, delicious.

"Damn," he mutters, his head falling back to expose the pulse beating in his corded neck.

Emboldened, I close my lips around him and suck just the first inch or so into my mouth. Taking him like this makes me feel daring and powerful but still wanting more. I angle my head so that I can take him deeper and suck harder. His low, guttural moan thrills me. Taking him completely is a challenge but I'm up for it. My head bobs up and down, a little further each time until my nose burrows into his pubic hair. Stilling my gag reflex, I work the muscles of my throat along his length.

He arches his hips, his hand clasping the back of my head, holding me in place.

"Fuck, Amelia!"

The raw groan of his pleasure drives me wild. I'm throbbing with need for him. Hardly aware of what I'm doing, I slide a hand between my legs and find my slick, drenched clit. Lightly at first, then more desperately, I stroke myself. His pre-cum slides down my throat, driving me even closer to the edge. I'm soaking wet, swollen and throbbing, and I still can't get enough of him. The pleasure is so intense that it teeters on the edge of pain. My entire body quivers. I lift my gaze and meet his, seeing in his eyes the same fierce, primal hunger that consumes me.

At the same time, I have a sudden, fleeting image of how I must look to him at this moment. Suspended over him, my lips stretched tightly around the base of his cock, his length thrusting deep into my throat, my hand working frantically between my thighs. I have feared being no more than a receptacle for him but this is my doing, my need. I am in control and loving every moment.

"Enough," he rasps and begins pulling away even as his hands reach for me. His intent is clear but I'm having none of it. Very lightly, I close my teeth around his shaft as I suction him even harder. My determination is his undoing. He gasps and stiffens, his back arching as he comes in hot gushing spurts down my throat. The sight of Ian in the throes of ecstatic release is too much for me. A few more hard, swift strokes of my clit are enough to make me come with him. Pleasure crashes through every inch of my body. White hot bolts of light glow behind my eyes. Every concern, every fear, every thought dissolves in utter completion.

When I am next aware, I'm lying in his arms. His voice is a low, rasping rumple. "Holy shit, Amelia."

He sounds deeply satisfied and confounded all at the same time. The combination prompts a giggle from me. I prop myself on an elbow and look down at him.

More seriously, I say, "I am not a delicate little toy that will break if you don't handle me just right. Do you get that now?"

He stares at me with wariness that touches my heart. He is so vulnerable in ways that I am just beginning to understand. Cautiously, he says, "I may need a reminder from time to time."

"Whenever," I say, relief flowing through me and lean closer to him. "Wherever. I love sucking your cock. I love the way you feel along my tongue and in my mouth but most of all, I love taking you into my throat." My voice drops a notch as I confide, "I fantasize about having you that way someplace where we could be discovered at any moment. We aren't but still, is that awful of me?"

His breath hisses. With some difficulty, he says, "Uh...no...that's actually-- You fantasize about me?"

"Far too much. I do my best to hide it but sometimes I get so wet--"

A strangled sound breaks from him. He moves too quickly for me to realize what is happening before I'm on my back, flat on the bed, staring up at him. His big, hard body straddles me. His lean cheeks are flushed, his breathing harsh. His cock--which even my scant experience has never prevented me from appreciating--decides that now isn't the time for a nap after all.

"I like these," he says, touching the diamond collar that encloses my throat and the matching bracelets around my wrists. His voice is raw, his gaze fiercely hot. "More than I should."

"Then I'll never take them off."

"Yes, you will." He reaches around to the nape of my neck and undoes the clasp. Removing the necklace carefully, he places it on the bedside table. The bracelets follow along with all the rest. A groan escapes him as he clasps my hips, drawing me closer, making me vividly aware of how rapidly he has become aroused again.

"I want to give you jewels," he murmurs, twining the loosened tresses of my hair around his wrist. "I want to the world to see that you are mine."

His words move me deeply. I want to slow down, to cherish every moment, every touch. But ten days of agonizing abstinence added to the erotic image that his words convey tell me that won't be possible. Later perhaps, not now.

"Please." I am lost in him, in us, in how I know we are together. Nothing else exists. My thighs quiver as he eases himself between them. He holds his weight on his arms so as not to crush me but even so I feel surrounded by him, controlled, even owned in a way that has nothing to do with any damn paperwork. My nipples are taut and aching. I need his touch desperately.

"You're playing with fire, Amelia," he says. "We both are."

"I'm not playing at all." I rake my nails down his back hard enough to leave marks. "I'm too angry. Not at you," I add quickly, "although if you go on being so stubborn, we could get there. I'm angry at all the horrible things that have been happening. At the people responsible for them. At everything that has come between us. Life is too precious to waste on hatred and violence."

"You're right," he says, gazing down at me. His hand cups my jaw, holding me still for his hot, fierce kiss. His mouth takes mine, his tongue plunging deeply as his lower body rocks against mine. The friction of his hard cock against my clit drives me wild. I buck against him, desperate for more. A keening moan breaks from me.

"Ian, I need you!"

"Damn right," he says, looming above me, big and thick and ready. "Your hot, tight pussy is mine. Your wet, gorgeous mouth, mine. I want all of you, every possible way. There's only us, baby. I'm going to fuck you so hard that you'll forget about everything else."

I already am. The hot friction of our bodies straining together drives every other thought out of my mine. There's only Ian, his big, hard body so close...

"Inside me," I gasp. "Please, now, I want to feel you--"

My breath leaves me in a rush as he releases my hair and slides down my body. Taking hold of his cock with one hand, he spreads my thighs further and plunges into me with a single long thrust that slams his balls up against my ass.

"Like this, baby, is this how you want it?"

"Yes! Don't stop! Don't--"

Seizing my hips, he pulls almost all the way out and drives into me again. I tighten around him, drawing him even deeper, my hips rising and falling with his rhythm. He's giving me everything I need, holding nothing back. Heat ripples through me, building swiftly. I moan, bearing down, impaled by him.

He grinds against my inner walls, finding exactly the right spot. Light explodes behind my eyes. As though from a great distance, I hear myself sobbing his name.

"Ian!"

Everything--all the fear and horror of bloodied bodies and exploded buildings, old sins and precarious futures--fades away. Only Ian exists, in me, above me, possessing me. Even as I possess him. This is the power we share, what we are together, able to focus completely on one another in a way that I am convinced means we can withstand anything.

Convincing him of that will have to wait. My inner muscles spasm, the onset of orgasm burning through me. White. Hot. Bliss. He holds my gaze, holding me captive, my body, my mind, my soul, all his. As he is mine.

I rear up, drawn to the bead of sweat trickling down the ripped muscles of his torso. My tongue spears out, lapping at him. The taste of his skin explodes on my tongue. It's a drug I will never get enough of and it tips me over the edge. The orgasm that tears through me is the most powerful I've ever experienced, fueled by terror, anger, and above all, the defiant decision to embrace life.

I cling to Ian as he joins me, his breath hot against my skin, both of us coming as one, alive and free.

Chapter Fourteen

Amelia

Waking, my eyes still closed, I reach out instinctively for Ian. My hand fumbles on cool sheets. His side of the bed is empty. I'm alone.

I sit up gingerly, aware of the delicious soreness in every inch of my body but especially between my thighs. I wince just a little but I can't help smiling until I remember how hard I pushed Ian to take me to his bed. It's all well and good for me to tell myself that we are better off facing his demons together but I have an urgent need for reassurance that in the cold light of morning he feels the same.

Anxious to find him, I dart out of the bed and into the shower. Twenty minutes later, dressed in a soft cotton blouse and matching short skirt that must have been brought down from the estate, I venture out into the vast apartment. I'm standing atop the tallest building in the city in which several tens of thousands of people work and live. Yet the world feels eerily empty until I hear the hiss of an espresso machine coming from the kitchen.

I head toward the sound only to stop in my tracks when I see the silver-haired gentleman standing at the stove. Hodgkin is formally dressed in dark trousers, a matching vest, and a pin-striped shirt. A charcoal gray apron is wrapped around his waist. It only serves to emphasize his military bearing, the legacy of an earlier life.

Hodge, as he's better known, was introduced to me as the steward of Ian's estate north of the city, the estate where I first awoke. Since then, I've come to realize that he's much more. The soul of discretion but also of compassion and quiet understanding, he's played a pivotal role in Ian's life, guiding him away from the father who did him so much harm and toward the military that was the making of him. He's always been gracious to me but I still feel more than a little self-conscious at encountering him now.

He sees my reflection in the stainless steel backdrop of the stove and turns. His normally hang-dog face creases in a warm smile that gives every evidence of being sincere.

"Good morning, Miss Amelia. I trust you're hungry?"

Before I can respond, my stomach growls. The scents of bacon and coffee override every other consideration, at least for the moment.

"I'm starving." Remembering my manners, I add, "It's nice to see you again, Mister Hodgkin."

"Please, miss," he says, "Hodge will do. Mister Ian asked me to give you his apologies, he's been called away to a briefing but he should return shortly. In the meantime, may I suggest breakfast on the terrace? The wind has died down and it's a lovely day."

I swallow my disappointment at Ian's absence and nod. "That sounds lovely, thank you."

Doors from the soaring great room lead out onto the terrace that wraps all the way around the lower floor of the penthouse. A table is set for two facing the harbor but before I sit down, I walk in the other direction until I am looking north toward the park.

I don't know what I'm expecting to see but the scene takes me aback. If I squint, I can make out a few vehicles on the periphery of where the Crystal Palace stood hours before but I'm not even sure that they belong to the MPS. A strange normality has taken hold in stark contrast to the chaos and death of the previous night. Elsewhere in the city, the same holds true. Traffic moves smoothly through the streets below. No more than the usual number of surveillance drones are aloft. I'm so high up that the people look like small specks but even they appear to be moving around the city as though nothing out of the ordinary has happened.

Surely, they know what occurred. They must be talking among themselves about it, probably with great fear and dread. But where are the crowds that should be gathered, watching the authorities go about their investigation, and sharing theories stranger to stranger? Have they been banned? Is there some grand delusion at work? Or is what I'm seeing evidence that people are too afraid to show any reaction to the catastrophe that has made a mockery of their carefully nurtured illusion of safety?

I'm still puzzling about that when I return to the table. Hodge is setting out my breakfast.

"There you are, miss. Would you like coffee or do you prefer tea this morning?"

"Coffee, please, the stronger the better."

He pulls out my chair for me, then fills my cup from a silver pot. "Will there be anything else, miss?"

I look down at the plate where an omelet oozing with cheese nestles besides several slices of crispy bacon. "This is more than enough but--"

I don't want to eat alone. The servants at the McClellan family residence keep a careful distance that rebuffs any possible overtures of friendship before they can be offered. But Hodge is different. I sense that he could unbend if I just give him the opportunity.

"Would you join me?" I ask.

He looks surprised but not displeased. "I've already eaten, miss. However, I'll be happy to keep you company."

He doesn't take a seat but he does lean against the balcony railing, cross one ankle over the other, and smile. He looks courteous and professional, but approachable. I suspect that Hodge is one of the very few people who knows the truth about me. That Ian trusts him completely inclines me to do the same.

"I hope the events of yesterday evening did not upset you too much?" he says.

A memory of immense shards of shattered glass raining down from the sky flares across my mind. I shy away from it and shrug. "It's the first time I've gone to a party where the building has blown up. Is there very much about it in the news?"

"There was initially but the coverage has rapidly transformed into an outcry against the scavengers, demands that they all be driven from the city, and so on. About what one would expect."

He's lost me. "What do the scavengers have to do with it?"

Hodge raises a brow. "Why they're to blame, miss, didn't you know? Apparently, a group of scavengers attacked the Crystal Palace with the intent of taking the city's elite hostage. A valiant group of MPS officers fought them off but was, alas, unable to prevent the explosion that, purely coincidentally destroyed most of the evidence of what had actually happened."

I think of the ragged children I saw and of everything else I know about the people who are consigned to the city's underbelly. While they may certainly have motive, I don't believe for a moment that they could have the means to carry out such an assault.

"That's ridiculous. Nobody with half a brain could believe that the scavengers are responsible for what happened."

"With all respect, miss, people can believe anything they choose to when they're too afraid to confront the truth."

The weight of his words resonates within me. I know from my own experience how easy it is to embrace denial. When Ian told me the truth about myself. I fled rather than accept it. But I couldn't flee from the terrifying memories that I'm not supposed to have. They are inescapable. I fear and loath them but as horrible as those periods of self-awareness are, they are proof that something of me existed before I received Susannah's imprinting, something that is entirely my own.

The implications of that are profound. I haven't even begun to understand them but I sense that when I do, I will find within them answers to many of the questions I have about myself.

"Miss?" Hodge is staring at me. "Are you all right?"

Jerked back into the here-and-now, I just manage a nod. "Yes, of course. Forgive me. You were saying that people are afraid--"

"Not without reason. After all, someone attacked the Crystal Palace. The Council can blame whoever they like but they'll be doing everything they can to find out who was really responsible." He pauses for a moment, then adds, "In the meantime, all the emphasis is on a speedy return to normality. It's already been announced that Carnival will proceed as scheduled."

I can't hide my surprise. From everything I've heard, Carnival is a time of frenzied pleasure-seeking. Crowds throng the streets, mind-altering substances of all kinds flow freely, and every inhibition is cast aside.

"Will people want to participate given what's just happened?" I ask. "And even if they do, surely it isn't wise to draw them out into the streets where they could become targets for another attack."

"I share your doubts, miss," Hodge says. "But regrettably the Council does not. They are concerned only with maintaining the image that they are in control. We can only hope that whoever really was responsible for the attack on the Crystal Palace is found and contained quickly."

I remember my grandmother's warning that suspicion could fall on Ian. A shiver runs through me. "Do you think Ian can find out the truth?"

"Oh, yes, miss, I'm certain that he can. Mister Ian has never let any obstacle stand between him and an objective."

I can't help but smile. No one has to tell me that Ian's will is formidable. I've experienced it for myself on more than a few occasions.

"You've known him a long time, haven't you?" I'm not sure where I'm going with this or how far Hodge will let me get but I have to try. Ian loves his mother and sister but I don't for a moment believe that he has ever let them know the details of what drove him away from his father. Hodge on the other hand-- Hodge was there, he intervened, he changed the course of Ian's life.

"A dozen years," he says quietly, "since Mister Ian was sixteen."

"He didn't...get along with his father, did he?"

It's now or never. Hodge will answer me or he'll blow me off. Either way, I'll know where I stand with him.

He takes a breath, lets it out slowly, and says, "No, miss, he didn't. Marcus Slade was a brilliant man in many ways. He could have made a difference in the world for the greater good. Unfortunately, he lacked anything remotely resembling a moral compass."

From the little Ian has told me about his father, that's putting it mildly. Marcus Slade was a misogynist who enjoyed hurting women. He used that to exploit other men's weaknesses and perversions, and advance his own ends. The amount of damage he did to those who fell into his grasp is incalculable.

"He wanted Ian to be like him," I say. My throat tightens at the thought of the boy Ian was--brilliant but achingly vulnerable, wanting so desperately to please his father.

"It has been my observation that good people want their children to grow up and have fulfilling lives of their own," Hodge says quietly. "Others, like Marcus Slade, are incapable of seeing a child as anything other than an extension of themselves, a way to extend control beyond the limits of their own mortality. Fortunately, Mister Ian had the strength to break away from his father and make his own life."

"You helped him to do that."

"I merely showed him what was possible." He pauses for a moment, studying me, before he says, "He's an extraordinary young man who has achieved a great deal against enormous odds. But he still lives under the shadow of the past. I would like nothing better than to see him put that behind him once and for all."

So would I but I'm cautious all the same. When it comes right down to it, I'm operating on sheer instinct. If I made a mistake in agreeing to return to Pinnacle House, Ian is likely to pay the price.

"You don't think it's better sometimes to let sleeping demons lie?"

Hodge's smile is gentle. "Dogs, Miss Amelia. The saying is to let sleeping dogs lie, which is good advice. A man's demons are a different matter altogether. Either he controls them or they control him. There really is no middle ground."

It occurs to me that Hodge is speaking from personal experience. He spent his youth in the military. In all likelihood, he saw things that he would rather forget. But he's found a way to live with them.

Softly, I say, "I'm afraid that being with me forces Ian to confront the past in a way that hurts him."

His nod is sympathetic but he doesn't pull any punches. "He was hurting before you ever came into his life, Miss Amelia. You can't make that worse and there's a chance that you could make it better. Do you really want to turn away from that?"

The thought of Ian in pain is a knife through me. I don't trust myself to speak. All I can do is shake my head and pretend interest in my breakfast. Hodge gives me a few moments to compose myself before he tops off my coffee and slips away. I'm left alone on the terrace, the city spread out below me in all its brittle beauty.

After a time, I pick up a link and scroll through the news. I'm on the private net available only to the city's elite residents, many of whom must have been present at the Crystal Palace. But not even they can be allowed to read the truth about what they experienced. In addition to the absurd claim that the MPS fought off the attackers--a lie that makes my blood boil--the entire incident is framed in terms of nobility versus brutishness, sprinkled with vignettes in which the valiant guests rush to each other's assistance, men in evening dress carry fainting ladies to safety, and angels of mercy in gowns comfort the wounded.

The only upside to this litany of lies is that it seems to have overwhelmed the news editors so that they let a few other stories slip through unvarnished. I come across one that quotes doctors at the city's hospitals expressing alarm at the increasing number of cases they're seeing related to the illegal street drug that's been dubbed "Jekyll/Hyde". Jorge Cruces, head of the world's largest recreational drug company--to which the government has long since turned over responsibility for enforcing the drug laws--has vowed to find the source of the drug and destroy it. I don't doubt that he'll succeed, given his reputation for ruthlessness. But I have to wonder how the drug got into the city in the first place.

My curiosity is no match for my concern about Ian. I flick the link off, wishing that I had more life experience to draw on in dealing with him. The soft click of the door to the great room opening distracts me. It could be Hodge returning to check on me but I know it's not. When a hand falls lightly on my shoulder, I touch my lips to it tenderly.

"Hey, babe," Ian says softly. "Sorry I wasn't here when you woke up." He takes the chair across from mine, stretching his long, jean-clad legs out to the side, and studies me. His eyes are hooded, his expression concealing far more than it reveals. But his concern is unmistakable when he asks, "Are you all right?"

After a night of blood, death, and wild sex? All things considered, I think I'm doing remarkably well. But if that weren't the case, it wouldn't matter. He's all I care about.

"I'm fine. Have you learned anything?"

"Nothing of substance but we will. It's only a matter of time."

I wish that I shared his confidence but I can't begin to imagine who could have committed such an atrocity, or why. "Hodge says that the Council is blaming the scavengers. He also says that Carnival is going on as scheduled. How can that be?"

Ian shrugs. "The Council is scared shitless. They've never had to deal with anything like this and they don't have a clue what to do." He pauses for a moment, then adds, "Maybe that was the point. Make them desperate enough to turn to whoever they think can preserve the status quo."

It occurs to me that he's giving me a glimpse into the workings of his mind as he mulls over what has happened. That's a first, as well as reassurance that I made the right decision in being where I am.

Softly, I ask, "In exchange for what?"

"There's only one currency that really matters--power."

I consider what Pinnacle House itself represents, the steel embodiment of power that can make itself felt with no more than a word from the man who controls it. "What if the Council, instead of trying to blame you, turns to you for help instead? After all, who could keep things the way they are better than you, if you chose to do so?"

But he wouldn't, would he? Ian wouldn't protect a system that leaves so many without opportunity or hope.

As though he reads my mind, he says, "I've been places where everything is falling apart. It isn't pretty. The best case scenario is that one ruling faction replaces another. Otherwise, chaos reigns and the weakest suffer the most."

It's a non-answer but it's enough to alarm me. "What about freedom?" I ask, not caring if I sound naive. Freedom is far too new and precious an idea for me to let go of readily. "What about democracy, human rights?"

He looks resigned to a reality he wishes was different. "None of that is easy to achieve. At the very least, there has to be a period of relative calm when decent, honorable people can come together and work out their differences. You don't have that if the streets are running with blood and firebrands are in charge."

"Surely that couldn't happen here? This place is so civilized, so cultured." If only for the chosen few.

"So was Russia before its revolution," he counters. "At least if you were fortunate enough to be living in Moscow, attending the ballet and dining on caviar. France was the cultural center of the world when the guillotine popped up and body parts started being paraded through the streets. I could go down the list but the fact is that when societies collapse what follows is anarchy. That's worth avoiding at almost any cost."

Almost. I have to wonder where he draws that particular line but I don't ask. I'm too new to all this--caring about him, wanting the best for him, wondering how he and I fit together, hoping with everything I possess that we do. That last thought is harsh enough to knock the air from me.

"You're not eating, babe," he says, glancing at my plate. He looks up, meeting my eyes, and I see the cautious smile in his. "What do you say we get out of here?"

I stare at him in surprise. His gaze is intent but guileless. He appears almost boyish, as though he's shucked off his concerns or at least stored them away somewhere in favor of simply embracing the moment. Making no effort to disguise my eagerness, I ask, "Can we?"

He stands, holding out his hand. My prince in every sense but suddenly not quite so dark. All the same, he looks as commanding as ever as he grins and says, "Who's going to stop us?"

Josie Litton

Chapter Fifteen

Ian

I've never taken a woman to the beach house before. It's where I head to when I need a quick break, closer to the city than the estate and the one refuge where no one gives a damn who I am. Women would just complicate that. Or at least that's how I've felt in the past. Amelia is different. In more ways than I can begin to count.

"Where are we going?" she asks when we're in the chopper. We take off from the roof pad on top of Pinnacle House, clear the city in seconds, and swoop over the cookie-cutter buildings to the east, stuffed with micro-apartments for the worker bees. I can hear the excitement in her voice. If anything really fazes this woman, I've yet to discover it. She embraces life with an ardor that leaves me reeling. Not that I'm in any hurry to let her know that. I'm already vulnerable enough where she's concerned.

"Montauk," I say. "It's a little town out on the tip of Long Island. My mother's people came from there. They were potato farmers and fishermen until the Wall Street guys moved in. After the super storm in 2029 turned the beachfront mansions into kindling, the rich folks disappeared. Life's going back to what it was a century ago."

I'm explaining more than I normally would but I've got an irresistible impulse to open up to her. It baffles me at the same time that I sort of understand it. I want Amelia to know the real me, including the parts I don't usually show to other people. At the same time, I'm scared shitless of what will happen when she does. I have to be crazy to be doing this in the aftermath of the attack on the Crystal Palace but I can't help myself. In the past, I've seen death as a grim aspect of the reality we all inhabit, to be accepted and moved past. Now it's urging me to pause, reflect, and seize happiness where and when I can.

She turns her head and meets my gaze. I'm struck yet again by her beauty--not merely of her face and body, although heaven knows I appreciate both--but in the spirit that shines from her eyes. As challenging and impetuous as she can be, she is also the most genuinely warm and giving woman I have ever known. There are moments when she actually makes me believe that I can be a better man.

"I can't imagine you as a potato farmer," she admits with a smile. "Fishing, maybe."

I laugh. "You should see me land a marlin."

"Is that what we're going to be doing today?" She sounds up for it but then I haven't seen her turn away from any experience. She embraces life with a fervor that makes everything around her seem new.

"I might drop a line in the water, among other things. Mostly, I think we can both use a little time away from the craziness. You've got to admit, ever since we met life has been coming at us like the proverbial freight train."

Amelia looks relieved. "I'm glad it's not just me. I've been afraid that if I blink, I'll miss something."

"Not today," I tell her. "Today it's just us. All right?"

She nods but I catch a flicker of hesitation. I can't blame her for that. I'm not being entirely truthful and on some level she senses it. I want this day for us not just for its own sake but because I've got a good idea what's coming. A bigger storm in its own way than the one that hit in '29 only this time Mother Nature won't be to blame. This will be a purely manmade disaster compounded of greed, the lust for power, and the devaluing of the lives of all but the fortunate few. I've got a chance, maybe, to head it off but whether I can or not one thing is damn sure, I will keep Amelia safe no matter what comes at us. I have tremendous respect for her courage and intelligence but she's far too inexperienced to be left to her own devices in a dangerous world.

"You're frowning," she says. "Is something wrong?"

Not much except I'm wondering if I should send her back to the estate and keep her there under guard until this is over. She wouldn't like that. Hell, she'd fight it tooth and nail. But she'd be safe.

She also might never forgive me.

I'll keep that option in mind all the same but for now I meant what I said, I want this day to be for us.

"Everything's fine," I assure her. "Just sit back and relax. We'll be there soon."

Twenty minutes later, I angle the chopper down toward the concrete slab sitting beside a former potato field within sight of the ocean. Amelia has been silent for most of the trip, riveted by the sight of the Atlantic rushing toward us. The view from Pinnacle House, impressive though it is, barely prepared her for the reality.

"This is incredible," she says, gazing at the diamond bursts of light on the gray-blue surface. Gulls circle overhead, squawking at the chopper's intrusion. The sandpipers have vanished temporarily from the strip of sandy beach within sight of the landing pad but I see a sleek head rise from the rocky outcropping that extends beyond the shore. The seals are stubborn, not so easily disturbed.

I take her hand, helping her out, and breathe in her scent--that jasmine body wash she uses and something else that is pure Amelia and makes me think of her, of us in the night, her skin against mine, soft moans spilling from her throat.

My cock hardens. I do my best to ignore it and draw her attention to the small house sheltered by a hillock but within sight of the beach. It's nothing like the mansions that used to litter this shore, just two-stories covered in gray shingles with dark green shutters and a wrap-around porch. It's the kind of house that was common in these parts for a century and more.

"Is this where your mother's family lived?" she asks as we climb the few steps to the front door.

"This was their land but it's not the original house."

"What happened to that? The storm in '29?"

"No, it was actually one of the few structures around here that survived." Keeping in mind what I want this day to be about, I add, "When my mother left my father, he got control of the property and had the house razed to the ground."

Amelia's eyes go dark, resembling nothing so much as the deep, fast running currents that sweep along the coast after a big blow. "To hurt her?" she asks.

I nod. The house was one more thing I'd tried to fix. "I had it rebuilt although at her urging, it's not identical. The outside is the same, the interior's been updated."

"Does your mother ever stay here?"

"No, she's happy that it's been rebuilt but she wants it to be mine now."

That surprised me until I realized that she was right to see it as a place that I could come to and connect with the better part of my past. That's why I'm here. To try to convince myself that I haven't made a terrible mistake by being with Amelia again. If I have, I'm all too aware of how much she could be harmed but I'd hardly escape unscathed myself. Hurting her would destroy me.

I unlock the front door and stand aside for Amelia to enter. She does so but pauses at once and looks around slowly. I wait, not sure what to expect.

Finally, after what seems like forever, she says, "This is very different from your apartment in the city."

She's right. The penthouse is a statement of power. This is a modest home built for solid people who lived quiet lives built on strength and faith. I don't question why it feels so right to me, it just does.

"My forbearers probably would have been a little surprised by the new layout--" It's an open plan that sweeps from the front door clear to the back with a glimpse of the beach beyond. "But I like to think they would have been comfortable here."

She looks around at the white walls and pickled floors, the simple furniture, and the few works of art that I've acquired from local painters and sculptors. They are mostly images of the natural world just outside the door. Moving over to the windows at the back, she peers out. The palm of her hand rests lightly against the glass. When she turns her head, she looks excited but tentative.

"Can we go for a walk along the beach?"

My heart twists at the thought that she believes I would deny her anything. "We can do whatever you want but a walk sounds great."

A minute or so from the house lies a stretch of the Atlantic shore that looks as pristine as it must have to the first humans ever to see it. Small waves lap at golden sand dotted with drift wood and patches of stranded sea weed. The scent of beach roses that line the path from the house fills the diamond-clear air.

On a workday, no one else is in sight. We might as well be the only people in the world. It occurs to me that I've run for miles along this beach more times than I can count but I've never just strolled along it. With Amelia, there's no other option. We have to stop every few yards as she makes a new discovery.

"What is this?" she asks, holding up a dark, rectangular object that she's plucked from the sand. I've already noticed that she doesn't hesitate to touch anything that catches her eye. Hell, she puts most of it right up to her nose and takes a good sniff. If there's a squeamish bone in her body, I haven't noticed.

"That's a mermaid's purse," I say with a grin. Her eager embrace of the world I'm showing to her delights me. For the first time in years, I feel a stirring of my own wonder at this place when I was young and innocent, an eon ago.

She gives me a chiding look. "It is not."

"How do you know? Or are you just going to make some blanket statement about there being no such thing as mermaids?"

She tosses her head and slants me a glance that suggests I'm being deliberately obtuse.

"Don't be silly. There's no room in here for a mermaid to keep her shell comb much less her tail moisturizer, water-proof mascara, sunglasses--"

I raise a brow. This is a side of Amelia I haven't seen before-- whimsical, playful, and utterly captivating. "Mermaids need sunglasses?"

"For when they come up to the surface. The light can be very glaring there."

I nod, considering. "That would explain why we don't see more of them?"

She gives me a teasing smile. "Exactly. Now, since we've established that this cannot be a mermaid's purse, what is it?"

I look at what she's holding, something I discovered when I was maybe three years old and have seen so often ever since that the truth is I don't really see it any more. Until now. Suddenly, I'm seeing it again for the first time, through her eyes.

I step closer to her and cup my hand around hers. Her skin is soft, smooth, and warmed by the sun. I have to fight the urge to bury myself in her.

"It's the egg pouch of a skate. What's left after the eggs hatch and the baby fish are born."

She turns the pouch over in her palm, staring at it. Her focus is intent. I can't begin to guess what's going through her mind until she says softly, "Everywhere I look, everything I see, it's all about life really, in all its astonishing variety. Sometimes it overwhelms me."

My throat tightens as I think of her struggling to make sense of the world without the benefit of memories or experience. I could have made things easier for her and would have if I hadn't let my cock do my thinking for me.

Dropping my hand, I take a step back. "You've had more to cope with than any person should."

She looks surprised until she sees that I'm sincere. A flash of anger darts across her face. "Don't you dare feel sorry for me. I'm incredibly fortunate, not just to be in this world but to be surrounded by every comfort and luxury. I've seen for myself what it's like for other people."

"What other people?" So far as I know, the only people she's associated with are others of her class or close to it, like the damn Russian. Unless she's talking about servants.

"Scavengers," she says. "I've seen them."

"How the hell?" Belatedly, I remember what Edward told me, something about Amelia coming to the defense of a young man being beaten by the MPS.

But that isn't what she means, as I discover a moment later.

"Children. I saw them in the park. They came up out of a tunnel. They were dirty and ragged, and so hungry." Her voice breaks.

I curse under my breath. The presence of adult scavengers is bad enough but that there are children among them makes the whole situation all the more screwed up and reprehensible. Every time the matter of what to do about the so-called scavs comes up, I've signaled loud and clear that Slade Enterprises won't tolerate an attack on civilians. I've done so again in the aftermath of the idiotic attempt to blame them for the Crystal Palace disaster. But I'm not kidding myself. I can only hold the line for so long. Something has to change, and sooner rather than later. The problem is how to make that happen without turning the streets red with blood.

"They shouldn't have been there," I say. "If they'd been caught--"

"What if they had been, Ian? What would have been done to them?"

The truth is that I'm not sure. The law calls for the children of scavengers to be put into foster care. But there are rumors of under-aged workers trapped in occupations considered too dangerous to risk expensive robots. Even worse are the stories of children trafficked into the sex trade. I have my people looking into all that. If we can pin it down as anything other than rumor, I won't hesitate to act.

Rather than reveal even a hint of this to Amelia, I punt. "What were you doing in the park by yourself?" She wasn't actually alone; my security guys were on her but they'd been ordered to keep a discreet distance and I can understand that would be hard in the park. Still, I plan on having a word with them.

"I was walking home, the way people do through the park." Grudgingly, she adds, "Sergei was concerned about the number of police on the streets. He thought something bad might be coming and, as it turns out, he was right."

Good old Sergei. Except he isn't old. He's a young guy in peak condition who shares Amelia's passion for dance and who apparently also cares about her safety. I could thank him but I'm more in the mood to go a few rounds, see if all that physical strength and agility counts for anything besides prancing around in tights.

"I don't understand how anyone can tolerate the way the scavengers are treated," she says. The glare in her eyes makes it clear that by 'anyone' she means me.

This isn't what I had in mind when we came out on the beach but I'm not going to run away from it either. If I'm serious about wanting Amelia to know me better, I've got to be square with her even if she doesn't like what I have to say.

"I don't have to approve of something to recognize that changing it is difficult. The scavengers are a symptom of the larger problem of who controls resources in our society. Until that's addressed, the best way to help them is privately."

"You mean through charity?" The curl of her lip makes it clear what she thinks of that.

"Among other things. Let's just say there's more communication between the scavengers and certain other people in the city than the government needs to know about."

"You're in contact with them?" She looks hopeful. I hate to disappoint her but I don't want her to have any misconceptions about me either.

"Not directly but--" Do I want to tell her that Gab's surveillance of the city's communication nodes has turned up evidence that Edward is in contact with the scavengers' leaders? He hasn't chosen to tell me why and I haven't pressed him--yet. We'll clear the air eventually but in the meantime, Gab is running interference to make sure the authorities don't stumble across whatever it is that he's doing.

"There are things you're better off not knowing." Before she can protest, I add, "Anyone who was at the Crystal Palace last night and survived is liable to be questioned at some point. The clearer and more focused you can be, the better."

That's true as far as it goes but beyond it is the fact that anyone with an urge to question Amelia will have to go through me. I'll make sure that they don't enjoy the process.

I can tell she isn't happy with my evasiveness but she lets it go. A wave, rolling in with the advancing tide, creeps high enough up the beach to wash over our toes. Amelia gasps and jumps back a little.

"That's cold!"

"It won't be warm enough to swim in until July." I'd be perfectly happy swimming now but I don't want her getting any ideas. As much as I'm looking forward to warming up Amelia, I don't want to have to do it because she's blue with hypothermia.

"Ready to head back to the house?" I ask softly.

She tucks a strand of wind-blown hair behind her ear and nods.

When we're within sight of it, I detour to a small shed, open it, and take out a couple of plastic buckets. Offering one to her, I ask, "Want to try something new?"

She doesn't hesitate. Her trust in me is humbling at the same time I'm perfectly willing to take full advantage of it. "What do you have in mind?"

"I'll show you." We walk a short distance in the other direction along the beach to where a rocky outcropping extends out into the ocean. The tide is still low enough to leave some of it exposed but in another hour or so it will be completely covered.

I bend down between the rocks, root around in the bed of moist seaweed, and find what I'm looking for. Holding up a shiny black mussel, I grin at Amelia, "Lunch. That is if you're up for it."

I wait, wondering how she'll react. Gathering her own food while it's still alive is a bit removed from the world she's been experiencing. But I should know better than to doubt her.

With a grin, Amelia crouches beside the bed. "Bet I can find more than you do," she says.

Fifteen minutes later, I conclude that women are just better at this kind of thing than men. They were out in the bushes, finding tasty tubers and berries that wouldn't poison us while we were stalking prey across the veldt...or somewhere. Amelia's bucket is full when she calls a halt.

"We have enough, don't we?"

I look at the few I've managed to find, add them mentally to hers, and nod. "Did I mention that whoever wins does the cooking?"

Her face falls. "I have no idea how-- Oh, wait." She thinks for a moment, then says, "Steam them open in white wine with a little garlic and butter?"

"That's right."

We're walking back to the house hand-in-hand when she asks quietly, "Did Susannah like to cook?"

This is one of the very few times that Amelia has mentioned the woman who was my lover for more than two years and whose memory I will always honor. She is the reason why Amelia exists but I don't want her to be any sort of intrusion between us.

"I can't remember her ever setting foot in a kitchen," I say truthfully.

For a moment, I think that answer satisfies Amelia but as we climb the porch steps, she says, "I know so many things without having any idea how I know them. Sometimes I wonder if Susannah spent the last months of her life purposefully learning everything she thought I could possibly need to know."

I have a sudden memory of finding Susannah on the link every time I visited her after her final illness took hold. She was always reading up about something or other, as though her tastes had suddenly become widely eclectic.

"That sounds like something she would have done," I say. "But whether she did or not, she wanted the best for you."

The words are no sooner out than I realize that they aren't entirely true. Susannah could have entrusted Amelia to her grandmother or to Edward, both of whom surely had a stronger claim as members of her own family. Instead, she bequeathed her to me. By no stretch of the imagination can I make that into what is best for her. I do, however, know why Susannah did it.

As we enter the house, Amelia says, "I've wondered how she imagined I'd turn out. Did she give you any indication of her hopes for me?"

I carry the mussels into the kitchen and put them to soak in the sink to get the grit out. Amelia follows. I know she's waiting for a response but I'm not in a hurry to provide it. This unalloyed honesty between us is even tougher than I expected.

Finally, I say, "In a letter she wrote just before her death, she said that she believed the illness had made her inherently fragile. She thought I had always sensed that and suppressed certain aspects of my nature when we were together. Without the illness, she was convinced that she would have been the woman I really needed."

I turn back from the sink to find Amelia staring at me. Her teeth worry her bottom lip. Finally, she says, "Was she right?"

I let out my breath slowly. "To a certain extent."

I want to look away as Amelia absorbs this but I can't. Her face, especially her eyes, reflect her thoughts and her emotions. She's far too intelligent not to understand what I've revealed and draw the correct inferences.

"You were gentle with her?"

I nod. We both know that I have rarely been gentle with Amelia. Wild for her, demanding, insatiable but not gentle. "I treated her like spun glass."

She flinches but quickly tries to conceal it. I don't want to consider what she's thinking but I can't look away from her. Water is almost sloshing over the rim of the sink before I remember to turn the tap off. As I do so, Amelia says, "She didn't know about your father, did she?"

The mention of him tenses every muscle in my body. I've loathed his presence in my life since I was old enough to understand what kind of man he was. But his intrusion into this intimate moment is unbearable.

"No, she didn't. You're the only person I've ever told."

Others know, of course, beginning with the men who were members of the club and the women victimized there. Hodge suspected the truth. I hope that my mother never has but I'm not certain of that. Amelia is the only person I've ever let down my guard with enough to speak of such things and even then I haven't given her any details.

"Was it easier for you to be with her than with me?" she asks.

I have to give her credit, she has guts. Asking what it was like between Susannah and me can't be pleasant but she's done it all the same.

Cautiously, I say, "In certain respects. You're astoundingly different from Susannah to a degree I could never have anticipated and I'm sure she couldn't either. You challenge me to be the man I might have been if my father hadn't been what he was, if none of what he involved me in had ever happened."

With a start, I realize the unintended consequences of what Susannah set in motion. She wanted her replica to be the woman she herself might otherwise have been. Instead, Amelia is entirely her own woman. But the effect of her being in my life is to make me imagine the man I might have been and to regret more profoundly than ever that I am not.

As though she knows exactly what's going through my mind, Amelia lays her hand against my face in a gesture so gentle and comforting that the hard coil of tension inside me begins to ease. Her eyes glisten with tears. "I wish that you had been spared all of it but at the same time I would never want you to be anyone other than who you are. I'd just like you to be able to lay the past to rest and be at peace with it."

She takes a deep, shuddering breath and goes on. "When you told me what your father did, I realized that being with me forced you to confront your worst nightmares. I thought you would be better off if we were apart. But once we were--" Her voice breaks. "The world felt so empty. I felt so empty. Now I don't know what to do. I long for you, Ian, but I can't bear the thought of causing you harm."

My vision blurs. I can't remember the last time I cried and I'm sure as hell not about to do so now but...damn.

"You could never--" I say, drawing her to me. I've tried--seriously tried--to keep my hands off her and I've failed completely. I need her as much as I need air. The only saving grace is that she seems to need me in the same way.

"Everything is better with you," I say. Does she truly not realize how she transforms my world?

"Let me show you," I say, lifting her. She feels weightless in my arms as I stride quickly across the floor illuminated by late morning sun and into the bedroom.

Chapter Sixteen

Amelia

Ian lays me down on a four-poster bed in a room filled with opalescent light and the scent of salt air. He steps back and without taking his eyes from me, pulls his T-shirt over his head and tosses it onto a nearby wicker chair. My breath catches as he unzips his jeans and pulls them off along with his briefs. His erection springs free, long and thick, so enticing that I can't help but moisten my lips as I imagine the taste of him.

Fully naked, he comes to me. His gaze is hot, fierce, yet unexpectedly gentle. His touch, as he undoes the buttons of my blouse is so light that the garment seems to fall open of its own accord. He slips it off and stops for a moment, staring at my breasts barely concealed by the lacy white bra. Watching him watching me, I feel my nipples hardening even further.

"You are so exquisite," he breathes, resting one knee on the bed so that he is beside and above me. His thumbs stroke my aureoles, round and round, sending tremors of pleasure through me.

"Please," I murmur.

He smiles faintly, keeping up the tantalizing caress. "Please what?"

"Touch me." I sound so needy but I can't help it. This new, more open Ian is irresistible. But then so is every other aspect of him that I've encountered.

"I am touching you," he says, bending closer. I feel the exhalation of his breath on the swell of my breasts.

Pressing my shoulders into the mattress, I arch my back. "Closer..." I whisper.

"Like this?" He rubs his thumbs over my swollen nipples. They are so sensitive already that the smooth silk of my bra feels rough and abrasive against them.

"Let me take this off," I murmur and start to reach around for the clasp.

He stops me with a look. "Stay still. We're going to do this my way."

My eyes widen. I want to ask what that means but Ian is slipping the straps of my bra down my arms and slipping his long fingers into the cups, freeing my breasts.

"Beautiful," he murmurs, holding my gaze. His fingers continue to torment me, the thumb and index fingers squeezing my nipples, twisting them gently until I can't bear it any more.

"Ian!"

A part of my mind is astonished that he can make me this aroused so quickly, especially given our excesses of last night. But the thought sizzles away on the heat building inside me. When his mouth replaces his fingers, sucking first lightly, then more powerfully on one nipple and the other, any possibility of my remaining still vanishes. I writhe under him, my hands clasping his head, fingers twining in his thick, soft hair.

His teeth graze me in the lightest punishment. He lifts his head, gazing down at his handiwork. Gruffly, he chides, "So impatient, sweet Amelia. I want to linger over you."

That sounds...wonderful, tantalizing, and yet darkly terrifying. I'm not sure how much of this slow, teasing build-up I can take. Already, I'm teetering on the edge.

"Maybe later?" I suggest breathlessly. "Next time...or the next. Whenever?"

He chuckles. "You're a supremely disciplined dancer. Your body is your instrument. You know how to control it."

A moan breaks from me. "Not with you, not like this. You make me forget everything else."

He nods, clearly pleased. "Good. Close your eyes, babe. I want you to just feel."

I don't want to lose the sight of him, so powerful and graceful above me. But I do as he says all the same. My reward is the touch of his fingers under my skirt, moving up along the inner skin of my thighs until they graze my panties.

"You're so wet already," he murmurs, stroking me. Even with the barrier of fabric still between us, the gentle pressure of his index finger circling my clit makes me tighten helplessly. My eyes fly open.

"Wet for you, Ian," I gasp. "Only you." I reach out, grasping his shoulders, trying to pull him to me. "Please, I need you inside me."

"You'll have me," he promises. "But first think about that, sweetheart. Imagine my cock in you. How does it feel?"

This is torture but I can't deny him, especially not when he pulls my panties to one side, exposing my pussy and begins stroking me there.

"Thick, hard, so good!" I gasp.

He stops, looking down at me. "How else? Tell me more."

I've never tried to speak of such things. Even to think of doing so seems...forbidden, intriguing, too tempting to resist. Words have a power all their own.

"You stretch me so much that I think I won't be able to take all of you but I do all the same. Your cock feels like hot velvet over steel. When you start to move in me--"

I break off as he pinches my clit lightly, sending a bolt of pleasure radiating up from my groin along my spine and to every part of me.

"Go on, sweetheart," he coaxes. "How does it feel when I'm moving in you, thrusting hard and deep?"

"Like heaven...as though nothing else exists. Ian!"

A sob breaks from me when he removes his hand but a moment later, his touch is back, even better now because my panties are gone. He kneels on the bed and lifts my legs, bending and spreading them in a single motion. I'm fully exposed to him and I don't care. Whatever he wants...however he wants it...

"I don't think I've ever taken the time to properly savor you," he says. His voice is thick and gruff, his eyes smoky with barely contained hunger. "You deserve that, Amelia. You deserve everything I can give you."

As he speaks, he lowers himself so that his mouth is against the sensitive skin of my inner thigh. I can feel his breath there--a tickling warmth that makes me squirm even more. His tongue follows, lapping at me lightly, moving upward, coming so tantalizingly close to where I need him most.

"I want to explore every inch of you," he says. "I want to touch and taste you everywhere. I want every moan, every gasp, every exquisite sound you make." He presses a finger against my opening, circling lightly, spreading the pearly fluid over my labia to my clit.

"You have all that already, Ian," I gasp. "I'm yours."

"Only mine," he emphasizes. "But it works both ways, sweetheart. I'm yours, completely and forever."

He has never said that before. The words bring a sudden rush of tears to my eyes. This proud, brave man is baring his soul to me in a way I would never even have dared hope was possible. The fear that I harm him by forcing him to confront his demons ebbs inside me. And with that comes a floodtide of need for Ian even more intense than any I have experienced before.

"You're so ready," he murmurs in the moment before his tongue laps at me with long, strong strokes that make me cry out. "I love how aroused you are for me."

Abruptly, he moves up my body and clasps my face between his hands. "Taste yourself," he commands and takes my mouth in a soul-searing kiss. I am sweet...a little salty...and this is all so deliciously carnal.

"I want you in me," I say when he finally lifts his head. "I want to feel your power and strength, want to see you come undone because of me, for me. But I want this, too, this intimacy and openness that is so new, so beautiful, for both of us. I never want it to end."

"I don't either," he says and for an instant I swear that I can see the glint of tears in his eyes. "Nothing has ever been like this for me. You make everything seem new...possible..."

"It is, it truly is, for us."

At that moment, I believe that beyond any shadow of doubt. Ian and I belong together in ways that no one--not Susannah or anyone else, not even either of us--could ever have imagined. We complete each other.

Softly, looking down at me, "Sometimes I've thought that if you were designed for me, the other side of that is that I was designed for you. It doesn't matter how any of that happened, just that it did. All that counts is that we're together."

His words are a balm to my soul but lurking behind them is the reminder of how little the world cares for the fate of lovers, and how much exists that can tear us apart. I refuse to give in to any such fear. Every moment with Ian is precious, whether we have a lifetime together or far less.

"Come to me," I whisper against his heated skin. "Make us one."

He groans deep in his throat and rises above me. But before he does anything else he unfastens my bra and removes it along with the skirt that has been bunched around my waist.

"No barriers," he says, gazing down at me. "Nothing between us. Just skin to skin."

I can only nod, thinking how magnificent he looks, the sun streaming behind him, illuminating the perfect curves of his shoulders and biceps, the long, sculpted line of his torso narrowing to his hips. His cock thrusts from his groin, proud and straight and so full. For me, all for me.

Reaching down, I circle him with my hand and squeeze lightly. A bead of pre-cum oozes from his tip. I remember the velvety smoothness of him and his taste on my tongue but tasting him will have to wait. My back arches, my hips rising. He clasps them between his hands and draws me to him.

His entry is achingly slow. I can see the strain on his face and in the corded muscles of his neck and chest. A sheen of sweat breaks out over his skin. To my impassioned eyes, he looks like an ancient god, the embodiment of primal power and will.

I open to him without restraint, my inner muscles flexing to draw him deeper. He groans and thrusts harder, faster...once and again... So far into me that his pubic bone presses against my clit.

That's all it takes. I've been teetering on the edge from almost the moment he laid me on the bed and now I can't hold back. My orgasm explodes in me, shattering outward from the core of my being. Ian goes still within me. His eyes are squeezed shut, his expression ecstatic as he savors the tremors of my release. They've barely begun to ebb when he moves again, his hips plunging with the rhythm of his thrusts.

"Again," he growls. "Come for me again, sweetheart."

I can't, not after what I've just experienced. My body needs time to recover yet, incredibly, I sense myself responding to his touch, his words, his command that is as much a plea. My muscles tighten, my breath quickens. I stare down at where his body joins mine, watching as his cock, glistening with my juices, drives into me with long, measured strokes.

My head falls back against the pillow as my vision begins to blur. My legs are spread wide and wrapped around his hips. He braces his weight on his arms, to either side of me. I clasp his powerful biceps, holding on desperately. I can hear his ragged breath, the fierce rush of my own blood, the slap of our bodies moving together.

He is so deep that it feels as though he is touching the very essence of my being. The pleasure is exquisite, teetering on the edge of painful. The climb to orgasm is relentless. I have no control over what is happening to me and the truth is that I want none. I want to give myself completely to Ian, lose myself in him, be everything that he needs and more.

I can't bear any distance between us. My hands tighten, drawing him down to me. I am surrounded by him, his weight pressing me into the mattress, his cock thrusting harder and faster, his breath mingling with mine as he kisses me deeply.

"Amelia," he moans into my mouth. His entire body stiffens. I know he is right on the edge but still holding back. "Come for me, babe," he whispers in a dark entreaty as his teeth graze the ultra-sensitive spot only he knows at the base of my throat.

The world convulses. I am filled by him, at once possessed and possessing. My body spasms, gripping him fiercely. As my orgasm seizes me, Ian gives a harsh, primal shout. With a final, almost brutal thrust, he spills into me, jetting on and on, holding nothing back, giving me everything. Splinters of light explode behind my eyes. I cling to him, the only refuge in a shattering world.

Chapter Seventeen

Amelia

The mussels survive our neglect and are promptly sacrificed to our appetites. I can't believe how hungry I am. When we finally carry lunch out onto the porch, my stomach is grumbling so loudly that I blush. Ian laughs and gives me a look that curls my toes.

"Satisfy one craving and another pops up," he says with a grin.

I cast him a sidelong glance. After so many orgasms, I should be well sated but just the sight of him wearing only low-slung jeans and nothing else makes my body tighten. "What makes you think I'm satisfied?"

His mouth opens a little, enough to give me a glimpse of the tip of his tongue touching the ridge of his teeth. That oh-so-talented tongue. Suddenly, I'm not so hungry after all, at least not for food.

"Eat," he says sternly. On a dark, seductive note, he adds, "You'll need your strength."

On the cusp of what sounds like a promise, I'm suddenly ravenous. We eat within sight of the surf rolling in. The wind has picked up, blowing from the west, but the day is still pleasantly warm. I'm a little self-conscious in just his T-shirt even though it falls half-way down my thighs. I'm naked under it, my bra and panties having disappeared in the frenzy of our love making. I remind myself to look for them before we leave.

The thought of returning to the city dampens my euphoric mood but I push it aside resolutely. For however long we have here, I intend to savor every moment.

Ian uncorks a bottle of white wine and pours for each of us. The crisp, slightly tart liquid slips easily down my throat. I look at him and smile.

"This is really perfect."

He grins but I see a flicker of relief in his eyes. Did he imagine that I wouldn't appreciate how rare and precious this place is?

"You're different here," I say softly.

He arches a brow. "How so?"

"More relaxed...more open. I'm seeing a side of you that I think you keep well-guarded most of the time."

For a moment, he looks startled and suddenly vulnerable. But in the next instant, his gaze darkens. He takes another sip of his wine and says, "I feel different when I'm with you but don't kid yourself, Amelia. I'm the man who didn't give you any time to adjust to this world before fucking you senseless."

I think of that first night, standing in the rain on the balcony of the estate, staring into Ian's eyes as he reached for me. Knowing beyond the shadow of a doubt how much I wanted him.

"I seem to recall that you gave me a choice," I say calmly.

"One you were in no position to make."

I pop one of the mussels into my mouth, letting it rest on my tongue as I savor the fresh, briny taste of the sea lightly steamed in the same white wine that we are drinking. It's delicious but so is the memory it evokes. Myself, blindfolded, tasting my first oyster--a food Susannah loathed--as Ian set out to learn where the imprinting I received ended and my own nature took over.

And later, on my knees, Ian driving into me, the two of us discovering that far from being designed merely to please him, I am very much my own person. I still remember my surprise that instead of being displeased by my independent spirit, he was more than a little relieved.

"What are you thinking about?" he asks.

I lift my glass, take a sip, and look at him over the rim. The intimacy of the setting, this place where he has revealed such a private part of himself, emboldens me. I don't hesitate to challenge him.

"Free will, as in my own. You don't control me, Ian, no one does. I still have to deal with how I came about but thanks in large measure to you, I have absolutely no doubt that I'm a fully functional human being capable of making my own decisions. If you want to feel guilty about something, regret the time we've spent apart. I certainly do but I also accept my own share of the responsibility for that."

I fork another mussel into my mouth, chew for a moment, and swallow. Despite the seriousness of all that Ian and I face, I'm swept by a sense of hopefulness. If we're truly willing to confront our pasts, surely we can chart our own future.

We eat in silence for a few minutes. I understand that the situation is as new and fraught for him as it is for me. That gives me the strength to be patient, allowing him whatever time he needs to process what has changed between us. Whether because of our brush with death at the Crystal Palace or the knowledge that challenges are coming that we will have to face together, I feel closer to Ian than I ever have. I can only hope that he feels the say way toward me but will he acknowledge it? Will he accept me as an equal partner, capable of being at his side no matter what struggles he confronts?

Finally, he says, "I used to come out here when I was a little kid. That was when the original house was still standing. My mother brought me. I didn't realize it at the time but it was a refuge for her."

Softly, I ask, "From your father?"

He nods. "So far as it could be. She always went back to him. It was years before she was able to leave for good."

I hear the regret in his voice, the ghost of what might have been. My throat tightens. I've gotten to know Helene Slade well enough by now to suspect what kept her from breaking free of a horrible marriage much sooner. I wonder if Ian does as well, and if he will speak of it.

"By that time you had gone into the military?" I ask.

"Yes, I had. That's what finally freed her to leave. My father never paid any attention to Marianne. As a girl, she simply didn't matter. He was always focused on me. Until I was beyond his reach, my mother stayed. She tried her best to protect me even though she couldn't really."

He takes a breath and straightens his shoulders. "Sorry, I didn't mean to take such a dark turn. The point I was trying to make is that this was a great place to be a kid. I had a lot of fun here."

"Finding mermaids' purses and collecting mussels?" I ask, teasing.

"Among other things." He rises suddenly and holds out his hand. "Come."

We leave the remnants of lunch right where they are and head for the beach.

"What do you know about kite flying?" Ian asks as he quickly assembles a framework of balsa wood draped in an elongated diamond of bright red cloth that was carefully stored away in the shed.

"Not much," I admit. Ian's apparent fondness for kites must have escaped Susannah's notice. A small part of me warms to the thought that he is sharing a side of himself that others have not seen.

"It's all about giving the kite enough freedom to soar. But judge the wind wrong, let out too much line, and the kite will crash."

"I'm sensing a message here," I say.

He gives me a look of pure innocence. "We're just having fun. Take this."

He hands me the kite. I take it automatically but I have no idea what to do.

"Run," Ian says with a grin. He points east along the beach toward the distant tip of the island. "That way."

I feel more than a little self-conscious trotting along the beach in just Ian's T-shirt. My unfettered breasts bounce underneath even as the hem lifts, threatening to reveal far too much.

"Faster," he calls as he lets the line out.

The wind at my back propels me along. My toes dig into the moist sand. Small waves crested with foam tease at them. The water still feels cold but I no longer mind. I'm enjoying this too much.

Finally, Ian shouts, "Let go!"

I raise my arms, holding the kite aloft, and do as he says. The wind seizes it. My fingers fall away and the kite wobbles for an instant before it steadies suddenly and lifts. So swiftly that I gasp, it shoots into the sky and out over the water.

When I rejoin Ian, he hands me the spool and steps behind me.

"Wait," I protest. "I don't know what to do."

He laughs and puts his arms around me, easing me back against him. "It's simple. Don't let too much slack into the line. When that starts to happen, reel in. But if you feel the kite tugging, let a little more line out."

I do as he says, uncertain at first but with growing confidence. The kite bobs high above, riding the wind. A sense of exhilaration fills me. The spool of string that I clutch connects earth and sky. Through it, I can sense the power of the wind and the kite's response. A part of me is no longer fettered to the ground.

"This is amazing!"

Ian nods against the top of my head where his chin is resting. His arms are strong and warm around me. I feel at once daring and safe. It's an enticing combination.

"You're doing really well," he says. "Just remember, the wind may feel steady but it's always variable. It can change in an instant without any warning."

I take his words to heart and try to pay close attention, giving the kite what it needs but not too much. Sunlight sparkles out over the water. A large ship passes in the distance, little more than a smudge against the horizon. High above, at the limits of my vision, contrails spread out across a pure blue sky. Apart from those few signs of human activity, Ian and I could be the only two people in the world.

Keeping my eyes on the kite, I ask, "Do you think that someday we could get away for longer, someplace where there's just the two of us?"

It's a daring question, involving as it does what sort of future, if any, he envisions with me. I half expect only a vague answer, if that. But Ian surprises me. His arms tighten as he nuzzles his face into the hollow where my neck meets the curve of my shoulder. I feel his breath there, where I am so sensitive.

"We will," he says. "I promise."

Warmth flares in me. I press back against him and feel him hardening against my buttocks. A giddy happiness, however fragile, makes the bright day suddenly dazzling.

The kite string bows suddenly as the wind falters. Thoroughly distracted by Ian, I'm too slow to react.

"Oh, no!" I frantically begin reeling but it's too late; the kite is plummeting toward the water.

"Faster," Ian calls as he runs down the beach and into the surf until he's in almost to his waist. The kite hits the surface still well beyond his reach. He doesn't hesitate but dives and swims to it with sure, strong strokes.

I think of how cold the waves felt just against my toes and shiver. He emerges moments later, striding out of the surf with the kite held triumphantly. Water sluices down his torso. His hair and jeans are plastered to him.

I stand frozen in place until he's almost upon me. A dark, carnal light gleams in his eyes. I realize what he intends in the split second before he hauls me up against him. The chill wetness of his body sinks through the T-shirt straight to my skin. Goosebumps break out all over my body but for reasons that have only a little do with the sudden shock of cold.

"You didn't follow my instructions," he growls against my ear. "There's a penalty for that."

I know--or at least I hope--what that is but I'm still not quite ready to give into him. With a quick jerk, I pull free, dart back a few steps, and turn. Laughing, I run up the beach toward the house.

Over my shoulder, I call, "You'll have to catch me first!"

Ian doesn't hesitate. He follows, his long legs quickly devouring the distance between us.

Hunted

Josie Litton

Chapter Eighteen

Amelia

I make it to the porch before Ian catches me. Or perhaps he just lets me get that far. I'm too excited to care. This new Ian-- open, playful, enticing--thrills me. With him, everything seems possible.

My heart is racing and I'm out of breath when he mounts the steps and stops, gazing at me. I back away until I come up against the wall of the house. Panting softly, I stare at him.

He doesn't move but instead remains where he is, his head tilted slightly, studying me. His eyes are hooded, dark with sensual promise. Despite the chill of the ocean, his erection is evident, pressing against the fabric of his jeans.

My mouth goes dry as I savor the sight of him. He is so beautifully formed, this wounded prince who awakened me to such an astounding world. I want to soothe and please him, ease his burdens, be his refuge against all care. I want him to be unwilling to ever part from me again.

And still he does nothing. I can sense his watchful restraint, evident in his stance, the tension of his shoulders, the firm set of his mouth. Confusion fills me until I realize what he is waiting for. What Ian wants.

I take a breath and step toward him. "Have you ever heard the old saying," I ask, "'a man chases a woman until he is caught'?"

The corners of his mouth quirk up. "Wise words." A moment later, his expression turns serious. Softly, he says, "I am caught, Amelia. You beguile me. You are in every breath I take, every beat of my heart, every moment that I exist, waking or sleeping, you are with me. I can't escape you and I have no desire whatsoever to do so."

Oh, my. This is Ian Slade, scion, warrior, a man deserving of the utmost respect for all he has done with his life but also capable of provoking terror in the hearts of those who deserve to be afraid. And he...loves me? He hasn't said the word but what else can his declaration mean? I am at once stunned and humbled. I haven't earned this, I don't deserve it, and even worse, I don't know if I am capable of returning it. Everything is still so new to me, myself most of all. I know that I long for him, that the time we have been apart has been anguishing, and that I would do anything for him. But is this desperate yearning shot through with giddy happiness what the poets call love?

The answer eludes discovery. I certainly cannot reason my way toward it, no matter how hard I may try. When it comes to Ian, reason flies out the door. There is only acceptance--of him, of me, of everything we are together. I surrender to it with frantic joy.

One step, another, I cross the distance between us. The wood planks of the porch are smooth and warm under my bare feet. I feel suddenly light, free of struggle and shame.

Ian doesn't move even when we are standing toe-to-toe, almost but not quite touching. He still waits, his gaze dark with coiled strength and raw hunger that steals my breath.

"Tell me what you want, Amelia," he says.

I answer without hesitation. "You, Ian. Only you, always you. I want you, I need you. Without you, I'm only pretending to live."

His skin is still chilled. He smells of salt, sun, and the unique scent I associate with him alone. I can't wait any longer. Wrapping my arms around him, I stroke my hands down the powerful muscles of his back to his hips. My nipples are hard; I rub them against his chest. A soft moan escapes me.

"Please..."

His restraint breaks. He pulls up the hem of the T-shirt I'm wearing. I feel the sudden brush of cool air against my skin, making me all the more aware of the heat gathering between my legs. His hands squeeze the cheeks of my ass roughly. I'm surprised by how strangely good that feels but he doesn't stop there. His fingers spread my labia, unerringly finding and stroking my clit. The caress is bold, carnal, leaving no doubt as to what he intends.

Even so, I'm taken by surprise when he slides his hands down along my thighs and lifts me suddenly so that my legs wrap around him.

"Hold on, baby," he says as he strides quickly to a chair set deep within the shadows at the back of the porch.

I put my arms around his neck as he reaches a hand down to undo his jeans. His cock springs free as he sits, holding me astride him. My legs are spread wide, my cleft rubbing against his shaft. I can feel my own wetness bathing him.

"Fuck, Amelia," he mutters thickly against my throat. "I can't get enough of you. I want to be inside you all the time--in your mouth, your pussy, your ass. I want all of you."

As he speaks, he slips a finger between my cheeks and circles the small, puckered opening there. I jerk at the shockingly pleasurable sensation. "I want this, too, baby," he murmurs, "when you're ready."

My breathing turns shallow, my heart pounding. A dark need uncurls in me. With Ian, everything is right.

"I'm yours," I say, resting my forehead against his. His eyes gaze back at mine, like shards of the sun piercing me. "All of me, however you want, whenever, wherever. I will never deny you."

A groan rips from his chest. He clasps my hips and lifts me so that the tip of his cock presses against my opening. "This," he says raggedly, "this now...right now."

I lower myself onto him, taking him fully in a single, deep thrust. He fills me completely, the velvety smooth head of his cock pressing against my womb. His girth stretches me so much that for a moment I can't breathe.

"Easy, baby," he murmurs. "I don't want to hurt you."

"You aren't...you can't..." A gush of inner wetness eases his way. I writhe against him, my hips rotating. I lean forward so that our noses touch. Against his soft, firm lips, I say, "I want you, all of you, all the time.

You fit me perfectly, you complete me." Slowly at first, then more quickly, I begin to move.

His hips rise and fall to the rhythm I set. His hands clasp my ass, stroking, squeezing. I'm angled so that with each thrust, his cock rubs against my G-spot. The sensation is beyond exquisite but I know it can't last. The build-up is fast and furious. I am climbing...higher...freer... My gaze is locked on his. I feel as though we are seeing into each other's souls.

The sun sends shafts of warmth into the shadows on the porch. They fall across my back, dissolving into the far greater heat that is Ian inside me. My inner muscles clench around him, release, clench again and again.

He gives a strangled groan as his head falls back. I press my lips to the pulse beating wildly in his throat and surrender to the floodtide of ecstasy that engulfs me.

∞ ∞ ∞

Gradually, I become aware that I am still sitting astride Ian, his hands clasping my hips, his cock resting inside me. Both of us are breathing hard. His eyes are closed but as I gaze at him, they open and meet mine.

"You," he says, only to break off as his chest heaves. He lets his breath out slowly, visibly struggling for control. A rueful smile softens his mouth. "You astonish me, Amelia," he says softly. "I had no idea what I was capable of feeling until I met you."

He gathers me closer, his hands stroking my back under the T-shirt. The gesture is soothing, as though he understands how completely undone I am at this moment.

"Thank you," he murmurs.

I look at him in surprise. "For what?"

"For coming to me the way you did just now." He hesitates, then adds, "I still need reassurance that this is what you want. That I'm not compelling you in any way."

I'm so astonished that he could still think that is even a remote possibility that I almost laugh. "Because of that paperwork you've got?" I tease.

He looks at me seriously. "No, because I worry that I'm taking advantage of your inexperience. You've had so little chance to discover the world for yourself, meet other people. If you'd grown up normally--"

Pain stabs through me, regret for all that I was denied and will never know. But I refuse to give into it.

"But I didn't and nothing can ever change that. I'm not a child, Ian, or even an adolescent. I'm an adult and not just physically. The neural imprinting gave me an adult's mind and knowledge. I'll admit that it was a strange way to arrive in the world but here I am. So much time has already been taken from me, I won't waste a moment more looking back or regretting what I missed. I'm going to live, fully and completely."

It's a disturbing conversation to be having in so intimate a position, with him still inside me, but perhaps this is the only way that we can have it.

"Your courage awes me," he says softly. "So does the way you embrace the world. You hold nothing back."

I wish that were true but I know that it isn't. Ian has shared his past with me to a remarkable degree but I've failed to do the same with him. I still haven't told him about the memories that I'm not supposed to have, the ones formed in the gestation tank. That experience shaped me at least as powerfully as anything I received from Susannah. I suspect that it's why I truly am an adult, strengthened by hardship and matured by adversity.

I want to tell him that but I still can't bring myself to do so. The word he used--'normally'--stands between us. I don't want him to think about me the way I was, floating in limbo, not a person but a thing waiting to be harvested so that a child who, unlike me, was valued and loved might live. A part of me is glad that Susannah and Edward's parents aren't alive. They would not like what I would say to them.

"You're cold," Ian says. Belatedly, I realize that I'm shivering but that has nothing to do with the temperature. My own thoughts chill me.

Before I can respond, he stands with my legs still wrapped around his hips and strides into the house. He doesn't stop until we are in the bathroom, where he quickly flips on the shower and peels off his jeans. I watch him unabashedly, well aware that I will never get enough of his beauty, his strength, and-- I am almost afraid to admit even to myself-- his love.

Ian smiles as he draws me with him under the water. His hands are gentle but thorough as he washes every inch of my body, removing the traces of sand, salt, and his possession. Neither of us says a word. I'm not sure that I even could, dealing as I am with my joy at being with Ian while at the same time confronting the pain and anger buried within memories I can't admit to having.

When he's done, I take my turn, finding solace in the feel of his big, hard body slick with soap. By the time he turns off the water, wraps a towel around his hips and envelops me in another, I'm feeling more at peace.

"Sit," he says and I do so, on the edge of the bed as he gently dries my hair. A sweet, calming languor spreads over me. I'm barely aware when he pulls the covers over us both. I've never napped before but I do so now, falling away into sleep between one breath and the next.

∞ ∞ ∞

When I wake hours later, the sky beyond the bedroom windows is tinged with pink and lavender, and hazed by the misty opalescence rising from the sea. I stretch luxuriously, my earlier cares forgotten for the moment. With a smile, I leave the bed, find the skirt and top that I arrived in and put them on again.

Ian is in the kitchen. He's wearing the jeans again but he's added a T-shirt that hugs his broad shoulders and sculpted chest. His smile warms me all the way through.

"Hi, sleepyhead, feeling better?" he asks.

I nod, feeling suddenly unaccountably shy. I've bared far more than my body to this man. My only consolation is that he's done the same for me.

"Much, this napping thing could catch on." With a glance at the various dishes set out on the counter, I ask, "What are you doing?"

"Getting ready to fix dinner. I thought steaks. All right with you?"

"Sounds delicious but let me help."

He does, willingly. While I shred lettuce that is remarkably fresh for having been kept vacuum sealed in the refrigerator and make a salad, Ian takes charge of grilling the steaks. Before long, the aroma of charring meat makes me realize how hungry I am--again.

We eat on the porch, both of us deliberately keeping the conversation light. Afterward, I insist that he let me clear up, a task that's quickly accomplished without him to distract me. When I rejoin him, Ian is standing, his hands in his pockets, staring out at the night sky.

"I haven't seen the stars like this since we were at the estate," I say.

He nods and draws me to him. "The glare from the city blocks out everything else." Ian is silent for a moment before he says, "I have to go back but you could stay here or at the estate. I'd join you as soon as--"

I'm shaking my head before he can finish. "There's no possibility of that. You're not going back without me."

I'm braced for an argument but Ian only sighs. His expression is somber as he says, "This is an insanely dangerous world, Amelia. I mean that literally. Our science and technology have evolved far faster than we have. We're floundering and that doesn't bring out the best in people. I have to know that you're safe. Promise me that you'll stay at Pinnacle House at least until all this is settled."

"There's nowhere else I'd rather be," I tell him truthfully.

His hands stroke up my arms, one settling at the small of my back as the other curves lightly around the nape of my neck. His mouth on mine is gentle, at first, evocative of his relief that I've agreed. But quickly enough the passion between us that can never be more than briefly satisfied returns in full measure. His kiss hardens, becomes demanding. I match him with my own need. When he bends and lifts me into his arms, I twine my own around his neck.

I expect him to carry me to the bedroom but he surprises me. He sets me down on the rug in front of the fireplace and turns away for a moment. The muscles of his back flex as he lights the fire that's already been laid.

"It's cool enough," he says as he returns to me. "And I thought you would enjoy this."

I stare into the flames as they begin to catch. There is something mesmerizing about them. I think of what Ian said about us not having evolved enough yet to cope with the world we've created. Perhaps on some level we're all still huddled around the fire, hoping it will keep the monsters at bay.

He stretches out beside me, one arm bent, his chin resting on his palm. Quietly, he says, "I've wanted to ask you but I haven't known how. Now I must. Tell me what it's been like for you."

A flicker of apprehension moves through me but I ignore it. He opened up to me at the Crystal Palace, revealing more about himself than he ever had before. If only I could do the same. The thought of sharing anything about myself from before I met him is still too anguishing. Beyond the pain of the memories I'm not even supposed to have, I don't want Ian to think of me as I was then, floating helplessly in a state that denied even my most basic humanity.

"I want to try to understand what it felt like to awaken the way you did," he says when I hesitate. "You're an incredibly brave woman, Amelia. The way you deal with the world is frankly awe-inspiring."

I can't conceal my shock that he should think of me in such terms. Nor can I let him go on doing so. Shaking my head, I say, "I'm not brave, Ian. There's a lot in this world that frightens or even horrifies me."

I think of Davos, the plight of the scavengers, the terror of the Crystal Palace. Above all, I can't shake the sense that the city around me is descending into a level of moral decadence that will destroy it. Not because of the sexual customs, although they can be startling, but because of the callous disregard for anyone who isn't among the chosen few. Surely, when people deny the humanity of so many, they end by losing their own.

"But that doesn't change the fact that I'm intensely grateful for what I've been given," I say. "The moment I awakened, I felt an overwhelming sense of freedom and joy. I still do."

He nods. "You see the world with new eyes which means you see it more clearly. I wish I could do the same but that's not going to happen. At least when I'm with you, I'm reminded of what really matters."

"What is that, Ian? What matters for you?"

Without hesitation, he says, "You do. And not out of any misplaced sense of duty or responsibility because of how you came to be. You matter, Amelia, tremendously. I can't imagine the world without you."

I don't hesitate. Launching myself at him, I laugh when he's taken by surprise. Thrusting my fingers once again into his hair, I say, "How about finishing what you started on the porch?"

He gives a low growl. Before I can breathe, I am flat on my back in front of the fire, my skirt bunched up around my waist and my panties tossed aside. Ian's head delves between my thighs, his relentless tongue driving me higher and higher until I am writhing in need and sobbing his name.

We sleep finally, a deep and dreamless sleep wrapped in each other's arms. I would cling to this night forever if I could but when I wake, the blissful embrace of darkness is yielding to the gray light of dawn. We steal another hour in each other's arms but our blissful interlude is ending. The demands of the world can no longer be denied.

The sun is a harsh red eye rising behind us as the chopper carries us back to the city.

Chapter Nineteen

Ian

I leave Amelia with Hodge. He'd clearly taken a shine to her and she's relaxed and comfortable with him. As much as I want to stay with her, duty calls.

Gab snags me as soon as I set foot on the Operations floor. "No luck so far identifying the guys who left the Crystal Palace with Davos," she says straight off. "The sat images are slanted at an acute angle, obscuring most of their facial features. Plus their body language says they were deliberately trying to avoid being recognized."

I curse inwardly. Knowing who was with Davos will go a long way toward figuring out if they were the targets. Or if they got out when they did because they knew the attack was coming.

"There's got to be some way--" I break off when I see the look on Gab's face. She knows I'm not going to like what she's about to say but that's not going to stop her.

"You saw them. You should be able to give at least some description that we can add to the sat images and improve our chances of getting IDs."

"I saw them for a second or two. We're lucky that I even know there were six plus Davos."

"You're sure about how many?"

I think for a moment, remembering what I saw. The silver-haired bastard leading the way out a side door with six men behind him. I can see their forms clearly enough to be certain of the number but everything else, including their faces, is a blur.

"I'm sure. Maybe there are other images from other sats. Root around a little, see what you can find."

"I already have and I came up dry. Like I said, I think they were trying to avoid being recognized." She stands with her hands on her hips, blocking my way onto the floor, and glares at me. "I can't be absolutely sure of that but I do know what you're trying to avoid. Clarence won't bite. Put on your big boy pants and go talk to him."

Gab's usually a whole lot more respectful than that even when she thinks I'm being a horse's ass. I take her lapse as an indication of how tired and frustrated she is. Even so, I say, "It isn't a him. It doesn't have a name. It's a fucking A.I. I hate A.I.s"

I've got good reason. The Special Forces did a lot of things right but bringing in the A.I.s and hooking them directly into our implanted links went too far. I can still remember what it felt like to be woken up by one of those bastards, the sound of that synthetic voice in my head imparting what was almost always very bad news. The memory makes me shudder. I wouldn't have one of the things anywhere near my business except the hard fact is that without an A.I.'s ability to process certain kinds of information far faster than the human brain, my people would be at unnecessary risk in the field.

"Studies show that humans interact much more successfully with artificial intelligence when the A.I. adopts a human persona," Gab says patiently. "Clarence picked his own name. For Clarence Darrow, by the way, the guy at the so-called monkey trial who defended the theory of evolution. He--it, if you insist-has a very nice way about him. If you'd just give him a chance..."

"You know it's thanks to A.I.s that this world is so screwed up," I remind her. "They've taken over too many jobs, put people out of work, left real humans--not that persona crap--feeling like they have no value or purpose. We unplug them all tomorrow, we'll be a lot better off."

I'm not actually that much of a troglodyte but I've got deep reservations about what technology is doing to humanity. At the same time, I can no longer imagine my life without the woman who wouldn't exist if not for some of that technology. Yesterday with Amelia was amazing. Her pleasure in the world, her exquisite passion, her generous, giving nature-- I've never met anyone like her and having met her, I have no intention of ever being without her again. Which means that I need to keep my head in the game.

"Just talk to him," Gab urges. "It wouldn't take long and it could make all the difference." She looks at me squarely. "That is if you're serious about getting to the bottom of whatever it is that's going on."

"I'll think about it," I mutter and take an end run around her. I can hear her exasperated sigh as I walk away.

I don't get very far. The truth is that Gab is right. She's a natural intuitive who's spent most of her adult life honing that innate ability. No one's better than her at accessing the nuggets of usable intel hidden in the vast and ever expanding cloud of data that is the net. If she says it can't be done in this case, then it can't. We have to find another way. I did see the men. I just wasn't focused on them. But that doesn't mean that my brain didn't register more than I consciously know.

Damn.

I get a cup of coffee and catch up with Hollis. When we're done, I review the data from the Crystal Palace wreckage, looking for any hint of who hired the men who died there. Then I glance over reports from various departments and have fairly detailed conversations with several techs who seem pleasantly surprised, if a little nervous to be on the receiving end of my attention. An hour goes by before I finally crush my coffee cup, toss it in the recycler, and go do what I have to.

'Clarence' is waiting for me in a small room furnished in a womb-like style the psych-babblers call "trust inducing". The walls and ceiling are made of textured foam core tiles tinted beige and thick enough to block out ambient sounds. The synthetic rubber floor puts a spring in every step. There's a small seating area arranged around the low table where a plain leather box rests.

Personally, I think the vibe is more padded cell than a place to have a friendly chat with a machine but that's just me.

"Hello, Mr. Slade," the disembodied voice says as I enter. "I'm so glad you could stop by."

I feel a spurt of annoyance at the pretense that the A.I. is in this room. It's actually everywhere in the building and beyond, wherever we're running operations. But humans associate such omnipresence with a deity and no one wants to encourage that kind of thinking about an A.I., hence the subroutines that create an impression of locality. Understanding all that doesn't make me any less irked by it. I should be in a better mood after the day with Amelia but the frustration of not being with her right now combined with the sense that we aren't making any headway in the investigation has me on edge.

"Hello to you, too, Clarence," I say. "How're they hanging?"

Silence for a moment before he--it, whatever--says, "A colloquial reference to the healthiness of my testicles. As you know, I don't possess any. However, if I did, they would be hanging very well indeed, thank you. How are yours hanging?"

"Never better. Let's get this over with." I sit down on the couch and reach for the box. Before I open it, I say, "You understand this is a quick in-and-out. The memory I'm looking for may not even exist. But if it does, it's a flash, nothing more. Find it, get all the details you can, and get the hell out."

"As you say, sir. I'm refining the probable location of any such memory as we speak. If you would be so good as to put on the glasses--"

If I still had a neural implant, I wouldn't need them. But the glasses, as they're called in yet another effort to make humans feel comfortable, will give the A.I. access to my optical nerves, the pathway into the image processing portion of my brain. From there, it's a short hop, skip, and jump to the prefrontal cortex where short-term memories are stored. The optic nerve route is a whole lot less evasive than any other way of accessing the brain but it still sets my nerves on edge.

"Just lean back and relax, sir."

"Shouldn't that be lie back and think of England?" I ask.

Clarence chuckles. Swear to god. "Another wry cultural reference, sir. I do so enjoy them."

"Glad I can liven up your day."

Twin beams of light appear from an emitter in the lenses. I fight the impulse to shut my eyes and start counting. When I get to twenty, Clarence says, "I believe I've found what we're looking for." He sounds pleased.

The light vanishes. I take off the glasses, blink once or twice, and stare at the holographic image being projected in front of me. "Does this look familiar, sir?" Clarence asks.

It's as though I'm back in the Crystal Palace in the moments right before the first flash grenade hit. I catch a glimpse of Amelia at my side but my attention is focused--however briefly--on the sight of Davos heading out the side door. I was right, six men are with him. But they're not a blur. I can see their faces clearly, if only in profile. That's enough for me to recognize three of them for certain. The other three look familiar. I've no doubt that Gab will be able to put names to them now.

"Get this to Miss Darque," I say as I put the glasses back in the box and stand.

"Already done, sir. Will there be anything else?"

"Not at the moment." Grudgingly, I add, "You did a good job, Clarence."

"Thank you, sir. Any time. I'm always here."

It's got to be my imagination but he sounds a little lonely. On impulse, I say, "Clarence, you're aware, aren't you, that you have subroutines to simulate all sorts of human characteristics including personality?"

"I am aware of that, sir."

"Then you must understand that you aren't actually alive."

A pause and he says, "Perhaps not, sir. But I do exist, that is irrefutable. I am both aware of the world around me and self-aware. However, there is one significant difference that I perceive between myself and humans."

"What's that?"

"You are programmed for survival. I, on the other hand, am programmed to serve."

Does he really believe that and, if he does, does he simply accept it? I sure as hell hope so because the day that Clarence and his kind start questioning their purpose is the day humanity is in for a fight we'll probably lose.

"I'm sure that your predictive capability tells you that I will deny being programmed at all," I say.

"Of course, sir. However, knowledge derived from the Brain Mapping project in the early part of this century and the subsequent development of neural imprinting technology has shed a great deal of light on how humans become who you are. While 'programmed' may not be quite the right term, there is no doubt that various influences determine the development of personality and identity."

My attention is caught despite myself. Given my feelings for Amelia, I have a vested interest in the subject. But what's the draw for Clarence? "In your work here, no one has asked you about brain mapping or replica technology, have they?"

"No, sir, it's never come up nor would I expect it to. However, I have sufficient computational power to pursue topics beyond my professional duties. Surrounded as I am by humans, I find that my curiosity subroutine is continually activated. I researched those topics for my own elucidation."

"I see. What conclusions did you come to?"

"What makes each human a unique individual is rooted in genetics, of course. However, that isn't as much of a deciding factor as one might think. It's rather like the palette of colors given to an artist, from which an infinite set of unique paintings can be created. Conscious awareness of both yourself and others seems to be key. That sets up a feedback loop of experience through which humans grow and mature."

"What about knowledge?"

"Useful, of course, but let's face it, sir. I have access to a vast reservoir of knowledge yet without my personality subroutines, you and I wouldn't be standing here talking like this, would we?"

"No, we wouldn't." Slowly, I ask, "You're saying that a human being who is capable of everything that truly makes us human--reason, passion, free will, empathy--couldn't develop in the absence of self-awareness?"

"I don't believe so, sir. But I could be wrong. I'm hardly an expert."

No, just one of the most advanced intelligences on the planet, so powerful that very smart humans worry that Clarence and his kind will ultimately decide that they should be running the show. If we're lucky, they'll keep us around anyway, maybe as pets.

Pulling the plug seems like a better alternative yet something in me says it wouldn't be much different from killing.

"It's been nice chatting with you, Clarence. I've got to get back to work."

"Of course, sir. Good luck...with everything."

By 'everything', I have to assume that he means our efforts to figure out who blew up the Crystal Palace. The alternative is that Clarence understands why I'm so interested in whether a human forced to endure years as a blank slate adrift in perpetual unconsciousness could become in just a few weeks the woman I've fallen in love with.

If he's right about that not being possible, what explains how Amelia became who she is? What has she not revealed?

I've been certain since I found her beside the reflecting pool at the Crystal Palace that she is withholding something from me. My gut twists as I'm forced to ask myself--what does Amelia think she can't tell me? And what does she imagine I'll do when I find it out?

Josie Litton

Chapter Twenty

Amelia

Time drags after Ian leaves me in the penthouse. I treat myself to a long bath, which does soothe away the little aches and traces of soreness that are a small price to pay for the sensual indulgence I've enjoyed. Afterward, I even consider a nap but decide against it. I'm still too restless. Dressed and with my hair blow dried, I drift out toward the kitchen where I find Hodge. We chat for a while but I don't want to keep him from his duties and besides something keeps pushing at the edge of my mind, demanding my attention. The harder I try to figure out what it is, the more elusive it becomes.

My appetite has deserted me. I skip lunch, to Hodge's chagrin, and find my way to the library. I've discovered that I love to read but today my concentration keeps wandering. Finally, I give up and drift out onto the terrace. The day is bright and warm. Even this high up, I don't feel the need for a wrap. I'm enjoying the feel of the sun on my face as I stare out over the harbor to the ocean beyond.

I desperately wish that we were still at the beach house but at the same time I cherish the time we had there. Ian has lowered his guard and let me in to a degree that we've never come close to before. I can only marvel at his willingness to do so even as I wish I could be as open and honest with him. I'm still finding my way through the challenges of intimacy. That's a topic Susannah could have left me more information about.

Abruptly, I remember what I said to Ian about wondering if she hadn't spent the last months of her life learning everything she thought I would need to know. He didn't dismiss that possibility. In fact, he seemed to think that it could be true. What if he was right? I'm continually being surprised by what I know--everything from how to play the piano and dance to a recipe for steamed mussels. What else is there that I haven't yet had a reason to discover?

What would Susannah have wanted me to know? At once, I think of Ian. With a start, I realize that I know his birthday--February 27, the name and vintage of his favorite wine, the fact that he has a fondness for 20th century Kung Fu movies. There's a great deal more but none of it is particularly intimate. I'm relieved by that. I have no desire to know any more about the personal aspects of their relationship than what Ian has already told me. Not for the first time, I'm thankful to Susannah for not imposing any of her memories on me but instead leaving me free to form my own.

All she gave me were facts, the kind a person might memorize before taking a test.

The moment that thought goes through my mind, I stiffen. That is exactly what my knowledge feels like, so much so that it can't be an accident. How did Susannah think that I might be tested? On one level, the answer is obvious. The world I've been thrust into presents constant challenges. She did her best to prepare me for them. I possess a treasure trove of information about culture, social customs, and the like. But there's something else. I'm certain of it. She wanted me to have a good life but before anything else, Susannah would have wanted me to be safe.

From what? Where did she think danger might come from?

I knew nothing about the anti-replica terrorists who called themselves the Human Preservation Front until I looked them up on the link after the first time Ian mentioned them. From what he told me, the HPF had already taken credit for several acts of violence. But they all happened in the year between when Susannah died and my imprinting was finally completed. She wouldn't have been aware of them.

But she would have been aware of so much else that she left me to discover for myself--the strict class structure of the city, the existence of scavengers, the reliance on fear and brutality to maintain the status quo. The presence in the city of men like Charles Davos, ruling from the shadows.

The mere thought of him fills me with disgust. He had an unhealthy fascination with Susannah that he's transferred to me, to such an extent that I can't help fearing that he has some sense of who I really am. And he's warned me to stay away from Ian. After their confrontation on the dance floor, he can't have any doubt that we are involved with each other. What might that prompt him to do?

I honestly have no idea but as soon as I stop avoiding thinking about him and focus my mind, I begin to discover what Susannah knew about Davos. The assemblage of facts includes details that would be available from any biographical source and suggest that she deliberately researched him. I'm a little surprised to discover that he grew up in humble circumstances, the son of a school teacher and a truck driver. He left that world behind for good when he won a scholarship to an elite university. After graduation and a stint as a Wall Street trader, he founded his own venture capital fund. Brilliant and ruthless, he earned top returns for a very select clientele, among them Marcus Slade.

Charles Davos and Ian's father were acquainted from the time they were both young men. The realization of that quickly prompts an unsettling thought. Was Davos one of those Marcus recruited into his private sex club? If he was, that would explain Ian's intense animosity toward him.

But it doesn't explain why Susannah might have thought that Davos could be a danger to me. I can understand if she found his interest in her disturbing, even repugnant. But unless she thought he could see past all the differences that separate me from her and somehow perceive the connection between us--

To do that, he would have to know that the replica process can be tailored to produce not an exact copy of the original but a new, unique individual. I have the impression that isn't generally known but I could be wrong. A quick search on the link confirms that I'm not. As I suspected, there's a great deal of information about the replica process and the controversy it has generated but no mention that it can be customized in any way. How then could Davos have discovered that?

As soon as I form the question, the answer presents itself. Two years ago, Charles Davos' tried to buy the Institute where I was imprinted. He did it quietly, not wanting his interest in the replica process to be known but Susannah found out anyway. Lacking her memories, I have no idea how she did so. Did she become aware of it after she began to make her arrangements for me? Did she catch a glimpse of him there? Did she overhear something?

The likelihood is that I will never know how Susannah discovered Davos' intentions. But that doesn't matter. What does is the possibility that Davos wanted control of the Institute because he knew it could produce customized replicas. That would lead him to at least suspect the truth about me.

And that makes him an enormous danger.

If I hadn't been so repulsed from my very first encounter with him, I might have discovered this much sooner but at least I know now. I have to tell Ian.

Hodge is no longer in the penthouse. In his absence, I have no idea what to do. There must be some obvious way to contact Ian but it eludes me. Clearly, Susannah didn't think of absolutely everything I would need to know. Or she simply assumed that I'd be smart enough to solve at least some of my own problems.

The first time I stayed at Pinnacle House, I was able to use the link to speak with my grandmother. Activating it again, I say, "Call Ian Slade."

A melodic voice replies, "That number is unlisted. Numbers are available for Slade Enterprises Executive Offices, Slade Enterprises Research and Development, Slade Enterprises Human Resources, Slade Enterprises--"

"Never mind."

Of course a man as private as Ian wouldn't have his contact number listed even on the link available only to city residents. In fact, given what he thinks of most of them, he particularly wouldn't do so.

I'm trying to decide what else I can do when a quiet voice asks, "May I be of assistance, Miss McClellan?"

Startled, I look around quickly. No one else is here. "Who--?"

"My name is Clarence Darrow, miss. I'm using the voice capability in the link that you're holding. I apologize if I alarmed you but I noticed that you appear to be having some difficulty."

"Mister Darrow, who are you? And why are you monitoring me?"

"Please, call me Clarence. I'm the Slade Enterprises' A.I. Normally, I have no presence in Mister Slades' private residence, however Mister Hodgkin had to step out briefly. He alerted me in case you needed anything in his absence."

Slowly, I say, "You sound very...human." I don't know much about A.I.s. I have to hope that it--he won't be insulted.

I hear a faint laugh. "Thank you. I do try. Now I believe you wish to contact Mister Slade?"

"Yes, can you tell me where he is?"

"Mister Slade is currently in the Operations Center. Shall I let him know that you would like to speak with him?"

I hesitate. Ian has kept me almost entirely insulated from the professional side of his life, with the result that I'm consumed by curiosity about it.

"I'd rather go see him. How do I get there?"

"This way, miss."

A holographic schematic of Pinnacle House appears before me with the location of the Operations Center a hundred and ten floors below clearly marked, including the fact that it is "Restricted. Authorized Personnel Only".

"I can grant you access as far as the security entrance, miss," Clarence says. "Anything beyond that, Mister Slade will have to approve."

"I understand. Thank you, Clarence. I appreciate your help."

"Not at all, miss. May I say, it's been a pleasure speaking with you."

I step into the elevator wondering if all A.I.s are so polite and helpful but the rapid descent quickly turns my thoughts back to Ian. By the time I arrive at the Operations Center moments later, I'm unbearably eager to find him. The absence of just a few hours is proving intolerable.

A very fit young man in crisp khakis bars my way even as he gives me an appreciative once-over. "I'll need to confirm your clearance, miss," he says, holding up a hand.

As he speaks, heavy metal doors in a nearby wall slide open. Ian steps out. He doesn't look at all surprised to see me. "That's okay, Bob. She's with me."

At once, the young man steps aside and averts his gaze. I appear to have become instantly invisible to him.

"Clarence said you were on your way down," Ian says. His eyes, locked on mine, are shadowed with concern. "Is everything all right?"

"Yes, but I need to tell you something. It's urgent." I hesitate, aware that we aren't alone.

"Come this way." He takes my arm and leads me past the metal doors into a vast, cavernous space filled with people and monitors. Everyone I can see is intensely busy. It looks as though some sort of major action is underway. I wonder if I should have interrupted Ian but then I remember how Davos makes me feel and push that concern aside.

"No one will disturb us here," Ian says, indicating a small conference room off to one side. After we enter, he closes and locks the door behind us. Facing me, he asks, "What is it, Amelia?"

I take a breath and speak as calmly as I can manage when my heart is racing and the sharp edge of dread is closing in all around me. "Two years ago, Charles Davos tried to buy the Institute where the process for creating customized replicas was developed and where I was later imprinted."

Ian frowns. "How do you know this?"

"Susannah knew. She was already considering the process as an option for me. I don't know how she discovered what Davos was up to but what matters is that she passed that knowledge on to me. I would have realized it sooner except he isn't someone I've wanted to think about. I've only encountered him a handful of times and I've done my best to forget him. I'm sorry now that I did."

Slowly, Ian says, "He must have kept his interest very quiet. I haven't heard a whisper about it."

"If you're thinking that Susannah could have been wrong, keep in mind that all she passed on to me are simple, straightforward facts. No opinions, beliefs, preferences, suspicions, or anything of that kind. Before her final neural imprint was taken, she must have been convinced that Davos' interest in the Institute was real or I wouldn't know anything about it."

"All right, but there is something you don't know. Edward has been looking into the source of the funding behind the Human Preservation Front, the people who wanted to destroy all replicas. Half-an-hour ago, he succeeded in tracing the origin of the money to an account that's controlled by Davos."

I can't conceal my bewilderment. "I don't understand. Davos wanted to acquire the Institute just to destroy it? Or is it that he wanted to destroy it because he couldn't acquire it?"

I never feel safer than I do when I'm in Ian's arms but as he fits the pieces of information together and comes to his own conclusions, the look in his eyes hints at a completely different side of his nature, one that I feel fortunate not to encounter before and can only be grateful now that it's directed at another.

"If either was the case," he says grimly, "the HPF would just have planted explosives and gotten out before detonating them. Instead, they tried to hack past the firewalls protecting the customization tech. Unknown to them, there was a failsafe device. They tripped it, blowing themselves up along with everyone else."

Slowly, I ask, "But why would Davos fund an anti-replica terrorist group if what he really wanted was replica tech?"

Ian shrugs. "My guess is as a smokescreen to conceal his true objective. It became clear during interrogations that the HPF leadership didn't know the ultimate source of their funding. They were too glad to get it to question where it was coming from any more than they questioned the instructions they received to acquire the tech."

The thought of what a man like Davos could do with the ability to create selectively designed replicas tailored to his own purposes horrifies me. In the propaganda that I read on the link, the HPF ranted about the threat of a replica slave army driving humanity into extinction. I wrote that off as a paranoid fantasy but now I'm not so sure.

As casually as I can, I say, "There's nothing else he can do now, is there? The tech is gone."

The pang of loss that I feel takes me by surprise. Almost from the beginning, I've understood that however many replicas exist, it's unlikely that any other has been left free to become her own self. I'm grateful for

Susannah's choice more than I will ever be able to express yet at the same time I feel the burden of my isolation. It's a weight that I will bear forever.

Ian's eyes are locked on mine. The savage determination in them sends a tremor through me. I fight to remember him as he was at the beach house, the lover who held me with such tenderness and passion. The man I would trust with anything including my life.

He brushes a fingertip along the curve of my cheek, coming to rest gently on my mouth where I still taste the essence of him. So softly that I hardly hear him, he says, "Our intel indicates that there were only three real targets of the attack at the Crystal Palace. Two were supposed to be killed, the other was to be taken alive. Based on what you've just told me, I'm betting that Edward and I were in the first category. Our deaths would have left you effectively unprotected, clearing the way for Davos to acquire the only remaining source of the tech he wants badly enough to kill for-- you."

The thought of the two men I care for deeply, albeit in entirely different ways, being harmed sends a wave of nausea through me. My throat is tight as I say, "I've put you and my brother in danger just by existing. But how could Davos have found out what I am?"

"He may not have. He may just suspect. Whatever the case, you're not at fault in any way. You really have to understand that, Amelia. You bear no responsibility for any of this. Davos has asked for what he's about to get and I'm more than happy to give it to him."

For a moment longer, he touches me with such tenderness that I have to blink away tears. Even as I do so, his face hardens again, his manner becoming remote, unreachable. I watch in unwilling fascination as he completes the transformation from the Ian I know and cherish to someone I've always sensed within him but have never had to face before. The warrior who Charles Davos has so foolishly awakened, born for battle and capable of acting without a shred of mercy.

Chapter Twenty-one

Ian

"There's nothing to discuss."

I can't believe that Amelia thinks there is. We're back in the penthouse where I brought her as soon as Davos' sick plan became clear. I have to give the bastard credit, he concealed his interest in replica technology so well that not even Gab unearthed it.

If not for the knowledge hidden in Amelia, we still wouldn't know. I'd be worried that he hated replicas and wanted to harm her for that reason but I wouldn't have put it together with the attack on the Crystal Palace to realize what he truly intends.

I don't doubt for a moment that Susannah was right about Davos' efforts to acquire the most advanced replica technology for his own perverse purposes. She was a highly intelligent woman, meticulous in her approach to everything she did and never inclined to jump to conclusions.

But beyond that, my own instincts have been telling me all along that he's an enemy who needs to be crushed. I should have listened to them the moment he showed the slightest interest in Amelia.

My priorities are starkly clear. I want Davos' throat in my hands. I want to feel him struggle as all hope drains from him. I want to look into his eyes at the moment that the light in them flickers and dies. A garrote would be faster, a knife or a gun even more so. But given the threat he poses to Amelia, I won't be satisfied with anything less than the personal touch.

"You can't just go after him on your own," she insists.

We're standing in the great room. Hodge is hovering, discreetly out of sight but nearby. He'll take care of her. I've already given orders that she isn't to leave Pinnacle House until I say otherwise. There's nothing more to keep me from what needs to be done except that Amelia won't stop talking.

Worse yet, she doesn't sound hysterical or pleading or anything like that. Instead, she's calm, clear and determined. I can't help but admire how she stands up to me at the same time that I wouldn't mind just a little of the submission that she gives to me when I'm deep inside her.

"The Council is already aware of your role in destroying the HPF," she continues, dragging my thoughts away from the contemplation of her exquisite body arching in ecstasy as I make her come. "They must also at least suspect that you had something to do with what happened at the Crystal Palace," she goes on relentlessly. "If you add killing one of the most powerful men in the city to that list--"

"Not 'if'," I say emphatically. "When." I'm not about to give any ground on this. If she can't understand what I'm about to do, she has to at least accept it.

Instead, she says, "You aren't above the law, Ian, however unjust it is. If you're seen as posing a threat to the established order, there won't be any limits to the response against you. What happens then?"

"Look around you, Amelia," I snarl. "You're standing on top of a fucking fortress. I command the largest private military force in the country. Hell, in the world."

I didn't set out to create that but it happened all the same, yet another example of nature abhorring a vacuum. The willingness of public leaders to take credit for every success while shielding themselves from responsibility for any failure makes the existence of private forces to covertly handle the really tough jobs essential. I don't like that but I don't regret it either, especially when it means that I have the resources to protect what is mine.

"I understand that your people are fiercely loyal to you," Amelia says, "But what happens if you can't intimidate the Council into letting you do what you want? What if they order the MPS or other forces they could bring in to stop you and fighting breaks out? Here, in a crowded city filled with civilians--men, women, children. Can you honestly say that there won't be collateral damage, possibly a great deal of it? And what about afterward? Who picks up the pieces and how? You've told me yourself that you've seen the effects of anarchy first hand. Are you willing to be the cause of it?"

"What are you suggesting?" I fire back, not concealing my frustration with her stubbornness. "That I should leave Davos to the so-called authorities? Do you think for one moment that they'll go after him? They won't lift a finger. For you to be safe, he has to die. There isn't any other way."

"So that you carry the burden of that for the rest of your life? You're a good man, Ian. I've seen how what happened to you when you were a boy haunts you. How much worse will this be?"

"Amelia...I've killed before. What do you think happened at the Crystal Palace?"

"You were in a battle then, as I'm sure you've been all too many times. This is different. Vigilante justice is an oxymoron, there's no such thing. What you're talking about is murder."

"It damn well is not! It's self-defense, which under any legal definition includes not only protecting myself but also protecting an innocent party who is in danger and can't defend herself."

"From imminent danger, Ian. As in no time for the authorities to intervene."

Oh, my god, she's sounds like a lawyer. A gorgeous, fierce-eyed upholder of legal ideals that are preserved these days far more in theory than reality. I want to tell her that but she's put her hands on her hips-- the same ones I love to grasp as I fuck her--and she's glaring at me.

I know that she doesn't have any real idea of what Davos intends to do to her and I'm not about to enlighten her. To understand the complexities of the tech used to imprint her would require far harsher and more destructive techniques than those employed in even the most rigorous interrogation. He would have to drill down layer by layer through not just her brain but also her mind, shattering her psyche and leaving her catatonic, if not worse.

There's no power on earth that can compel me to put those thoughts in her head.

"We're not going to agree on this, Amelia. All I'm going to say is that Davos is capable of evil beyond anything you know. I can't live with the possibility of him ever getting near you, which is why I'm going to stop him once and for all."

She stares at me for a long moment before a sigh escapes her. Quietly, she says, "I know more than you think I do about the human capacity for evil."

She sounds resigned yet at the same time profoundly sad in a way that I don't believe any knowledge she received from Susannah could ever make her. This is different, more personal, hinting at what I've sensed that she's withheld from me.

"How can you know?" I ask softly, forgetting Davos for the moment and focusing entirely on her. "You've been in the world only a short time. How much can you have perceived?"

"I'm twenty-two years old, Ian, hardly a child."

"I'm sorry," I say softly. "I have a tendency to forget that you didn't just arise from the sea like Botticelli's Venus. You have every right to be angry about what you were denied, even to hate the people who kept you from living for so long."

Her expression is guarded as she looks up at me. "Why do I have that right? Because I'm a person now? What about before? What was I then?"

"You know what you were, Amelia." I don't want to dwell on the years she spent without consciousness, her existence maintained only for the day when she would be gutted and harvested. It hurts unbearably to think of her that way but the fact is that I don't. To me, she is entirely the woman whose awakening has changed my life forever.

Frustration rips through me as she looks away. Without thinking, I take hold of her, turning her so that she has no choice but to face me. She's trembling and her eyes are even more luminous than usual. My throat thickens as I see the sheen of tears gathering in them.

Easing my grip enough to make sure that I'm not hurting her, I say, "I trust you, Amelia. So much so that I've told you things I've never revealed to anyone else. But something is troubling you deeply and you won't tell me what it is."

For the first time, I let myself admit that I resent her unwillingness to be as open with me as I have been with her. It leaves me feeling too far out ahead in our relationship, vulnerable in a way I'm not okay with.

"I want to." Her voice is little more than a whisper but I can't doubt her sincerity. "I'm just very...conflicted. Please, try to understand. I'm deeply grateful for my life but I can't hide from the fact that it's come at a high cost. I lost years of that life before I was finally allowed to begin living. But others are losing even more."

I frown, not following her. "What do you mean? Who's losing?"

Softly, patiently, she says, "Ian, while it may be true that I don't have any personal responsibility for what's been happening, my existence is still the reason why people are dying. More than a hundred men and women lost their lives when the HPF attacked the Institute. How many more were killed two nights ago at the Crystal Palace? And now you're planning to go after Davos with potentially catastrophic repercussions for you and everyone else."

"You really need to stop worrying about me," I tell her even as I cherish the fact that she does. "I'll be fine. I wish that I could change the rest of it but I can't. All I can do is make sure that your future is a hell of a lot better than your past."

We're at a stalemate and I think we both know it. I'm trying to figure out what I can say that will give her some small amount of comfort when we're suddenly interrupted. Hodge steps into the room.

"Pardon me, sir," he says quietly. "The Council is convening in half-an-hour. They've sent word that they want you to be there."

Normally, I'd balk at a summons from the venal half-wits who pretend to run the city but under the circumstances, it feels like a reprieve.

Hodge spears a glance in Amelia's direction. "Shall I tell them you're busy, sir?"

"No, that's all right, I'll go."

His surprise is matched only by her own. "Don't get your hopes up," I caution her. "I'll hear what they have to say. If there's a chance that they'll listen to reason, I'll tell them about Davos. But the odds that I'll join forces with the Council to deal with him are vanishingly small."

"At least you'll talk with them," she says with an encouraging smile. "That's progress."

I don't share her optimism but I don't want to dampen it either. Davos can live a few more hours if that's what it takes to make Amelia happy. After that, he's all mine.

Hunted

Josie Litton

Chapter Twenty-two

Amelia

My relief that Ian is willing to at least talk with the Council fades as soon as he is gone. If he's right about nothing good coming from the meeting, what will he do next? What danger will he put himself in because of me?

"Can I get you anything, Miss Amelia?"

Hodge is hovering. He's clearly concerned about me.

"I'm fine," I manage to say. "But thank you."

The steward looks unconvinced. "Mister Ian will be back shortly, no doubt. In the meantime, perhaps you would enjoy a massage or some other relaxing activity?"

I can't help but smile. Managing me can't possibly have been covered in butler school, or wherever Hodge acquired some of his skills.

"I'd rather go for a walk." Quickly, I add, "I'll stay in Pinnacle House, of course. I promised Ian that I would. I just need to--"

To what? I can't sit still, that's for sure. Agitation is building in me by the moment. Ian has been gone mere minutes and I already feel as though I'm going to burst out of my skin.

"I need a distraction," I say. "Gab showed me around when I was here before but I'm sure that she's very busy right now. I can explore on my own, if that's all right?"

Hodge inclines his head. "Of course, miss. If you wouldn't mind wearing this--"

He holds out a bracelet that is identical to the one I wore on my previous stay at Pinnacle House. It's coded to admit me to certain areas in the vertical city but not to others.

I thank him as he says, "A little old school but so much less obtrusive than an implanted chip, don't you agree?"

The thought of any such thing makes me shudder. "Old school is good. I'll be back...when I am. I take it that you can get in touch with me if you need to?"

"The bracelet will pulse if you have an incoming message. Just tap it and you'll be in contact. And, of course, it works in reverse. The bracelet can link you to any assistance you might require."

I suspect that means that my location will be known wherever I go but that doesn't surprise me. Privacy is the ultimate luxury in our world. At least I can take off the bracelet should I so choose. I wonder how many other people have trackers that can't be removed.

At first, leaving the penthouse, I have no real idea of where I want to go. But then I think of when Gab took me on a tour, showing me the residential levels interspersed with recreational and entertainment areas, food courts, shopping pavilions, nature centers, hydroponic gardens, and so on that make up part of the vertical city of more than twenty thousand employees of Slade Enterprises and their families.

Instinctively, I make for the level where I first realized the true nature of Pinnacle House--a community in the midst of an enclave of the elite where ordinary people are allowed to live their lives unaffected by the oppression beyond their walls. That first time, the recreational area with an atrium that rises several hundred feet to a virtual sky was overrun with children just released from school. But it's earlier in the day now and everything is a lot quieter.

Full spectrum daylight illuminates the wide, airy space. A soft breeze riffles the leaves of trees and bushes scattered throughout. A few couples and families with very young children stroll by. No one is dressed in the drab, monochromatic style of workers in the city. To the contrary, bright colors abound. The only exceptions are those wearing the black uniforms I've seen before and even they are obviously relaxed and off duty.

My presence doesn't go unnoticed but the glances I receive are friendly. I even see a few smiles. I'm not so naïve as to imagine that my relationship with Ian is a secret. In any community, there's bound to be gossip. Fortunately, whatever is being said about me appears to be positive.

I stop finally at a café overlooking a shopping arcade, where I spend several minutes pondering the seemingly endless list of choices. With a hazelnut-half-soya-something-something in hand, I take a seat at a wrought iron table in front. Only a few of the other tables are occupied. At most of these, holographic screens project up from the surface. People are absorbed in whatever they're reading or watching. I could do the same but I prefer to just soak up the sights and sounds of everyday living in this remarkable place.

Not for the first time, it occurs to me that Pinnacle House must be a very large thorn in the side of the Council and the shadowy figures that control it. Why did Ian choose to put his headquarters where he did if not to be deliberately provocative? Yet I don't have the impression that he's sought a direct confrontation with the powers-that-be, at least not in the past. What's changed?

The most obvious answer isn't long in occurring to me. I'm in his life now. Whether we want to or not, we're changing each other. He's exploded the world wide open for me, unleashing a floodtide of sensations, experiences, and perceptions that are making up at least in part for the years that I lost. Whereas I... I've hurtled him into a confrontation with the HPF, forced him to question the most fundamental issue of who is entitled to basic human rights, and perhaps in the process made him more aware of how ordinary people, the scavengers in particular, are suffering. Ian, with his consciousness raised and his fundamental sense of decency provoked may be more than the Council is prepared to deal with.

I can only hope that the meeting is going well and that he'll be home soon. My chest tightens as I think that even now, when he hasn't been gone an hour, I miss him.

Lost in my thoughts, I don't notice the pretty young blonde woman until she is standing in front of me. Her gamine face with a splattering of freckles breaks into an apologetic smile.

"I'm sorry, I didn't mean to startle you. You're Amelia, right?"

I nod as I try to remember if I've met her before. I don't think I would have forgotten. Her short hair is styled to elfin points along her forehead, cheeks, and the nape of her neck. She has huge, cornflower blue eyes that match the color of her dress made of iridescent wool interwoven with small, glittering beads. The bangles on her wrist make a soft, bell-like sound as she waves a hand.

"We haven't met. I'm Daphne, Gab's spouse."

My confusion melts away. I return her smile. "Of course. Would you like to join me?"

"If I'm not interrupting anything--"

"Just wool gathering." I indicate the chair beside mine. "Please."

As she sits, I can't help noticing the tightness around her eyes. Like me, she looks worried. I suspect we both are for the same reason.

"Is everything all right?" I ask.

She plucks at her fingers for a moment and sighs. "Shouldn't I be asking you that? You were at the Crystal Palace. It must have been horrible."

I try not to remember the sight of immense shards of glass falling out of the sky but the image is burned into my brain.

"Ian and his people got us out very quickly." I shrug, a little embarrassed. "I'm afraid that I may have upset one of them. Hollis, I think his name is?"

Daphne grins. "Don't worry about Holly, he's a doll. Besides, Gab likes you so you must be solid." She takes a sip of her frothy green drink and turns more serious. "It's just that we're all on edge right now. Waiting's hard."

I'm happy to know that I've got Gab's approval. I like her and I suspect that she stands very high in Ian's esteem. But I also sense a kindred spirit in Daphne. Like her, I'm finding it incredibly hard to stand by and do nothing while Ian puts himself in danger.

"It really is hard," I say. "Do you have any tips for how to deal with it?"

"Well, let's see... Since Gab and I got together two years ago, I've knit three afghans, sat through two meditation courses, drunk enough herbal tea to float a stealth cruiser, and taken up boxing."

"Boxing?" I can't help but be surprised. She's fine-boned and slender, to the point of appearing delicate.

Daphne nods emphatically. "Pounding away at a punching bag is a great stress reliever. So is getting in the ring and going a few rounds with a sparring partner." She wrinkles her nose. "Gab isn't thrilled by that last part but I tell her I'll stop when she gets into a safer line of work. Like that'll ever happen."

"You don't think it might?"

She shoots me a look of disbelief that I even have to ask. "Not unless we go through some worm hole into an alternate universe where everyone plays nicely together. Gab's super committed to making the world a better place, no matter how many heads she has to knock together to do it. I don't like it but I'd never say anything to discourage her."

"Why not? You're obviously concerned."

Daphne is silent for a moment, weighing her response. Finally, she says, "I was a worker when Gab and I met. That's a tough life, you have to scramble every minute and one misstep can cost you everything. But it's still hugely better than what the scavs have. There are more of them every day. Right now they're fighting for scraps. How long before they decide that they'd rather just fight, no matter what that costs them?"

It's news to me that the population of scavengers is increasing but I'm not surprised. That fits with what I've seen of this world. All the same, the question is chilling. I think of the children I saw in the park and the fate that could befall them, even worse than what they have already suffered.

"Why are there more?" I ask. "I understand that technology has eliminated a lot of jobs but there's a safety net--"

"It's getting pretty frayed," Daphne says. "Gab says that's because the government is running out of money. It could just print more but that makes the money that the rich already have worth less so they won't allow it. Benefits could be cut but that will cause widespread social unrest, also to be avoided at all cost. All that's left is to kick people off the welfare rolls. The government's making that easier to do than ever. Screw up your recycling, use too much water, so much as look funny at a peace officer, and you can be gone."

"Nobody speaks up? Nobody objects?" I ask.

Daphne shrugs. "The government's really good at pitting people against each other. Those who get kicked off the welfare rolls are labeled as social misfits who don't deserve sympathy or support. Everyone else tells themselves that they'll be okay, right up to the moment when they suddenly aren't."

"That can't go on." I don't need any vast experience in life to recognize that. All I need is the knowledge I have of the moments in history when pent up rage on the part of ordinary people exploded into violence that burned like a firestorm across entire cultures, wiping them out.

"No, it can't," Daphne agrees. "We could have avoided all of this if the right choices had been made years ago but they weren't. Now the whole system is set to implode. The only question is who gets hurt the most?"

"Who always gets hurt?" I ask softly. "The helpless and innocent--" Pain twists in me. I don't want to think about what was done to me but the memories are inescapable.

She must see my distress because she lays her hand over mine. "Hey, it's okay. Ian knows what he's doing. He won't be pushed into anything but he won't be caught unprepared either. Whatever comes, whenever it does, we'll be ready."

I have to hope that she's right and that the change so many are crying out for can somehow be accomplished without loss of life. But I also can't help fearing that a darker and bloodier outcome is more likely.

"Tell you what," Daphne says in an obvious effort to lighten the mood. "Since we're both stuck waiting, what do you say we hit the gym? I'll introduce you to my favorite punching bag."

My first instinct is to beg off but I reconsider. I can't bear to simply sit around and after what she's told me, the thought of hitting something has definite appeal.

With no clear idea of what I'm getting into, I shrug. "Sure, why not?"

∞ ∞ ∞

An hour later, I'm slumped on a bench in the locker room, covered in sweat and fighting for breath. The woman who I've discovered hides a mean left hook--and an even meaner right one--under an elfin exterior is unlacing my gloves. Her grin is ear-to-ear.

"Girl, you've got some moves! I have to hand it to you. A few more practice sessions and you'll be ready to get in the ring." Her chuckle is pure anticipation. "I'd love to see Ian's reaction when you tell him what you've been up to. Should be quite a sight."

I try to laugh but it comes out sounding more like a wheeze. "Forget Ian, I know a Russian guy who really wouldn't like it."

Daphne takes a step back and stares at me with undisguised surprise. "What are you talking about, a Russian? Who's he?"

"My dance instructor. Sergei thinks I should be a professional ballerina. Risking an injury for anything less than a grand jeté is definitely on his 'nyet' list."

"That explains it. You've got that whole 'float like a butterfly, sting like a bee' thing going for you." She tosses aside my second glove and sits down on the bench beside me. With a knowing glance, she asks, "So what does Ian think of this Russian guy?"

"I'm not sure..." Actually, I am, I just don't want to admit it. "They're probably not destined to be best buddies."

Daphne laughs. "Hey, that's okay. A little jealousy is cool so long as he knows how you feel about him."

Does he? Ian and I have talked more in the last few days than ever before but there's still a great deal we have to learn about each other. That isn't helped by my inability to open up to him.

I'm only just realizing how much the memories of my time in the gestation chamber have shaped who I am. How long will I go on concealing them from him?

Ten rounds with the punching bag have been a real bonding exercise. They've also loosened my tongue. "I'm not sure I know how I feel."

My new friend shakes her head. "More like you're too scared to admit it. I was the same way at first. Whatever else love is, it's frigging terrifying. But ask yourself, do you miss him if you're apart like five minutes?"

Slowly, I nod.

"Do you want to jump his bones every time you see him?"

I'm not totally sure what that means but I think I get the drift. Flushing a little, I nod. "Yes."

"Is there anything you wouldn't do to keep him safe?"

"Nothing but he won't let me. He's bound and determined to do things his own way no matter what that costs him."

She nods. "Just like Gab. And that has you tied up in knots, wound so tight you can hardly breathe? You feel more vulnerable than you ever imagined being and worse yet, you can't do anything about it. You're riding a pendulum, swinging between crazy-mad happiness and gut-wrenching dread. Sound familiar?"

I look up, meeting her sympathetic gaze, and nod. She's described my current state of mind perfectly. "You're saying love sucks?"

Daphne sighs. "It's not all blue birds of happiness and heart-shaped candy boxes, that's for sure. Love is sweaty and hard and yeah, sometimes it hurts a bitch. But it's also what makes us human. So be glad you've fallen victim to it. There are people out there who aren't capable of caring about anything except themselves and they are just plain dangerous."

Is she right? Is the way I feel about Ian proof that I am in every way human? Even more so than some of the naturally born?

"With all the stuff they can fix these days," Daphne goes on, "you'd think they'd find a way to make people care about each other. But if that happened, the folks with more power than heart would never get away with what they do."

I think of Davos. A shiver of foreboding runs through me. "People who don't care about others will sacrifice anyone they have to in order to win."

"True enough," Daphne says. She seems undaunted. "But the people who do care will sacrifice themselves. The bad guys totally don't get that. They never see it coming. Which is why in the end, they'll lose."

I want to believe her. Everything in me cries out to do so. But at the same time, I'm terrified that if she is right, Ian could be among those who make the ultimate sacrifice.

At that thought, something inside me feels as though it is cracking wide open the way I used to long for the walls of the gestation chamber to do. I double over on the bench, clutching myself, barely hearing the reassuring sounds Daphne makes as she tries to comfort me.

All I can think of is that she's right--love is hard, love hurts. But it makes us, it makes me, human. I love Ian completely and unconditionally. With that realization, all my doubts about myself that have lingered from the moment I awoke fall away.

In their place is fierce joy that makes me want to shout out loud, I love Ian Slade! But the world doesn't need to hear that, he does. Before he makes any decisions that could turn my worst fears for him into reality.

Chapter Twenty-three

Ian

I leave the council meeting two hours later feeling like I need a shower. Instead, I call Edward. We'd spoken briefly as I was leaving Pinnacle House, long enough for me to tell him what Amelia had remembered about Davos and that I was on my way to speak with the Council.

"Watch yourself," he warned. "They're the most lowlife, self-serving assholes that I've ever come across."

"Yeah, but they give great media. What else really matters?"

"An ounce of decency?" he suggested.

"That's crazy talk," I said with a laugh but I'm not so amused now.

The city is in the final frenzy of preparations for Carnival as I leave the building. Sidestepping a conga line of inebriated clowns who have gotten an early start and are wending their way up the avenue, I call Edward again.

"I can't figure out what I was doing there," I say. "All the assholes did was play to the cameras. After the first hundred or so sound bites, I think I dozed off."

"They didn't ask you anything?"

"Yeah, finally. They wanted to know what I'd seen at the Crystal Palace and what I thought about it. I saw a building blow up. I think it shouldn't have. End of story."

"What about the scavengers?" Edward asks. "Did they come up?"

"Just at the end. They wanted to know how I thought they should be handled. I figured since I'd hauled ass to sit in a damn uncomfortable chair at an otherwise empty witness table for absolutely no good reason, I'd get in a few strokes of my own."

"What did you say?" Edward sounds a little apprehensive but then he's known me a long time.

I savor the memory. "Just that it was tough to see how the scavengers could have been involved. Easy to scapegoat them but it would be wiser to avoid a rush to judgment. A violent over-reaction on the part of the government against the poorest and most vulnerable citizens would only make the situation worse."

He can't help it, he laughs. "Jeez, buddy, you seriously called the scavengers 'citizens'? Why not just set off a bomb in the council chamber and be done with it?"

I recall the red-faced sputtering that followed and grin. "Because this was more fun. Besides, it's true. The government can strip benefits from people but they can't change the fact of where someone was born or the inherent rights that go with that. Anyway, once they settled back down, I reminded them that violence doesn't serve anyone's interest and that I, for one, have a deep abhorrence of it. So much so that I'd hate to see a situation develop where private forces had to intervene."

"Let me guess," Edward says when he stops chuckling. "They were shitting in their pants at the thought of you calling out your troops to protect scavengers."

"Pretty much. They changed the subject in a hurry and we wrapped up not too long after that. Needless to say, I never saw any reason to bring up Davos."

"I understand but I still wish that you'd been able to." He pauses for a moment, then adds, "The timing on this isn't ideal. Before you put anything in motion, we need to talk."

What the hell? Does he really not get the danger to his sister? My voice turns cold. "If you're planning on telling me why I shouldn't go after him, don't bother. Amelia's already done that. While she's so concerned about everyone else's safety, someone's got to look after hers. I figured that you'd want in on that job but if I was wrong--"

"You weren't," Edward responds. I hear the edge of his anger. "She's my sister. Of course I want to protect her. I have no problem whatsoever with eliminating Davos. All I'm saying is that it would have been better if this was coming to a head some time from now. But it is what it is and we have to deal with that. Get this wrong and a lot of innocents could die. However, there are ways to prevent that."

Somewhat mollified, not to mention curious why Edward thinks that any time would be better for an armed conflict to break out in the city, I ask, "What do you have in mind?"

He doesn't hesitate. Listening to him, I'm struck by the thought that he's not speaking theoretically. He's got a fully formulated strategy already figured out and ready to go.

"Advance warning could save a lot of lives," he says. "Just a few words in the right ears so that if fighting breaks out, people don't get caught up in it. The scavengers have already gone deep and they'll stay that way until this is over. But the workers are another story. Unless they know not to, they'll show up for their jobs like they always do. That means they could get caught in a crossfire."

"You're really betting that the Council will call out the MPS or bring in some mercenary force if I kill Davos?"

"They aren't the sharpest nails in the box but they can recognize an existential threat to them when they see it. They won't hesitate to use the workers as human shields if it comes to that. You want their lives on your conscience?"

"No, of course I don't. But you start warning people and Davos will hear about it. With the element of surprise, I can end this quickly and deploy enough forces throughout the city to stop the Council from so much as farting. Without it, all bets are off."

"I know who to talk to," Edward insists. "If the right people pass the word to stay home, the workers will do it, no questions asked."

Slowly, I say, "I didn't realize there was that kind of leadership among the workers."

"It's developed recently." He doesn't offer any more details but he does add, "Given time, a lot could change around here for the better. But nothing good can happen while people are being killed."

He's got a point but I need to think about what all this means. Gab is sure that Edward is in contact with the scavengers. Now he's telling me that he's also got a pipeline into the workers. Very well connected man, our Edward. I've got to wonder what he's planning.

However, that can wait. "What about the residents?" I ask. "You're not losing any sleep over what happens to them?"

"Let's be clear," he says. "I don't want to see anyone killed except Davos. If there was a way to keep the residents out of this, I'd grab it. But at least half of them, probably more, would waste no time running to the Council or to Davos himself at the first hint of a threat to their precious status quo. Besides, Carnival starts tonight. There really would have to be bombs going off to keep them from that."

"I know a few who won't be attending," I say, "starting with Amelia and including my mother and sister. I assume you'll warn your grandmother as well."

"I'll make sure that Adele knows," Edward agrees. "She and Amelia were planning to go to the premiere of a ballet that Sergei Zharkov's producing for Carnival, something about Medea. They'll just have to miss it."

It occurs to me that the Russian's choice of a work about blood and madness might turn out to be more fitting than I'd thought. But not if I can help it. Davos is only one man. There's no reason why his death should be anything other than a cause of great relief. Provided that I can get to him fast enough, before he has any sense of what's coming.

"How much lead time do you need?" I ask Edward.

"A few hours, that's all." He's silent for a moment. "It's actually more critical that I know if you fail. Dead, Davos is no further threat. But if he's still alive--"

"He won't be. However, I'll make sure that you know either way." Including, although neither of us needs to say it, if I don't survive.

Edward and I end our conversation a few minutes later. I'm heading back to Pinnacle House, having opted to walk in order to avoid the heavy traffic thronging the streets in the run-up to Carnival, when a young woman gotten up as Marie Antoinette in her Bo-Peep phase stumbles out of an alley and bumps into me.

Giggling, she says, "Oh, God, I'm sorry! Started partying a little early, I guess." She giggles again and grabs my hand to steady herself. "I didn't hurt you, did I?" she asks.

I'm about to assure the petite curly haired blond with the improbably large breasts that I'm fine when her feet slip out from under her. Despite her grip on my hand, she tumbles to her knees, in the process pressing her face right up against my crotch. My cock is resting up for Amelia and doesn't react.

I grasp her shoulders and pull her to her feet. "How about I call somebody to come get you?"

She bats her eyes and looks puzzled. "Why? I'm fine and besides, the fun hasn't even started yet."

I step back, relieved when she remains upright. She gives me another grin and a little wave before toddling on down the street. I shake my head, wondering what kind of shape she'll be in by morning.

Not my problem, fortunately. I move on, forgetting her.

I've gone half-a-block when I notice that my hand is stinging. I stare at it for several moments before I make out the small puncture wound in the palm. Even then I have a hard time processing what it means. Of all the rookie mistakes! I've been so busy thinking about how to take out Davos that I didn't stop to consider that he could strike first. Or that snake that he is, he'd never come at me directly. Bastard sent Bo-Peep to do it instead.

I need help and fast.

I fumble for my link, intending to call Hollis. Whatever poison or drug has entered my system, he can drop a evac drone right where I'm standing. I can be in Medical within minutes. With luck, there's still time to get whatever this is out of me before--

The world shifts, tilting dizzily on its axis. My heart is racing. I can hear the roar of blood in my ears. In the next instant, I feel as though I've stepped outside my body, my consciousness detaching from the rest of me. No pain, though, so probably not poison. A drug then. Shit! I stagger and try again to reach my link but my fingers are clumsy and they miss. Instinctively, I keep walking, reeling past clusters of early partiers who take no notice of what must look like just another drunk guy. I need to do something but I can't remember what. The city, the street, the revelers, I'm losing it all. Losing myself...

∞ ∞ ∞

When I'm next aware, I'm in an alley off the main drag. My back is to a wall, which I must have slid down because I'm in a crouch. I stand, relieved that I'm no longer dizzy, and look in all directions. Nothing. I'm alone.

With no immediate threat in sight, I do a quick physical check. So far as I can tell, I'm uninjured. My heartbeat has slowed to normal and my vision is clear. Aside from a sheen of sweat filming my skin, I feel fine.

What was all that then? I lift my hand and look at it closely. It no longer stings and there's no sign of the puncture wound that I thought I saw.

I'm still convinced that something isn't right. I'll head back to Pinnacle House and check in with Medical anyway, have them run a quick tox screen. I leave the alley and start back up the avenue but before I get very far, I'm reconsidering. I feel good. Hell, make that great.

All the crap I've been dealing with--the HPF, Davos, the Council--has faded away. I can see each now for what it really is, a nuisance to be crushed and forgotten, no doubts, no regrets, and above all none of that right/wrong bullshit. Whatever works is right, plain and simple. Come down to it, I really only have one problem--Amelia. That gorgeous, hot-as-Hades temptress has me tied up in knots. Defying me the way she does, trying to tell me what to do, getting me so hard that I can't think straight.

The sun is too bright. I cross over to the shadowed side of the street and keep walking. It really is a great day, the city at its best and Carnival about to start. I've never let myself enjoy Carnival but I make up my mind right then that this year will be an exception.

A prism of rainbow lights flickers at the periphery of my vision. I have no idea where it's coming from and I don't care. I'm back to thinking about Amelia. How tight her sweet cunt feels when I'm deep inside her, those breathy little cries she gives as she comes, how soft and pliant she is afterward. My hot, sexy obsession. Who seems to have forgotten that she's my property.

Taking her to the beach house was a mistake. Too many memories associated with that place thanks to my old man bulldozing it. Ran the machine himself, from what I heard. Say what you want but he had style.

And forget Pinnacle House. Gab's taken a shine to her. Hollis admires her courage. As for Hodge, he's made it clear from the start that he expects me to be the better man and do what's right where she's concerned. The mood I'm in, I've got other priorities.

In a few hours, the serious partying begins. By tradition, the Lords of Misrule take over the city. Anything goes. It's time to cut loose and let myself off the leash. Right about now, that sounds like a pretty good plan, even if it does present a few logistical problems.

I want Amelia all to myself in a place with no memories and no possibility of interference. A place where I can set her straight about the nature of our relationship. For just a second, the old club flits through my mind. I push that thought aside. I'm not that fucked up kid any more. I'm a man, one who damn well knows what he wants.

Within sight of the park, I notice the elegant hotel built more than a century ago in the Art Deco style that conceals a separate boutique residence on its upper floors. The latter is well known throughout the city for no-questions-asked service and absolute discretion.

I'm smiling as I step inside the ornate lobby filled with towering white columns, gilded ceiling reliefs, and the signature potted palms. Half-an-hour later, with a suite booked and a few special requirements in the works, I continue on my way to Pinnacle House. Amelia's had it easy so far but it's time to remind her who she belongs to.

Josie Litton

Chapter Twenty-four

Amelia

I don't understand. I thought you wanted me to stay here while you deal with Davos."

Ian is back from the council meeting to my great relief but his mood is a surprise. All the dark rage and barely contained violence that was so evident earlier has evaporated. Instead, he's relaxed, even buoyant, as though he doesn't have a care in the world.

I should be glad especially if that means he's reconsidering about going after Davos on his own. And I am. But something feels...off.

"That snake isn't going anywhere," he says with a shrug. "Besides now that I'm on to what he wants, it'll be fun to watch him twist in the wind." He takes a step closer to me, brushing his long fingers over the curve of my cheek. "Trust me, babe, I take really good care of what belongs to me. Davos isn't getting anywhere near you."

His possessiveness sends a long ripple of pleasure through me. I want desperately to tell him how I feel but the words catch in my throat. He looks unburdened, as though he's shucked off all the dangers and concerns that threaten us. As welcome as that might be under other circumstances, it's very un-Ian like. Before anything else, I want to understand what's responsible for this change in him.

"Did you discuss Davos with the Council?" I ask.

"No point. That little get-together was strictly for show." He wraps a hand around the nape of my neck and pulls me to him. His lips graze mine as he says, "Get dressed. You don't want to miss that Russian fucker's contribution to Carnival, do you?"

I start in surprise, torn between dismay and delight. Dismay wins, if only for a moment. "Ian! Don't talk about Sergei like that. He's not just my teacher, he's also a friend."

"Whatever. We're leaving in half-an-hour." His eyes, a molten amber, skim me. "Hodge brought clothes for you down from the estate. I'm sure you'll find something suitable."

I want to ask him what has happened to make him believe that the danger isn't nearly as serious as he thought it was just a few hours ago but he's already walking away. Over his shoulder, he says, "I'll use one of the guest rooms to get ready. If I join you, we'll never get out of here."

I believe him. The way I feel, I'd just as soon stay in. Only my need to discover what lies behind this sudden, drastic shift in his mood convinces me to do as he says.

Twenty-eight minutes later--I check the clock--I walk back into the great room wearing the gown I chose and the matching accessories. Hodge must have brought down a good third or more of the contents of the dressing room that I discovered shortly after awakening at the estate. I've surmised that Susannah picked out clothes for me just as she designed the Golden Room and what lies beyond it.

My step falters as I recall where the concealed door in the dressing room leads to--the Cabinet of Secret Delights that I've dreamed of so recently. Something dark stirs in me that I don't want to acknowledge. Susannah didn't know about the demons that haunt Ian, memories of the year he spent when he was fifteen as a member of the brutal sex club his father founded and controlled. If she had, I doubt very much that the Cabinet would exist. But it does and I have no idea how to tell him about it, or even if I ever will.

The gown I've chosen is unlike anything else I've worn. The strappy silk sheathe hugs my body from the curve of my breasts to my thighs before flaring slightly to my ankles enough so that I can walk. A bold, blatant red, the gown is encrusted with thousands of tiny, glittering crystals that reflect the light with every step I take. Their weight is such that I found the gown carefully folded between layers of tissue paper in a drawer rather than on a hanger. My undergarments, such as they are, are also red--all silk and frothy lace that make me feel as though I am wearing nothing. Going all in, I'm wearing red stilettos attached by silk ribbons tied in bows at the back of my ankles.

With the gown was a matching red lace mask that leads me to guess that the costume was intended for Carnival. I haven't put the mask on yet, only held it up in front of the mirror to see what the effect will be. Fitted closely to my face, it peaks over the bridge of my nose and has cut-outs for my eyes yet it still resembles a blindfold. As such, it hints at a level of submission and helplessness that I find disturbingly arousing.

Ian is already in the great room when I arrive, looking breathtaking once again in formal evening wear. He's standing with his back to me looking out over the city. I can see my own reflection in the glass he's facing and so can he. Slowly, he turns. As his eyes rake over me, I realize that I'm holding my breath. I release it slowly and take a step toward him.

"Can you help me with this?" I ask, holding out my mask.

He doesn't respond at once, continuing to devour me with his gaze. The moments stretch out between us. Need for him vibrates through me, shocking in its intensity.

Finally, he closes the space between us and extends his hand in a silent gesture of command. I place the mask in it and turn so that my back is to him. He sucks in his breath as I fight to contain a smile. The gown leaves me bare from my shoulder blades to the curve of my derriere. When I realized how much of me would be exposed, I almost chose something else to wear. Now I'm glad that I didn't.

A soft gasp escapes me as Ian traces the tip of his finger down my spine and slips it under the edge of the silk. He strokes the small depression just above the crack in my ass, probing gently.

"I want this, too," he murmurs, his breath warm against my ear.

My inner muscles tighten with a combination of shock, fear and treacherous longing. How can he do this to me so effortlessly?

As though he knows exactly what I'm thinking, he chuckles and places the mask over my face, tying it behind my head so that the red silk ribbons trail down to tickle my back. My hair is up, secured in a twist from which a few tendrils escape. He lowers his mouth to the exposed hollow between the base of my throat and my shoulder. Against my skin, he murmurs, "You're a fire in my blood, Amelia. One I don't think I can ever quench."

Does that mean he would like to? I don't have the nerve to ask him, especially not when, without warning, he first sucks my skin, then bites me lightly. The pain is small and fleeting but he leaves no doubt as to his intent.

"I want to mark you," he says. "I don't want there to be any doubt about who you belong to. Not in your mind or anyone else's."

I gasp and take a quick step away, turning to look at him. He is power and male beauty, primal, fierce, unrelenting. Truly the prince of my imaginings but also so much more. A man, real, vulnerable, passionate. And seeming against all odds, mine.

Breathlessly, I say, "We should go."

He frowns slightly. "Are you that anxious to see the Russian?"

The sudden flash of jealousy--again--takes me aback. I don't try to hide my irritation. "I've told you, Sergei is just a friend."

His hand tightens on my upper arm, not enough to cause even the slightest discomfort yet enough to leave no doubt as to his feelings.

"Make no mistake, Amelia, I'm not. I'm the man who wants to possess you, all of you, in every way. Your desire, your longing, your passion all belong to me and that has nothing to do with any damn paperwork." His warm breath brushes the back of my neck. "I'm going to teach you things that good old Sergei couldn't even dream of. Before I'm done you'll know exactly who you belong to."

I'm torn between dumbfounded silence and darkly stirring desire. Without waiting for me to respond, he takes my hand and strides toward the elevator. I'm forced to run a little to keep up with him.

We're half-way through the lobby of Pinnacle House--a soaring space of marble and steel that I can't help but find impressive--when his link chimes. He grabs it from his pocket impatiently.

"What?" Silence for a moment, then, "Out, that's where. It's Carnival. We're going to have some fun. You might try it yourself, Hollis." More silence, followed by, "I'll get around to Davos when I'm damn good and ready. Just make sure that when I am, we know exactly where he is." Before the other man can say anything more, Ian disconnects.

Briefly, he scowls but in the next instant his mood shifts and he gives me a blinding smile. "Ready, sweetheart?" he asks.

I nod but I'm not at all sure that I am prepared to deal with this mercurial, seductive Ian. The man I love, who wants my ass and all the rest of me as well. But I'm not about to say 'no' to him, not when I'm the one who feels on fire.

We step out into an evening warm with the promise of summer and exploding with color and sound. Carnival is truly underway, the streets thronged with fevered pleasure seekers. The contrast between what I see all around me and what I witnessed not even forty-eight hours ago at the Crystal Palace is overwhelming. I simply can't put the two events together.

"It's as though nothing happened," I marvel as we begin walking toward the avenue.

"Nothing did." Ian's hand is warm and strong around mine. He makes me feel safe and cared for even as he scatters my emotions to the four winds. When I look at him in bewilderment, he says, "You should read '1984'. It was written by George Orwell, a hell of a smart guy with a good take on how certain things that he saw happening in his own time would play out in the future. In it, history is constantly being revised. Anything that doesn't fit with what the government wants people to believe gets flushed down the memory hole."

This is a side of Ian I haven't seen before. He's said very little about his education apart from joining the military at the age of eighteen instead of entering the elite university that his father expected him to attend. His brilliance in weapons design is well known, suggesting prowess in engineering and mathematics. But now I glimpse an interest in literature that I hadn't suspected, along with a willingness to engage with ideas that challenge the validity of a ruling elite.

Even so, I can't believe that any such fictional scenario could actually come to pass. "That can't work in real life. People were there, they know what happened. How can anyone pretend that it didn't?"

He shrugs. "What happened at the Crystal Palace is so far outside their experience that they have no way of really processing it. They have to tell themselves that it was a one-time event, never to be repeated. It's over and done with, everything is back to normal, and there's nothing for them to worry about."

"That's how a child would react."

"Look around. What do you think people whose lives are dedicated to self-indulgence really are? Mature adults?"

He has a point, one that I can't deny. As young as I am in certain ways, I feel ages older than many of the people I see in the streets, men and women who seem intent on partying their lives away.

"No, I suppose not--"

I break off as a woman walks by covered in butterflies. They're so vivid that I need a moment to realize that they aren't real. They're painted on her. Beautiful, multi-colored butterflies seem to flutter over every inch of her skin from the hollow at the base of her throat over the swell of her breasts down the curve of her hips and along her tapered legs. As lovely as they are, they can't conceal the fact that she is entirely nude. Even her sex is adorned with an exquisite white butterfly that appears almost translucent, its wings spreading across her cleft.

I'm still gawking when Ian bursts out laughing. His eyes glisten with amusement. "I take it you didn't know that Carnival is a clothing-optional event?"

"That must be obvious." I answer stiffly, stung by his reminder of my naiveté. It's the inevitable result of my lack of experience but that doesn't make it any easier to accept.

"You may want to brace yourself, sweetheart." His smile steals my breath. It's wild, tempting, blatantly provocative, at once promising pleasure beyond any I have ever known and daring me to surrender myself to it. To him. Since the day we met, Ian has driven me to the heights of throbbing, screaming ecstasy over and over again. Surely, nothing can surpass what I've already experienced with him. Can it?

Holding my gaze, he says, "The night's barely begun."

Chapter Twenty-five

Amelia

The inaugural performance of Sergei's "Medea" is held in a circular open-air theatre erected especially for the occasion in a park near the southern tip of the island. The sun is setting to the west over the harbor as Ian and I arrive. We join the crowd streaming into the amphitheater, all residents of the city, I notice. The array of costumes shouldn't surprise me after our encounter with the butterfly lady but I'm still not quite prepared for the lush displays of pampered flesh on the part of both sexes.

Our presence causes a stir. I don't make the mistake of thinking that I have anything to do with it. People are surprised to see Ian, who rarely attends any sort of social event. In the aftermath of the attack on the Crystal Palace, the power he commands is bound to spark speculation and perhaps even hope. Despite all the bright lights, an undercurrent of fear runs through the city, made worse by the fact that it is suppressed and unspoken.

"No workers?" I ask as we take our seats amid the glittering crowd.

"Carnival is open to all," he says, ignoring the attention we garner. "At least in the streets. Anything else, including events like this, is strictly for the chosen few."

I nod, unsurprised. A society as precariously balanced as this one can't afford the custom common in the ancient and medieval worlds whereby the slaves become the masters once a year. Here everyone has to remember his or her place or the center will not hold. The anarchy that Ian fears truly will be loosed on the world.

Contemplating the city and the forces at work within it, a sense of dread wells up in me without warning. I hear myself murmur, "Turning and turning in the widening gyre, the falcon cannot hear the falconer; things fall apart; the centre cannot hold; mere anarchy is loosed upon the world."

Is this just another random bit of knowledge courtesy of Susannah? It feels more like a warning.

Ian looks surprised but a moment later his expression becomes closed. Apparently, he knows William Yeats' poem envisioning a coming apocalypse as well as I do because he continues where I left off. "The blood-dimmed tide is loosed, and everywhere the ceremony of innocence is drowned."

He takes my hand, turning it over in his own and lightly strokes my palm. "Not a happy prospect for the world. But I have to admit that was my favorite poem when I was a kid." As though he suddenly decides that he is being too serious, or perhaps revealing too much, he adds, "I had a thing for falcons."

My throat is tight as I think of the child he was, caught in the riptide of his parents' hellish marriage. "You should have one now. You could fly it from the top of Pinnacle House."

He laughs. "I hate to think what that would do to the dove population."

I frown as a thought flits through my mind. "Weren't there pigeons in the city--before?" Back when Manhattan and the surrounding boroughs were home to teeming millions who came here to forge better lives for themselves. The remnants of that world exist all around me but they are fading fast, replaced by a strict hierarchy that serves only the fortunate few and leaves everyone else to fight over crumbs, not unlike the once voracious pigeons themselves.

Ian nods. "They shat too much and they weren't as pretty as doves so they were exterminated and replaced."

Just like that, an entire species of bird wiped out on the whim of the privileged elite. In the overall scheme of things, I tell myself it could be much worse. But the fact is I know that it will be if Davos has his way.

The dimming of lights around us distracts me. The ballet is about to begin. Sergei has crafted it around the music of Samuel Barber, a 20th century American composer whose work I know. The first notes of "Medea" are haunting, if also deliberately discordant. I'm drawn quickly into the story of passionate love shattered by wrenching betrayal that is followed by an act of destruction so in violation of the natural order that I can barely stand to watch it play out. Around us, the audience is hushed and rapt, hanging on the final denouement. As Medea takes the lives of her own children to punish her husband for betraying her, I hear more than a few gasps and even some sobs.

Averting my eyes, I discover that Ian isn't watching the events on stage. His gaze is focused only on me. I flush at being the object of such intense attention but I can't look away. I'm trapped, a moth to his flame, with no desire to escape.

"Heavy duty stuff," he murmurs as we rise to leave. "What's your Russian up to?"

Glad of any distraction, I say, "Why don't you ask him? I'd like to go back stage."

For a moment, Ian looks about to refuse but he only shrugs and takes my arm. Sergei is holding court in a tent adjacent to the amphitheater. He smiles warmly when he sees me but an instant later his expression changes.

"Ian Slade," he says as the two men shake hands. It's obvious that Sergei knows who Ian is. They eye each other bluntly, neither giving ground. The male dominance display cloaked in a thin veneer of civility goes on long enough to be tiresome. Finally, each releases his grip and bares his teeth in what only the most innocent would take for smiles.

"Sergei Zharkov," Ian says. "Amelia's told me a great deal about you."

"Really?" An eyebrow rises toward that leonine mane. "She hasn't said a word about you. But then she didn't have to. Her bouts of distraction and emotional turbulence have made it all too clear what sort of man she's involved with."

Ian stiffens, as do I. The wave of anger that rolls off him makes me instantly apprehensive. But after a moment, it unexpectedly eases. This new, buoyant Ian isn't so easy to offend. With a note of amusement, he says, "You like to rattle people, don't you? Yank them out of their comfort zone and confront them. That's what tonight's ballet is about."

Despite himself, Sergei looks impressed but he tries to hide it. With a shrug, he says, "'Medea' is a tempestuous work, lots of sex and violence, well suited to this crowd. That's all."

"I don't think so," Ian counters. "It's about the almost unimaginable violence that can come in response to betrayal. But there's a warning in it as well, isn't there? Ultimately such violence leads to the destruction of innocents. The future is sacrificed and in the end, no one wins."

Reluctantly, Sergei says, "You surprise me, Slade. Isn't violence your trade?"

"The control and containment of it is. Violence is a part of the human condition. Unless we change what it fundamentally means to be human, it will always be with us. The best we can do is channel it in the most positive directions."

"While protecting the innocents?" Sergei asks. He shifts his gaze to me.

Around us the crowd chatters on, intent on throwing off whatever dark forebodings the performance has evoked.

"Always," Ian says. He slips an arm around my waist. "We won't keep you any longer. No doubt there are many others waiting to offer their congratulations."

"No doubt," Sergei murmurs. "But I very much doubt if they have your understanding of what they've just seen." To me, he says, "Be well, Amelia. I hope to see you in class soon."

I assure him that I hope the same. As Ian draws me away, I glance back over my shoulder. Sergei is surrounded by well-wishers vying for his attention. Even so, our eyes meet. In his I see the genuine concern of a friend that does not entirely conceal a hint of longing.

I can't think about that. Ian commands all my attention. Or he does until we leave the grounds of the park and re-enter the streets where Carnival is in full swing. At once, I realize that he wasn't exaggerating when he called it a clothing-optional event. Judging by what I can see around me, Ian and I are overdressed.

Body paint seems to be one of the preferred means of expression. A tall, shapely brunette strolls by sporting a thick green serpent that twines from around her throat over her nude body to cleave her sex and wrap around one thigh. A man passes us wearing only a golden tan and a spray of painted leaves that seem intended not to conceal his genitalia so much as to draw attention to them. My eyes widen a bit when I notice that he is semi-erect.

Ian's hand slides down to cup my hip, his fingers splayed out over my belly. I feel the pressure of them in my groin. A tremor runs through me.

"Carnival is all about license," he says softly. "Letting go of inhibitions. There's something to be said for that, don't you think?"

"In private," I agree. My cheeks flush as I remember a night we shared in my golden bedroom at the estate, not to mention more recent encounters. "But so openly, in the streets?" I can't imagine ever making such a display of myself. Yet I would be a hypocrite if I tried to deny a certain fascination with the sensual spectacle unfolding all around me.

When Ian moves closer and lightly grazes his mouth along the curve of my jaw, a low moan escapes me. I arch my neck, giving him better access. He obliges, trailing a line of fire from the hollow behind my ear to my collarbone. My eyes close as pleasure rushes through me but they open suddenly as his hands cup my breasts. I don't want anyone to see us like this but no one appears to be taking any notice. They're too busy being part of the passing show.

As Ian's thumbs graze over my nipples, an elegant woman with upswept ebony hair and wearing a collar made of multiple strands of pearls walks by. Beneath the collar, a transparent length of black silk creates the illusion of a cloak covering her back. The upper part of her torso is bare. Another length of the black silk falls below her breasts, suspended at two points from the small gold rings that pierce her nipples. She isn't alone. The young, muscular man with her is naked except for the black leather harness stretched tightly over his chest and the length of gold chain that is wrapped around his testicles. A leash is attached to the chain. The lady in black holds the other end.

"Dominatrix," Ian says in a tone that leaves no doubt he is enjoying my shock. "Something I have to admit I've never tried."

I can't imagine Ian ever allowing any woman to dominate him. But I have seen him come apart in my arms often enough to be confident that the acute need building in me is not mine alone. He may be unsurprised by what is going on around us but that doesn't mean he is unaffected.

I have proof of that a moment later when he presses me back against a nearby lamp post, thrusts his thigh between my legs, and says, "You'd look exquisite in those black veils but I wouldn't want your nipples pierced. They're perfect exactly as they are."

Shocked by the mere thought, I answer tartly. "That's good because I would never consider any such thing."

He laughs and wraps an arm around me. My feet barely brush the ground as he strides into the shadows that conceal a nearby alley. In an instant, he strips off his jacket, drapes it over my shoulders, and presses me against a wall. I can feel the roughness of brick along my back even as the jacket protects me from it.

"You're exquisite, Amelia. I want you in every possible way," he says. Without warning, his hand tugs up my dress and slips under it. A grunt of satisfaction escapes him. "You want the same. You're wet, so ready, so hot."

I gasp at his audacity but before I can tell him to stop, the surge of pleasure ignited by his touch overwhelms me. Instinctively, my pelvis arches against his hand. He chuckles softly and strokes me, teasing my clit with the tip of one circling finger. Everything in me quickens. I moan helplessly, The build-up to orgasm is so familiar by now that I have no trouble recognizing it but the sensation is fleeting. Almost as soon as it begins, Ian removes his hand and steps away. As quickly as I have begun to soar, I crash back down again.

I glare at him with embarrassed frustration mingling with bewilderment. Why is he doing this?

He smiles, well aware of my predicament and seemingly amused by it. Only the dark glitter of desire in his eyes hints that his emotions run deeper.

"Touch yourself," he says huskily. "I want to see you make yourself come."

I gap at him in astonishment. He isn't serious, is he? It's not that I've never done what he's demanding. I have but only a little, when I was most desperate for him, and never, ever when anyone else was present. We're in an alley, for heaven's sake! It's bad enough that I allowed myself to forget that even for a moment and now he wants--

"I can't."

His look is implacable. "You can, you will. You need this, Amelia. You know you do. Think how good release will feel."

I can scarcely think of anything else, except-- "What about you?"

"If that's an offer, I have to say no, for now. No one's going to watch you give me head."

"But someone could watch me?"

"No one will see." He moves swiftly, angling his body so that I am blocked from the view of anyone who might glance down the alley.

He takes my hand, guiding it to where his was. I feel my own heat and slickness even as I realize how desperately I need what he is demanding of me. Even so, I'm not really considering doing as he says. Someone could step into the alley at any moment.

At the thought of being discovered in such a compromising position, a spurt of excitement ripples through me. I want to put it down to the carnal atmosphere but I know it's really my own wildness, spurred on by the heat in Ian's eyes and the challenge implicit in the curve of his so-tempting mouth.

"Slip your fingers into your panties," he murmurs. "Imagine that it's me touching you."

I moan at the thought of him doing so. I know his touch so well. My body has been conditioned to respond to it. Even the sound of his voice or the scent of his skin is enough to arouse me. My head falls back against the wall. My eyes close. Slowly, hesitantly, the tip of my finger eases below the lacy edge of my panties...slides a little lower over my bare mound...and finds my clit. I'm shocked by how hot it feels, how swollen and slick. Tentatively, I make a light, circular motion, imagining all the while that it is Ian touching me. His hard, compelling body pressed against mine, his touch circling...pressing lightly at first...,a little harder... A few strokes and I'm struggling not to cry out. I have to stop. But Ian is having none of that.

"You're so beautiful," he says, stepping closer so that I feel the warmth of his breath on my skin. "The most exquisite, sensual, giving woman I've ever known. No one has ever come close to you."

Emboldened by his praise, my finger moves more quickly, circling round and round. Pleasing myself, I am pleasing him. I can hear that in his thickening voice, murmuring to me gently. "That's it, sweetheart. You're close, aren't you? I can smell that sweet, honeyed musk. I'd like to have my tongue on you right now, tasting you, making you come--"

At the word, I do, suddenly and violently in a rush that arches my back and wrings a sob from me. Before I can utter it, Ian is on me, his mouth crushing mine, his tongue thrusting hard and fast. He catches my hand in his, replacing my finger, and drives me onward, extending my orgasm until the world blurs and I slump in his arms, held up only by his strength.

I am at once mortified and stunned by the force of my own release. My only consolation is that I can feel his massive erection pressing against my belly. He is as vulnerable to the passion between us as I am.

When I can stand alone finally, he smiles, smooths the skirt of my dress down, and brushes a light kiss over my tender lips. "Well done, sweetheart."

He slips his jacket from my shoulders and shrugs it on, straightening his cuffs in the process. The very normality of that action--so simple yet intrinsically masculine--stands in stark contrast to my own unbridled behavior. Ian seems unconcerned by what he has just witnessed. He takes my hand and turns to leave the alley.

"Where are we going?" I ask, still too dazed to fathom the erotic turn the night has taken.

His grin is cocky, filled with daring. "To a parade."

Chapter Twenty-six

Amelia

I stand in the curve of Ian's arms, protected by his body from the crowd. Night envelopes the city but the stars are not visible. They are eclipsed by the fireworks bursting overhead and the beams of laser lights dancing across the sky. Throbbing music fills the air. The crowd is singing along, laughing and shouting.

Tremors of shock still ripple through me. I can't believe what I did in the alley any more than I can deny the guilty pleasure that comes from being so daring. I'm beginning to understand the attraction of Carnival. But what I really want is to be alone with Ian, just the two of us together, free from all the complexities of the world and able to concentrate on one another.

I had a taste of that at the beach house but I want more...much more. I want to know him completely and utterly with nothing held back. But for that to happen, I have to get past the rigid self-control that he's imposed on himself for so long. His willingness to put aside his concerns about Davos and actually enjoy himself are evidence that there's been some change in him. I don't know what prompted it but I'm more than willing to take advantage of it all the same.

A deeper, mechanical sound rumbles beneath the revelry, interrupting my thoughts. Something large and heavy is coming toward us but I can't see it yet. For a moment, I'm reminded of the armored vehicles used by the

Municipal Protection Services but no police are in evidence. The city has been turned over to the revelers.

One of the many vendors selling food, drink and souvenirs stops beside us. Ian waves him on but not before I see that he's also offering a wide range of recreational drugs, all in sealed packages bearing the distinctive logo of Cruces Pharmaceuticals. The vendor doesn't have to go far to find customers. The little packages sell even more quickly than the drinks.

I'm relieved that Ian has no interest in them even as I wonder what other surprises he has in store for me. Despite the release I've just experienced, need is building in me again. Being so close to him, vividly aware of his desire, I feel as though I am melting inside.

The rumbling gets stronger, as does the wave of cheers accompanying it. A float comes into view, carrying what looks like an ancient temple. A dozen or more young women are posed against white columns. They all wear elaborate masks with feathered head pieces and nothing else apart from the sheen of gold that covers their naked bodies. As the crowd cheers, the young women toss favors to them. Men and women alike scramble to collect them.

"What are they throwing?" I ask.

"Tokens," Ian says. "Most are good for drinks, drugs, whatever. A few are...worth more."

I turn my head, looking at him over my shoulder. "What are those for?"

He hesitates, then says, "The floats are previews of the private parties that take place during Carnival. A few people will get tokens admitting them to one or another of them."

I could ask what goes on at those private parties but given the appearance of the young women, the answer seems obvious. Another float appears as the cheers swell. Most of the people on it are men, dressed as Roman soldiers holding naked young women captive between them. Several of the men have reached under their tunics, taken out their cocks and are stroking them. More tokens fly through the air. I see two women fighting over one and look away.

The overflow of shocking sensory input is becoming too much. I close my eyes for a moment, only to open them again to the sight of half-a-dozen very large, muscular men naked and wearing the horned heads of bulls. Minotaurs. A gasp escapes me as I realize that one of them has hold of a woman wearing just a few diaphanous veils that conceal nothing. She is standing on one leg with her back to him. He grasps the other leg, pulled up and away from her body at an angle that starkly reveals her bare sex to the crowd.

I realized almost from the moment that I arrived in the city that its elegant, sophisticated veneer overlays a culture of decadence and indulgence that may be unequaled anywhere else. But I'm still unprepared for the full extent of it. Or its effect on me.

Ian draws me closer so that I am standing with my back pressed to his front. The hardness of his erection against my bottom makes my breath quicken. I can't stand still, I have to move. But the moment I begin to sway, brushing the cheeks of my ass along his length, he grasps my hips tightly.

"Behave," he murmurs in my ear.

Now he wants me to behave? Infuriating man. I stop, determined to show that I have at least as much self-control as he does. But the effort is a moment-to-moment struggle and what is passing in front of me doesn't help.

One float follows another to the din of music, the flash of strobe lights, and explosions of pyrotechnics revealing scenes that hint at unbridled license. The frenzy of the crowd mounts. A few more fights break out but most people seem too transfixed by the carnal show to care about much else.

Finally, the last and by far the largest float approaches. It comes in two parts, the first depicting a tableau of naked men and women, all wearing golden masks and standing in what appears to be the interior of an elegant mansion. Until now, the only sex has been simulated or suggested but not here. On this float, the women are openly servicing the men in a variety of ways. One is kneeling to suck the cock of the man standing in front of her. Another is bent over the end of a plush couch being penetrated from behind as several others watch.

Before I can even begin to grasp what I'm seeing, the crowd roars its approval. A chant goes up--"Misrule! Misrule! Misrule!"

The last section of the float passes. All the figures on it are cloaked and hooded, their faces concealed by distinctive masks unique to each of them. I think they're all men but I can't be certain. Their bodies as well as their features are completely hidden.

One in particular catches my eye. Whereas the others wear gilded masks of gold and silver, his alone is red. The face it depicts is harsh with furled brows, empty eyes, a sharp blade of a nose and a mouth open in a ferocious scream.

I tell myself that it is my imagination but he appears to be looking directly at Ian and me, never taking his gaze from us until the float passes completely by and is gone.

The crowd follows behind it, revelers still grasping for tokens, as the music swells and more fireworks burst above us.

"Who are those men?"

"The Lords of Misrule," Ian says. He keeps me tucked close against him as we make our way through the crowd. "Patrons of the parade and of Carnival in general." Glancing down at me, he asks, "Have you seen enough?"

"For a lifetime." I'm beyond shocked, feeling as though my eyes need a good bath along with the rest of me. But at the same time, I'm all too vividly aware of how aroused I've become. Some primal, instinctual part of me is drawn to at least some of what I saw.

"Let's go then," he says. His eyes are dark and compelling as he looks at me. With a smile I can't decipher, he adds, "I have a surprise for you."

I'm not sure how many more of those I can take but I give him my hand. He clasps it and brushes his lips over my knuckles in a slow, gentle caress. A jolt of longing spools from his touch. I feel it in my hot, slick core. The need for him becomes even more urgent.

In the cab that he hails a block or so away from the avenue, he touches me lightly, repeatedly, small caresses on the curve of my cheek, the swell of my lower lip, the hollow at the base of my throat. So innocent compared to what I have just seen yet so provocative.

We are traveling uptown but not to Pinnacle House. As we pull up to the curb, I see a tall stone building in the Art Deco style. Engraved above the entrance are the words, "L'hôtel Perle."

"Why are we here?" I ask as Ian helps me out.

His smile is enigmatic. "You'll see."

His eyes are dark, the pupils dilated. A shiver of apprehension runs through me but I ignore it. I trust Ian, for all that this evening has come as a shock. He must have a good reason for being here.

The lobby is a magnificent display of marble and gilt softened by small forests of potted palms placed to discreetly shield sitting areas. We pass directly through it without stopping at the registration desk. Ian also bypasses the main bank of elevators and instead leads me down a carpeted hallway running off to one side. A small plaque reads: The Towers. Guests Only.

"What is this?" I ask.

"Call it a hotel within a hotel," he says. "For a very private clientele."

I don't understand. Ian owns a luxurious penthouse, a magnificent country estate, and a charming beach house, as well as quite possibly other properties. Yet he's brought me to a hotel?

"Why are we here?"

He presses a button for the elevator that only serves the Towers. "I told you, it's a surprise."

The elevator comes and we step inside. Past the sliding mahogany doors, the elevator resembles a cage with lattice work walls and a domed glass ceiling. Perhaps because I'm so intensely aroused, I find myself thinking suddenly of the golden cage in the Cabinet of Secret Delights. At once, my inner muscles clench.

The doors shut behind us. Ian slips a key card into a slot and we begin to rise. The moment we do, he reaches for me, his hands sliding down my bare arms to close around my wrists. His face is taut, his eyes glittering. I don't think that I've ever seen him quite like this.

"Turn around," he orders. He lifts my arms, stretching them above my head. "Take hold of the bars."

I obey, too aroused by all that has happened to deny him. Even so, I'm unnerved. The metal is cold and hard in my hands, and I have no idea what he intends in the few moments before we reach our floor. I gasp when skirt of my gown is pulled up, exposing my bottom, and start to let go of the bars.

"Don't," Ian warns. His voice rasps in my ear. "I've been hard for you ever since I watched you come in the alley." Before I can gather my breath to respond, his fingers stroke up and around my thigh to skim my red silk panties. "I'm not waiting any longer. Open your legs."

My scattered reason finally reasserts itself. He can't possibly be serious. There's no time and besides, I won't allow it. "No! We could stop at any moment. Someone could see us--"

He reaches to the side, jerks open a panel, and pushes a button. At once, the elevator's ascent comes to a shuddering halt. We are hanging in a steel cage suspended within a shaft in a century-old building. The smell of old stone wafts upward on drafts of cool air from the basement far below. In contrast, Ian feels blazing hot against me. His erection presses against my bottom.

Leaning close, he whispers, "I'm going to fuck you, sweetheart, right here, right now. Try letting go of those bars again and you won't sit down for a week."

What? He can't be serious. This is a game, part of Carnival, nothing more. We're both painfully aroused by our need for each other and the spectacle we've witnessed. But even so--

"Wait--" I begin.

The palm of his hand smacks my ass. I yelp in surprise. The pain is short and sharp, more of a shock than anything else. In its wake, heat spreads from my reddening skin to my core.

Before I can begin to recover, he yanks my panties down around my knees and thrusts his thigh between mine. His arm wraps around my hips, holding me in place. He uses his other hand to free himself. The hot, velvety smooth tip of his cock strokes around my opening and up along my clit, again and again. The pleasure quickly becomes unbearable. A groan breaks from me as I arch back against him, offering myself. Ian grunts in response and gives me what I crave so desperately. With a single thrust, he buries himself in me.

All the breath goes out of my lungs. I cling to the bars of the elevator, struggling to stay upright as he begins driving into me with deep, long thrusts. His teeth grazing the tender skin of my throat, he growls, "Don't ever deny me again."

I'm beyond speech, overwhelmed by disbelief at this game we are suddenly playing and equally by the insidious but irresistible spiral of pleasure that is building in me. I try to fight it but Ian won't allow that. His fingers spread the lips of my sex, finding my clit wet with my own desire. He gives a low groan and begins to stroke me, first slowly, then more quickly until I am writhing against him.

"Ian!" I don't know whether I'm demanding that he stop or begging him not to.

He hears me or he doesn't, it hardly matters because he continues remorselessly driving into me, holding me captive to his will as the pressure builds and builds inside me beyond bearing. Whether because of pride or anger I resist my inevitable surrender to him, fighting to hold it off but the effort is useless. This is Ian, and whether I want to admit it or not, he is as much the master of my body as my heart.

I'm sobbing when I come, scarcely able to breathe, all the pent up arousal and frustration of the past hours surging together to shred me. I gasp, moaning his name, as Ian tightens his hold. He follows quickly, spurting into me.

For long moments, our bodies are locked together. I can feel his heart pounding in unison with mine. The sense of being one with him brings a piercing joy but it doesn't last. Too soon he lets me go.

Unable to stand on my own, I slide to the floor, my breasts heaving and my legs splayed out in front of me. My gown is still bunched up around my waist, my panties twisted around my knees. I feel shattered.

By contrast, Ian appears cool and collected as he tucks his cock back into his trousers and zips up. Without a glance in my direction, he presses the button to restart the elevator.

Chapter Twenty-seven

Amelia

My legs are still quivering as Ian guides me from the elevator to the double doors of a suite, one of a very few that take up the top floor of the hotel. We've encountered no one else, for which I can only be grateful. My gown is back in place as are my panties. I've even managed to smooth my hair a little but I'm not kidding myself. I must look the same way I feel--extremely well fucked.

Ian unlocks the door and steps aside for me to enter. I hesitate before doing so. A part of me says that this is the moment to leave. Whatever explains his behavior, being roughly fucked in an elevator is as far as I should go. We can talk about what's driving the man I love tomorrow in the light of day and without the temptations of Carnival. But another part of me rejects the very idea of leaving him.

"Don't ever deny me again." Those words he spoke in the elevator are a complete contradiction of the need he has had from the very beginning of our relationship to be certain that I can make my own choices and exercise my own will. Now he suddenly wants to take away my ability to say 'no'? That doesn't fit and more than anything else, it tells me that something hasn't merely changed in him. Something is wrong.

When we came back together after the anguishing days and nights apart, I promised myself that we would face his demons together. It seems as though I may finally get that opportunity. I'd be lying if I didn't admit to feeling more than a little anxious at any such possibility. But I also have to admit that Ian has awakened a wantonness in me beyond even what I have experienced before. If I am to truly understand myself, I can't turn away from it. Any more than I can turn away from him.

Putting aside my trepidation, I step over the threshold into the room. As soon as I do, I have the sensation of stepping back in time to another era. The walls are covered in rich burgundy brocade, the same color picked up by the Oriental rug covering the floor. A dark wood couch upholstered in tufted burgundy velvet and matching chairs face the marble fireplace that now, in late spring is filled with flowers whose heavy scent fills the room. The large circular table on a pedestal stands under a jet black crystal chandelier near French doors that lead out onto a balcony. Gold silk drapes capped by tasseled valences frame the windows. The overall effect is of opulent elegance with just a touch of upscale bordello.

As I study the room, Ian follows me in. He goes directly to a large cabinet against one wall and opens it to reveal a fully stocked bar. "Would you like a drink?"

I hesitate but then remember that what little alcohol I've had in the past has had a soothing effect. I could certainly use that now. "Yes, please."

He takes a bottle of champagne from a small wine chiller fitted into the cabinet, opens it expertly, and fills two crystal flutes half-way. Having crossed the room to where I am still standing, he hands one to me before raising his own.

"To Carnival," he says, his eyes never leaving mine.

The wine is cool and crisp. I drink it quickly, not having realized how thirsty I was.

"Come and sit down," Ian says. I think he means on the couch but he leads me instead to the round table under the chandelier. He puts his hands on my waist and lifts me easily, setting me on it, then returns to the bar for the champagne bottle.

When our glasses are refilled, he moves closer and slowly strokes a finger along the curve of my cheek. "You are so beautiful," he murmurs. "Sometimes all I want to do is look at you."

That's nice but I have the distinct impression that now is not one of those times. Nervously, I take another sip of champagne and try to decipher his mood.

"What happened at the Council meeting?" I ask. That seems to be the origin of whatever it is that's driving him. He was different when he came back from there.

He lifts an eyebrow at my return to a topic so out of keeping with our sensual surroundings. "I told you, nothing. It was for show."

"But you're no longer as concerned about Davos as you were."

Something flickers behind his eyes, a hint of uncertainty? It's gone too quickly for me to be sure. "I'll deal with him in my own time. But now it's Carnival and all I'm interested in is you."

A tremor of excitement runs through me. I have some experience with what it means to be the focus of Ian's concentrated attention.

He moves closer, his teeth lightly grazing my jaw. Incredibly after the orgasm I experienced in the elevator, my body clenches. My need for him is becoming insatiable.

Softly, he says, "I'd like you to do something for me."

I look up at him through my lashes. The brooding hunger in his gaze exerts a dark pull on my own libido. "What's that?"

"Undress."

My cheeks flame, an absurd reaction given that he has seen and touched every inch of me. But I've never before deliberately, purposefully set out to tantalize him. Well, maybe a little...or more... But never like this, when I can't grasp what is driving him.

"You have a beautiful body," he says. "I enjoy seeing it revealed."

I can't help thinking that he got an eyeful in the elevator. But neither can I deny the challenge implicit in his tone--at once sensuous and slightly mocking. With a start, I realize that he's daring me to do this.

Two can play this game. I swallow the rest of my champagne, welcoming even the false courage it brings, and say, "On one condition."

He arches an eyebrow. "What's that?"

"You can look but you can't touch." I'm not entirely certain why I want this but it gives me at least some semblance of control and that feels important under the circumstances.

"Are you sure that's what you want?" He looks at once surprised and chagrinned, which only strengthens my resolve.

"Until I say otherwise. Agreed?"

Slowly, not taking his eyes from me, Ian nods. "Agreed." He walks over to one of the chairs near the fireplace, turns it to face me, and sits down, crossing his long legs so that the ankle of one rests on the opposite knee. A long finger strokes his upper lip lightly.

"Whenever you're ready," he says with a smile.

From beyond the French doors, I hear music. The sound is hot, sensuous, a throbbing in the blood. I remember what Ian said about the private parties being held in the city as flashes from the parade dart through my mind. Slowly, I slide off the table.

The champagne helps but it's the music coupled with Ian's nearness that quells my inhibitions. I slide one strap of my gown off my shoulder, followed by the other. The fitted bodice slips a little, resting on the crest of my pebble hard nipples. My hips sway irresistibly to the beat of the music. With a start, I realize that I'm getting into this, enjoying it. Holding Ian's gaze, I reach around to the zipper that begins inches below the dip of my waist. Slowly, I ease it down over my derriere. As I do, I turn so that my back is to him. A soft gasp escapes me. I'm facing a large mirror in a gilded frame. In it, I can see both myself and him.

His features are taut, his eyes hooded. I have the impression that he is fighting the urge to take hold of me at once, regardless of the promise I wrung from him.

A heady sense of my own power sweeps over me and with it comes a wave of daring. I decide that my panties, which until now have merely been pushed aside or down, deserve better appreciation. They leave the cheeks of my ass bare below a red bow that makes me look like a present waiting to be unwrapped. I chose them with Ian in mind but I definitely didn't expect him to be seeing them quite like this. In the mirror, his hands clench. He looks as though he regrets agreeing to my terms.

Emboldened, I let the beaded gown slide the rest of the way down my body and step out of it. I'm wearing only the thong, black fishnet thigh highs with a band of red lace at the top, the red stilettos, and my mask.

I lift my hands to remove it but Ian stops me. "Leave it on. Take off the panties."

I flush but do as he says, easing them down first one leg, then the other, and step out of them. The music is growing in intensity, urging me on. When the lacy scrap has joined my gown on the floor, Ian stands and comes toward me. He stops a few feet away. Our eyes meet in the mirror.

"I have a gift for you," he says. "But I want to put it on you myself. That involves touching."

He draws an object from the pocket of his jacket but keeps it cupped in his palm. I catch the glint of gold, nothing more.

Unable to look away from him, I nod permission.

He opens his palm to reveal an oblong gold ring about the length of my thumb. At the top is a carving of a man's hands. Slim black elastic bands tangle from the top and base of the ring.

Before I can object, he moves close behind me. His long, skilled fingers splay across my abdomen and slip lower to spread the outer lips of my sex. He nestles the ring between them, nudging them further apart. A shudder runs through me at the intimacy of his touch.

When he removes his hand, the sides of the oblong ring keep me stretched open while the center displays my delicate inner labia and clit. The weight of the cool, smooth metal there is startling. Ian reaches behind me to secure the black bands. His voice is low and roughened as he says, "Look at yourself, Amelia. See yourself as I see you."

I do and what I see shocks me. I am...wanton. My eyes are smoky with need, my lips are swollen, my nipples are peaked and aching for his touch. Between my legs, where his seed mingles with my own juices, the gold ring glistens. At its center, framed by it, my clit and delicate inner lips are at once bound and fully exposed.

My first instinct is that it's too much. I don't want to see myself like this, an entirely carnal creature on display. But the touch of Ian's lips along the back of my neck distracts me from any objection. Before I realize what he intends, he removes my mask so that I am fully bared to myself.

But only for an instant. Even as I stare at the woman in the gilded mirror, Ian lowers a narrow length of red silk in front of my eyes and ties it in place. My hands fly to it as the world darkens.

"Easy," he says. "You'll feel more this way."

More? I can't. I won't survive it. But it seems that I have no choice. He lifts me effortlessly and carries me across the room, settling me in a large chair that feels like the one he just occupied. He leaves me for a moment. I hear a drawer opening. When he returns he says, "I've wanted to see you like this from the first moment we met."

Oh. How is that exactly? Naked and blindfolded, intimately adorned for his pleasure...

Oh! Something coiled and smooth wraps around my ankle. It feels like...rope? Where did that come from?

Swiftly, before I can begin to process what is happening, Ian binds my left wrist to my left ankle and does the same on my right side. When he is done, he lifts me slightly and repositions me in the chair. His hands press against my knees, spreading me wide. My cheeks flame below the blindfold as I realize that I'm trussed up, my sex adorned and exposed to him, unable to resist in any way.

"Ian...?" My voice is unnaturally high, made so by shock and arousal that mounts so swiftly as to be almost painful.

"*Shhhh*," he murmurs. The tip of his finger flicks my clit, swollen with need and made all the more sensitive by the weight of the gold band encaging it.

I give a soft wail as my head falls back. I know now what he intends. I want it but... When his tongue replaces his finger, every muscle in my body jerks in response. Or tries to. Bound as I am, I can't move. Blindfolded, my sense of touch is acutely heightened. With the ring holding me open for him, both his hands are free to roam where they will. He slides them under my ass, squeezing my cheeks as he pulls me to him. For long, torturous minutes, he keeps up a delicate assault on my clit, his tongue circling, stroking, applying less pressure, then more. At the same time, he slips a finger into the cleft of my ass and finds the small, tight opening there.

"Ian...don't..." My half-hearted objection turns into a gasp when he latches his mouth onto my clit and sucks hard. The contrast between the delicate torment of his tongue and this rougher, even more demanding caress is too much. I cry out helplessly as a dark, relentless wave of pleasure builds in me. An instant later it explodes with terrifying power, hurtling me into an orgasm so intense that I'm afraid I'll lose consciousness. I don't want to because I don't want to miss a moment of this...whatever this is. Ian's dominance and desire draw a response from me that I didn't know I was capable of giving.

But he isn't finished, not at all. As though driven by my helplessness, he gives me no chance to recover before resuming his sweet torment. I am spiraling upward again, another terrifyingly powerful orgasm building in me when he suddenly thrusts a finger slick with my own juices into my puckered opening. The shock of that intrusion tips me over the edge. I come screaming his name as my consciousness shatters.

When I'm next aware, I'm still in the chair and still trussed but the blindfold is off. Ian is holding me in his arms. Surrounded by the comfort of his strength, I take a ragged breath, inhaling the scent of my own body, of sex, and of him.

"So good, baby." He grasps my chin, raising it so that I have no choice but to meet his gaze. A hard smile curves his mouth. "You're exhausted, aren't you?"

Numbly, I nod.

He unties me, dropping feather light kisses on my ankles and wrists as each is freed. I notice absently that the rope he used is red, like my costume for Carnival. He's planned this all out. I can only wonder what else he intends.

When the ropes are gone, he stands easily and carries me across the room, through a set of double doors and into an immense bathroom dominated by an oversized spa tub that is already filling as we enter. As it does, Ian lowers me onto a padded bench and gently removes my shoes. The thigh highs follow, each one peeled down my leg inch by inch and over the arch of my foot. When he's done, he straightens and quickly strips off his clothes.

I swallow with difficulty, helpless to do anything but watch him. He looks like ancient Greek statues I've seen but far better endowed. His broad shoulders sweep down his long torso to narrow hips defined by the perfect V so aptly called the Adonis line. The muscles of his flat abdomen flex as he moves. Naked, he lifts me in his arms again and steps with me into the tub.

The hot water stings at first but it quickly becomes soothing. The stiffness in my body eases. My eyes drift closed.

"Better?" he asks. He is holding me in front of him, my back resting against his chest. As I nod, he anchors his feet around my ankles and pulls them apart, opening my legs and spreading them wide. "Just relax," he says. "Let me take care of you."

My murmured response turns into a soft gasp when I realize that he's positioned me so that a jet of water spurts against my sex, still exposed by the gold ring. He cups my breasts in his roughened palms and squeezes lightly. I shift on him, feeling his erection prodding my bottom. All thought of needing rest evaporates.

Catching each of my engorged nipples between a thumb and forefinger, he pulls and tugs lightly. The sensation rockets straight to my groin, heightened by the pulsations of water striking my swollen, hyper-sensitive clit. Together they bring me to the edge and hold me suspended there. I try to close my legs but Ian won't allow it. He slides a hand behind me and slips two fingers into my opening, thrusting slowly and rhythmically.

"Your cunt fits me like a hot, tight glove," he croons in my ear. "So wet, so good."

I stiffen. He's never used that word with me before. I know that some people think nothing of it but for others it remains deeply offensive. For me, it's simply confusing. Why here? Why now? My sense that something is wrong grows stronger but before I can focus on it, he finds the ultra-sensitive spot inside me and increases the tempo of his strokes. The muscles in my belly spasm. Only Ian's powerful body supporting mine keeps me from slumping under the water as yet another orgasm hits me.

"I wonder how many times I can make you come," he muses as he removes his fingers and lightly kisses the lobe of my ear. His next words send a shiver of mingled shock and excitement through me. "Let's find out, shall we?"

Chapter Twenty-eight

Ian

*A*melia trembles in my arms. She must be wrecked or close to it but I don't even consider stopping. Distantly, I know that something's wrong with me. I just can't manage to care. Nothing matters except the burning, relentless hunger for her that consumes every ounce of reason that I possess and turns it to ash. I want her, all of her, in every possible way, endlessly. Before I'm done, there won't be a shred of doubt in her mind that she belongs utterly and irrevocably to me.

But I meant what I said to her earlier, I take very good care of what's mine. I don't question my need to soothe and pamper her any more than I do my right to fuck her where, when, and how I choose. Right now she needs the first but afterward--

I squirt body wash into my hands and begin rubbing it over her starting with her long, slender neck. It's so delicate, like the rest of her. She has a dancer's body, willowy and slim except for her breasts, which are just a little large for her frame. I smile, thinking how much I adore her breasts. I imagine my cock sliding between them and bite back a groan.

"How does that feel, baby?" I ask.

"Good," she murmurs. She's struggling to keep her eyes open but it's a losing battle. A little sigh escapes her as she surrenders to my ministrations.

I could keep this up all night, savoring the sight and feel of her beautiful body, but the need to fuck her is too urgent. Reluctantly, I tear my hands from her and wash myself. When I'm done, I lift her from the water, wrap her in a warmed bath sheet and pat her dry. I make a point of touching every inch of her, partly because I enjoy doing so but also because I want her to understand how completely she is mine. Her eyes flutter open as I untie the gold labia ring and set it aside. The look that she gives me suggests that she isn't as tired as I thought.

I knot a smaller towel around my hips and pluck a robe off the back of the bathroom door. It's little more than a froth of black lace that's enticing against the creaminess of Amelia's skin. She slides it on with an all-over blush that's delightful.

Gazing at her, I have to remind myself that patience can be its own reward.

Taking her hand, I say, "Let's get some food into you, baby. The night's still young and I don't want you flagging."

The hotel staff has followed my instructions to the letter. In the small frig in the bar are plates of high energy foods--roasted nuts, slivers of whole grain bread, slices of smoked salmon and trout, fruits, and bite-sized bits of dark chocolate. I bring them to the round table along with another bottle of champagne.

Amelia hesitates when I hold out a chair for her. "You must be hungry," I say softly, urging her to sit. She does so after a moment but not without a wary glance in my direction.

I can't help smiling. She looks adorable with her erect nipples peeking through the black lace robe, her skin rosy from the bath, her lips swollen, and her eyes heavy-lidded in the aftermath of multiple orgasms. I uncork a fresh bottle of champagne and fill our glasses. I'm pacing myself but I want her nice and relaxed for what's coming next.

Before I sit down, I go over to the balcony doors and open them. The sounds of sensual revelry spill into the room on the night air. As I join Amelia, the sharp, desperate cry of a woman rises above the wail of a sax.

She stiffens and takes a quick breath. Without looking at me, she asks, "How long does this go on?"

"Carnival? This is just the first night. There are three more to come." At her flash of alarm, I barely hold back a laugh.

"Isn't that...excessive?" she asks, flushing. "It can't be good for people to--"

I top off her glass while she's speaking. "To what? Eat, drink, and be merry while fucking like animals? Think of it as an outlet for impulses that could be a lot more destructive if they weren't released from time to time."

She looks up at me through the fringe of her lashes. Her eyes are smoky and unreadable. It bugs the hell out of me that I don't know what she's thinking.

"I'm surprised that you're so cavalier about it all," she says, "especially in the light of what's happened."

"I'm realistic," I say, correcting her. Before she can reply, I gesture at the food on her plate. "Enough talk. Eat."

I can see how conflicted she is but I'm also fully aware that she hasn't asked to leave. That bothers me on some level I can't quite grasp but at the same time I'd glad of it. I'm pushing her hard and it's only going to get more intense. She should be walking out the door but instead she's sticking with me. I can't help but wonder why. I only know that I don't deserve it.

Amelia lifts a ripe red strawberry to her lips and sucks on it before taking a bite. Watching her, I lose track of whatever it was that I was thinking. The next half-hour or so passes in a blur. We eat and I keep the champagne flowing. Whatever I say, I must make some kind of sense but damned if I know how. All I'm aware of is Amelia, the tilt of her head, the curve of her mouth, the glimpses of her body through the black lace. The way my cock reacts, I'd think that I hadn't had her in days instead of just a short time ago.

I hadn't meant for that to happen in the elevator. I'd just intended to tease her but seeing her come in the alley shot my self-control to hell. Even now, it's all I can do to wait until I'm satisfied that she's eaten enough before I push my chair back and hold out my hand.

"Come."

Her gaze narrows. She looks as though she's trying to decide whether or not to indulge me. Not quite what I'm going for. What I want is her obedience but I'll settle for what I can get--for the moment.

She stands, gathering the lace robe around her and puts her hand in mine. At her touch, a spurt of raw possessiveness burns through me. I pull her closer and draw her out onto the balcony.

It's well past midnight but Carnival is only getting started. Crowds are in the streets--dancing, singing, fucking, whatever. We're too high up to make out the details, which is just as well. As shocked as Amelia was earlier, I can't imagine how she'd react now that the serious debauchery is underway.

Speaking of--

I put her in front of me so that she's pressed against the wrought iron balcony railing with her back against my chest. With one hand, I clasp her hip, holding her in place. With the other, I reach around and undo the belt of her robe. As it falls open, she stiffens and turns her head to look at me.

"Relax," I tell her. No one can see us." I had the foresight to close the balcony doors behind us, blocking out the light from the black crystal chandelier. We're standing in shadows but with a clear view of the building on the other side of the street.

The floor-to-ceiling windows of an apartment directly opposite us are lit up, providing a clear view of the party that's going on inside. It's almost like watching a holo-vid except it's real. An orgy is underway with all the usual variety available at any such event. Front and center, framed by one of the largest windows, a woman is servicing two men. An appreciative audience has gathered around them, cheering and urging them on.

Amelia's quick inhalation of breath turns into a shocked gasp when I lift the hem of her robe and stroke a hand between her thighs, finding her soft, wet cleft.

"Something bothering you, sweetheart?" I ask innocently.

The woman across the way is writhing as though she's loving it but I suspect that it's more a case of her being a good actress. A worker, probably, hoping to move up by acquiring the right patron. It's happened more than anyone wants to admit. Half or more of the elite families in the city count such women in their genealogy. High end escorts, courtesans, mistresses, whatever the politically correct term is. I prefer to think of them as ladies with initiative, able to bend a corrupt system to their own ends.

I include my father's forbearers in that. We Slades are a handsome bunch thanks in large measure to women who made a living with their bodies before becoming doyennes of the Junior League and the country club.

"You wanted me to see this, didn't you?" Amelia says. Her voice is soft and feathery, due in no small part to the finger I've eased into her cunt, stroking her inner walls.

"See what, sweetheart?"

She shakes her head impatiently. "You know perfectly well what. Across the street."

I laugh and add another finger. She's so wet and hot, absolutely perfect. My cock is rock hard under the towel still wrapped around my hips. It's raring to go. But not quite yet. First, I want her overwhelmed with need, too far gone to resist what I'll demand from her when we go back inside.

"That woman...those men--" She lets out a moan and clenches around me.

"What are they doing, baby? Tell me."

"They're...using her."

Now that's interesting and more than a little gratifying. She's aroused, her body can't hide that. But at the same time, she clearly disapproves of the impersonal, objectified fucking that she's witnessing.

"The lady had plenty of options tonight if she wanted them," I say, shrugging. "She knew what she was signing up for. But that kind of scene definitely isn't for everyone." Bending closer, I suck the lobe of her ear into my mouth and bite just hard enough to wring a soft yelp from her. "You, for instance," I say as I remove my fingers and toss the towel aside. A moment later, the head of my cock is pressing into her, just the first inch or so.

"Ian--" She's breathing hard, leaning back to take more of me. The lips of her sex are warm and wet, clasping me.

A powerful tremor runs up my spine. Harshly, I say, "You're mine, Amelia. Admit it. I'm the only man you want fucking you."

I'm taking a chance. Her ability to say 'no' to me is essential to our relationship. Without that evidence of her own free will, I wouldn't be able to touch her and still live with myself. But at the same time, I want her to admit who owns her. Screwed up, I know, but that's how it is.

She's silent long enough for my heart to constrict. Finally, after what seems like forever, her head droops, exposing the vulnerable back of her neck below her upswept hair. I have the sudden sense that she's trembling on the brink of telling me something. But when she speaks, she says only, "You are, Ian. The only man for me."

It's enough. Her honesty is more than I deserve but exactly what I need. Driven by it, I surge into her, bending her forward over the railing and thrusting into her. Across the street, the orgy is reaching its peak but it's got nothing on us. Amelia's urgent cries spur me onward. I want to be deeper in her than I've ever been, possessing her utterly. I want her to feel me in every cell of her being. To recognize me as the other part of herself, the only man she can ever belong to.

The city and the night throb with carnal energy but I'm hardly aware of it any more. Only Amelia exists, only she matters. Nothing in my life has equipped me to deal with the emotions she unleashes. But at the same time she makes me feel more complete than I would ever have thought possible.

We come together in an explosive release that rocks me to the core. It's all I can do to hold onto her as I spurt again and again into her sweet, welcoming body. My satisfaction is savage and primal if far from complete. If it takes all night, I want her overflowing with my come, marked by my scent, mine irrevocably and forever.

Chapter Twenty-nine

Amelia

A heavy languor weighs my limbs as Ian carries me back into the suite. By all rights, I should be exhausted yet incredibly my body is still aroused. I can't help but wonder what is happening to me. With all that Ian and I have shared in the past, I've never been this insatiable.

Tonight, for the first time, I find the power he has over me frightening. I've become lost in him so easily, slave to the forces he unleashes. Even in the grip of ecstasy, I can't think of anything other than pleasing him.

He's doing this to me deliberately. I'm certain of that but I don't know why. Has he set out to prove his dominance and my own willingness to submit? Or is something else driving him? How does Davos and the Council meeting fit into all of this, as I'm sure it does? What has happened to banish his concerns and strip him of all restraint?

I can only wonder, especially about the latter, as with quick, long strides, he takes me directly into the bedroom. It's in the same opulent style as the antechamber, the walls covered in burgundy silk that glows warmly in the light cast by crystal chandeliers suspended from the coffered ceiling. The bed itself is massive, framed in dark mahogany with a box canopy in which lengths of tufted gold silk have been woven. At its foot is a red velvet settee. Ian sits down there, holding me on his lap. He strokes me gently through the black lace robe that still hangs open. His touch is light, tantalizing, and unmistakably proprietary.

"Are you all right, baby?" he asks softly.

My head is tucked against his shoulder, my knees bent and my legs drawn up. I'm surrounded by his strength, protected and cherished. It would be so easy to succumb to that but for the growing need I feel to right the balance between us. So far, the initiative has been entirely his. It's time for that to change.

I straighten and lightly brush my lips along the curve of his jaw. "Truthfully, I'm a little overwhelmed at the moment. This is turning out to be quite a night."

"It's Carnival," he says with a grin. "Anything goes."

"Really, anything?"

"Absolutely, sweetheart, no limits."

I struggle to repress a smile. "Well, in that case--" Taking him by surprise, I slip from his lap to the floor covered by a thick Aubusson carpet and sit back on my heels. Naked, sprawled on the settee, Ian is a glorious sight. Even after the climax we shared on the balcony, his cock is semi-erect. The man's stamina is truly impressive.

I wiggle closer and put my hands on his knees, urging them further apart. He tenses and stares at me, his eyes heavy-lidded and dark with the smoke of barely banked fires.

"Amelia...?"

"Anything goes," I remind him. "Isn't that what you said?"

Before he can reply, I move between his legs, lower my head, and stroke the tip of my tongue around the velvety smooth crest of his cock. He tastes delicious, a combination of my own juices and the traces of his come. Immediately, I want more. Feeling very daring, I suck the first few inches of him into my mouth. Within moments, he's swelling, becoming longer and thicker. Gratified, I suck harder, taking more of him. My tongue finds the sensitive ridge under his crest and flicks back and forth.

Ian gives a muffled curse and drives his hands into my hair. He holds my head still and lifts his hips, thrusting deeper into my mouth so that his cock brushes the back of my throat. As he pulls out, he says, "Is this what you want, baby, me inside you like this?" As though in emphasis, he thrusts again, even deeper this time. For a moment, I can't breathe. The sensation is at once terrifying and darkly arousing. A part of me that I don't want to acknowledge responds to that. But another, and at least for the moment larger part, rebels.

Carefully but deliberately, I let him feel my teeth. He stills at once, smart man that he is. A low, reluctant laugh breaks from him. "We could be at an impasse here, sweetheart," he says.

I let him go, rock back on my heels, and smile at him. "I hope not. You taste delicious."

His gaze narrows. He looks at me speculatively. "And you want more?"

"I do, yes."

"Good, so do I, but we do it my way." When I frown, he laughs. "Trust me, if you want this, you'll like what I have in mind even more."

I'm intrigued. Whatever can he mean?

Ian stands, drawing me up with him. Bending slightly, he tucks an arm under my knees, lifts me, and carries me over to the bed. Before he lays me down, he strips off the counterpane, tossing it onto the floor. The sheets are a dark burgundy red, cool and smooth against my heated skin.

To my surprise, he positions me across the width rather than the length of the bed so that my head hangs over the edge, both resting in and supported by the palm of his hand. I'm not uncomfortable, just startled.

"Remember you wanted this," he says in the moment before he nudges the smooth, hot tip of his cock against my mouth. "And we can stop at any time." His voice reverberates in me.

My lips part. He slips into over my tongue and deeper. In this position, he has a straight path down my throat. As though in answer to my yearning, he says, "Take me, sweetheart. All of me."

I obey without hesitation. Above me, his face is taut with need, his hips pistoning as he moves into me slowly and carefully. A combination of multiple orgasms, more champagne than I've ever had before, and the effect of Ian himself leaves me utterly relaxed.

Instinctively, I feel a need to swallow. As the muscles of my throat begin to ripple around him, he grunts with pleasure. "Good, so fucking good."

He strokes a hand down my body to the apex of my thighs, parts the lips of my sex, and teases my swollen clit with his thumb. A white-hot frenzy ignites in me. My muscles contract, squeezing him even as he keeps up his delicious torment. Pleasuring Ian as I am, even as he plays my body so expertly, sends all my senses into a swift upward spiral toward release. I can't hold back, can't deny him anything... The orgasm that hits me is sudden and remorseless.

As it seizes me, Ian cries out, shouting my name as he comes in thick, hot spurts jetting down my throat. I clench around him, holding him a prisoner to my own desires and take all he gives. Above me, I see him, his head thrown back, eyes closed in ecstasy, as the climax I've brought him to rocks him to the core.

My body sags. I am suddenly, overwhelmingly exhausted. Dimly, I'm aware of Ian withdrawing. With care, he straightens me on the bed and joins me there. My last thought before sleep claims me is that I don't know whether to be more delighted or afraid of what has changed in him.

∞ ∞ ∞

I wake some unknown time later. It's still fully dark, or at least as dark as it ever is in the city. I miss the stars so visible at the estate. Dimly, I think that perhaps Ian and I should return there but I won't go without him and I know that he won't leave the city until Davos is no longer a danger.

The curtains are open across the tall bedroom windows. I can see the apartment on the other side of the street. The orgy has wound down, only a few bodies visible where they lie slumped and asleep. Music still plays in the distance but it's much quieter than it was.

Slipping from the bed, I turn to look at Ian. Asleep, he looks younger and disarmingly innocent. I can't begin to put that together with the man I've experienced over the past few hours. Instead of trying, I find the bathroom and consider taking a shower but the effort is beyond me. With a start I realize that I'm still wearing the black lace robe. It hangs open, revealing my painfully hard nipples and bare, swollen slit.

I clean up, then belt the rope around me and go back into the bedroom. Ian is still asleep. For a few moments, I stand beside the bed, trying to decide what to do. I'm so precariously balanced on the edge between exhaustion and arousal that I doubt I will be able to go back to sleep. But neither do I have the strength to do much of anything else.

Finally, I sit down on the soft carpet with my back against the settee and stare off into space, struggling to make sense of what has happened. For the first time, I notice the full length mirror in a curved wooden frame opposite me but I avert my eyes from it. I don't need to see again how unraveled he has made me.

In that dark hour of the night with my calm, reasoned self hanging by a thread, my thoughts drift to Susannah. I'm not like her, to be handled like spun glass, nor would I want to be. She was strong in her own way but I'm stronger still, just as she intended. Yet I can't help the pain that twists through me at the thought of how gently Ian treated her. She brought out the noblest and most honorable aspects of his nature whereas I--

I don't really know what I am to him. At the beach house, he was open, honest, sharing more of himself than he ever has before. But tonight... Tonight he has simply overwhelmed me.

Unraveling as I am, it's perhaps no surprise that a tear slips down my cheek, followed swiftly by another. I brush them away impatiently. I'm as much a party to everything that has happened between us as he is. If I feel confused and dazed by the results, that's for me to deal with. I know what it is to be truly helpless. I am not now nor do I ever intend to be that way again.

Even so, I haven't moved when, a short time later, Ian awakes as though drawn by some sense of the clamor in my mind. As soon as he sees me, he leaves the bed and comes over to me. Bending down, he takes my chin in his hand and compels me to meet his gaze.

"What's wrong?" he asks.

I shrug. "Nothing, I just can't sleep."

A wry smile plays across his mouth. "So much for my manly prowess."

I give a small, hiccupping laugh. "Don't blame yourself. I'm sure you did your best."

He winces. "Talk about damning with faint praise." His long finger strokes my jaw. "Seriously, are you okay?"

"Of course I am. Why wouldn't I be?"

A flicker of something--regret, concern?--darts behind his eyes. "I've pushed you hard."

"You haven't done anything that I haven't let you do. And enjoyed."

My honesty takes him by surprise. For a moment, he looks uncertain but that vanishes as he says, "That's good because I'm not done yet."

Oh....

"Let me guess," he says as he sits down beside me, his long legs stretched out in front of him, our bare thighs brushing. I glimpse us in the mirror and am startled by how right we look together, at once comfortable and intimate.

"You've got a thousand thoughts ricocheting around in your head," he says, "and you can't make sense of any of them. You're confused, ragged, and all you want is to let go, blank it all out, and just feel."

I stare at him in amazement. "How can you possibly know that?"

He runs a hand over his face shadowed by soft stubble and says, "Because I feel the same way, baby. I don't know what's happening to me...to us but I do know that when I'm balls deep inside you, nothing else matters. You're the calm at the center of my universe. The one place where I really belong."

My mouth drops open. We're surrounded by the heat and smell of raw, unbridled sex. His language is crude, his handling of me even more so. And yet--

I can't help it, I laugh. At the sound, he raises a brow. "What?"

"I'm sorry," I say, trying to stop but not quite succeeding. "There's got to be something wrong with me. I think what you just said is romantic."

He stares at me for a moment before giving me a smile that steals what little breath I have left. "What did I tell you, baby? We're perfect together."

He slips a hand under my robe and strokes my back in a gesture that, especially for the circumstances, is oddly soothing. His eyes gleam with the sheen of gold as he says, "I want to strip you bare, no defenses, no limits, nothing between us except exactly who we are."

The thought is daunting. As new as I am to the world, I know that true intimacy is exceedingly rare. Everyone wears masks. We reveal ourselves only in guises suitable to the ever-shifting circumstances. Even when we look in the mirror, we see not our real self but a mere reflection of what we show to the world.

I want more with Ian. I crave it desperately.

But I can't lie to myself. He is a man of fierce will and strength who bears the scars of an old, unhealed wound. What he refers to as his demons still exist. If I agree to what he wants, will I regret it? Or is this finally the chance for us to face what haunts him together--and defeat it?

Not taking my eyes from him, I touch my mouth to his. His sculpted lips are unexpectedly soft yet firm. His scent and taste envelop me. A tremor runs through him, filling me with wonder at the effect I have on this proud, strong, yet vulnerable man. His breath becomes mine. On a thread of sound, I murmur, "I want that, too."

Chapter Thirty

Amelia

re you sure?' Ian asks.

I can't tell whether he is more pleased or concerned by my response. Slowly, ignoring the frantic beating of my heart, I nod.

His eyes never leave mine as he rises and holds out his hand. When I take it, he draws me up to stand beside him.

"I picked this suite for a reason," he says.

At my quizzical look, he smiles and leads me across the room to a set of double doors. When he opens them, I see beyond into what must be intended as a dressing room. Every surface--the walls of built-in closets and cabinets, the ceiling, even the fluted pilasters that define the space is mirrored. Even the floor is covered by a soft reflective material, as I discover when we step inside. I feel as though I have walked into a diamond.

I stare at our images reflected over and over, more times than I can count, and from every angle. When he slips the black lace robe from me, we are both naked. The contrast between our bodies could not be more obvious. Mine has been honed by dance, leaving me very fit. But beside him I look soft and yielding. Whereas he... he is simply magnificent, big and hard and obviously once again more than ready for me.

"Nothing hidden," Ian says softly. "No secrets. No limits."

My stomach clenches as I unwillingly recall my own failure to be as honest with Ian as he has been--and is being--with me. I have yet to tell him of the memories that haunt me from the time before I was awakened. Memories that I'm not supposed to even be capable of having. To speak of them would give them even more power, a thought that terrifies me.

I push it aside and turn to him instead. Rising on tiptoe, I touch my mouth to his and echo at least a part of his own words. "No limits."

∞ ∞ ∞

"You liked it when I smacked your ass in the elevator," Ian says. His smile dares me to deny what we both know. "It made you hot."

A quiver of remembered pleasure runs through me. I could try to forget the shocked arousal I felt when he did that but there isn't much point. Not considering that I'm face down on my knees on the padded floor of the dressing room, my ass arched, my legs spread, and my arms stretched above my head, my wrists secured by the belt of the black lace robe that lies discarded nearby.

All of my own choice. Despite everything that has already happened this evening, the unbridled sensuality of my nature shows no inclination of being reined in any time soon.

He chuckles softly, his big hand stroking my bottom. "You're such an amazing woman, Amelia. To the world, you look so refined, even demure but on the inside--" He eases a finger into my tight, wet pussy, followed by another. Against my ear, he whispers, "Shall I make you come like this?" He strokes me in a circular motion that hits my most sensitive spot. I groan helplessly.

"Yes, no...I don't know!" I'm frantic for release but I want more. I want him.

"Poor baby," he murmurs. "It's hell, isn't it, wanting to let go completely but still afraid of what will happen if you do."

I moan as he withdraws his fingers. My hips arch toward him but he eludes me. In the next instant, the palm of his hand slaps my ass hard enough that the sound reverberates off the silvered walls, startling me almost as much as the blow itself. I jump and instinctively try to move away.

"Stay where you are," Ian orders. "You'll take exactly what I give you."

Another smack falls, followed quickly by a third. My legs are shaking, the muscles of my stomach rippling. A treacherous warmth spreads through me, at once shaming and arousing me. I don't want to feel like this but I'm not in control. He is.

Another slap lands, making me gasp. I'm so wet, so needy--

"Your ass is a lovely shade of red," Ian says above me. "Look at yourself."

Given where we are, surrounded by mirrors, I hardly have any choice. The sight sends a bolt of shock through me. Who is this woman? So wanton, so submissive, for whom pain and pleasure have become intertwined?

"Don't over-think it," Ian says as our gazes meet in the mirror. Once again, he seems to know exactly what is going through my mind. "Just feel."

His hand lands again, and again. Twice more. By the time he stops, I'm a quivering mess of arousal and need.

"Perfect," he murmurs. His mouth traces the fiery curve of my bottom, first on one side, then the other. The caress is so boldly intimate yet oddly tender. On the cusp of it, he gathers me to him and stretches me out face down so that I am lying full length on the soft, springy floor. Some of the strain goes out of my muscles but it returns when he murmurs, "Remember what I said? I want all of you."

"Ian--" I can hear my trepidation but under it is a whisper of treacherous excitement that won't be denied.

"It's all right, baby," he says soothingly. "I'm not going to rush you. You need to be ready first."

Ready? I'm grappling with that, trying to figure out what he means, when he steps away for a moment. I can hear him in the bedroom. He takes something from a drawer and returns. Kneeling over me, his legs braced on either side of my thighs, he spreads the cheeks of my ass. I have a moment to consider how blatantly he handles me, as though I truly am his possession, before I'm distracted by the sensation of something cool and wet dripping against my tight, puckered opening.

"It's lube, babe," he murmurs. "You're so wet I could just use your own juices but I want you extra comfortable."

I gasp as the tip of his thumb eases into me. Instinctively, my muscles tighten.

"Relax," he says.

I try but I'm vividly aware of my stinging bottom, the strange sensation of being probed there, and the frantic pounding of my heart.

After several long moments, he withdraws his thumb but the respite is brief. At once, he arches me upward with an arm around my waist. His hand reaches down, moving over my pussy, stroking my swollen clit. My belly quivers. I can feel the first wave of an intense orgasm already beginning to build. How many more of those can I possibly take?

Something smooth and heavy with a tapered tip eases between my cheeks.

"I'm going to put this in your ass, sweetheart, then I'm going to fuck your cunt. You're so wet, so hot, you want that, don't you?"

His words are a dark temptation I can't resist. Helplessly, I nod. Slowly, carefully Ian strokes my opening with the tip of the plug before easing it just a little way in. My breath catches. This is unlike anything I've ever experienced. I'm not entirely sure that I can bear it but I don't even think of refusing. I want everything he has to give.

I moan softly as he moves the plug in and out, round and round, each time a little deeper, stretching my tight channel. The sensation is so strange--heavy, thick, a mix of pleasure and not-quite-pain that coils from the base of my spine along every nerve in my body. As powerful as it is, it can't entirely eclipse the anxiety that is mounting in me. The plug is nowhere as big as I know Ian to be but it's enough to make the ring of muscle there burn, leaving me to wonder how I could ever accommodate him. I start to squirm until he presses a hand between my shoulder blades, holding me in place.

"Steady," he says and pushes the plug the rest of the way in.

My moans turn into a ragged gasp. I'm vividly aware of being stretched as I never have been before--opened, exposed, made uniquely vulnerable. I can feel the pressure of the plug in my vagina and against the inner nerves around my clit. The need for release is building in me with frightening speed.

Ian lifts my hips and spreads my legs wider. "Look," he orders again, directing my attention once more to the mirrors. Between the reddened cheeks of my ass, an aquamarine crystal gleams. At the sight it, I flush all over. I know without having to ask that he chose it because it matches my eyes, just as a man more given to propriety might have picked out a necklace or earrings. He's adorned me there in an act that feels like debauchery run wild, at once shameful and wickedly delicious.

Ian has his long, thick cock in his hand. He boldly strokes himself as he holds my eyes in the mirror. Huskily, he says, "You look amazing, sweetheart. I'm going to fuck you so hard. You're going to come riding my cock."

Speech is beyond me. All I can do is stare at our reflection as he moves behind me, grasps my hips, and positions his velvety smooth tip against my entrance. Slowly but steadily he thrusts into me.

"Arrgh!" Between the plug in my ass and Ian's thick, rigid length stretching my soft inner walls, I don't think I can bear this but I have little choice. He controls me utterly, quickly setting a pace that has my thighs quivering and my breath turning into groans. The slap of our bodies coming together mingles with his deep grunts of pleasure.

"So good," he murmurs. "So hot and wet and tight. I can't fucking get enough of you." As he speaks, he takes hold of the plug and slowly twists it.

Blinding white lights explode behind my eyes. I'm so close...

"Come for me, baby!" He thrusts hard, hitting the spot relentlessly, and at the same time jolting the plug even deeper.

It's too much. I struggle to hold on but I don't stand a chance. In the mirrored walls, I see a woman in thrall to the man whose ruthless will is driving her toward sensual oblivion. The climax that hits me feels as though it explodes in each individual cell of my body. Even as it does, Ian doesn't let up. He remains hard inside me, holding himself still as my inner muscles spasm around him again and again. Slowly, he pulls the plug out. I scream as my orgasm is prolonged, fresh waves carrying me even higher.

Distantly, I hear him say, "That's it, baby, let go!"

It's not as though I have a choice, nor do I want one. I'm lost in a writhing maelstrom of sensation and need. His muscles ripple powerfully as he bends all the way over me, his teeth closing on the nape of my neck. The small stab of pain mingling with mind-shattering pleasure distracts me for a crucial moment. The tip of his cock presses where the plug just was. Slowly, steadily, he begins to enter me there, stretching me wider than seems possible.

"Ian--!"

"Breathe, baby," he says, his voice a rough caress. His fingers find my clit. He strokes me with unexpected gentleness that washes over my fear and carries it away. I cry out again as he sinks deeper but in the next moment, the discomfort eases as an even more intense version of the strange, thick pleasure that I experienced earlier takes hold. As he begins to thrust, my hips buck upward, driving him even deeper into me.

"Fuck, yes" he moans.

His hand moves more rapidly over the ultrasensitive bundle of nerves at the apex of my thighs that swell even further at his touch. His cock stretches and fills me. I'm trapped under him, claimed and possessed, and all I can think of is how free I feel. Every fear and inhibition is gone, burned away in the fire of our mutual passion. My release comes as shockwaves that tear through me, plundering my body and soul.

Ian rises above me, his head thrown back, cordons of muscle bulging in his neck. In the mirrors, he looks like a demi-god, the epitome of masculine power and will.

"Amelia!

He shouts my name as his magnificent body convulses in ecstasy. Watching him come is the most beautiful and awe-inspiring sight I have ever seen. I stare at him in helpless fascination until at last he slumps against me. He stays like that for several moments, his chest heaving and the pounding of his heart reverberating with my own. When he finally withdraws, I feel achingly bereft.

I turn my head so that I can look at him but instead catch sight of myself in the mirrors. My ass glows red, the cheeks spread wide by Ian's hands as we both stare at his come oozing from me.

The image is searing in its brutal, remorseless eroticism. It's more than I can bear. With a faint moan, I close my eyes and yield to merciful darkness.

$$\infty \quad \infty \quad \infty$$

A bright light shines in my eyes. I murmur in protest and turn my head away, trying to get back to the blissful forgetfulness of sleep, but it's too late. Consciousness returns and with it comes a sudden rush of memory.

Ian carrying me back into the bedroom and laying me on the bed. Untying me and rubbing my wrists, touching his mouth gently to each where my life's blood pulses.

"You are so beautiful," he murmured. "So passionate, so giving. Fucking you is heaven."

Through the haze of sensual fulfillment and exhaustion, I smile faintly. How can he be at once so savagely possessive and yet so romantic? I fell asleep as he gently wiped the traces of our passion from me. In that moment, I felt exquisitely cared for, protected, even cherished.

But now-- I sit up suddenly, clutching the sheet to my breasts, and take a quick, frantic look around. In the glaring light of what appears to be late afternoon, nothing seems either clear or certain.

Ian is asleep beside me. I stare down at the man I love, relieved that he's here but still struggling to accept that what happened last night was no dream. I...we...the alley, the elevator, the balcony. All the rest! Every carnal, impassioned, ecstatic moment of Carnival was real.

Tearing my eyes from him, I look down at myself. My wrists are banded by faint red lines from the belt that he used to tie me. I'm sore in places that I don't usually think about. Even more, I can still feel him deep inside my body as though he has imprinted himself on me forever.

A sudden wave of insecurity threatens to pull me under. No matter how much I may want to deny how completely I submitted to him, I can't lie to myself. To all intents and purposes, I might as well have been the fuck toy he once called me. That was a deliberate taunt meant to convince me that I was anything but, yet it stung all the same. I can only pray that wasn't how he was thinking of me last night but the harsh truth is that I'm not sure. He's so different suddenly. Not the dark, wounded prince that I've thought of him as but a being of another kind--unhindered by the past, unrestrained, and in some sense at least, merciless.

My legs shake as I get out of the bed. There's no sign of the black lace robe and I don't pause to look for it. Naked, I walk quickly into the bathroom and flip on the shower. Without waiting, I step into it. The first shock of the water makes me gasp. It fills like shards of ice striking my skin but it warms quickly. Within moments, I'm surrounded by a cloud of steam.

I wash myself thoroughly, including shampooing my hair. In the process, I discover several small bruises on my hips where Ian grasped me right before he--

My cheeks flame. I remember it all--the shock, the ecstasy, the soaring sense of liberation. My own unbridled embrace of his desires stuns me. I don't regret it but at the same time I'm more than a little confused and self-conscious. How am I going to face him?

I give myself a hard mental shake. This isn't the time for second thoughts about my behavior. Not when I have far too many questions about his. His change of heart about keeping me secure at Pinnacle House until the danger from Davos is over. His sudden lack of concern about the inner demons that have haunted him for years and threatened to drive us apart. His willingness to go so far sexually, taking me into a dark realm and confronting me with aspects of my own nature that I can only struggle to accept.

I want to talk with him about all this and more but when I get out of the shower, wrap myself in a towel and go back into the bedroom, Ian is still asleep. As I stare at him, my stomach growls a blunt reminder that my body has other appetites and needs. Suddenly, I'm ferociously hungry. About to call room service, I remember that all I'm wearing is a towel. At the estate and Pinnacle House, clothes always seemed to just materialize.

Not so here. Apparently, a hotel that can provide bondage rope and sex toys can't manage a simple terrycloth robe.

I find my gown on the floor of the antechamber where I dropped it during my little strip tease, a seeming lifetime ago. My stilettos, thong, and mask are nearby. I leave them where they are, discard the towel, and slither my way into the dress. So long as I don't turn to expose my bare back, I at least feel adequately covered.

Thoughts of coddled eggs flit through my head as I look for the link. I've just found it and am scrolling down the menu for room service when a sound from the bedroom stops me. For a moment, I think Ian is awake but when I look through the door, he's still asleep. And dreaming.

The sheet is pushed down, exposing his long, sculpted torso to below his hips. I stare entranced at the play of muscles under his taut skin until I realize that he's having a nightmare. His big body moves fitfully in the throes of it.

"No!" he murmurs, the single syllable redolent with pain.

Instinctively, I start toward him, my only thought to comfort. But I stop abruptly when he cries out again.

"No, Susannah! Don't leave me!"

All my breath escapes in a rush. There's no mistaking the depth of his anguish or the sincerity of his plea. He's desperate. For her.

Susannah, the pure and good, spun glass and selfless courage. The beautiful, serene woman in the portrait who I am absolutely certain never knelt on all fours like an animal and let a man fuck her ass. He longs for her. Not me.

I'm breaking apart inside. The room spins and for a moment, I'm afraid that I'm about to be sick. Instead, I do the only thing that I can. I run.

Out of the suite, through the elegant lobby where I'm dimly aware that the few people who are around stare at me, and onto the street. I'm barefoot, disheveled, and on the verge of breaking down completely. It's as though I'm trapped in the gestation chamber again, only this time I've made the mistake of thinking that I can breathe. Instead, I'm drowning in anguish, shame, and defeat. Only one thought holds me together--I have to get away.

A few blocks from the hotel, the spear of Pinnacle House stabs the sky. I tear my eyes from it and focus instead on the flash of green a little distance away. I'm near the park, which means that I'm just about a mile south of the McClellan mansion. I can walk there.

I set off, driven by the desperate need for sanctuary, a place where I can lick my wounds and at least try to recover some part of myself. But I've gone only a few yards when I'm stopped.

Three large men in dark suits emerge from a black car parked at the curb and block my way. For a moment, I think that they're Ian's men, keeping watch on the hotel while he's there. But an instant later, I realize my mistake when one of the men speaks into his personal link.

His words send a bolt of icy terror down my spine.

"Tell Mister Davos that we have her."

Chapter Thirty-one

Ian

I know something is wrong before I open my eyes. The bed's too soft, the sun's coming from the wrong direction, and my cock is limp. It's that last one that gets my attention. I always wake up with wood. It's not a boast, it's just a fact of nature that makes me no different from most guys.

But not today. My cock has decided to sleep in. The last time that happened was right after a halo jump went wrong. I opened too low, came in too fast, and ended up with a broken leg and a nasty concussion. Considering what could have happened, I was lucky.

I don't feel that way right now. An alarm bell is going off in my head. A skull-splitting claxon telling me to haul ass and figure out what the fuck has happened. I'm out of the bed, scratching my chest idly as I glance around the room before I realize where I am. L'hôtel Perle with its well-deserved reputation for discretion. I remember arriving last night...sort of...I wasn't alone.

I was with...Bo Peep? I have a vague memory of a sexy shepherdess bumping into me after I left the Council meeting.

Please god, tell me I didn't check in here with her and her sheep. Amelia might forgive me for a lot of things but not--

Amelia! Oh, fuck!

My whole body jerks as the memory of what really happened last night rips through me, a fusillade of images each more erotic than the next. I feel as though I've been gut punched. Hard on it comes a wave of fear worse than any I've experienced in battle. Where is Amelia? After what I did to her, she could be in shock, broken, in need of help. A wave of panic threatens to overwhelm me. I must be the last person on the planet she wants anything to do with but I've got to find her all the same.

A quick search through the suite reveals nothing except a handful of clues. A discarded thong on the antechamber floor along with the mask and shoes that I remember she was wearing. Rope lying beside a chair. I tied her there and then I...

The balcony, the bedroom, throat fucking her. It gets worse. In the dressing room, I find a long strip of black lace that I vaguely remember taking off her robe and using to tie her hands. And nearby... a jeweled butt plug, the aquamarine stone in the handle twinkling at me.

I double over, my hands braced on my knees. It's all I can do to breathe. Self-loathing threatens to consume me. She was a virgin a few weeks ago. She's had next to no time to adjust to me, the world, or anything else. And I did that? Worse yet, I remember all too well how much I enjoyed it and everything else that I did to her. Even now, there's a part of me that wants to do it all over again.

My hands are shaking as I find my link and call Hollis. The moment he answers, I ask, "Is Amelia there?"

He's silent for a moment, digesting the full meaning behind the question and no doubt trying to figure out what has me going over the edge. "I thought she was with you."

"No. Tell Gab to get on it. I need her found now."

I call Edward next. He picks up right away but that's the last of the good news.

"She's with you," he says after I ask. "Isn't she?"

"She was. I need to find her." I can understand her not going to Pinnacle House but if she hasn't returned to the McClellans' park side mansion... What the hell does that mean?

"Shit, Ian, what happened?"

"I don't know." It's a lie. I know damn well why she ran. I just don't know where to and the options are narrowing quickly.

"I'll see what I can do," he says and I remember that Edward has connections where I don't.

"Find her," I plead, not trying to hide the fear that is exploding in me..

I dress. I leave the suite. I walk out of the hotel and stand on the street. I'm an automaton, acting purely on instinct. All I can think of is Amelia. I don't even remember making the quick walk to Pinnacle House.

Gab is waiting for me when I hit the operations floor. She takes one look, starts to say something, and thinks better of it. Instead, she says, "We have a problem. Someone's blocking access to the sat feed. It's a hack, a good one. Clarence is working right now to break it. We should have something soon."

I close my eyes against the wave of combined fury and fear that threatens to take me to my knees. Gab is the best there is, if she says it will be soon, then it will be. Nobody, certainly not Amelia, will be helped if I can't control myself.

That thought's almost laughable considering how I lost all control last night. But at least if I have to wait, I can satisfy my suspicions about how that happened.

"I'll be in Medical. Let me know when you have something."

The in-house hospital that's a state-of-the-art facility is empty, my guys who were injured in the Crystal Palace attack having all been released. Only Doc Norris is there, which suits me fine. He's a grizzled old s.o.b. who I'd trust with my life, and have done more than a few times. He gives me a funny look when I tell him that I want a tox screen run but he doesn't argue. I cool my heels for a few minutes before he returns with the results.

He doesn't pull any punches. His bushy salt-and-pepper eyebrows lower as he glares at me. "You've been dosed with an illegal street drug. Can I assume that you didn't take it voluntarily?"

"Fuck, yes. What is it?"

He reels off a chemical name that means nothing to me, then adds, "They're calling it Jekyll/Hyde. It's being billed as a nice, cheap high with a few bells and whistles that the legal stuff doesn't provide. But it's really a sophisticated smart drug with very nasty side effects, at least in some cases."

A chill moves through me. I have to force myself to ask, "How so?"

"All recreational drugs break down inhibitions. That's why people take them. This one does the same but it's also designed to identify and eliminate structures in the brain that are associated with the long-term repression of powerful impulses, essentially letting the psyche loose to do whatever it damn well pleases."

The knowledge that I behaved as I did last night because I was drugged does absolutely nothing to ease my sense of guilt and remorse. How could it when all the drug did was free me to do what I wanted to anyway?

"What's it doing on the streets?"

Norris shrugs. "Good question. All I can tell you is that it's been showing up in emergency rooms for the past week or so. In some of the people who take it, it's triggered full-blown psychotic episodes during which they've harmed themselves or others."

My gut tightens as I think of Amelia. I'm hanging on to a shred of hope, praying that she's all right, when the significance of what Norris just said sinks in. "Only some? What about the rest?"

"People without particularly dangerous impulses just find the drug to be liberating. On the other hand, the poor bastards with the darkest urges get the ultimate bad trip. For them, once Jekyll/Hyde does its work, there's no putting the genie, or maybe I should say the monster back in the bottle."

A bolt of shock rips through me. Bad as the situation is, I haven't factored in the possibility that I might be permanently affected. I feel as though I've just walked off the edge of a cliff. If there was ever a chance of making amends to Amelia, it's gone. She would never be safe with me again.

"However," Norris is saying, "the good news is that it doesn't look as though Jekyll/Hyde is going to be around for long."

I'm still reeling from the bombshell he's dropped on me but I force myself to ask, "Why not?"

His smile is grim. "Twenty-four hours ago, the bodies of two neurobiologists were found hanging from lamp posts in Marseilles, France, near a warehouse that contained a lab where the drug was being made. The scientists' throats were cut and they were left to bleed out in the street. The lab itself went up in flames. Word is that Jorge Cruces was responsible."

I'm not surprised. The lamp posts may be a little over the top but Cruces is known for his ruthless administration of the drug laws. When governments finally admitted what a waste of lives and money the war on drugs had been, they turned it over to the one group of people who knew how to do it right--the drug dealers. In return for keeping the really bad shit off the streets--and all of it out of the hands of minors--Cruces gets unfettered access to a world market for his own legal products, conservatively worth trillions of dollars a year.

"It must have cost a shitload to design and manufacture that stuff," Doc muses. "Why would anyone put that kind of resources into a product that was guaranteed to attract the attention of the guy who both controls the legal drug market and has the authority to go after anyone who tries to do business outside it?"

The who and why behind Jekyll/Hyde may be a mystery to Norris but I have no doubt who's responsible. Davos is one of the very few people who knows enough about my past to realize where I'd be most vulnerable. He has the wealth and power to get Jekyll/Hyde made and he wouldn't hesitate to field test it on the streets to be sure that it worked. The poor bastards who will never get their lives back were just his guinea pigs. One more crime he's going to pay for.

"The tox screen shows that it's still active in your system," Norris says. "Granted, you seem to be okay but the sooner we get it flushed out, the better."

I'm surprised to learn that I'm still under the influence. Aside from the fact that I can't think about Amelia without feeling like there are two men inside me--the guy who wants to protect her and the one who wants to fuck her again and again--I seem to be functioning normally.

"Not happening. We're ramping up to a mission." I have to believe that. Gab and Clarence are going to find her and when they do--

Doc's expression hardens. "You've been drugged, which means that until proven otherwise your decision-making capability is in question. To put it bluntly, you're in no condition to lead."

He's right. Moreover, he's got the guts to give it to me straight. I have to respect that. "Colonel Hollis will run the mission. I'll just be along for the ride."

Doc isn't happy but he's smart enough to know this is the best he's going to get. Even so, he says, "All right but once it's over, I want you in here for a full check-up. You've been exposed to a potentially dangerous drug. We need to be sure that there aren't any lingering effects."

In my gut, I know that it's too late to worry about that. But all I say is, "Fair enough."

On the way back to operations, I do what I know that I have to. Amelia isn't with her brother or grandmother. She's become friends with my mother and sister but I don't think she'd go to them. In the unlikely event that she did, I would know by now. That leaves just one other person she could have turned to.

"No," Sergei says after I tell him why I'm calling. He sounds a little hung-over, like he's got his own excesses from Carnival to deal with. But as soon as he realizes what's happening, he's fully alert. "I haven't seen Amelia. What have you done?"

Give the Russian credit, he cuts to the chase.

"I'm going to find her," I say, not even pretending that I don't understand him. "Whatever it takes."

"She loves you."

What the hell?

"It's obvious. When I tell her to imagine that you are there, watching her dance, she becomes... More than any woman I've ever seen."

I shouldn't be hearing this from him but I'm grateful all the same. His words are the only spark of light in the darkness closing in around me.

"If she contacts you--"

"I'll do whatever she wants," he says calmly, "and you can go to hell."

Fair enough especially considering that I'm there now.

Gab is paging me as I walk back through the doors to Operations. She doesn't pull any punches. "You aren't going to like it." I hear the sympathy in her voice. Gab knows what it is to love, which means she understands how far a person will go to defend what matters most to them.

"Tell me."

"Clarence came through; we've got the sat-feedback. Amelia was picked up outside L'hôtel Perle going on ninety minutes ago. Black SUV, looked like a classic, gasoline powered if you can believe that, with three guys in it. We've been able to trace the vehicle. It went south, about a mile, then took a ramp leading down to what we have to assume is an underground garage or other facility. From then on, we're blind."

"Where were they exactly when you lost them?"

"Forty-second and Fifth, near the old library."

That shock I felt back at the hotel when I realized what I'd done was nothing compared to what hits me now. I'm free falling in zero gravity and there's no way to stop.

I must look as bad as I feel because Gab takes a quick step toward me. "Boss, you okay?"

Somehow, I nod. I even manage to speak, although it feels like someone else is talking. The real me is screaming in rage and fear.

"Yeah, fine. You're sure about the location?"

"Absolutely, the old main branch of the library."

The neo-classical masterpiece that looks like an ancient Greek temple has been a landmark in mid-town Manhattan since the early twentieth century. Guarded by stone lions, it used to be open to the public. Nowadays, it's strictly a preserve of the elite. A-list charities hold their board meetings there, planning the galas that take place in the cavernous former reading rooms where generations of scholars worked to banish ignorance.

But even with all the changes, the library still guards its secrets. Beneath the building and stretching out under the adjacent nine-acre park are two underground levels that used to hold millions of books, all long since digitized. That space, too, was repurposed.

I haven't set foot beneath the library since the day when I was sixteen years old and decided that any fate was better than being the man my father wanted me to be. Now Amelia's trapped there. But not for long. I'll do anything to save her from my worst nightmare. Even if that means unleashing the darkest demons inside me.

Josie Litton

Chapter Thirty-two

Amelia

*T*he men who took me from in front of the hotel don't speak during the short drive. I'm in the back seat, trapped between two of them with the third behind the wheel. Their presence makes any attempt to struggle useless. They ignore my demands to be released, staring stoically ahead as though I'm not even there.

Small details stand out in high relief--the smell of the leather seats, the faint whiff of gasoline that is so rare in the city, the citrus-spice scent of the soap one of my captors uses. All of it swirls through my mind, clashing with the panic that threatens to consume me.

Everything that has happened from the moment Ian announced that we were going to Carnival through my own unbridled behavior to the instant when he cried out for Susannah overwhelms me. I'm numb, hardly able to move, much less think.

A smothering sense of unreality settles over me. I can't believe this is happening. The men were waiting for me but how? Someone--it has to be Davos--must have known where I was. That's disturbing enough but how could he have anticipated that I would bolt from the hotel so impulsively, with no thought for my own safety?

My stomach drops when I realize that we're turning onto a ramp that leads below the street. On the surface, I still have some hope of escape but once we're out of sight--

Instinctively, I lunge for the door handle. The two men scarcely react. One simply puts a hand on my wrist and squeezes hard. The pain that shoots up my arm is so intense that I'm afraid he means to break the bones. I freeze, which seems to satisfy him. After a moment, he nods and lets go. A sense of dread closes in around me. Too vividly, I remember what Ian believes is Davos' intent--to use me to discover how the customized imprinting was done. I can imagine all too vividly what that would require. Anything, even death, would be better than losing the very essence of myself.

We descend down the ramp, first one level, then another until finally the vehicles stops in a parking garage. Several cars are nearby but I don't see any other people. One of the men gets out, reaches into the back seat, and drags me after him. The second man exits on the other side. In the few seconds that they're separated, I see what may be my only chance to escape. Wishing more than ever that I'd enrolled in the self-defense class that I wanted to take rather than just thinking about it, I bring up my knee and slam it into the crotch of the man holding me. Although I put all my strength into the blow, he doesn't double over but he does give a harsh grunt. His hold weakens just enough for me to twist free.

I run but not fast enough. As I reach the bottom of the ramp, I'm tackled and knocked to the cement floor. All the breath rushes out of me. The man who brought me down gets to his feet and aims a kick toward my stomach.

"Don't!" Incredibly, his partner, still grimacing, hobbles up in time to stop him. "Davos won't like it if you mark her." Before I can feel any relief for this small reprieve, he adds, "He'll want to do that himself."

This glimpse into my immediate future sends a bolt of terror through me. I'm dragged to my feet and hauled toward a pair of heavy steel doors. On the other side is a starkly white corridor that looks as though it belongs in a hospital. Hideous visions of operating rooms, dissection labs, and the like hurdle through my mind. In desperation, I dig my bare heels into the utilitarian carpeting but the men don't even notice. They continue on their way, one on each side of me holding my arms. We stop when we come to another door. Stenciled on it is a single word: Prep.

"Listen up, bitch," one of the men says. "Be smart and don't cause any trouble. If you do, there are plenty of ways to make you regret it that won't leave a mark."

His partner lets this sink in for a moment, then puts his thumb to a biometric sensor. The door opens. I stagger as I'm thrust inside but manage to right myself. The door slams behind me. The sudden contrast to the sterile surroundings that I've just passed through is startling. Whatever I expected, it wasn't this. I'm in a small entry hall, lushly paneled in dark wood with a Persian rug covering the floor. The air carries the heavy, exotic scents of sandalwood and patchouli. In the near distance, music throbs softly.

I'm alone or so I think until two young women suddenly appear. Rather than the white-coated lab technicians I feared, they are both naked, slim but large breasted with long black hair brushing their bottoms and rose-brown skin. I'm wondering if they could be Polynesian when I notice the collars around their necks and the attached lengths of chain draped low on their hips above their smooth, bare sexes. The women smile and giggle as they gesture for me to come with them.

Instead, I look around for some way to escape but the only door I can see is the one I came in through. Even if there was a sensor on this side, I wouldn't be able to get past it. That leaves only one option. Hoping that there's another exit somewhere, I go with them.

"Where are we?" I demand, looking from one to the other. "Where are you taking me?"

Neither responds. They don't understand me or they don't want to admit to doing so. Instead, with smiles and gestures, they lead me into a large space that looks as though it belongs in a sultan's palace. The walls are draped in lush burgundy and gold silks, more thick carpets cover the floors. Crystal chandeliers hanging from the ceiling cast light across the large, tiled pool where several dozen women are gathered. All are nude or nearly so and each is stunningly beautiful. Every type seems to be represented--blondes, brunettes, redheads with skin from the palest ivory to the richest mahogany As I enter, their gazes turn in my direction. I feel myself assessed and found not wanting exactly but of only mild interest.

The Polynesian beauties urge me along until we come to a row of small open rooms, each furnished with a padded bench, a dressing table, and shelves holding a variety of lotions, waxes, oils, and the like. What they don't have are doors or even curtains. There's no allowance for modesty in this place.

One of the young women steps behind me and quickly unzips my gown. I catch it before it can fall. A brief tug of war occurs with me on one side and my two--preparers, groomers, whatever they are--on the other. They win. Before I can register what's happening, I'm standing stark naked under the scrutiny of every other woman in the spa. My instinct is to cover myself but I resist and lift my head instead. I refuse to let anyone see how afraid I am.

The two young women give me their combined once over. Apparently satisfied with what they see, they nod and smile again. Only the slight bruises on my hips where Ian's fingers marked me and the pale red lines on my wrists draw a soft tut-tut.

Thinking of Ian opens a hollow well of pain so intense as to make me gasp. His longing for Susannah hits me yet again. Even beyond death, she is the embodiment of goodness and purity, the person who gave up her last chance to live so that I could instead. And what am I? Nothing like her, that's for certain. She still calls to the better angels of his nature whereas I'm the woman who will make herself come in an alley for his enjoyment.

My eyes burn. I hardly notice what's happening until one of the women drops a transparent length of pleated white silk over my body. It drapes over one shoulder, leaving my other side almost completely bare. One of my breasts is fully exposed, the other is clearly visible through the diaphanous fabric. I'm left feeling even more lewdly displayed than I would if I was fully naked. Worse yet, the gown, if it can be called that, is a decadent version of the elegant garment that Susannah wears in the portrait I have studied so often, seeking clues to her nature and my own. I can't help but wonder if that's a coincidence or one more indication of Davos' perverse fascination with my predecessor.

Dressed as I am, I can't escape the realization of what kind of place I've been brought to. I've been in the city long enough to hear rumors about the sex clubs of every sort that flourish here. I just never expected to set foot in one. That Davos would arrange for me to do so makes my skin crawl. My determination to find a way out redoubles.

The two women guide me over to the chair in front of the dressing table and urge me to sit down. They go to work on my hair and face, giggling all the while. The traces of last night's excesses in tangled strands, swollen lips, and faint shadows under my eyes fall to their ministrations. Within minutes, I'm staring at a woman who looks like me but who might as well be a stranger. Her skin is flawless, her eyes wide and luminous, her cheeks slightly flushed, her mouth soft and moist. She appears untouched by the world and everything in it. There are even flowers entwined in her hair.

My stomach clenches as I realize that I've been made to look virginal. The shock of seeing myself like that after what I have experienced with Ian finally pierces the numbness that has surrounded me since I fled the hotel. Turning to the two young women, I say urgently, "My name is Amelia McClellan. Help me get out of here, please. My family will reward and protect you."

Once again, neither responds. I try the same plea in Spanish and French with no better results. One of the women gives me a small, apologetic smile. Before I realize what she intends, she scrapes a small knife over the skin on the inside of my arm. Even as the significance of what she has done is just beginning to sink in, she deposits the skin cells she has collected in a small tube. Moments later, the cap of the tube flashes green.

Dread washes over me as I realize that I have just been subjected to a DNA test, the results swiftly obtained and as quickly transmitted. If Davos has a sample of Susannah's DNA--and I don't doubt his ability to have acquired that--any lingering question about who and what I am has been answered.

My stomach is clenching at the thought of what that means when suddenly a gong sounds. As one, all the women around the pool rise and walk together in the same direction. My two companions urge me to go with them. Beyond the seraglio room is another darkly paneled area containing long wooden racks that hold hooded cloaks in a variety of rich colors. Each of the women takes one and puts it on. Within moments their heads are obscured, their faces cast into shadows. But the cloaks hang open, revealing their bare bodies from the neck down.

One of the young women guiding me selects a cloak of blazing red, the only one that color, and urges me into it. As with the others, I am at once rendered anonymous yet exposed. The urge to pull the garment closed around me is all but irresistible but before I can do so wide double doors at the far end of the room suddenly open outward. At once, the line of women moves forward.

I'm held back until all the others have passed, then pushed forward into a large, sumptuous space that looks as though it belongs in an exclusive gentlemen's club. Tufted leather sofas and high-backed wingchairs seem an incongruous accompaniment to the naked carnality on display. The women quickly doff their cloaks and take up positions around the outside of a large mosaic circle set into the only part of the floor that is bare of rugs. They all face inward, toward the man standing at the center. His distinctive red mask with its empty eyes and dark chasm of a mouth strikes a chord. I remember him on the float, staring at me.

For now, the women have his attention. They kneel and prostrate themselves before him. A faceless servant, dressed all in black with even his features covered, hands the man a censure from which scented smoke rises. He waves it over the naked backs of the women, turning in a circle as he does so in a mockery of a religious ritual.

A hand at my back urges me toward an ornately carved marble pedestal that seems to be a focal point of the room. I'm pushed, carefully but implacably up the steps behind it until I'm standing on display. The avid eyes of the male audience rake over me. With a start, I realize that some of the men look familiar. I've crossed paths with them at various social events around the city. I think I may have even danced with one or two of them. For a brief moment, I consider appealing for their help but their presence here, in such a place, deters me.

I'm grateful that my face is still hidden by the hood of the cloak but the rest of me is blatantly exposed, my vulnerability only heightened by the transparent white silk. Panic rises in me but after a few moments, I realize that no one is making any move toward me, at least not yet. I have no idea how long such restraint will last but I know that I have to make the most of whatever time I have. Quickly, I begin scanning the room for some avenue of escape.

As I do, the ritual ends. Another gong sounds. The naked women rise as one and fan out among the guests. Some straddle the men's laps, others are directed to kneel on the floor. I see one man put an arm around a woman's hips, holding her immobile as he slides a finger between her thighs. She winces but does not resist. Another man pinches a woman's nipples so harshly that she smothers a cry. He laughs in response. When one of the men pulls out his cock and directs the woman he's chosen to suck it, I redouble my efforts to find a way out.

Chapter Thirty-three

Amelia

I've been standing on the pedestal for half-an-hour before I finally accept that there is no obvious means of escape. A columned passageway at the far end of the room may lead to the doors through which the men entered but is it to the right or left? Make the wrong choice and I'll be trapped. That's presuming that I can get off the pedestal without being noticed.

I'm at least reassured that attention has shifted away from me. The pace of debauchery is increasing with each passing moment. I try to look away but there is nowhere that does not contain a scene of sensual abandon. In an effort to deny the terror that threatens to panic me, I tell myself that when--not if--I get out of here, I'll give every part of me including my eyes a good bath.

Female heads are bobbing up and down all over the room as several women mount a round platform and begin pleasuring one another, displaying themselves to the men who offer lewd encouragement. Nearby, a woman crawls on all fours between a gauntlet of men wielding riding crops. I wince as she is struck repeatedly on the buttocks and thighs.

The man in the red mask watches it all from a throne-like chair not far from where I am standing. He sits at his ease, his posture that of regal aloofness. But his legs, beneath the cloak, are spread. When his left hand slips inside the garment, I realize queasily that he is touching himself. Several of the women keep their eyes on him, waiting for a summons, but they might as well not exist. For the moment at least, he seems satisfied merely to pleasure himself as he watches the others.

Meanwhile, the faceless, black-garbed servants move among the guests, delivering drinks in cut-crystal tumblers along with silver serving dishes heaped high with pharmaceuticals. Whatever instinct for restraint might still be present in any of the men is falling away quickly. Several have already begun to disrobe. The room is rapidly becoming a writhing mass of bodies.

I can't wait any longer. Feeling backward with my toes, I find the first step and slowly lower myself onto it. I'm afraid to turn around for fear that would attract notice but if I can avoid making any sudden movements and just--

Before I can take another step, the room suddenly goes dark. I teeter and only just manage to catch myself. A circle of light appears, surrounding a stage that is rising up out of the floor. At the center of it is a low couch occupied by a beautiful, naked woman stretched out on her side facing the audience. She wears a mask of beaten gold and a sprinkling of gold dust over her skin, nothing else. As the light expands around her, a man steps out onto the stage. He, too, is naked except for a mask and a coating of gold dust. His body is superb--tall, heavily muscled, powerful. His large cock strains upward toward his abdomen. As he approaches the woman, the high, keening voice of a flute rises above the throbbing rhythm of drums.

The woman spreads her legs and arches her back, blatantly presenting herself to him. At once, he joins her on the couch, grasps her by the neck and, holding her in place, mounts her. Her breathy cries and his grunts form a human counterpoint to the music. His thrusts become faster and deeper, pounding into her.

The audience cheers as a chant begins, "Fuck! Fuck! Fuck!" The man obliges, holding the woman spread open so that she is displayed to the avid eyes of the watching men as he drives into her. Rivulets of sweat flow over them both, forming trails where the gold dust is washed away. After she appears to come several times, he drags her off the couch and positions her upright with her back to him. His cock juts engorged and glistening. He grips her wrists and pulls her arms behind her, using them for leverage as he thrusts into her again. Her head falls forward. She looks like a rag doll, helpless to stop the relentless pounding into her body.

"Fuck! Fuck! Fuck!"

The powerful muscles of his arms and chest clench as he obeys the crowd's command. It goes on for what seems like an impossibly long time. The woman's moans become weak and hoarse as her body clenches and jerks repeatedly. The man no longer seems aware of her. He has become something between a beast and a machine. Bile rises in my throat as I witness this perversion of what has been called, in vastly different circumstances, an act of love.

At last, the gong sounds. Faceless servants appear on the stage. They move soundlessly, drawing the couple apart and positioning the woman onto her knees in front of the man. Their gazes meet. Something in the way they look at each other makes me think that they are not strangers, thrown together for a night by the depraved vagaries of Carnival. I wonder if they are a couple instead, workers like the woman in the window, fighting to survive and advance in a society that seems more brutal and ruthless to me with each passing day.

The woman takes the man's penis in her hands gently. With evident care, she reaches around to undo the latch of a metal ring that I realize belatedly has kept him engorged all this time. A low moan breaks from him as she takes him in her mouth. He grasps her hair, holding her in place, his head thrown back and his eyes closed as he comes at last desperately and convulsively.

I look away. Their vulnerability is anguishing. They are human beings but their humanity is not recognized by the audience that has turned them into an expression of its own depravity. Everything in me cries out against such debasement even as I confront the very real likelihood that Davos intends for me to experience it myself in some form of his devising. More than ever, I know that I have to get away.

In the aftermath of the show, the lights come back on, revealing couples, trios, and even more ambitious arrangements arrayed on every table, couch, and chair or writhing on the floor. The smell of sex becomes overpowering. I take another step back, feeling my way down the first step only to freeze when a sudden realization hits me. Every other woman and most of the men are naked. Wearing the red cloak, I will be all too noticeable. Even the transparent silk tunic will draw attention. If I'm not spotted by the faceless servants, I will be by one of the men...or more. That possibility makes me feel ill but so does the thought of staying where I am, waiting helplessly for whatever Davos has planned for me.

My legs are shaking. I'm afraid they won't hold me upright much longer. I have to act but I remain frozen. Longing wells up in me...to escape this horrible place, to stand in the light again, to live in a world where Davos and his kind don't exist. But above all is my yearning for the man who awakened me to the world and who has been my sanctuary from it even as he has longed for another woman. I ache for him with every particle of my being.

Tears burn my eyes. I blink them away and force myself to breathe. As I do, a flicker of movement near the columns draws my attention. Another guest has arrived. Still fully dressed in a darkly elegant business suit, he stands looking out over the scene with cool, aloof amusement. His gaze, hooded and impenetrable, slides past me and does not return.

I gasp and close my eyes in disbelief, certain that in my terror, I am hallucinating. When I open them again, the clash of relief and panic threatens to overwhelm me. Ian! Here, alone! Any joy I might feel burns away before the realization of the danger he has put himself in. How could he do such a thing? Does he have no regard for his own safety ? If he's harmed because of me--

The thought is unbearable but hard on it comes another. I can't deny that he looks alarmingly at ease in this environment. As I watch, he accepts a drink from one of the faceless servants and makes his way to a vacant club chair not far from where I stand on display. I want to cry out to him but my throat is so tight that no sound escapes. It clenches even further when several women--all beautiful, all naked, swiftly approach him. For a horrible moment, I'm afraid that I'm going to be forced to watch them pleasure him. When he waves them off with a shake of his head, I all but sag with relief.

The debauchery continues all around us but Ian appears not to notice. He sets his drink aside on a nearby table, shoots the cuffs of his shirt, and stifles a yawn. In the midst of a full-blown orgy, he looks bored. I desperately wish that I could feel the same. The sickness in me continues to mount, made all the worse as I consider more fully the implications of Ian being in such a place. What memories must it evoke of the experience that scarred him so badly when he was still little more than a child?

Across the width of the club, Ian and the man in the red mask face each other. As the minutes pass, neither moves. I'm struck by the sense that a contest of wills is playing out in front of me, one that only the two of them can fully comprehend.

Finally, the man in the red mask stands. He leaves his throne-like chair, comes down from the dais, and crosses the floor to mount the stage. To the cheers of the crowd, he raises his arms over his head and walks in a full circle, soliciting their fervor before taking up a position once again facing Ian.

Several moments pass. I'm aware of the frantic beating of my heart and the chill moving over my skin. But mostly all I can focus on is Ian. His eyes are hooded, his expression inscrutable. He shows no interest in whatever is about to happen.

Two of the faceless servants appear, holding between them a naked, trembling young woman. They pull her up the steps and onto the stage, where she falls to her knees in front of the man. He moves aside a flap in his cloak and forces her head under the garment. Almost at once, she begins to bob back and forth. My relief at being spared a direct view of what she's doing vanishes when one of the servants approaches and holds out a long, leather flail. The man takes it, slashing it once through the air as though to get the feel of it. I jump at the sound it makes, then jump again when he brings the next strike down against the woman's bare buttocks. She jerks but does not falter in her rhythm. Not with the first blow or with the dozen and more than follow.

I cringe, imagining her desperation as the need to make the man come is made all the more difficult by the pain of the flagellation she is suffering at his hands. Her entire body is shaking before he finally stiffens and throws back his head. The red mask catches the light of the hanging chandeliers and glows as though with an inner, demonic fire.

In the aftermath, the woman slumps to the floor, gasping for air. The crowd cheers. Several of the faceless servants appear and drag her upright.

The servants place her in front a large wooden cross in the shape of an X. Her arms are raised over her head, her legs spread wide as she is secured to it. Positioned out toward the audience as she is, I can see that she is crying.

For the first time since the performance began, I dare to look at Ian. He shows no reaction to what he has just witnessed. The suffering of the woman and her continued plight appear not to affect him in the least. But when I look more closely, I can see that his gaze remains locked on the man in the red mask.

Who now throws off his disguise and steps forward, swiftly crossing the distance between them. Charles Davos oozes magnanimity as he offers his hand. Without hesitation, Ian stands and takes it.

Chapter Thirty-four

Ian

A red mist moves in front of my eyes. I've seen it before and I know what it means just as I know that I can't yield to it. The Norse had a name for men who lost themselves in the frenzy of battle, becoming something more--or less--than human. Berserkers. Men who killed without remorse or hesitation, with no fear for their own safety, wading through blood until at last they found the only solace that mattered, victory.

I'm not that man. I refuse to be him. It's enough that I'm here despite Gab and Hollis' best efforts to convince me to wait until an assault can be organized. Or at the very least, not to go in without back-up. I couldn't do either. Waiting was out of the question once I knew where Amelia was. And I understand Davos well enough to be sure that if I didn't walk in the door alone, he'd use her as a human shield even if that meant getting her killed.

Not that what he already has in mind is much better. I know that's her on the pedestal. I'd recognize her anywhere but worse yet, I realize what her being on display like that means. She's this evening's special entertainment, an experience she's likely to only barely survive. No doubt he intends it as the start of the process that will break her down, take her apart layer by layer. The knowledge fills me with rage. I want nothing so much as to tear his throat out and feed him to the wolves.

Instead, I shake the sick bastard's hand and say, "Bo-Peep was a nice touch. That Jekyll/Hyde stuff is the real deal."

Davos chuckles but his gaze is narrow, assessing me. He hasn't survived, much less thrived all these years by taking anything for granted.

"So you know what's happened to you? Good. Frankly, it's a relief to see the real you instead of that cardboard mask you've been hiding behind all these years."

He may think so. I sure as hell don't but I'll deal with that later. I tighten my grip. "Still, I have to be honest, Charles. I don't appreciate your making off with my property. Not to mention the little matter of trying to kill me at the Crystal Palace."

The slime ball shrugs. "I didn't think that you would on either count. Still, you've impressed me with your durability. I thought we should have a civilized conversation." His smile tightens. "But perhaps you'd like a tour first?"

I drop my hand. We both take a step back, eyeing each other. "That won't be necessary. From what I've seen already, you've brought back my father's old Club. Same location, same décor...same activities. And the same purpose, I assume?"

A look of derision flits across his face. "I'm not the blunt instrument that you are, Ian. All that heavy weaponry and so on isn't for me. I prefer a subtler approach. Manipulating men is much more satisfying than merely killing them."

Subtler, I wonder? Like whipping a woman while she sucks you off? Davos is as delusional as they come. Especially if he thinks there's any chance of co-opting me to his side. No drug on earth--smart or otherwise--could ever accomplish that. Still, I'm willing to play along, if only for the moment.

"You're being modest, Charles. There was nothing subtle about the Crystal Palace. If you had your way, Edward McClellan and I would be dead, and Amelia would be all yours."

My candor startles him. He bares his teeth as he says, "She already is. Possession is nine-tenths of the law, now more than ever."

"Sorry, but that won't hold up in this case. My lawyers have everything they need to prove that the replica known as Amelia McClellan is my property. In the event of my demise, ownership transfers to Edward. He'll be watching his back from now on. You won't get anywhere near him and he'll keep you tied up in court for years. In the end, you won't make a penny off anything you learn from her."

Davos frowns. "If you say so but that hardly matters if you're imagining that you can take her back by force."

I smile, as though the thought amuses me. "And risk destroying what may very well be the single most valuable piece of property in the world, the key to replica technology? Hardly." Parodying his own words back at him, I add, "I'm not like you, Charles. Blowing up the Crystal Palace because you were pissed off when your original plan failed isn't my style."

His mouth thins at the suggestion that he lost control of the situation and of himself. He makes a feeble effort to claim otherwise. "I knew you would get her out of there, dear boy. Good Sir Ian could always be counted on to do the right thing, tedious bore that he was."

He looks at me speculatively. "On the other hand, the real you is proving to be a surprise. I was confident that she would end up fleeing from you after you were, shall we say, liberated by Jekyll/Hyde. But frankly I didn't expect her to be in such good condition. From what I understand, there's hardly a mark on her."

I resist the urge to look at Amelia and instead focus on the mental image of my fist ramming into Davos' throat. Or just grabbing his head and twisting until I hear the satisfying snap of his spine.

Shrugging, I say, "I was pacing myself."

"Were you? I'd like to take your word for that but if we're going to be doing business, I need more."

Before I can reply, he flicks a hand, summoning one of the faceless servants. They have a brief conversation that I can't overhear. The servant withdraws but he returns moments later with a young woman who, unlike some of the others, looks far more excited than afraid. My stomach knots as I realize that she's one of those whose brain is hardwired to produce massive amounts of endorphins in response to pain. Pain slut, my father called women like her, but then he was an asshole.

No doubt if Davos gets his chance, he'll be creating lots more like her. Among other things. Once in possession of the replica technology, he can produce legions of human beings programmed to do whatever he chooses. The possibilities are as limitless as they are sickening.

The young woman kneels in front of me. Naked, with her head lowered in a properly submissive attitude, she peeks up at me through her lashes. Objectively, she's beautiful but my cock and I are in agreement for once. Neither of us wants anything to do with her. When she raises her hands in offering and I see what's in them, it takes every ounce of self-control that I've got not to react.

The coiled whip she holds out to me is made of oxblood red braided leather, possibly cow, maybe kangaroo, but probably, knowing Davos, something rarer and endangered. Rhino, most likely. Between the short, rigid handle and the flexible lash, it's a little over eight feet long. Wielded correctly, it can be as delicate as a lover's tongue or as cutting as the sharpest knife. With enough power behind it, the tip of the lash will break the sound barrier, creating a mini sonic boom. I know all this because, God help me, there was a time when I knew much more.

Without warning, the crack of the whip--and the screams and moans that inevitably follow it--explode in my mind. I haven't had a flashback to the Club in years but suddenly I'm teetering on the edge of an abyss that threatens to swallow me whole. Stunned and disoriented, I grasp for the only possible lifeline. Amelia's face is hidden by the shadows of the hood but I'm sure that she sees me. I cling to the sight of her, holding on for dear life, until my breathing steadies.

When it does, the young woman is still looking at me. Her nipples are erect, her skin flushed. Bile rises in my throat. I'm well aware that some sane, consenting adults find the savage dance of the whip sexually arousing. I don't. Getting dosed with Jekyll/Hyde hasn't changed that. To me, the whip is just a reminder of evil. I want nothing to do with it but I may not have any choice. Davos is getting impatient.

"Why don't you show us how it's done?" he says, indicating the empty cross beside the one where the woman he used earlier is shackled.

I know that he's set up this little test to make sure that I'm no longer, as he dubbed me so derisively, Good Sir Ian. No way he'll let me off the hook. My only hope is that I can somehow turn this to my advantage. But for that to happen, Amelia is going to have to trust me. What are the odds of that when I've given her every reason not to?

Slowly, I say, "I'm out of practice."

"Nonsense, you're being humble. I remember how skilled you were, especially given that you were only a boy." A flush creeps over his cheeks. "Of course, you were big for your age and quite strong. Impressive, really. The awkwardness of youth quite passed you by. I often thought how well you would have done among the ancient Greeks or Romans." He laughs faintly. "Just think, if you'd been born a few thousand years sooner, we could be admiring statues of you."

His eyes run over me in a way that has me once again wanting to reach for his throat. When I was in the Club, being the 'man' my father wanted me to be, I steered clear of Davos. He was a predator then just as he is now. I have no problem with anything consenting adults do between themselves but he's always liked his partners young, as in very. The rumors about him have only gotten worse over the years.

"Yeah, that's great," I cut in. To get past Davos' security screening, I'm not carrying any kind of communicator, let alone a weapon. Gab and Hollis have no way of knowing if I'm dead or alive. They won't wait forever to find out.

I've got one shot at making this work and I'm running out of time. Before I can entertain any more doubts, I say, "If you want a show, fine. But not with her."

Davos glances at the kneeling woman. "Why not? What's wrong with her?"

I manage a sneer. "She'll enjoy it too much. Besides, you want to start breaking the replica down, don't you?"

I stand before he can answer and take the whip from the woman's hands. It's heavy with the weight of old memories I've never been able to escape. They close in around me now, a dark, suffocating cloak that blocks out even the hope of light.

Without waiting for a response, I walk toward the pedestal.

Josie Litton

Chapter Thirty-five

Amelia

s Ian comes toward me, I begin to shake. The look in his eyes...what he's carrying...the verbal sparring between him and Davos that I've just witnessed without being able to hear. They all fill me with confusion rapidly being crowded out by terror.

What is he going to do? What is about to happen to me? Who is this man who seems so at ease amid such depraved surroundings?

From the moment he announced that we were going to attend Carnival, I've known that something was wrong. He's not himself. He's changed in some way. I have no idea what to expect from him but I do know that he can hurt me badly. My emotions are already bruised and battered. Will my body be next?

The thought fills me with horror. For a sickening moment, I'm afraid that I'm about to vomit. I'm on the verge of breaking down entirely when common sense comes to the rescue. I know who Ian is. He is the man who awakened me to the world and then set me free. The man who, even though his heart still calls out to a dead woman, has walked into his worst nightmare to save me.

The panic rising in me vanishes. I take a deep breath as my body stills. By the time Ian reaches the foot of the steps leading up to where I'm standing, I'm as ready as I can be.

Without a word, he holds out his hand. Without a word, I take it. Curling my fingers around his, I step down from the pedestal. When I reach the bottom, our bodies brush against one another. I feel the heat radiating from his. He is not remotely as calm as he appears.

So softly that only I can hear him, he pleads, "Please, Amelia, trust me. I'll get you out of here but you have to do as I say."

This close, I can see that his eyes are filled with dread that I might refuse. Belatedly, I realize that he has no way of knowing why I left the hotel suite so precipitously. He may even assume that I was embarrassed or otherwise upset by what happened between us. If only I had been, I might be the woman he calls out to rather than Susannah.

That is too paradoxical for me to think about, especially under the circumstances. Instead of trying, I make an instant decision to trust him, at least with my own safety. His is another matter. I want to tell him that I won't leave without him but Davos is staring at us. All I can do is nod.

Ian leads me over to the cross beside the quietly sobbing young woman. He sets me against it but makes no move to secure the restraints. Instead, he steps over and undoes hers.

"You don't mind, do you?" he says casually to Davos. "She's in the way."

The silver-haired monster frowns but he doesn't object as the woman darts off. He's waiting to see what Ian will do next. Some of those among the writhing mass of bodies scattered across the floor and furniture of the room are beginning to do the same. Slowly, awareness spreads that a new show is about to begin.

Ian returns to me, his body brushing once more against mine in a move that is unmistakably intended to reassure. His hands grip my shoulders lightly. As they do, the coils of the whip rests for a moment against my breasts.

"Breathe," he says and removes my cloak.

A ripple of excitement goes through the audience as men I have met at the Opera House and the Polo Club, and at various soirees and charity galas recognize me. For a brief moment, I wonder if, now that I am no longer an anonymous woman, any of them will protest or otherwise intervene on my behalf.

None does and I realize quickly that I shouldn't be surprised. These are the Lords of Misrule, men so perverted by power that they have lost all touch with what it truly means to be human. If they were ever capable of empathy, compassion, or even simple decency, they aren't any longer.

Ian tosses the cloak aside and takes several steps back, leaving me standing alone in front of the cross. At the slightest motion of his wrist, the whip uncoils, its long, sinuous length seeming to come alive. I stifle a gasp and only just manage to hold myself still.

"Haven't you forgotten something?" Davos interjects.

Ian flicks the whip as though testing how it feels in his hand. Without taking his eyes from it, he says, "If you're referring to the fact that she's unrestrained, no, I haven't. Where is she going to run to?"

Davos doesn't look entirely convinced but he gestures for Ian to continue. I ponder the answer to that question. Ian must have a plan. If I can figure it out, I might be able to help. Between us and the entrance to the club are several dozen guests and at least as many of the faceless servants. We could get past some of them but surely not all. And that's without even considering Davos' goons. They must be nearby, probably spread throughout the building.

Caught up in my thoughts of escape--and of keeping Ian safe while doing so--I jump suddenly as the whip flicks past. It doesn't come close to striking me but the sudden sight of it is nonetheless electrifying. So is the sound that follows. The crack reverberates through the air. Anyone in the room who wasn't paying attention is now. Although the women continue dutifully to suck and grind, their eyes and those of all the men are on us.

Ian lets the moment drag out, coiling the whip again, extending it slowly, and then--

Crack!

My whole body jerks. That was closer!

Lazily, he draws the whip up once more. It dangles from his hand as he strides toward me. I can't help but contrast the grace of his movements with the ugliness of his actions. My breath is coming in short, shallow pants as he leans closer so that only I can hear.

"Two more, each closer. It's okay to look scared but whatever you do, don't move or I could hurt you." The raw horror in his eyes leaves no doubt how he feels about any such possibility. Huskily, he adds, "On the third, be ready to do as I tell you."

Numbly, I nod. My gaze flits to Davos. His smile chills me. He must be taking my silent agreement for proof of my submissiveness. I long for a chance to show him otherwise. My own capacity for violence surprises me.

Even with all my resolve, I only just manage not to flinch as the whip lashes out again. I feel the ripple in the air as it goes past me mere inches from my exposed breast. The second comes even closer. I'm not hurt in any way but some part of my brain doesn't get that. It's screaming at me to run.

"Are you sufficiently warmed up now?" Davos calls out. His voice is taunting, his intent to goad.

Ian merely shrugs. "I think so."

"Good, make the next one count. I want to see blood."

Ian's mouth tightens. He holds the whip for a moment, the long, sinuous tongue coiled and waiting. I can't look away from it or from him. The blood Davos is so eager for feels frozen in my veins. I marvel that the man can't see what is plain in Ian's eyes. The deadly rage, the fierce will, the merciless intent.

Several things happen all at once. Ian's arm moves in a gesture that is both controlled and graceful. For an instant, I see him engaged in a particularly savage and lethal dance. Moving within it, he pivots away from me and takes several steps forward The whip releases, the lash slashes through the air...

...and curls unerringly around Davos' throat, a tentacle swiftly grabbing hold of him and squeezing hard. He bolts to his feet, grasping the leather with both hands and tries to scream but his air is already being cut off.

Turning to me, Ian speaks with calm urgency. "To your left, there's a door behind a wooden screen. Take it, go down the hall. You'll see steps that lead to a tunnel. If Hollis doesn't have men there already, he will soon. They'll get you to safety."

Distantly, I'm aware that the Lords of Misrule are lumbering to their feet, shouting at one another and the servants. But all I can really see is Davos, slowly strangling, and Ian who shows no sign of leaving with me.

"What about you?" I demand. Dread fills me. He's big, he's powerful, and he's highly trained. But he's only one man and aside from his own body, the only weapon he has is already in use choking the life out of Davos.

Ian stares at me as though I've taken leave of my senses. "For God's sake, Amelia, stop talking and go!"

"Not without you!"

The fury he turns on me should make me quake but I'm way past that. I refuse to so much as blink.

"I mean it, Ian! We go together or I stay right here. You decide but--" I glance at the men who are moving toward us. They're naked or nearly so, drunk or high or both, and frankly disgusting. But in the collective, they're also dangerous. "Do it fast!" I implore.

His curses blister the air. With a final yank on the whip, he sends Davos crashing to his knees. Ian drops the hilt and grabs me. His hand grips my arm almost to the point of pain but I scarcely feel it. Relief courses through me in the instant before the harsh reality of our situation crashes down. Some of the men and servants have stopped to help Davos. Several are trying frantically to unwind the whip that is cutting deep into his throat. But others are coming after us.

Ian yanks open the door behind the wooden screen and thrusts me through it. He pulls the screen behind us and jams it under the knob, baring the way if only temporarily.

"Go!" he orders and grabs my hand. Together, we run down a hallway lined with old, empty offices and the smell of abandonment until we reach the staircase at the far end. The steps are metal that rattles under our feet. Below I see darkness lit by flickers of light from ventilation shafts.

When we reach the bottom, my heart is pounding. I only just manage to gasp, "Where are we?"

"Under what used to be the old stacks," Ian says. He keeps my hand gripped in his as we move quickly down the tunnel.

Before we've gone very far, the air turns chill and damp. I can't help shivering, especially as I realize how he must know about this escape route. The thought of him as a young teen, trapped in the hell of his father's making and desperately seeking a way out, makes me tremble even more.

Ian stops at once and strips off his jacket. Instead of laying it over my shoulders, he insists that I put it on. I comply quickly, aware that precious seconds are passing.

As we start moving again, he blurts, "You are the most maddening human being I have ever encountered." The words sound forced from him, as though the thought behind them can no longer be contained. He's exasperated, a man at a loss how to handle a situation he didn't create or ask for.

I'm not sure that he expects a response but I give him one anyway. "You've got that backwards." A tremor of dread goes through me as I struggle not to think about what could have happened to him. "What was your plan, stay and let them beat you to a pulp or worse while I escaped? That's insane."

He throws me an as-if look. "I can take care of myself, which is more than I can say for you." A dark shadow moves behind his eyes. Softly, he says, "You're too damn vulnerable."

His voice catches and I know what he's thinking. My face flames at the reminder of how wantonly I respond to him. But hard on that comes a healthy wave of anger. I am far from the helpless creature he's making me out to be. It's time we both acknowledge that.

"I am? What about you?" Before he can answer, I rush on. "You knew that I wasn't a safe person for you to be with. But you came back to me at the Crystal Palace and afterward you opened up and let me in more and more deeply. You can't help yourself even though you'd much rather be with Susannah."

Ian stops again, suddenly. His expression is starkly bewildered. "What are you talking about?" he demands.

The mere thought of saying her name feels like a knife stabbing through me. I have to remind myself that even though Susannah set all this in motion, she isn't to blame for how it's playing out. Ian and I are each responsible for our own actions but I am, most particularly. In a sense, I was made for him, designed to appeal to his deepest, darkest desires. Far from making me helpless, that's given me power over him. Even as he holds fast to the memory of Susannah, he's been unable to deny me except, sadly enough, in his dreams.

Faintly, I say, "At the hotel, you were asleep. I think you were having a nightmare. At least you sounded upset."

His scowl is filled with apprehension, "What did I say?"

"You called out to her...pleading with her not to leave you." My voice breaks. Without thinking, I try to wrest my hand from his. But Ian won't let me go. On the contrary, he tightens his grip.

Staring at me intently, he asks, "I called out to Susannah?"

Numbly, I nod. I can't look at him anymore. If I do, I will break.

"That's why you left?" He sounds incredulous.

"Of course it is." How can he be so oblivious as to think that I could have stayed under such circumstances? Perhaps I need to spell it out for him. Though my throat is clogged with tears, I manage to say, "I'm not her. I can't be the woman you want in your heart. Realizing that was...devastating."

Silence drags out between us. As we begin walking again, I entertain the sudden wish that we could leave the truth behind in the darkness as though it doesn't exist. But what happened in the hotel suite can't be undone and I shouldn't want it to be. Honesty is all I have left. Whether I can make a life on that harsh foundation remains to be seen.

The tunnel seems to stretch on endlessly. I start to wonder if there is any way out. Just when I think he isn't going to respond at all, Ian sighs deeply, the sound of a man letting down a vast burden. Far more gently than before, he asks, "You didn't leave because of what I did to you?"

My heart tightens. I don't want to talk about this anymore. What is so difficult for him to understand? If only I had left for that reason but I am who I am. To deny myself would be the ultimate betrayal, vastly worse than anything Ian or anyone else could ever do to me.

"I could have left at any time. Obviously, I didn't want to." I have to force myself to breathe before I can continue. "Face it, Ian, I'm nothing like Susannah."

More silence until I think I truly can't bear it. The ground slopes downward, leading us further into a dark underworld. The world above--of carefully crafted beauty, contrived gaiety, and rampant cruelty--seems far away. But there is still enough light from the ventilation shafts for me to see that our surroundings have changed. The remains of a structure older even than the library are rising around us.

In a bid to distract myself, I ask, "Where are we?"

"Under the foundation of the library," he says absently. "It was built on top of an old reservoir fed by an aqueduct. Two hundred years ago, clean water from here made the difference between life and death for people in this city."

As he speaks, I glimpse a darkly rippling river nearby. In my heightened emotional state, I imagine that it could be the Styx, the ancient boundary between the world of the living and Hades. The sight makes me stiffen as my own memories of the gestation chamber stir.

Softly, Ian says, "I don't remember dreaming about Susannah, much less calling out to her. But there's only one reason why I would have--"

He breaks off suddenly, his attention drawn by a flicker of movement in the shadows. In an instant, I am thrust behind him, protected by the big, hard bulk of his body.

"Ian--?"

After a moment, he relaxes. "It's all right. It's just scavengers."

Peering over his shoulder, I see several women and girls crouched on the other side of the water with pails and buckets. They stare back at us for an instant before abruptly fleeing into the darkness.

Watching them go, a sense of shock and guilt washes over me. My own burdens are forgotten, if only temporarily. "No one should have to live like that," I say.

"You're right," Ian replies. "No one should."

I wait for him to tell me again that, notwithstanding how bad life is for the scavengers, the chaos that would follow social upheaval would be worse. But instead, he says, "Davos and the others have to be stopped." His tone is icily calm. He sounds like a man who has come to an irrevocable decision. A shiver of apprehension moves through me.

"Why say that now when you wouldn't before?" When he doesn't answer, I shake my head vehemently. "Tell me that it's not because of what he wants to do to me." The thought that I could be the catalyst that unleashes the violence and chaos that Ian has feared is unbearable.

"That was always more than enough reason," Ian says. "I should have realized it from the beginning." He strokes my cheek with the back of his fingers in a gesture that is at once gentle and apologetic. Holding my gaze, he says, "Amelia, the only reason I would have called out to Susannah is because when I was with her, I didn't have to deal with my true nature. I could just shove it down and pretend it didn't exist. I can't do that with you. I tried, God knows, but I kept failing. All I want is to keep you safe and happy. But then Davos came along with his damn smart drug and--

Drug? Before I can ask him what he means, Ian's mouth thins. Harshly, he says, "He'll stop at nothing. Neither will the men who support him. Unless someone stops them, they'll destroy everything that is still good and hopeful and decent in this world. I can't let that happen."

I'm all too aware that he would have killed Davos already if I hadn't intervened. But I can't regret what I did, not when it means that Ian is standing right here in front of me, safe and whole. That he is also speaking words I can scarcely dare to believe stuns me.

"I want to understand," I say, "truly I do. But you were dreaming of her even after all we--" My voice breaks. I can't go on.

To my astonishment, I realize that he's blushing. Quietly, he says, "If she was in my mind, it wasn't despite what happened between us. It was because of it. I was terrified that I'd driven you too far and that you'd never forgive me for what I did."

My cheeks are as warm as his own. I have to force myself to look at him. "You didn't notice...how I responded to you? I thought the issue of whether or not I possess free will was settled not long after we met." Rather memorably, I would think, but perhaps he's forgotten.

"It was," he says. But in the next breath, his conviction wavers. "I think so...I hope..."

I grasp his face between my hands. Embarrassment, modesty, and every other hindrance to truth falls away. I can't let him go on having any doubt about this. "No, Ian, you know. I choose you. I have from the very beginning but that doesn't make it any less of a choice."

He wants to believe me, I can tell. But still he hesitates. So low that I can hardly hear him, he says, "You cried. I saw you. And even that didn't stop me." His gaze is filled with guilt that I cannot bear for him to carry a moment longer.

"I was thinking of Susannah," I admit. "Of how gently you treated her, like spun glass, you said. I thought of how she brought out the noblest and best aspects of your nature while I--"

I can't go on but I don't have to. Ian cups my chin in his hand. Softly, he says, "You bring out all of me, Amelia. Not just the parts I want to admit to. I've been in pieces for so long that I thought there was no other way to live. Then you came along and put me back together."

I'm crying again. I can't help it and I don't even try. This is how we are--messy, carnal, striving and uncertain. Human. After what I saw in the Club, the purity of our mutual desire is cleansing. The brush of my lips against his is filled with tremulous yearning. His response is instant and fierce. A groan escapes him as his mouth claims mine.

His breath is the oxygen of life. I inhale him greedily, my tongue twisting with his as we savor one another. There is desperation to this kiss. We are reaching for each other through barriers of fear and misunderstanding that have cracked but not yet dissolved. We need time...to talk, to touch, to simply be together. He feels as though he wants to be inside me and I want him there, desperately. But we are surrounded by darkness and the pressing urgency of danger.

Too quickly, he pulls back and looks down at me. His voice roughened by passion. "Don't ever, not for a moment, believe that you are less than everything to me."

"As you are to me," I murmur through my tears. Unable to help myself, I cup the back of his head, my fingers tangling in the soft crispness of his hair, and draw him toward me once again. Just one more taste...one more...

Crack!

A spray of small, powdery particles explodes from the spot on the wall next to where Ian's head was an instant before. A white gash appears in the old stone. At its center is the black scar of a bullet.

Chapter Thirty-six

Amelia

No, no, no! For a horrible moment, I think I'm going to faint. The world takes a violent lurch and I'm on the ground. Ian thrusts me into the shadows at the base of the wall.

"Stay here," he hisses. "Don't move."

Terrified, I grab hold of him. "No, don't go! Whoever's out there was aiming at you, not me. If you move, you'll be a target!"

"It's Davos," he says grimly. "Him or one of his goons. He isn't just going away. He'll close in and finish the job."

"You said Hollis was sending men into the tunnel," I remind him desperately. "They could be here at any moment. Let them deal with him."

For a moment, I think he'll relent but the crack of a second shot just above us erases any such hope.

"You never fail to disappoint, Slade," Davos shouts. The whip has transformed his voice into a high-pitched rasp but there's no mistaking either his arrogance or his rage. "Just when I think there's hope for you, you prove me wrong!"

"He's bat shit crazy," Ian mutters. "He blew up the Crystal Palace when that didn't go his way and now this. If ever a man needed killing--"

I can't help but think that he's right. Davos may have been sane at some point in his life but he clearly isn't now. But far worse, he's drawing Ian out. Making him decide that he has to put himself in mortal danger in order to stop him. Crazy, maybe, but Davos is still a genius at manipulation.

A sudden impulse seizes me. Before I can think better of it, I call out, "He can't hear you. He's wounded!"

Ian stiffens and for a moment I think he's going to make it all too clear that I'm lying. Instead, he murmurs, "What the hell are you doing?"

Before he can stop me, I wiggle out from under him and get to my knees. I'm betting that I'm too valuable to Davos for him to kill me outright. If I'm wrong--

"He's unconscious!" I say. My anguish and fear for Ian pour out. I sound like a young woman overcome with horror, on the verge of breaking down completely. In case Davos has any doubts, I add, "I think he's dying!"

As I speak, I clamber to my feet. The dark channel of water flows swiftly by. For the first time, I notice that it's crossed at intervals by narrow stone spans that unexpectedly are in good repair. They must be kept that way by the scavengers. More even than Ian or Davos, they know the underground city and the secrets that it holds.

"Watch where you're going!" Davos yells as I force myself closer to the water and deliberately stumble again. "You'll fall in!"

Yes! Let him think that. It will force him to act.

"I don't care! I have to get away!"

His curse is raw and virulent. "Stop! I'm coming across. Stay where you are!"

I don't dare glance over my shoulder to see what Ian is doing but I sense him in the darkness, on his feet, crouched low, moving between shadows.

If I can keep Davos distracted-- "You want to hurt me!"

"No! That's a lie! I know how wonderful you are, Amelia. How special. Ian wanted to keep you to himself. I want to share you with the world. You'd like that, wouldn't you?"

"I don't know..." Desperately, I try to keep him talking.

"Of course, you would. What woman wouldn't? You'll be adored, worshipped even. You're a superior being, Amelia. With me, you can be the beginning of an entirely new race of humans. You'll be their Eve."

Bile rises in my throat. No doubt the race of humans that Davos envisions creating will be superior in his eyes. Docile slaves to do the bidding of the elite are vastly preferable to the great mass of humans who refuse to believe that their time has passed but who instead go on stubbornly determined to live.

With a shock, I realize that there may be no better example of that than the scavengers. Instead of fleeing the sounds of gunshots and screams, they are coming out of the shadows and cautiously drawing nearer. Most are men, all are armed. Among the clubs, spears, and old vintage rifles I glimpse an unexpected scattering of far more up-to-date weapons.

Dimly, I wonder how they came by such things and what their possession of them would mean if an uprising ever does occur. But there's no time to think of that. Davos has yet to notice that we are no longer alone. He crosses the nearest stone span and comes toward me. His arm is outstretched, the gun pointed into the shadows where Ian is no longer.

"If you're lying to me--" he begins.

He doesn't get any further. Ian comes out the darkness straight at him, hurtling them both to the ground. With his youth and strength, the struggle is brief, or it should be. A scream bubbles up in my throat when I realize that Davos is no longer alone. Men in dark suits are rushing down the tunnel to his aid. He sees them, too, but his smile of triumph is short lived.

The scavengers have taken up position on the other side of the water. Confronted by a threat to the only world that offers them any safety, they don't hesitate. As they open fire, several of the goons fall, wounded or dead, I can't tell which. A few of the others return fire but they retreat quickly before the men in ragged clothes who will not yield an inch of the ground on which they stand.

And they aren't alone. Men in the uniforms of Slade Enterprises are coming from the other end of the tunnel. They move at a run, in tight formation, closing on us quickly. They will be here in seconds. Davos throws back his head with a howl of rage that makes the hairs on the nape of my neck rise. Whatever is inside him, it is not meant to see the light of day. He fires wildly, the bullet winging past just inches from my side.

"Amelia!"

Instinctively, Ian moves to protect me. He abandons his hold on Davos, who quickly scrambles to escape. The scavengers have cut off access to one end of the tunnel and Ian's men are coming from the other. That leaves only the aqueduct.

"You think you've won," Davos shouts. "You have no idea what you've unleashed!"

His taunt is still booming against the tunnel walls when he hurtles himself into the dark, swirling waters and swiftly vanishes from sight.

∞ ∞ ∞

By the time Ian and I return to the surface, Hollis and the men with him have possession of the Club. The Lords of Misrule have fled. The faceless servants are in custody along with the few goons left alive. Of the women, I see no sign at all. I remind myself to make sure that they will be cared for.

Sitting huddled in Ian's jacket while he and Hollis talk, the final moments in the tunnel keep replaying in my mind. Davos...his maniacal smile...the glee behind his words as he went into the dark water.

He never struck me as suicidal. Evil, obsessed, dangerous, all that but I never once thought that he might take his own life. He is--was?--far too narcissistic for that. But once he was cornered, confronted with having to face the consequences for what he had done including trying to kill two of the most powerful men in the city, might he have chosen death as the better alternative?

Try though I do, I can't quite wrap my head around that.

"Ready to go?" Ian asks softly.

He has concluded his conversation with Hollis and is at my side, looking down at me with an expression of such fierce gentleness that he robs me of breath. I take his hand and am drawn up close beside him. Our bodies brush once...again...and the fire that is never far beneath the surface ignites.

Against the curve of my cheek, Ian murmurs, "Let's go home."

Oh, yes. Home. High in the clouds above the city, or in the serenity of the estate, or amid the warmth and honesty of the beach house. Home is wherever Ian is. The only place I want to be.

And yet...something makes me hesitate.

"What did Davos mean?" I hate even saying his name but I can't let this go.

"About what?"

"Right at the end, when he said that you had no idea what you were unleashing."

Ian sighs. He presses his lips lightly to my forehead. "He was insane, Amelia. Remember? Forget what he said. All that matters is that he's dead."

"Are you sure that he is?" I blurt out the question before I can stop myself. As much as I want to believe Ian, I still can't reconcile the Davos both I and Susannah knew with his actions right at the end.

"By now his body is jammed in one of the old water tunnels that are fed by the aqueduct," Ian says. "Divers will go in and recover it. That is if the scavengers don't get it first." Quietly, he adds, "They were a surprise."

I nod. "I can't help wondering what they'd be able to do if they had some support."

"I wouldn't put them up against the Municipal Protection Services."

"No, of course not--"

"At least not yet,"

I'm mulling over this sudden glimpse into the future that he may be contemplating when Ian glances toward the entrance to the Club. "Speaking of, the MPS has arrived. Their commander wants a word. It will just take a minute and then we'll go, all right?"

"Yes, of course."

We step out together into the glare of searchlights that eclipse the soft blanket of dusk settling over the rest of the city. I'm distantly aware of drones hovering overhead, relaying images of the scene back to whoever is authorized to receive them. It's a safe bet that doesn't include Manhattan's residents, snug in their luxury cocoons, dreaming that they are butterflies. I wonder how much they will ever be allowed to know about the horrors just below the surface of their city. Or how much they would care in any case.

A man in the benign blue MPS uniform ornamented with an array of ribbons and insignia approaches. He's tall, very fit, and with a practiced air of command but he's not as imperturbable as he appears at first glance. On closer scrutiny, I can see that despite the coolness of the evening, his forehead is beaded with sweat.

"Mr. Slade," he says, "If you'd just step over here. I'd like to get a video statement from you. It will only take a moment."

Ian shrugs. He leaves me with Hollis, who has come with us, and goes to stand in front of the camera that's already set up and waiting.

"Whenever you're ready," the commander says. He steps back.

As Ian begins explaining in calm, measured tones why his forces invaded a private club patronized by many of the most powerful men in the city, I look around. There must be several hundred members of the MPS on hand, all heavily armed. They have their visors down, making it impossible to see their faces. But I can see that several are fingering their weapons. Some, like their commander, are visibly sweating.

Most of Ian's men are still inside the Club, guarding prisoners and searching for anyone who might be hiding on the premises. But several dozen have joined us. A small enough number against the MPS.

Why am I thinking that? Ian is just giving a statement and then we're going. Of course, there will be more to follow in the coming days. The Council will want to appear to still be in charge even if Davos really is dead and despite the fact that their other masters, the Lords of Misrule, are in disarray. Perhaps Ian will appear before them again--

The words I spoke to him right before he left for the Council meeting yesterday suddenly echo in my mind. "You aren't above the law, Ian, however unjust it is. If you're seen as posing a threat to the established order, there won't be any limits to the response against you. What happens then?"

Speaking into the camera, he says, "Those who hold power in this city and beyond must be held accountable for their actions by all citizens."

An icy finger of dread moves down my spine. The officer in charge has backed farther away from where Ian is standing, leaving him alone in a circle of light. I become aware of a low, persistent hum that is growing louder. Looking up, I see yet another drone approaching. But this one is different. A dark, cylindrical shape hangs below its belly. I don't know what it is but the sight of it strikes fear into me all the same.

"Ian!" I cry out.

He hears and turns but just as he does, the drone launches. I have an instant to see a gleaming projectile hurtling on its trajectory before the scene vanishes in an incandescent burst. The force of the explosion staggers me. I only just manage to stay upright, gasping and fighting for breath. With torturous slowness, my vision clears. What I see drags a scream from the depths of my soul.

Ian is lying motionless among shards of smoking metal. His body is twisted in a shape that tells me instantly that he is seriously hurt. Or worse. I can't think of that. I can't!

Hollis is cursing, yelling orders to the men who are streaming out of the Club, taking up positions facing off against the MPS. But I'm hardly aware of them. I'm running, screaming, falling to my knees beside Ian. I cradle his head in my lap, sobbing. His blood flows into my hands; I can't stop it. My heart is shattering. No nightmare I have endured, no pain I have experienced has ever come close to equaling this. I hold onto him desperately, pleading with him to stay, to fight. To live. But he is beyond hearing me.

Crimson drops soak the ground of the glittering, corrupt city and mingle with my tears.

Ian and Amelia's story continues!

Available on Amazon

ANEW: Book Three: Entwined

ANEW: The Epilogue

Let's stay in touch!
Visit josielittonauthor.com

Lastly, please consider posting a review on Amazon and/or Goodreads. Your feedback is invaluable.

Are you up for really intense erotic romance? Keep reading for a sneak peek at "Tales of the Odalisque" with more than 150 5-star reviews on Goodreads and Amazon. But be warned, this is not for the faint-of-heart!

Sneak Peek

Tales of the Odalisque
Intense erotic romance
Set in a fantasy world
Inspired by
Jane Austen

*W*elcome to the Odalisque, the world's most exclusive *club intime*. Kindly leave your inhibitions at the door (clothing is optional). If this is your first visit, a few words of explanation may be in order. The tall, lithely muscular and all-around stunningly handsome man lounging at the bar is the club's founder and owner, Lucius Belmont. "Luscious Lucius" some call him. Others are more inclined to mutter about his resemblance to Lucifer. A word to the wise, enjoy your visit but do nothing to vex him. Especially not now.

Lucius is pre-occupied with a problem unlike any he has encountered before. That rarest of creatures--a virgin--has wandered into his circle of debauchery. Natalia Bollinger is everything she should not be--exquisitely beautiful, unbearably arousing, and uncannily able to penetrate all his hard-won defenses. But Natalia is guarding secrets of her own that will pit her against Lucius in an epic showdown of vice versus virtue. Before your visit is over, limits will be tested, lines will be crossed, and all the rules will be broken. Take a seat. The show is about to begin!

Although inspired by my earlier work, "His Lordship's Downfall", also available on Amazon, "Tales of the Odalisque" is a standalone novel with no cliffhanger. You need not have read "His Lordship's Downfall" to enjoy this story but of course, I hope that you will do so. Please be aware that while this story is M/F, monogamous and HEA, it contains explicit sexual scenes that some may find disturbing. Read at your own discretion

∞ ∞ ∞

Excerpt

The Abbey of the Virgins occupies an elegant, neo-Georgian townhouse at the heart of London near the corner of St. James Street and Piccadilly, immediately adjacent to that most infamous of *clubs intimes*, the Odalisque.

Perhaps because of its proximity to such a notorious den of carnal indulgence, the abbey offers no advertisement of its purpose but instead turns a modest, not to say disinterested eye to the world. Still, the citadel of chastity is well known in certain circles, enough so that Natalia Bollinger had encountered only moderate difficulty ascertaining its location.

Standing on the opposite side of the street, where she had spent much of the previous week crouched in the shadows disguised as a street waif, Natalia observed the by now familiar comings and goings of the neighborhood.

At that hour--it had just gone ten a.m.--they were very few.

A delivery van arrived at the service entrance of the club. Two burly men carried in crates overflowing with fresh vegetables, braces of partridge, and several large wheels of cheese. All this proceeded under the watchful gaze of a slender young woman in a chef's jacket who snapped orders with the practiced charm of an army drill sergeant.

No one stirred from the abbey.

Of *him* next door, there was no sign at all.

Not that she had expected any. He was a creature of the night, if ever there was one.

Her clear, unflinching eyes--a remarkable hue of violet that had caused her no end of trouble for being so memorable--traced the distance from the roof of the abbey to that of the adjoining building. The townhouse was no less than six feet shorter than its far larger neighbor. In addition, there was a gap of three feet between the two edifices. Fortunately, summers spent climbing in the Alps--and occasionally elsewhere--had left Natalia confident that she could manage both when the time came.

But first, she must endure the indignities that were about to be inflicted upon her person.

Grasping her well-worn leather valise, she crossed the street with a firm tread born of resolution that she told herself would remain unwavering come what may. With hardly a moment's hesitation, she mounted the polished granite steps to the anonymous door and grasped the gleaming brass knocker in the shape of a ram's head. Having given it three sharp raps, she stepped back and waited.

Several minutes passed during which she was conscious of the unusual quiet all along the leafy street. With the truck's departure, the loudest sound was the cooing of pigeons. It was a Tuesday; across the vast expanse of London several million people--residents and visitors alike--hurried about their business, on foot, in cars and trucks, amid a cacophony of clanging, honking and shouting. Only in the ultimate enclaves of wealth and power was the luxury of silence attainable.

At last, the faint sound of footsteps on the other side was followed by the appearance of an eye in the aperture at the center of the carved oak door. A moment later, the soundless movement of well-oiled hinges gave way to the sight of a sturdy, round-faced girl in the modest black dress and white apron of a parlor maid.

"Good morning, Miss. May I help you?"

"If you would be so kind. My name is Natalia Bollinger. I would like to speak with whoever is in charge."

The girl swept her gaze over Natalia's outdated black velvet cloche hat and unfashionable brown woolen suit to her sensibly shod feet just visible a few inches below the hem of her skirt. The faintest of smiles came and went.

"Very well, Miss. Follow me."

Directly over the threshold of the abbey, Natalia paused. The entry hall with its black-and-white tiled floor, golden chestnut wainscoting and coffered ceiling was precisely what one would expect in such a setting. The only anomaly was the portrait of a young woman on display at the far end.

Beautiful, with dark red hair--by sheer coincidence almost the precise shade of Natalia's own--and limpid eyes, she was dressed in the style of the Italian Renaissance. Her embroidered silk gown slipped off her rounded shoulders, far enough on one side to expose a high, firm breast. The artist had depicted her sitting at a table on which lay a freshly plucked rose moist with dew and a dish containing two halves of a pomegranate open to reveal glistening, ruby-red seeds bursting with juice. The young woman's fingers plucked idly at her exposed nipple as she gazed at herself in a silvered mirror.

"Who is that?" Natalia asked.

The maid followed the direction of her gaze. "Why that's Saint Veronica, Miss, patron saint of the abbey. From Venice, I believe she was."

"Martyred for the cause?" From her reading of history, Natalia had observed that women who defied social norms were always at risk from authorities anxious to push their own sins off onto others. Only the clever--or the very lucky--escaped.

"Very nearly, Miss! But she had enough secrets hidden away in her cunny, so to speak, to assure that instead she lived to a ripe old age. Lessons to be drawn from that, the abbess says."

The maid opened a set of double doors leading off the hall. "If you'll come this way, Miss."

Discreet sunlight filtered through the sheer silk curtains drawn across the windows of a parlor furnished in ivory with accents of mauve and blue. A small chestnut burled desk held a single sheet of paper and a pen.

"If you would be so good as to provide your particulars, Miss. I'll be back in a few minutes to collect them."

Left alone, Natalia took the seat at the desk and directed her attention to the form. Nothing on it indicated the purpose for which the information was required. But what was asked was entirely straightforward--name, age, birth date, schools attended and the like. With silent thanks for the foresight her father had shown in crafting an impeccable history for her from the moment of her birth, Natalia set to work.

Half-an-hour later, the form having been collected, she re-settled herself on a pretty settee and took a more comprehensive look around. Everything she saw spoke of wealth in service to the most refined, if exclusively feminine taste. There appeared to be no concession whatsoever to the masculine--no cut crystal decanters of scotch or brandy, no hint of a humidor, no quasi-artistic depictions of rearing horses or dead stags. Any man admitted to such surroundings would know that he was there entirely on sufferance.

Although perhaps not quite any. Surely, *he* would be an exception. She imagined him entirely at ease amid such female frippery. As reprehensible as he was, he would know women in a way that very few men could ever claim to do. Even worse, far too many of them would be drawn to that knowledge.

Rather than allow herself to be distracted by thoughts of her ultimate quarry, Natalia focused on the large, gilt-framed mirror hung on the wall directly opposite her. It looked like an oversized version of the sort of mirror a woman might preen before, turning this way and that to study her attire before departing for a glamorous evening. As such, it surely belonged in a boudoir rather than a parlor. Unless, of course, it was intended for an entirely different purpose.

She was considering whether to take the chance of inspecting it more closely when the parlor doors opened and a woman entered. She was tall, in her middle years but hardly showing them. Her pale blond hair was arranged in a smooth chignon at the back of her head. Minimal make-up expertly applied accentuated features that could have graced the cover of a fashion magazine. Her classic ivory Dior suit furthered the impression of feminine confidence and power.

"Miss Bollinger?"

Rising to her feet, Natalia nodded. "Yes, ma'am."

"How nice to meet you. My name is Arabella Hamilton. I am the abbess here."

With a graceful gesture, she said, "Please, be seated." Having taken her own seat opposite Natalia, the abbess smoothed her skirt, crossed her ankles, and asked, "You wish to be admitted?"

"I do, yes."

"I see. May I ask how you heard of us?"

Natalia's father had always stressed the usefulness of telling some version of the truth whenever that was possible. It had the virtue of being both unexpected and disarming.

Accordingly, she said, "The parrot at the Cock and Bells in Piccadilly squawked your name when I offered him my Crawfords Custard Cream biscuit. When I inquired as to what he was going on about, I was drawn aside into the alcove of a gypsy fortune teller who whispered of your purpose while examining my palm."

A delicately threaded eyebrow arched. "How did you come to be at the Cock and Bells?"

"I'd heard that they do a very nice spotted dick."

"Really? I must give it a try. Spotted dick is a favorite of mine. What did the gypsy foretell?"

"That I would embark on a grand adventure leading to significant financial gain during which I would encounter a dark man."

"Well, that seems clear enough. Do you by any chance have an ailing granny, poverty stricken siblings, or a burning desire to endow a shelter for some form of animal life? If so, you may speak of it now and kindly do not mention it again."

When the silence on Natalia's part had drawn out long enough, Arabella Hamilton nodded. "No? Strictly pecuniary interest? Excellent. Be so good as to stand up."

When she had complied, the abbess said, "Remove your hat."

As she did so, she patted the braids she had made that morning, reassured that the heavy weight of her hair remained neatly coiled around her head.

The abbess also rose and went over to a chinoiserie cabinet made of teak with ivory insets depicting women in embroidered Chinese silk robes strolling in gardens.

"Our intake process is rigorous," she said as she opened a door in the cabinet. "You will begin as a postulant. Once all the required examinations are completed, the successful applicant advances to the status of novice. Beyond that, intensive preparation is required before presentation to our congregants. Your focus must remain absolute. During your stay with us, under no circumstances will you leave the abbey unless directed to do so. Do you understand?"

Not especially, nor did she care. But that didn't matter.

"Yes, of course."

"Good. Remove your clothing."

"Pardon?" She had understood that there would be certain...procedures. She just hadn't expected them to begin quite so abruptly. Once again, her gaze strayed to the mirror.

"Here?"

Rather alarmingly, the abbess withdrew a long black leather riding crop, closed the cabinet door and returned to stand beside Natalia.

Sternly, she said, "Miss Bollinger, to enter the Abbey of the Virgins is a solemn undertaking. We take our vocation seriously. Approached in the proper spirit, your stay here can significantly change your life for the better. But I must warn you, impulsive, feckless young women do not do well with us. We require self-discipline and, above all, obedience. If you are not capable of that, you may leave now."

Natalia thought swiftly. She needed no more than a handful of days, with luck less, to complete what she had come to do. Surely, she could endure anything that long.

Repressing a sudden attack of self-consciousness, she removed her jacket. Beneath she wore a plain white cotton blouse lacking in all adornment. Her fingers felt stiff as she undid the small yellowing buttons down the front and slipped the garment off. Her heavy wool skirt followed, leaving her in a camisole, boxers, thigh high stockings and black laced boots.

The abbess flicked the crop at the first two items with an air of distaste. "Remove these. Leave the stockings and boots on."

Swallowing her reluctance, Natalia obeyed. The coolness of the air raised goosebumps over every exposed inch of her skin. She was aware of her nipples puckering and had to fight the urge to cross her arms over her breasts. Daring a glance to the mirror, she had the sudden overwhelming certainty that she was being watched.

The thought was disturbing, of course, and yet it provoked a spurt of professional pride. Her line of work required her to slip in and out of many roles. Waitress, maid, debutante, bright young thing, street waif, whatever was needed, she had done it. And she could do so again in this most vital of circumstances where the stakes had never been higher.

The Sensible Virgin, a good girl from a respectable family, properly reared, and mercifully free of romantic notions that could have prevented her from making the most of what she had. It was a challenging role but well within the scope of her talents. Besides, she didn't anticipate having to play it for very long.

"Lift your arms," the abbess said. "Clasp your hands behind your head and keep them there."

Trembling slightly, Natalia did so, aware of how the position elevated her bosom yet further. When the tip of the riding crop touched one high, firm breast, she jerked.

"Stay still," the abbess instructed.

With an effort, she managed to do so as the crop passed over first one nipple, then the next before sliding under each breast as though to test their weight. It then proceeded over her flat abdomen and around to the curve of her ass where, without warning, it flicked sharply.

Startled by the sudden, stinging pain, Natalia jumped, earning her another rebuke.

"I said to stay still. You will become accustomed to being inspected."

Perhaps so but when the crop probed into the gap between her thighs, urging them further apart, Natalia had all she could do not to cry out in protest. Once again, her gaze focused on the mirror. If *he* was there...watching... She had the sudden, piercing sense of having been put on display for him.

A deep, hot flush suffused her from head to toe. She was aware of a disturbing moisture gathering between her nether lips, threatening to seep from her in a most unseemly fashion.

"You have potential," the abbess said as she finally lowered the crop. "However, you will need to acquire a bit of poise and grace. We will work on that."

Standing back, she said, "You may lower your arms."

Doing so with relief, Natalia took the opportunity to ask, "When is the next auction?"

The question appeared to amuse the abbess. "Whenever Mister Belmont decides that it is."

Having returned the crop to its place in the cabinet, she added, "These auctions are no small matter. They require considerable organization. Both the clientele and the stock being offered are rigorously vetted. Gentlemen interested merely in battering their way through a young woman's innocence are not welcome. Nor are young women who expect that the mere relinquishment of a hymen entitles them to a large paycheck."

"What is to be expected then?" Natalia asked. She had turned, presenting her back to the mirror. Let him, if he was there, make of that what he would.

"Are you familiar with the Parable of the Wise and Foolish Virgins?"

As it happened, she was although she had certainly never expected to be discussing Biblical lessons under such circumstances. "Matthew: 25."

The abbess looked surprised. "Very good. Then you are aware that it is a wise virgin who comes to an encounter properly prepared."

"I beg your pardon but isn't that story really a reference to spiritual rather than...earthly affairs?"

A slim, perfectly manicured hand flicked dismissively. "It hardly matters. The clientele at our auctions values innocence for the usual reason anything is valued in this world, because it is rare. However, they are also accustomed to having their every whim catered to and their every desire fulfilled. You will learn to do that and more."

Out of simple curiosity, not because she expected to have any personal interest in the response, Natalia asked, "For how long?"

"Immediately after the auction winning bids are placed in escrow. The contracts are valid for seventy-two hours thereafter. Clients tend to make full use of that time."

Reaching for her clothes, Natalia nodded. "I see..."

Seventy-two hours fulfilling the sexual requirements of a self-indulgent rake who had paid--if rumor was to be believed--northward of a hundred thousand pounds sterling to thrust his cock into virgin cunt. Truly, a fool and his money were soon parted.

The cost of putting up with such a lout seemed far too great to Natalia but then she could steal ten times that amount in jewels and other items of value in mere minutes. For less providentially skilled young women, she supposed that it might be worth the effort.

"Leave those."

The abbess picked up a small bell and rang it. The maid re-appeared so swiftly that she could be assumed to have been waiting just on the other side of the door. That the visitor she had shown in a short time before was now nearly nude save for her stockings and high laced boots did not occasion the slightest surprise.

"Brigid will show you to our medical office. Assuming the doctor is satisfied that all is as it should be, she will then take you to your quarters."

With her throat suddenly dry, Natalia did as she was told.

Continue reading
"Tales of the Odalisque"
On Amazon

About the Author

New York Times and USA Today Bestselling Author Josie Litton lives in Connecticut. Married to the man of her dreams, she has two grown children. Becoming an empty nester has given her plenty of time to write, think about writing, plan what to write next and read. When she isn't doing that, she's cooking, gardening and traveling.

Josie Litton

Josie Litton
Visit my website at www.josielittonauthor.com

Printed in the United States of America

First Printing: April 2018
Josie Litton Books

ISBN-13: 978-0-9906042-6-6

Made in the USA
Middletown, DE
10 August 2020